THE KREUTZER SONATA
THE DEVIL
AND OTHER TALES

THE KREUTZER SONATA
THE DEVIL
AND OTHER TALES

By LEO TOLSTOY

Translation of FAMILY HAPPINESS by

J. D. DUFF

and of the other stories by

Aylmer Maude

GYAN

Published by

GYAN

Gyan Publishing House
5, Ansari Road
Daryaganj, New Delhi-110002
Phone: 011-47034999, 9811692060
E-mail: books@gyanbooks.com

Distribution Network
gyanbooks.com
India, USA, Canada, UK, Australia

ISBN: 978-93-6208-542-9 (HB)
First Published, 1889

2nd Impression 2024

Printed at: Gyan Press, Delhi.

THE KREUTZER SONATA THE DEVIL AND OTHER TALES
Author: LEO TOLSTOY, AYLMER MAUDE, Translator: J. D. DUFF

THE KREUTZER SONATA, THE DEVIL, &c.

THE KREUTZER SONATA
THE DEVIL
AND OTHER TALES

By LEO TOLSTÓY

Translation of FAMILY HAPPINESS *by*
J. D. DUFF

and of the other stories by
AYLMER MAUDE

With an Introduction by
AYLMER MAUDE

GEOFFREY CUMBERLEGE
OXFORD UNIVERSITY PRESS
LONDON NEW YORK TORONTO

CONTENTS

INTRODUCTION

THE stories in this volume, though not autobiographical, are so closely connected with Tolstóy's life that some mention of the events that prompted them is called for, especially as Tolstóy wished them to be mentioned, and because his emphatic and repeated statements that he led a disorderly life in his youth, may give a wrong impression to readers unacquainted with the actual facts. He did, it is true, misbehave before marriage, but did not do so habitually, and he was never unfaithful to his wife.

When P. I. Birukóv visited him three months before his death, Tolstóy said to him: 'You always write only what is good about me. That is misleading and incomplete. The bad should also be told. When I was young I led a very bad life, and there were two occurrences in particular that torment me even now. I tell you this, and ask you to write it in my biography. Those occurrences were: an affair with a peasant woman in our village before my marriage—which is referred to in my story *The Devil*. The other was the crime I committed much earlier with a maid-servant, Másha, who lived at my aunt's. She was a virgin. I seduced her, and she was dismissed and perished.'

The seduction scene in *Resurrection* was no doubt based on that occurrence. There is also reason to believe that the feelings expressed by young Nekhlyúdov, in *A Billiard-Marker's Notes*, after his companions had taken him to a house of ill-fame, were those Tolstóy himself experienced after a similar experience which occurred at Kazán, where he went to live at his aunt's when he was about fourteen years old.

Tolstóy's attitude towards a girl he thoroughly

respected is shown by what happened when he was on his way to the Caucasus before he was twenty-three. He then stayed for a week in Kazán and renewed acquaintance with Zinaída Molostvóna, a girl of twenty-one whom he had known when he was at that University. They were mutually attracted, and danced together nearly all the mazurkas at balls they attended.

After reaching the Caucasus he noted in his *Diary*:

'Love and religion are two pure and lofty feelings. I do not know what people call love. If it is what I have read and heard about it, then I have never experienced it. I had formerly seen Zinaída when she was a pupil at the Institute. I liked her, but knew her only slightly . . . I have now stayed a week in Kazán, and how pleasant it was. If I were asked why I stayed there, what I found so pleasant, and why I was so happy, I should not say it was because I was in love. I did not know that. It seems to me that just that unconsciousness is the chief feature of love and forms its whole charm. *How morally at ease I was at that time! I did not then feel this burden of mean passions that spoil all the pleasure of life.* I did not utter a word of love, but I am sure that she knows my feelings and that if she loves me it is due only to the fact that she understood me. All the first impulses of the soul are pure and lofty. Actual life destroys their innocence and charm.

'*My relations with Zinaída remained at the stage of a pure attraction of two souls to one another.*

'But perhaps you doubt that I love you, Zinaída? Forgive me if that is so, I am to blame and could by a single word convince you.

'Is it possible that I shall never see her again? Is it possible that I shall some day learn that she is married to some Bekétov, or, what would be still more distressing, shall see her in a cap [indicating a married woman], merry, and with those same wise, open, happy, and loving eyes? I do not abandon my plans of going to marry her. *I am not sufficiently convinced that she would constitute my happiness, but for all that I am in love.* What else do these joyful recollections mean that animate me, and what is this vision that always appears as soon as I see or feel something beautiful? Should I not write her a letter? I do not know her patronymic [her father's name—without the use of which it was impossible to address anyone politely] and perhaps on that account am depriving myself of happiness . . .

'Do you remember the Bishop's garden, Zinaída, the little side path? It was on the tip of my tongue to declare myself, as it was on yours also. It was for me to take the initiative, but do you know why, as it seems to me, I said nothing? I was so happy that I had nothing to wish for and feared to spoil my—no, not my, but our—felicity.

'That gracious time will ever remain the best of my life's recollections.'

His new surroundings and the army life around him in the Caucasus no doubt quickly dispersed the impression Zinaída had created, and the *Diary* does not mention her again for a year, when we read: 'Zinaída is marrying Tile. I am distressed by this, and still more by the fact that it has not upset me much.'

Apart from his general disapproval of dissolute conduct, his feeling was very much that of Eugène in *The Devil*, who found it impossible to refrain from women while he was a bachelor, but always looked forward to a strictly moral marriage, was careful not to let himself become entangled with society women, and avoided affairs with women on his own estate, except on one or two occasions.

Tolstóy's *Diary* must not be counted on to give a complete record of his lapses, for he sometimes neglected to post it up, as, for instance, for a couple of months after his return from the Crimean War. But in general the day-by-day notes in his *Diary* (allowing for a few deletions made by his literary executors) show how he behaved; and from January 1853, when he had begun his army-service in the

Caucasus, for a period of five years, they indicate that —for a young man of his class and race and time— his conduct was not such as would be reckoned dissolute.

Here are some of his characteristically abrupt entries:

'April 16th 1853. o.s. If I didn't misbehave myself on the Tuesday of Passion Week it was only by God's grace.

'May 8th. To-day wrote a good deal . . . I must have a woman. Sensuality gives me not a moment's peace.

'June 25th. I am not consistent or persistent in anything. As a result I have latterly become intolerably repulsive to myself. . . . In small things and in great this defect ruins my happiness. Had I been persistent in my desire for women I should have had success and reminiscences. Had I been consistent in continence I should have been proudly tranquil. This damned army detachment has completely knocked me out of the path of goodness on which I had entered so well, and to which I wish to return at any cost because it is the best path.'

'July 9th–15th. . . . Yesterday I was attracted by a handsome gipsy girl, but God saved me. Avoid the society of women you can easily have, and try to exhaust yourself by physical labour when you feel strong desire.'

Several entries indicate that he had only been saved from transgression by lack of opportunity or by bashfulness. For instance, on July 11th, 1854, he notes: 'The landlady's very pretty married daughter, who coquetted with me most stupidly and beyond all bounds, despite my efforts acted on me as used to be the case: that is to say, I suffered terribly from bashfulness.'

Tolstóy was in fact one of those artists of whom it has been well said that they are 'not less self-controlled than other people, but have much more to control'. Had he not been so frank and so dissatisfied with his own conduct, those who now reproach him would not have had the opportunity to do so, for as he justly says in his *Confession*, despite his misconduct, 'people praised my conduct and my contemporaries considered and consider me to be a comparatively moral man'.

It was only when in later years he expressed aims and aspirations much beyond the accepted customs and standards of society, that people began to insinuate that he had been so bad a man that no one need now attend to anything he wrote.

In 1856 and 1857, after long contemplating family life, Tolstóy was on the verge of proposing to a ward of his, Valérya Arséneva—a story told in my *Life of Tolstoy*. It was this experience which, after it was over, set Tolstóy to work on *Family Happiness*, a story in which he considers what he might have expected from marriage with such a girl. He was so little satisfied with the work that he wrote to his friend V. P. Bótkin:

> 'It is only now, here far from all the world, that I realize what I have done in *Family Happiness*. After reading the proofs of the second part I see what a sorry thing it is—it is a wretched work. It is a real torment to me to see it, read it, or remember it.'

In that same year 1859 he wrote to A. V. Druzhínin:

> 'I have written nothing more since *Family Happiness* and it seems to me that I never shall write any more. . . . Were I haunted by ideas that tormented me, forced themselves to leap out, and aroused boldness, audacity, and force in me—that would be different. But at the age of thirty-one to write very pretty stories agreeable to read —no on my word I am incapable of lifting a finger to do it!'

I have in this volume been very glad to avail myself of Mr. J. D. Duff's kind permission to use his excellent translation of that story.

After this episode Tolstóy was attracted by a succession of ladies, including a Miss Tyútchev, a Princess Sherbátov, a Miss Chechérin, a Princess Lvov, and others. None of these attractions however led to a proposal, and Tolstóy's attitude in all such cases was impeccable.

Some months after his retúrn from a visit to western Europe in 1857, he formed, on the other hand, a connexion with a peasant woman, Aksínya, at Yásnaya Polyána, which influenced him much, lasted for a considerable time, and to which his story *The Devil* owes its origin.

We learn something of the affair from the disjointed entries in his *Diary*, in which he notes: 'A wonderful Trinity. Fading wild-cherry blossoms held in horny hands. Vasíli Davýdkin's choking voice. Had a glimpse of A.—very attractive. Have waited vainly all these days. To-day in the big old wood. I am a fool, a brute. Her bronzed flush and her eyes . . . I am in love as never before in my life. Have no other thought. Am tormented. To-morrow with all my strength.'

A month later he writes: 'She has become repulsive to me.'

A year later: 'I only remember A. with repulsion. Her shoulders.'

Again six months later: 'I continue only to see A.'

Half a year later still: 'I had not been seeing her, but yesterday . . . [the dots are in the *Diary*] it even frightens me to feel how near she is to me.'

And next day: 'She is nowhere to be found—I have looked for her. It is no longer the feeling of a stag, but of a husband for a wife. It is strange that I try to arouse my former feeling of satiety and cannot do so. Efforts to be tranquil arouse that irresistible feeling more than anything else.'

Formerly his desire had extended to casual women and, despite his lofty conception of marriage and of what his future wife should be, had at times amounted to physical suffering. But now what was commonly regarded as the very usual and irresponsible relations of a landlord with a peasant-woman had gradually acquired such strength as to absorb his whole attention and concentrate his desire entirely on one woman without arousing the protest of conscience that had formerly always been in evidence. Previously he had sought for chaste love and had suffered from direct manifestations of instinct in complete contradiction to that desire. But this time he was content to regard what had happened as merely an episode of bachelor life. Nature herself, however, gave more weight and warmth to this union, and his necessity to marry, if he was ever to attain his cherished desire for a family and a home life of his own, became urgent.

After at last breaking loose from his thraldom to Aksínya, he remarked one day to his sister Mary: 'Máshenka, the Behrs family please me very much, and if I should ever marry it would certainly be into that family.'

Tolstóy, though several years younger, had as a child been a playmate of Madame Behrs, who now had three charming daughters, Lisa, Sónya, and Tánya. From the time of his return from Sevastopol Tolstóy missed no opportunity of visiting them in Moscow, and a rumour spread that he intended to marry the eldest daughter Lisa. If he ever had such an idea he abandoned it, and suddenly fell desperately in love with the second daughter, eighteen-year-old Sónya, being then himself thirty-four. On August 23rd, 1862, he noted: 'I am afraid of myself. What if this is only a *desire* for love and not real love? I try to notice only her weak points, but yet I love.' On September 3rd: 'Never has my future with a wife presented itself to me so clearly, joyfully, and calmly. . . . Above all it seems that it would be so simple and timely, with no passions, fears, nor a single moment of regret.' On September 13th: 'I am in love as I did not believe it possible to love. I am a madman and shall shoot myself if it goes on like this. . . . I should have been on my guard sooner, but now I cannot stop.' And next day: 'Every day I think that it is impossible to suffer more and at the same time be so happy, and every day I become more insane. . . . Tomorrow I will go as soon as I am up and will say everything or will shoot myself.'

It was, however, not till three days later, on September 16th, that he actually proposed and was at once accepted. He insisted on having the marriage immediately, and it was fixed for the 23rd of that same month. He did not sleep the night before, but was tormented by doubts and full of 'fear, distrust, and a wish to run away'. The wedding was to take place at eight o'clock in the evening, and though it was not the proper thing for a bridegroom to call on his fiancée on their wedding-day, Tolstóy infringed that rule, visited Sónya, and questioned her closely as to whether she was sure she loved him, whether the remembrance of a flirtation she had had with a certain Polivánov was not troubling her, and whether it would not be more honourable and better for them to separate before it was too late. Sónya wept, assuring him of her love and that he had nothing to be disturbed about; and conscious of the unreasonableness of his behaviour Tolstóy took the decisive step. Nor did he run away after the marriage, but on the contrary wrote in his *Diary* three months later: 'No one has had or will have such happiness.'

Having on previous occasions been extremely cautious and careful in weighing the pros and cons when contemplating marriage, he was in this instance swept away by the strength of his feelings and everything was done hastily and with little reflection.

The first months of married rapture were followed by gradual disillusionment and disappointment, though it was sixteen or eighteen years before there was any direct admission of failure, and during those years nobody suspected that the marriage was not entirely satisfactory. It is now not difficult, however, to detect indications of what was happening.

Only six months after his marriage Tolstóy wrote *The Porcelain Doll*—a letter addressed to his sister-in-law Tatiána Behrs (the Natásha of *War and Peace*), which is the earliest intimation we have of the disenchantment he felt when he began to realize the existence of a mental and spiritual gulf separating his wife from himself. Again in an early chapter of *War and Peace*, the first novel he wrote after his marriage, the reader is struck by Prince Andrew's vehement exclamation to Pierre:

> 'Never, never marry, my dear fellow! That is my advice: never marry till you can say to yourself that you have done all you are capable of and until you have ceased to love the woman of your choice and have seen her plainly as she is, or else you will make a cruel and irrevocable mistake. Marry when you are old and good for nothing—or all that is good and noble in you will be lost. It will all be wasted on trifles. Yes! Yes! Yes! Don't look at me with such surprise. If you marry expecting anything from yourself in the future, you will feel at every step that for you all is ended, all is closed except the drawing-room, where you will be ranged side by side with a court lackey and an idiot!'

Towards the end of the same novel we are told of Pierre—into whom, as also into Prince Andrew, Tolstóy put much of himself—that:

> 'The general opinion was that Pierre was under his wife's thumb, which was really true. From the very first

days of their married life Natásha had announced her demands. Pierre was greatly surprised by his wife's view, to him a perfectly novel one, that every moment of his life belonged to her and to the family. His wife's demands astonished him, but they also flattered him and he submitted to them. . . . At home Natásha placed herself in the position of a slave to her husband, and the whole household went on tiptoe when he was occupied—that is, was reading or writing in his study.'

We need not here follow the course of Tolstóy's married life further. Thirty years later, in May 1893, we find him noting in his *Diary*: 'I remembered what marriage has brought me—it is terrible!'

The occurrences in *The Kreutzer Sonata* do not very closely resemble what actually happened between Tolstóy and his wife, but it is evident that his conviction that life is poisoned by intimate relations springing from physical desire and that to yield to such desire is disastrous, was the result of experience. The book is so powerfully written that it attracted very general attention and aroused much discussion. Antón Chékhov, the author and playwright, who was also a medical practitioner, wrote of it to a friend:

'Did you really dislike *The Kreutzer Sonata*? I would not say it is a work of genius destined for eternity—I am no judge of that—but in my opinion, amid all that is now being written here and abroad, it is hardly possible to find anything of equal importance in conception and beauty of execution. Apart from its artistic merits which are in places amazing, we should be grateful for the story alone, for it stimulates thought extremely. When reading it one can hardly refrain from exclaiming: "That is the truth!" or "This is absurd!" True it has very annoying defects. Apart from the things you mention, it has something for which one does not readily forgive its author—namely the audacity with which he treats matters he has no knowledge of and from stubbornness does not wish to understand. For instance, his remarks about syphilis, Foundling Hospitals, women's aversion to conception, &c., are not merely open to dispute, but frankly reveal an ignorant man who during his long life has not taken the trouble to read a couple of books by specialists. But for all that the defects are blown away like feathers before the wind. The quality of the story obliterates them, and if one notices them it is only to feel rather annoyed that the story should not have escaped the fate of all human work—none of which is perfect or free from blemish.'

There are no doubt drawbacks to any frank discussion of such a subject, and the late Sir Paul Vinogradoff told me that, to his knowledge, discussion of the book between young men and women when it appeared had sometimes led to results the very reverse of those Tolstóy desired. Baron A. F. Meyendorff, on the other hand, tells me that his experience was that *The Kreutzer Sonata* had a very good influence on students who, like himself, were about nineteen when the book appeared and they read it.

He writes:

'I was deeply impressed by the passage which then seemed to me the *leit motif* of the whole story, in which Tolstóy says that it is evil to "know" a woman without love.' [The passage referred to is probably this: 'Real debauchery lies precisely in freeing oneself from moral relations with a woman with whom you have physical intimacy.'] 'It seems to me that Tolstóy thus gave expression to a moral urge which leads to a distinction between love and libido, the latter being, as I think Pascal had noticed, more like hatred than like tender feeling. Needless to add that Tolstóy's description of the personal problems in man lends itself to the fashion of Freudian interpretation or *mis*interpretation, but *The Kreutzer Sonata* has not been regarded by Russian readers as one of the books that appeal to the "lower instincts". It is my personal impression, shared by many others, that its influence runs in the opposite direction.'

The danger referred to of Freudian, or schadenfreudian, misinterpretation would be even greater were it not that the customary stock-in-trade of that school of thought on encountering any disapproval of loose living is to assert that the author they criticize suffered from a reaction from previous excesses, was insincere, or cried sour grapes after himself losing the power of enjoyment—and none of these things can plausibly be said of Tolstóy. He married at thirty-four and had lived faithfully with his wife for twenty-seven years before he wrote *The Kreutzer Sonata.* The discord that had arisen between them was caused by the disposal of his property and not by any physical incompatibility. Suggestions of insincerity are equally wide of the mark, for Tolstóy's power always lay in the outspoken frankness with which he expressed his views regardless of whether they accorded with his own conduct or not; and had he wished to write a sex-novel from motives other than those alleged, it would obviously have been easy to do so in ways more accordant with the taste of his public, and therefore more calculated to secure approval and applause. Nor does the 'sour grapes' suggestion meet the case, for Tolstóy retained his physical and sexual vigour long after *The Kreutzer Sonata* was written—in fact it was not till 1909, the year before his death, when he was eighty-one and very ill, that he was able to tell me that he was no longer troubled by physical desire. When he wrote *The Kreutzer Sonata* the grapes were still very tempting to him and remained so for many years.

Besides a translation of the usual text of the story, the present volume, in an appendix, gives passages that appeared in the lithographed copies that circulated subterraneously during the time that the book was banned by the censor.

The next story in this volume, *The Devil*, is on a similar theme—one to which Tolstóy returned again and again in different forms. *The Devil* is less well known, for owing to its intimately autobiographical nature its publication would have annoyed Tolstóy's wife, and it was not even included in the three-volume edition of Tolstóy's posthumous works published in this country soon after his death. It had been written at about the same time as *The Kreutzer Sonata* and was evidently prompted by memories of his affair with Aksínya.

The following extract from the memoirs of V. I. Alexéev throws a side-light on the story. Writing of 1870, when he was a tutor in Tolstóy's family and Tolstóy had been married nine years, Alexéev says:

'One day Tolstóy came up to me in agitation and asked me to help him. I looked up and saw that he was out of countenance, and I wondered how I could help him. He said in an agitated voice: "Save me, I am falling!" I saw that something had gone wrong with him and I felt frightened.

' "What is the matter, Leo Nikolaévich?" I asked.

' "I am overcome by sensual temptation and feel quite powerless. I fear that I may yield to the temptation. Help me!"

' "I am myself a weak man. How can I help you?" said I.

' "You can help. Please don't refuse!"

' "But what can I do to help?"

' "This: don't refuse to accompany me when I go for my walks. We will walk together and talk and the temptation won't come into my mind."

'We went for a walk and he told me how almost every day during his walk he met Dómna the servants' cook (a young woman whose husband had been taken as a soldier. She was twenty-two or three, not particularly handsome, but "blood and milk" as the peasants say of that sort of complexion—a tall, healthy, and attractive young woman with a fine figure.) At first for some days he had watched her and that had been pleasant. Then following her he had begun to whistle to her; then he had taken to accompanying her and talking to her, and at last it had come to his giving her an assignation. (The rendezvous was to be in the further alley in the park. To go there it was necessary to pass the windows of the room where the children did their lessons.) But just as he was passing those windows on his way to the rendezvous he experienced a terrible struggle between sensual temptation and his conscience. At that moment his son Ilyá, seeing him through the window, called to remind him of a Greek lesson arranged for that day, and thereby detained him. That was the decisive moment. Tolstóy woke up as it were, did not go to the rendezvous and was glad to have avoided it. But the matter did not end there. Sensuality continued to torment him. He tried prayer, but that did not free him from the temptation. He suffered and felt himself powerless, felt that by himself he might yield at any moment, and resolved to try one more means—that of confessing to someone, telling all the details of the strength of the temptation that oppressed him and of his spiritual weakness in face of this ordeal. That was why he had come to me and told everything—to make himself as much ashamed of his weakness as possible. Also, to escape from a continuation of the temptation he asked me to accompany him every day during his walk which he had been accustomed to take quite alone. Moreover he arranged that Dómna should go away to another place.'

This occurred more than twelve years after Tolstóy's affair with Aksínya and about nineteen years before *The Devil* was written, but it has an obvious relation to the latter story.

The next story in the present volume is *Father Sergius*, which again treats of the same theme, but in a quite different setting—that of a hermitage. That story, too, was published posthumously.

The very short story *Françoise*, adapted from Guy de Maupassant, is of a similar kind, and naturally recalls Tolstóy's admirable Introduction to Maupassant's works. That Introduction is a perfect model of what such things should be, and those who tell us that Tolstóy though a great artist was not a clear thinker, might profitably read it for the light it throws not only on de Maupassant's merits and defects but on the whole surrounding domain of literature, and because it reveals the mental and moral calibre which placed Tolstóy head and shoulders above his contemporaries and gave him a predominance in literature unmatched by any of his successors.

AYLMER MAUDE.

FAMILY HAPPINESS

FAMILY HAPPINESS

A NOVEL

PART I

CHAPTER I

We were in mourning for my mother, who had died in the autumn, and I spent all that winter alone in the country with Kátya and Sónya.

Kátya was an old friend of the family, our governess who had brought us all up, and I had known and loved her since my earliest recollections. Sónya was my younger sister. It was a dark and sad winter which we spent in our old house of Pokróvskoe. The weather was cold and so windy that the snowdrifts came higher than the windows; the panes were almost always dimmed by frost, and we seldom walked or drove anywhere throughout the winter. Our visitors were few, and those who came brought no addition of cheerfulness or happiness to the household. They all wore sad faces and spoke low, as if they were afraid of waking someone; they never laughed, but sighed and often shed tears as they looked at me and especially at little Sónya in her black frock. The feeling of death clung to the house; the air was still filled with the grief and horror of death. My mother's room was kept locked; and whenever I passed it on my way to bed, I felt a strange uncomfortable impulse to look into that cold empty room.

I was then seventeen; and in the very year of her death my mother was intending to move to Petersburg, in order to take me into society. The loss of my mother was a great grief to me; but I must confess to another feeling behind that grief—a feeling that though I was young and pretty (so everybody told me), I was wasting a second winter in the solitude of the country. Before the winter ended, this sense of dejection, solitude, and simple boredom increased to such an extent that I refused to leave my room or open the piano or take up a book. When Kátya urged me to find some occupation, I said that I did not feel able for it; but in my heart I said, 'What is the good of it? What is the good of doing anything, when the best part of my life is being wasted like this?' And to this question, tears were my only answer.

I was told that I was growing thin and losing my looks; but even this failed to interest me. What did it matter? For whom? I felt that my whole life was bound to go on in the same solitude and helpless dreariness, from which I had myself no strength and even no wish to escape. Towards the end of winter Kátya became anxious about me and determined to make an effort to take me abroad. But money was needed for this, and we hardly knew how our affairs stood after my mother's death. Our guardian, who was to come and clear up our position, was expected every day.

In March he arrived.

'Well, thank God!' Kátya said to me one day, when I was walking up and down the room like a shadow, without occupation, without a thought, and without a wish. 'Sergéy Mikháylych has arrived; he has sent to inquire about us and means to come here for dinner. You must rouse yourself, dear Máshechka,' she added, 'or what will he think of you? He was so fond of you all.'

Sergéy Mikháylych was our near neighbour, and, though a much younger man, had been a friend of my father's. His coming was likely to change our plans and to make it possible to leave the country;

and also I had grown up in the habit of love and regard for him; and when Kátya begged me to rouse myself, she guessed rightly that it would give me especial pain to show to disadvantage before him, more than before any other of our friends. Like everyone in the house, from Kátya and his god-daughter Sónya down to the helper in the stables, I loved him from old habit; and also he had a special significance for me, owing to a remark which my mother had once made in my presence. 'I should like you to marry a man like him,' she said. At the time this seemed to me strange and even unpleasant. My ideal husband was quite different: he was to be thin, pale, and sad; and Sergéy Mikháylych was middle-aged, tall, robust, and always, as it seemed to me, in good spirits. But still my mother's words stuck in my head; and even six years before this time, when I was eleven, and he still said 'thou' to me, and played with me, and called me by the pet-name of 'violet'—even then I sometimes asked myself in a fright, 'What *shall* I do, if he suddenly wants to marry me?'

Before our dinner, to which Kátya made an addition of sweets and a dish of spinach, Sergéy Mikháylych arrived. From the window I watched him drive up to the house in a small sleigh; but as soon as it turned the corner, I hastened to the drawing-room, meaning to pretend that his visit was a complete surprise. But when I heard his tramp and loud voice and Kátya's footsteps in the hall, I lost patience and went to meet him myself. He was holding Kátya's hand, talking loud, and smiling. When he saw me, he stopped and looked at me for a time without bowing. I was uncomfortable and felt myself blushing.

'Can this be really you?' he said in his plain decisive way, walking towards me with his arms apart.

'Is so great a change possible? How grown-up you are! I used to call you "violet", but now you are a rose in full bloom!'

He took my hand in his own large hand and pressed it so hard that it almost hurt. Expecting him to kiss my hand, I bent towards him, but he only pressed it again and looked straight into my eyes with the old firmness and cheerfulness in his face.

It was six years since I had seen him last. He was much changed—older and darker in complexion; and he now wore whiskers which did not become him at all; but much remained the same—his simple manner, the large features of his honest open face, his bright intelligent eyes, his friendly, almost boyish, smile.

Five minutes later he had ceased to be a visitor and had become the friend of us all, even of the servants, whose visible eagerness to wait on him proved their pleasure at his arrival.

He behaved quite unlike the neighbours who had visited us after my mother's death. They had thought it necessary to be silent when they sat with us, and to shed tears. He, on the contrary, was cheerful and talkative, and said not a word about my mother, so that this indifference seemed strange to me at first and even improper on the part of so close a friend. But I understood later that what seemed indifference was sincerity, and I felt grateful for it. In the evening Kátya poured out tea, sitting in her old place in the drawing-room, where she used to sit in my mother's lifetime; Sónya and I sat near him; our old butler Grigóri had hunted out one of my father's pipes and brought it to him; and he began to walk up and down the room as he used to do in past days.

'How many terrible changes there are in this

house, when one thinks of it all!' he said, stopping in his walk.

'Yes,' said Kátya with a sigh; and then she put the lid on the samovar and looked at him, quite ready to burst out crying.

'I suppose you remember your father?' he said, turning to me.

'Not clearly,' I answered.

'How happy you would have been together now!' he added in a low voice, looking thoughtfully at my face above the eyes. 'I was very fond of him,' he added in a still lower tone, and it seemed to me that his eyes were shining more than usual.

'And now God has taken her too!' said Kátya; and at once she laid her napkin on the teapot, took out her handkerchief, and began to cry.

'Yes, the changes in this house are terrible,' he repeated, turning away. 'Sónya, show me your toys,' he added after a little and went off to the parlour. When he had gone, I looked at Kátya with eyes full of tears.

'What a splendid friend he is!' she said. And, though he was no relation, I did really feel a kind of warmth and comfort in the sympathy of this good man.

I could hear him moving about in the parlour with Sónya, and the sound of her high childish voice. I sent tea to him there; and I heard him sit down at the piano and strike the keys with Sónya's little hands.

Then his voice came—'Márya Alexándrovna, come here and play something.'

I liked his easy behaviour to me and his friendly tone of command; I got up and went to him.

'Play this,' he said, opening a book of Beethoven's music at the *adagio* of the Moonlight Sonata. 'Let me hear how you play,' he added, and went off to a corner of the room, carrying his cup with him.

I somehow felt that with him it was impossible to refuse or to say beforehand that I played badly: I sat down obediently at the piano and began to play as well as I could; yet I was afraid of criticism, because I knew that he understood and enjoyed music. The *adagio* suited the remembrance of past days evoked by our conversation at tea, and I believe that I played it fairly well. But he would not let me play the *scherzo*. 'No,' he said, coming up to me; 'you don't play that right; don't go on; but the first movement was not bad; you seem to be musical.' This moderate praise pleased me so much that I even reddened. I felt it pleasant and strange that a friend of my father's, and his contemporary, should no longer treat me like a child but speak to me seriously. Kátya now went upstairs to put Sónya to bed, and we were left alone in the parlour.

He talked to me about my father, and about the beginning of their friendship and the happy days they had spent together, while I was still busy with lesson-books and toys; and his talk put my father before me in quite a new light, as a man of simple and delightful character. He asked me too about my tastes, what I read and what I intended to do, and gave me advice. The man of mirth and jest who used to tease me and make me toys had disappeared; here was a serious, simple, and affectionate friend, for whom I could not help feeling respect and sympathy. It was easy and pleasant to talk to him; and yet I felt an involuntary strain also. I was anxious about each word I spoke: I wished so much to earn for my own sake the love which had been given me already merely because I was my father's daughter.

After putting Sónya to bed, Kátya joined us and

began to complain to him of my apathy, about which I had said nothing.

'So she never told me the most important thing of all!' he said, smiling and shaking his head reproachfully at me.

'Why tell you?' I said. 'It is very tiresome to talk about, and it will pass off.' (I really felt now, not only that my dejection would pass off, but that it had already passed off, or rather had never existed.)

'It is a bad thing,' he said, 'not to be able to stand solitude. Can it be that you are a young lady?'

'Of course, I am a young lady,' I answered, laughing.

'Well, I can't praise a young lady who is alive only when people are admiring her, but as soon as she is left alone, collapses and finds nothing to her taste—one who is all for show and has no resources in herself.'

'You have a flattering opinion of me!' I said, just for the sake of saying something.

He was silent for a little. Then he said: 'Yes; your likeness to your father means something. There is something in you . . . ,' and his kind attentive look again flattered me and made me feel a pleasant embarrassment.

I noticed now for the first time that his face, which gave one at first the impression of high spirits, had also an expression peculiar to himself—bright at first and then more and more attentive and rather sad.

'You ought not to be bored and you cannot be,' he said; 'you have music, which you appreciate, books, study; your whole life lies before you, and now or never is the time to prepare for it and save yourself future regrets. A year hence it will be too late.'

He spoke to me like a father or an uncle, and

I felt that he kept a constant check upon himself, in order to keep on my level. Though I was hurt that he considered me as inferior to himself, I was pleased that for me alone he thought it necessary to try to be different.

For the rest of the evening he talked about business with Kátya.

'Well, good-bye, dear friends,' he said. Then he got up, came towards me, and took my hand.

'When shall we see you again?' asked Kátya.

'In spring,' he answered, still holding my hand. 'I shall go now to Daníilovka' (this was another property of ours), 'look into things there and make what arrangements I can; then I go to Moscow on business of my own; and in summer we shall meet again.'

'Must you really be away so long?' I asked, and I felt terribly grieved. I had really hoped to see him every day, and I felt a sudden shock of regret, and a fear that my depression would return. And my face and voice must have made this plain.

'You must find more to do and not get depressed,' he said; and I thought his tone too cool and unconcerned. 'I shall put you through an examination in spring,' he added, letting go my hand and not looking at me.

When we saw him off in the hall, he put on his fur coat in a hurry and still avoided looking at me. 'He is taking a deal of trouble for nothing!' I thought. 'Does he think me so anxious that he should look at me? He is a good man, a very good man; but that's all.'

That evening, however, Kátya and I sat up late, talking, not about him but about our plans for the summer, and where we should spend next winter and what we should do then. I had ceased to ask that terrible question—what is the good of it all?

Now it seemed quite plain and simple: the proper object of life was happiness, and I promised myself much happiness ahead. It seemed as if our gloomy old house had suddenly become full of light and life.

CHAPTER II

MEANWHILE spring arrived. My old dejection passed away and gave place to the unrest which spring brings with it, full of dreams and vague hopes and desires. Instead of living as I had done at the beginning of winter, I read and played the piano and gave lessons to Sónya; but also I often went into the garden and wandered for long alone through the avenues, or sat on a bench there; and Heaven knows what my thoughts and wishes and hopes were at such times. Sometimes at night, especially if there was a moon, I sat by my bedroom window till dawn; sometimes, when Kátya was not watching, I stole out into the garden wearing only a wrapper and ran through the dew as far as the pond; and once I went all the way to the open fields and walked right round the garden alone at night.

I find it difficult now to recall and understand the dreams which then filled my imagination. Even when I *can* recall them, I find it hard to believe that my dreams were just like that: they were so strange and so remote from life.

Sergéy Mikháylych kept his promise: he returned from his travels at the end of May.

His first visit to us was in the evening and was quite unexpected. We were sitting in the veranda, preparing for tea. By this time the garden was all green, and the nightingales had taken up their quarters for the whole of St. Peter's Fast in the leafy borders. The tops of the round lilac bushes had a sprinkling of white and purple—a sign that their flowers were ready to open. The foliage of the birch avenue was all transparent in the light of the setting sun. In the veranda there was shade and freshness. The evening dew was sure to be heavy on the grass. Out of doors beyond the garden the last sounds of day were audible, and the noise of the sheep and cattle, as they were driven home. Níkon, the half-witted boy, was driving his water-cart along the path outside the veranda, and a cold stream of water from the sprinkler made dark circles on the mould round the stems and supports of the dahlias. In our veranda the polished samovar shone and hissed on the white table-cloth; there were crack-nels and biscuits and cream on the table. Kátya was busy washing the cups with her plump hands. I was too hungry after bathing to wait for tea, and was eating bread with thick fresh cream. I was wearing a gingham blouse with loose sleeves, and my hair, still wet, was covered with a kerchief. Kátya saw him first, even before he came in.

'You, Sergéy Mikháylych!' she cried. 'Why, we were just talking about you.'

I got up, meaning to go and change my dress, but he caught me just by the door.

'Why stand on such ceremony in the country?' he said, looking with a smile at the kerchief on my head. 'You don't mind the presence of your butler, and I am really the same to you as Grigóri is.' But I felt just then that he was looking at me in a way quite unlike Grigóri's way, and I was uncom-fortable.

'I shall come back at once,' I said, as I left them.

'But what is wrong?' he called out after me; 'it's just the dress of a young peasant woman.'

'How strangely he looked at me!' I said to myself as I was quickly changing upstairs. 'Well, I'm glad he has come; things will be more lively.' After a look in the glass I ran gaily downstairs and into the veranda; I was out of breath and did not disguise my haste. He was sitting at the table, talking to Kátya about our affairs. He glanced at me and smiled; then he went on talking. From what he said it appeared that our affairs were in capital shape: it was now possible for us, after spending the summer in the country, to go either to Petersburg for Sónya's education, or abroad.

'If only you would go abroad with us—' said Kátya; 'without you we shall be quite lost there.'

'Oh, I should like to go round the world with you,' he said, half in jest and half in earnest.

'All right,' I said; 'let us start off and go round the world.'

He smiled and shook his head.

'What about my mother? What about my business?' he said. 'But that's not the question just now: I want to know how you have been spending your time. Not depressed again, I hope?'

When I told him that I had been busy and not bored during his absence, and when Kátya confirmed my report, he praised me as if he had a right to do so, and his words and looks were kind, as they might have been to a child. I felt obliged to tell him, in detail and with perfect frankness, all my good actions, and to confess, as if I were in church, all that he might disapprove of. The evening was so fine that we stayed in the veranda after tea was cleared away; and the conversation interested me so much that I did not notice how we ceased by degrees to hear any sound of the servants indoors. The scent of flowers grew stronger and came from all sides; the grass was drenched with dew; a nightingale struck up in a lilac bush close by and then stopped on hearing our voices; the starry sky seemed to come down lower over our heads.

It was growing dusk, but I did not notice it till a bat suddenly and silently flew in beneath the veranda awning and began to flutter round my white shawl. I shrank back against the wall and nearly cried out; but the bat as silently and swiftly dived out from under the awning and disappeared in the half-darkness of the garden.

'How fond I am of this place of yours!' he said, changing the conversation; 'I wish I could spend all my life here, sitting in this veranda.'

'Well, do then!' said Kátya.

'That's all very well,' he said, 'but life won't sit still.'

'Why don't you marry?' asked Kátya; 'you would make an excellent husband.'

'Because I like sitting still?' and he laughed. 'No, Katerína Kárlovna, too late for you and me to marry. People have long ceased to think of me as a marrying man, and I am even surer of it myself; and I declare I have felt quite comfortable since the matter was settled.'

It seemed to me that he said this in an unnaturally persuasive way.

'Nonsense!' said Kátya; 'a man of thirty-six makes out that he is too old!'

'Too old indeed,' he went on, 'when all one wants is to sit still. For a man who is going to marry that's not enough. Just you ask her,' he added, nodding at me; 'people of her age should marry, and you and I can rejoice in their happiness.'

The sadness and constraint latent in his voice was not lost upon me. He was silent for a little, and neither Kátya nor I spoke.

'Well, just fancy,' he went on, turning a little on his seat; 'suppose that by some mischance I married a girl of seventeen, Másha, if you like—I mean, Márya Alexándrovna. The instance is good; I am glad it turned up; there could not be a better instance.'

I laughed; but I could not understand why he was glad, or what it was that had turned up.

'Just tell me honestly, with your hand on your heart,' he said, turning as if playfully to me, 'would it not be a misfortune for you to unite your life with that of an old worn-out man who only wants to sit still, whereas Heaven knows what wishes are fermenting in that heart of yours?'

I felt uncomfortable and was silent, not knowing how to answer him.

'I am not making you a proposal, you know,' he said, laughing; 'but am I really the kind of husband you dream of when walking alone in the avenue at twilight? It would be a misfortune, would it not?'

'No, not a misfortune,' I began.

'But a bad thing,' he ended my sentence.

'Perhaps; but I may be mistaken . . .' He interrupted me again.

'There, you see! She is quite right, and I am grateful to her for her frankness, and very glad to have had this conversation. And there is something else to be said'—he added: 'for me too it would be a very great misfortune.'

'How odd you are! You have not changed in the least,' said Kátya, and then left the veranda, to order supper to be served.

When she had gone, we were both silent and all was still around us, but for one exception. A nightingale, which had sung last night by fitful snatches, now flooded the garden with a steady stream of song, and was soon answered by another from the dell below, which had not sung till that evening. The nearer bird stopped and seemed to listen for a moment, and then broke out again still louder than before, pouring out his song in piercing long-drawn cadences. There was a regal calm in the birds' voices, as they floated through the realm of night which belongs to those birds and not to man. The gardener walked past to his sleeping-quarters in the greenhouse, and the noise of his heavy boots grew fainter and fainter along the path. Someone whistled twice sharply at the foot of the hill; and then all was still again. The rustling of leaves could just be heard; the veranda awning flapped; a faint perfume, floating in the air, came down on the veranda and filled it. I felt silence awkward after what had been said, but what to say I did not know. I looked at him. His eyes, bright in the half-darkness, turned towards me.

'How good life is!' he said.

I sighed, I don't know why.

'Well?' he asked.

'Life is good,' I repeated after him.

Again we were silent, and again I felt uncomfortable. I could not help fancying that I had wounded him by agreeing that he was old; and I wished to comfort him but did not know how.

'Well, I must be saying good-bye,' he said, rising; 'my mother expects me for supper; I have hardly seen her all day.'

'I meant to play you the new sonata,' I said.

'That must wait,' he replied; and I thought that he spoke coldly.

'Good-bye.'

I felt still more certain that I had wounded him, and I was sorry. Kátya and I went to the steps to see him off and stood for a while in the open, looking along the road where he had disappeared from view. When we ceased to hear the sound of his horse's hoofs, I walked round the house to the veranda, and again sat looking into the garden; and all I wished to see and hear, I still saw and heard for a long time in the dewy mist filled with the sounds of night.

He came a second time, and a third; and the awkwardness arising from that strange conversation passed away entirely, never to return. During that whole summer he came two or three times a week; and I grew so accustomed to his presence, that, when he failed to come for some time, I missed him and felt angry with him, and thought he was behaving badly in deserting me. He treated me like a boy whose company he liked, asked me questions, invited the most cordial frankness on my part, gave me advice and encouragement, or sometimes scolded and checked me. But in spite of his constant effort to keep on my level, I was aware that behind the part of him which I could understand there remained an entire region of mystery, into which he did not consider it necessary to admit me; and this fact did much to preserve my respect for him and his attraction for me. I knew from Kátya and from our neighbours that he had not only to care for his old mother with whom he lived, and to manage his own estate and our affairs, but was also responsible for some public business which was the source of serious worries; but what view he took of all this, what were his convictions, plans, and hopes, I could not in the least find out from him. Whenever I turned the conversation to his affairs, he frowned in a way peculiar to himself and seemed to imply, 'Please stop! That is no business of yours;' and then he changed the subject. This hurt me at first; but I soon grew accustomed to confining our talk to my affairs, and felt this to be quite natural.

There was another thing which displeased me at first and then became pleasant to me. This was his complete indifference and even contempt for my personal appearance. Never by word or look did he imply that I was pretty; on the contrary, he frowned and laughed, whenever the word was applied to me in his presence. He even liked to find fault with my looks and tease me about them. On special days Kátya liked to dress me out in fine clothes and to arrange my hair effectively; but my finery met only with mockery from him, which pained kind-hearted Kátya and at first disconcerted me. She had made up her mind that he admired me; and she could not understand how a man could help wishing a woman whom he admired to appear to the utmost advantage. But I soon understood what he wanted. He wished to make sure that I had not a trace of affectation. And when I understood this I was really quite free from affectation in the clothes I wore, or the arrangement of my hair, or my movements; but a very obvious form of affectation took its place—an affectation of simplicity, at a time when I could not yet be really simple. That he loved me, I knew; but I did not yet ask myself whether he loved me as a child or as a woman. I valued his love; I felt that he thought me better than all other young women in the world, and I could not help wishing him to go on being deceived about me. Without wishing to deceive him, I did deceive him, and I became better myself while deceiving him. I felt it a better and worthier course to show him the good points of my heart and mind than of my body. My hair, hands, face, ways—all these, whether good or bad, he had appraised at once and knew so well, that I could add nothing to my external appearance except the wish to deceive him. But my mind and heart he did not know, because he loved them, and because they were in the very process of growth and development; and on this point I could and did deceive him. And how easy I felt in his company, once I understood this clearly! My causeless bashfulness and awkward movements completely disappeared. Whether he saw me from in front, or in profile, sitting or standing, with my hair up or my hair down, I felt that he knew me from head to foot, and I fancied, was satisfied with me as I was. If, contrary to his habit, he had suddenly said to me as other people did, that I had a pretty face, I believe that I should not have liked it at all. But, on the other hand, how light and happy my heart was when, after I had said something, he looked hard at me and said, hiding emotion under a mask of raillery:

'Yes, there *is* something in you! you are a fine girl—that I must tell you.'

And for what did I receive such rewards, which filled my heart with pride and joy? Merely for saying that I felt for old Grigóri in his love for his little granddaughter; or because the reading of some poem or novel moved me to tears; or because I liked Mozart better than Schulhof. And I was surprised at my own quickness in guessing what was good and worthy of love, when I certainly did not know then what *was* good and worthy to be loved. Most of my former tastes and habits did not please him; and a mere look of his, or a twitch of his eyebrow was enough to show that he did not like what I was trying to say; and I felt at once that my own standard was changed. Sometimes, when he was about to give me a piece of advice, I seemed to know beforehand what he would say. When he looked in my face and asked me a question, his very look would draw out of me the answer he wanted. All my thoughts and feelings of that time were not really mine: they were his thoughts and feelings, which had suddenly become mine and passed into my life and lighted it up. Quite unconsciously I began to look at everything with different eyes—at Kátya and the servants and Sónya and myself and my occupations. Books, which I used to read merely to escape boredom, now became one of the chief pleasures of my life, merely because he brought me the books and we read and discussed them together. The lessons I gave to Sónya had been a burdensome obligation which I forced myself to go through from a sense of duty; but, after he was present at a lesson, it became a joy to me to watch Sónya's progress. It used to seem to me an impossibility to learn a whole piece of music by heart; but now, when I knew that he would hear it and might praise it, I would play a single movement forty times over without stopping, till poor Kátya stuffed her ears with cotton-wool, while I was still not weary of it. The same old sonatas seemed quite different in their expression, and came out quite changed and much improved. Even Kátya, whom I knew and loved like a second self, became different in my eyes. I now understood for the first time that she was not in the least bound to be the mother, friend, and slave that she was to us. Now I appreciated all the self-sacrifice and devotion of this affectionate creature, and all my obligations to her; and I began to love her even better. It was he too who taught me to take quite a new view of our serfs and servants and maids. It is an absurd confession to make—but I had spent seventeen years among these people and yet knew less about them than about strangers whom I had never seen; it had never once occurred to me that they had their affections and wishes and sorrows, just as I had. Our garden and woods and fields, which I had known so long, became suddenly new and beautiful to me. He was right in saying that the only certain happiness in life is to live for others. At the time his words seemed to me strange, and

I did not understand them; but by degrees this became a conviction with me, without thinking about it. He revealed to me a whole new world of joys in the present, without changing anything in my life, without adding anything except himself to each impression in my mind. All that had surrounded me from childhood without saying anything to me, suddenly came to life. The mere sight of him made everything begin to speak and press for admittance to my heart, filling it with happiness.

Often during that summer, when I went upstairs to my room and lay down on my bed, the old unhappiness of spring with its desires and hopes for the future gave place to a passionate happiness in the present. Unable to sleep, I often got up and sat on Kátya's bed, and told her how perfectly happy I was, though I now realize that this was quite unnecessary, as she could see it for herself. But she told me that she was quite content and perfectly happy, and kissed me. I believed her—it seemed to me so necessary and just that everyone should be happy. But Kátya could think of sleep too; and sometimes, pretending to be angry, she drove me from her bed and went to sleep, while I turned over and over in my mind all that made me so happy. Sometimes I got up and said my prayers over again, praying in my own words and thanking God for all the happiness he had given me.

All was quiet in the room; there was only the even breathing of Kátya in her sleep, and the ticking of the clock by her bed, while I turned from side to side and whispered words of prayer, or crossed myself and kissed the cross round my neck. The door was shut and the windows shuttered; perhaps a fly or gnat hung buzzing in the air. I felt a wish never to leave that room—a wish that dawn might never come, that my present frame of mind might never change. I felt that my dreams and thoughts and prayers were live things, living there in the dark with me, hovering about my bed, and standing over me. And every thought was his thought, and every feeling his feeling. I did not know yet that this was love; I thought that things might go on so for ever, and that this feeling involved no consequences.

CHAPTER III

ONE day when the corn was being carried, I went with Kátya and Sónya to our favourite seat in the garden, in the shade of the lime-trees and above the dell, beyond which the fields and woods lay open before us. It was three days since Sergéy Mikháylych had been to see us; we were expecting him, all the more because our bailiff reported that he had promised to visit the harvest-field. At two o'clock we saw him ride on to the rye-field. With a smile and a glance at me, Kátya ordered peaches and cherries, of which he was very fond, to be brought; then she lay down on the bench and began to doze. I tore off a crooked flat lime-tree branch, which made my hand wet with its juicy leaves and juicy bark. Then I fanned Kátya with it and went on with my book, breaking off from time to time, to look at the field-path along which he must come. Sónya was making a dolls' house at the root of an old lime-tree. The day was sultry, windless, and steaming; the clouds were packing and growing blacker; all morning a thunderstorm had been gathering, and I felt restless, as I always did before thunder. But by afternoon the clouds began to part, the sun sailed out into a clear sky, and only in one quarter was there a faint rumbling. A single heavy cloud, louring above the horizon and mingling with the dust from the fields, was rent from time to time by pale zigzags of lightning which ran down to the ground. It was clear that for to-day the storm would pass off, with us at all events. The road beyond the garden was visible in places, and we could see a procession of high creaking carts slowly moving along it with their load of sheaves, while the empty carts rattled at a faster pace to meet them, with swaying legs and shirts fluttering in them. The thick dust neither blew away nor settled down—it stood still beyond the fence, and we could see it through the transparent foliage of the garden trees. A little farther off, in the stack-yard, the same voices and the same creaking of wheels were audible; and the same yellow sheaves that had moved slowly past the fence were now flying aloft, and I could see the oval stacks gradually rising higher, and their conspicuous pointed tops, and the labourers swarming upon them. On the dusty field in front more carts were moving and more yellow sheaves were visible; and the noise of the carts, with the sound of talking and singing, came to us from a distance. At one side the bare stubble, with strips of fallow covered with wormwood, came more and more into view. Lower down, to the right, the gay dresses of the women were visible, as they bent down and swung their arms to bind the sheaves. Here the bare stubble looked untidy; but the disorder was cleared by degrees, as the pretty sheaves were ranged at close intervals. It seemed as if summer had suddenly turned to autumn before my eyes. The dust and heat were everywhere, except in our favourite nook in the garden; and everywhere, in this heat and dust and under the burning sun, the labourers carried on their heavy task with talk and noise.

Meanwhile Kátya slept so sweetly on our shady bench, beneath her white cambric handkerchief, the black juicy cherries glistened so temptingly on the plate, our dresses were so clean and fresh, the water in the jug was so bright with rainbow colours in the sun, and I felt so happy! 'How can I help it?' I thought; 'am I to blame for being happy? And how can I share my happiness? How and to whom can I surrender all myself and all my happiness?'

By this time the sun had sunk behind the tops of the birch avenue, the dust was settling on the fields, the distance became clearer and brighter in the slanting light. The clouds had dispersed altogether; I could see through the trees the thatch of three new corn-stacks. The labourers came down off the stacks; the carts hurried past, evidently for the last time, with a loud noise of shouting; the women, with rakes over their shoulders and straw-bands in their belts, walked home past us, singing loudly; and still there was no sign of Sergéy Mikháylych, though I had seen him ride down the hill long ago. Suddenly he appeared upon the avenue, coming from a quarter where I was not looking for him. He had walked round by the dell. He came quickly towards me, with his hat off and radiant with high spirits. Seeing that Kátya was asleep, he bit his lip, closed his eyes, and advanced on tiptoe; I saw at once that he was in that peculiar mood of causeless merriment which I always delighted to see in him, and which we called 'wild ecstasy'. He was just like a schoolboy playing truant; his whole figure, from head to foot, breathed content, happiness, and boyish frolic.

'Well, young violet, how are you? All right?' he said in a whisper, coming up to me and taking my hand. Then, in answer to my question, 'Oh, I'm splendid to-day, I feel like a boy of thirteen—I want to play at horses and climb trees.'

'Is it wild ecstasy?' I asked, looking into his laughing eyes, and feeling that the 'wild ecstasy' was infecting me.

'Yes,' he answered, winking and checking a smile. 'But I don't see why you need hit Katerína Kárlovna on the nose.'

With my eyes on him I had gone on waving the branch, without noticing that I had knocked the handkerchief off Kátya's face and was now brushing her with the leaves. I laughed.

'She will say she was awake all the time,' I whispered, as if not to awake Kátya; but that was not my real reason—it was only that I liked to whisper to him.

He moved his lips in imitation of me, pretending that my voice was too low for him to hear. Catching sight of the dish of cherries, he pretended to steal it, and carried it off to Sónya under the lime-tree, where he sat down on her dolls. Sónya was angry at first, but he soon made his peace with her by starting a game, to see which of them could eat cherries faster.

'If you like, I will send for more cherries,' I said; 'or let us go ourselves.'

He took the dish and set the dolls on it, and we all three started for the orchard. Sónya ran behind us, laughing and pulling at his coat, to make him surrender the dolls. He gave them up and then turned to me, speaking more seriously.

'You really are a violet,' he said, still speaking low, though there was no longer any fear of waking anybody; 'when I came to you out of all that dust and heat and toil, I positively smelt violets at once. But not the sweet violet—you know, that early dark violet that smells of melting snow and spring grass.'

'Is harvest going on well?' I asked, in order to hide the happy agitation which his words produced in me.

'First-rate! Our people are always splendid. The more you know them, the better you like them.'

'Yes,' I said; 'before you came I was watching them from the garden, and suddenly I felt ashamed to be so comfortable myself while they were hard at work, and so . . .'

He interrupted me, with a kind but grave look: 'Don't talk like that, my dear; it is too sacred a matter to talk of lightly. God forbid that you should use fine phrases about that!'

'But it is only to *you* I say this.'

'All right, I understand. But what about those cherries?'

The orchard was locked, and no gardener to be seen: he had sent them all off to help with the harvest. Sónya ran to fetch the key. But he would not wait for her: climbing up a corner of the wall, he raised the net and jumped down on the other side.

His voice came over the wall—'If you want some, give me the dish.'

'No,' I said; 'I want to pick for myself. I shall fetch the key; Sónya won't find it.'

But suddenly I felt that I must see what he was doing there and what he looked like—that I must watch his movements while he supposed that no one saw him. Besides I was simply unwilling just then to lose sight of him for a single minute. Running on tiptoe through the nettles to the other side of the orchard where the wall was lower, I mounted on an empty cask, till the top of the wall was on a level with my waist, and then leaned over into the orchard. I looked at the gnarled old trees, with their broad dented leaves and the ripe black cherries hanging straight and heavy among the foliage; then I pushed my head under the net, and from under the knotted bough of an old cherry-tree I caught sight of Sergéy Mikháylych. He evidently thought that I had gone away and that no one was watching him. With his hat off and his eyes shut, he was sitting on the fork of an old tree and carefully rolling into a ball a lump of cherry-tree gum. Suddenly he shrugged his shoulders, opened his eyes, muttered something, and smiled. Both words and smile were so unlike him that I felt ashamed of myself for eavesdropping. It seemed to me that he had said, 'Másha!' 'Impossible,' I thought. 'Darling Másha!' he said again, in a lower and more tender tone. There was no possible doubt about the two words this time. My heart beat hard, and such a passionate joy—illicit joy, as I felt—took hold of me, that I clutched at the wall, fearing to fall and betray myself. Startled by the sound of my movement, he looked round—he dropped his eyes instantly, and his face turned red, even scarlet, like a child's. He tried to speak, but in vain; again and again his face positively flamed up. Still he smiled as he looked at me, and I smiled too. Then his whole face grew radiant with happiness. He had ceased to be the old uncle who spoiled or scolded me; he was a man on my level, who loved and feared me as I loved and feared him. We looked at one another without speaking. But suddenly he frowned; the smile and light in his eyes disappeared, and he resumed his cold paternal tone, just as if we were doing something wrong and he was repenting and calling on me to repent.

'You had better get down, or you will hurt yourself,' he said; 'and do put your hair straight; just think what you look like!'

'What makes him pretend? what makes him want

to give me pain?' I thought in my vexation. And the same instant brought an irresistible desire to upset his composure again and test my power over him.

'No,' I said; 'I mean to pick for myself.' I caught hold of the nearest branch and climbed to the top of the wall; then, before he had time to catch me, I jumped down on the other side.

'What foolish things you do!' he muttered, flushing again and trying to hide his confusion under a pretence of annoyance; 'you might really have hurt yourself. But how do you mean to get out of this?'

He was even more confused than before, but this time his confusion frightened rather than pleased me. It infected me too and made me blush; avoiding his eye and not knowing what to say, I began to pick cherries though I had nothing to put them in. I reproached myself, I repented of what I had done, I was frightened; I felt that I had lost his good opinion for ever by my folly. Both of us were silent and embarrassed. From this difficult situation Sónya rescued us by running back with the key in her hand. For some time we both addressed our conversation to her and said nothing to each other. When we returned to Kátya, who assured us that she had never been asleep and was listening all the time, I calmed down, and he tried to drop into his fatherly patronizing manner again, but I was not taken in by it. A discussion which we had had some days before came back clear before me.

Kátya had been saying that it was easier for a man to be in love and declare his love than for a woman.

'A man may say that he is in love, and a woman can't,' she said.

'I disagree,' said he; 'a man has no business to say, and can't say, that he is in love.'

'Why not?' I asked.

'Because it never can be true. What sort of a revelation is that, that a man is in love? A man seems to think that whenever he says the word, something will go pop!—that some miracle will be worked, signs and wonders, with all the big guns firing at once! In my opinion,' he went on, 'whoever solemnly brings out the words "I love you" is either deceiving himself or, which is even worse, deceiving others.'

'Then how is a woman to know that a man is in love with her, unless he tells her?' asked Kátya.

'That I don't know,' he answered; 'every man has his own way of telling things. If the feeling exists, it will out somehow. But when I read novels, I always fancy the crestfallen look of Lieut. Strélsky or Alfred, when he says, "I love you, Eleanora", and expects something wonderful to happen at once, and no change at all takes place in either of them—their eyes and their noses and their whole selves remain exactly as they were.'

Even then I had felt that this banter covered something serious that had reference to myself. But Kátya resented his disrespectful treatment of the heroes in novels.

'You are never serious,' she said; 'but tell me truthfully, have you never yourself told a woman that you loved her?'

'Never, and never gone down on one knee,' he answered, laughing; 'and never will.'

This conversation I now recalled, and I reflected that there was no need for him to tell me that he loved me. 'I know that he loves me,' I thought, 'and all his endeavours to seem indifferent will not change my opinion.'

He said little to me throughout the evening, but in every word he said to Kátya and Sónya and in every look and movement of his I saw love and felt no doubt of it. I was only vexed and sorry for him, that he thought it necessary still to hide his feelings and pretend coldness, when it was all so clear, and when it would have been so simple and easy to be boundlessly happy. But my jumping down to him in the orchard weighed on me like a crime. I kept feeling that he would cease to respect me and was angry with me.

After tea I went to the piano, and he followed me.

'Play me something—it is long since I heard you,' he said, catching me up in the parlour.

'I was just going to,' I said. Then I looked straight in his face and said quickly, 'Sergéy Mikháylych, you are not angry with me, are you?'

'What for?' he asked.

'For not obeying you this afternoon,' I said, blushing.

He understood me: he shook his head and made a grimace, which implied that I deserved a scolding but that he did not feel able to give it.

'So it's all right, and we are friends again?' I said, sitting down at the piano.

'Of course!' he said.

In the drawing-room, a large lofty room, there were only two lighted candles on the piano, the rest of the room remaining in half-darkness. Outside the open windows the summer night was bright. All was silent, except when the sound of Kátya's footsteps in the unlighted parlour was heard occasionally, or when his horse, which was tied up under the window, snorted or stamped his hoof on the burdocks that grew there. He sat behind me, where I could not see him; but everywhere—in the half-darkness of the room, in every sound, in myself—I felt his presence. Every look, every movement of his, though I could not see them, found an echo in my heart. I played a sonata of Mozart's which he had brought me and which I had learnt in his presence and for him. I was not thinking at all of what I was playing, but I believe that I played it well, and I thought that he was pleased. I was conscious of his pleasure, and conscious too, though I never looked at him, of the gaze fixed on me from behind. Still moving my fingers mechanically, I turned round quite involuntarily and looked at him. The night had grown brighter, and his head stood out on a background of darkness. He was sitting with his head propped on his hands, and his eyes shone as they gazed at me. Catching his look, I smiled and stopped playing. He smiled too and shook his head reproachfully at the music, for me to go on. When I stopped, the moon had grown brighter and was riding high in the heavens; and the faint light of the candles was supplemented by a new silvery light which came in through the windows and fell on the floor. Kátya called out that it was really too bad—that I had stopped at the best part of the piece, and that I was playing badly. But he declared that I had never played so well; and then he began to walk about the rooms—through the drawing-room to the unlighted parlour and back again to the drawing-room, and each time he looked at me and smiled. I smiled too; I wanted even to laugh with no reason; I was so happy at something that had happened that very day. Kátya and I were standing by the piano; and each time that he vanished through the drawing-room door, I started kissing her in my favourite place, the soft part of her neck under the chin; and each time he came back, I made a solemn face and refrained with difficulty from laughing.

'What is the matter with her to-day?' Kátya asked him.

He only smiled at me without answering; he knew what was the matter with me.

'Just look what a night it is!' he called out from the parlour, where he had stopped by the open French window looking into the garden.

We joined him; and it really was such a night as I have never seen since. The full moon shone above the house and behind us, so that we could not see it, and half the shadow, thrown by the roof and pillars of the house and by the veranda awning, lay slanting and foreshortened on the gravel-path and the strip of turf beyond. Everything else was bright and saturated with the silver of the dew and the moonlight. The broad garden-path, on one side of which the shadows of the dahlias and their supports lay aslant, all bright and cold, and shining on the inequalities of the gravel, ran on till it vanished in the mist. Through the trees the roof of the greenhouse shone bright, and a growing mist rose from the dell. The lilac-bushes, already partly leafless, were all bright to the centre. Each flower was distinguishable apart, and all were drenched with dew. In the avenues light and shade were so mingled that they looked, not like paths and trees but like transparent houses, swaying and moving. To our right, in the shadow of the house, everything was black, indistinguishable, and uncanny. But all the brighter for the surrounding darkness was the top of a poplar, with a fantastic crown of leaves, which for some strange reason remained there close to the house, towering into the bright light, instead of flying away into the dim distance, into the retreating dark-blue of the sky.

'Let us go for a walk,' I said.

Kátya agreed, but said I must put on goloshes.

'I don't want them, Kátya,' I said; 'Sergéy Mikháylych will give me his arm.'

As if that would prevent me from wetting my feet! But to us three this seemed perfectly natural at the time. Though he never used to offer me his arm, I now took it of my own accord, and he saw nothing strange in it. We all went down from the veranda together. That whole world, that sky, that garden, that air, were different from those that I knew.

We were walking along an avenue, and it seemed to me, whenever I looked ahead, that we could go no farther in the same direction, that the world of the possible ended there, and that the whole scene must remain fixed for ever in its beauty. But we still moved on, and the magic wall kept parting to let us in; and still we found the familiar garden with trees and paths and withered leaves. And we were really walking along the paths, treading on patches of light and shade; and a withered leaf was really crackling under my foot, and a live twig brushing my face. And that was really he, walking steadily and slowly at my side, and carefully supporting my arm; and that was really Kátya walking beside us with her creaking shoes. And that must be the moon in the sky, shining down on us through the motionless branches.

But at each step the magic wall closed up again behind us and in front, and I ceased to believe in the possibility of advancing farther—I ceased to believe in the reality of it all.

'Oh, there's a frog!' cried Kátya.

'Who said that? and why?' I thought. But then I realized it was Kátya, and that she was afraid of frogs. Then I looked at the ground and saw a little frog which gave a jump and then stood still in front of me, while its tiny shadow was reflected on the shining clay of the path.

'You're not afraid of frogs, are you?' he asked.

I turned and looked at him. Just where we were there was a gap of one tree in the lime-avenue, and I could see his face clearly—it was so handsome and so happy!

Though he had spoken of my fear of frogs, I knew that he meant to say, 'I love you, my dear one!' 'I love you, I love you' was repeated by his look, by his arm; the light, the shadow, and the air all repeated the same words.

We had gone all round the garden. Kátya's short steps had kept up with us, but now she was tired and out of breath. She said it was time to go in; and I felt very sorry for her. 'Poor thing!' I thought; 'why does not she feel as we do? why are we not all young and happy, like this night and like him and me?'

We went in, but it was a long time before he went away, though the cocks had crowed, and everyone in the house was asleep, and his horse, tethered under the window, snorted continually and stamped his hoof on the burdocks. Kátya never reminded us of the hour, and we sat on talking of the merest trifles and not thinking of the time, till it was past two. The cocks were crowing for the third time and the dawn was breaking when he rode away. He said good-bye as usual and made no special allusion; but I knew that from that day he was mine, and that I should never lose him now. As soon as I had confessed to myself that I loved him, I took Kátya into my confidence. She rejoiced in the news and was touched by my telling her; but she was actually able—poor thing!—to go to bed and sleep! For me, I walked for a long, long time about the veranda; then I went down to the garden, where, recalling each word, each movement, I walked along the same avenues through which I had walked with him. I did not sleep at all that night, and saw sunrise and early dawn for the first time in my life. And never again did I see such a night and such a morning. 'Only why does he not tell me plainly that he loves me?' I thought; 'what makes him invent obstacles and call himself old, when all is so simple and so splendid? What makes him waste this golden time which may never return? Let him say "I love you"—say it in plain words; let him take my hand in his and bend over it and say "I love you". Let him blush and look down before me; and then I will tell him all. No! not tell him, but throw my arms round him and press close to him and weep.' But then a thought came to me—'What if I am mistaken and he does not love me?'

I was startled by this fear—God knows where it might have led me. I recalled his embarrassment and mine, when I jumped down to him in the orchard; and my heart grew very heavy. Tears gushed from my eyes, and I began to pray. A strange thought occurred to me, calming me and bringing hope with it. I resolved to begin fasting on that day, to take the Communion on my birthday, and on that same day to be betrothed to him.

How this result would come to pass I had no idea; but from that moment I believed and felt sure it would be so. The dawn had fully come and the labourers were getting up when I went back to my room.

CHAPTER IV

THE Fast of the Assumption falling in August, no one in the house was surprised by my intention of fasting.

During the whole of the week he never once came to see us; but, far from being surprised or vexed or made uneasy by his absence, I was glad of it—I did not expect him until my birthday. Each day during the week I got up early. While the horses were being harnessed, I walked in the garden alone, turning over in my mind the sins of the day before, and considering what I must do to-day, so as to be satisfied with my day and not spoil it by a single sin. It seemed so easy to me then to abstain from sin altogether; only a trifling effort seemed necessary. When the horses came round, I got into the carriage with Kátya or one of the maids, and we drove to the church two miles away. While entering the church, I always recalled the prayer for those who 'come unto the Temple in the fear of God', and tried to get just that frame of mind when mounting the two grass-grown steps up to the building. At that hour there were not more than a dozen worshippers—household servants or peasant women keeping the Fast. They bowed to me, and I returned their bows with studied humility. Then, with what seemed to me a great effort of courage, I went myself and got candles from the man who kept them, an old soldier and an Elder; and I placed the candles before the icons. Through the central door of the altar-screen I could see the altar-cloth which my mother had worked; on the screen were the two angels which had seemed so big to me when I was little, and the dove with a golden halo which had fascinated me long ago. Behind the choir stood the old battered font, where I had been christened myself and had stood godmother to so many of the servants' children. The old priest came out, wearing a cope made of the pall that had covered my father's coffin, and began to read in the same voice that I had heard all my life—at services held in our house, at Sónya's christening, at memorial services for my father, and at my mother's funeral. The same old quavering voice of the deacon rose in the choir; and the same old woman, whom I could remember at every service in that church, crouched by the wall, fixing her streaming eyes on an icon in the choir, pressing her folded fingers against her faded kerchief, and muttering with her toothless gums. And these objects were no longer merely curious to me, merely interesting from old recollections—each had become important and sacred in my eyes and seemed charged with profound meaning. I listened to each word of the prayers and tried to suit my feeling to it; and if I failed to understand, I prayed silently that God would enlighten me, or made up a prayer of my own in place of what I had failed to catch. When the penitential prayers were repeated, I recalled my past life, and that innocent childish past seemed to me so black when compared to the present brightness of my soul, that I wept and was horrified at myself; but I felt too that all those sins would be forgiven, and that if my sins had been even greater, my repentance would be all the sweeter. At the end of the service when the priest said, 'The blessing of the Lord be upon you!' I seemed to feel an immediate sensation of physical well-being, of a mysterious light and warmth that instantly filled my heart. The service over, the priest came and asked me whether he should come to our house to say Mass, and what hour would suit me; and I thanked him for the suggestion, intended, as I thought, to please me, but said that I would come to church instead, walking or driving.

'Is that not too much trouble?' he asked. And I was at a loss for an answer, fearing to commit a sin of pride.

After the Mass, if Kátya was not with me. I

always sent the carriage home and walked back alone, bowing humbly to all who passed, and trying to find an opportunity of giving help or advice. I was eager to sacrifice myself for someone, to help in lifting a fallen cart, to rock a child's cradle, to give up the path to others by stepping into the mud. One evening I heard the bailiff report to Kátya that Simon, one of our serfs, had come to beg some boards to make a coffin for his daughter, and a rouble to pay the priest for the funeral; the bailiff had given what he asked. 'Are they as poor as that?' I asked. 'Very poor, Miss,' the bailiff answered; 'they have no salt to their food.' My heart ached to hear this, and yet I felt a kind of pleasure too. Pretending to Kátya that I was merely going for a walk, I ran upstairs, got out all my money (it was very little but it was all I had), crossed myself, and started off alone, through the veranda and the garden, on my way to Simon's hut. It stood at the end of the village, and no one saw me as I went up to the window, placed the money on the sill, and tapped on the pane. Someone came out, making the door creak, and hailed me; but I hurried home, cold and shaking with fear like a criminal. Kátya asked where I had been and what was the matter with me; but I did not answer, and did not even understand what she was saying. Everything suddenly seemed to me so petty and insignificant. I locked myself up in my own room, and walked up and down alone for a long time, unable to do anything, unable to think, unable to understand my own feelings. I thought of the joy of the whole family, and of what they would say of their benefactor; and I felt sorry that I had not given them the money myself. I thought too of what Sergéy Mikháylych would say, if he knew what I had done; and I was glad to think that no one would ever find out. I was so happy, and I felt myself and everyone else so bad, and yet was so kindly disposed to myself and to all the world, that the thought of death came to me as a dream of happiness. I smiled and prayed and wept, and felt at that moment a burning passion of love for all the world, myself included. Between services I used to read the Gospel; and the book became more and more intelligible to me, and the story of that divine life simpler and more touching; and the depths of thought and feeling I found in studying it became more awful and impenetrable. On the other hand, how clear and simple everything seemed to me when I rose from the study of this book and looked again on life around me and reflected on it! It was so difficult, I felt, to lead a bad life, and so simple to love everyone and be loved. All were so kind and gentle to me; even Sónya, whose lessons I had not broken off, was quite different—trying to understand and please me and not to vex me. Everyone treated me as I treated them. Thinking over my enemies, of whom I must ask pardon before confession, I could only remember one—one of our neighbours, a girl, whom I had made fun of in company a year ago, and who had ceased to visit us. I wrote to her, confessing my fault and asking her forgiveness. She replied that she forgave me and wished me to forgive her. I cried for joy over her simple words, and saw in them, at the time, a deep and touching feeling. My old nurse cried, when I asked her to forgive me. 'What makes them all so kind to me? what have I done to deserve their love?' I asked myself. Sergéy Mikháylych would come into my mind, and I thought for long about him. I could not help it, and I did not consider these thoughts sinful. But my thoughts of him were quite different from what they had been on the night when I first realized that I loved him: he seemed to me now like a second self, and became a part of every plan for the future. The inferiority which I had always felt in his presence had vanished entirely: I felt myself his equal, and could understand him thoroughly from the moral elevation I had reached. What had seemed strange in him was now quite clear to me. Now I could see what he meant by saying that to live for others was the only true happiness, and I agreed with him perfectly. I believed that our life together would be endlessly happy and untroubled. I looked forward, not to foreign tours or fashionable society or display, but to a quite different scene—a quiet family life in the country, with constant self-sacrifice, constant mutual love, and constant recognition in all things of the kind hand of Providence.

I carried out my plan of taking the Communion on my birthday. When I came back from church that day, my heart was so swelling with happiness that I was afraid of life, afraid of any feeling that might break in on that happiness. We had hardly left the carriage for the steps in front of the house, when there was a sound of wheels on the bridge, and I saw Sergéy Mikháylych drive up in his well-known trap. He congratulated me,* and we went together to the parlour. Never since I had known him had I been so much at my ease with him and so self-possessed as on that morning. I felt in myself a whole new world, out of his reach and beyond his comprehension. I was not conscious of the slightest embarrassment in speaking to him. He must have understood the cause of this feeling; for he was tender and gentle beyond his wont and showed a kind of reverent consideration for me. When I made

* It is the custom in Russia to congratulate anyone on his or her birthday, and also on receiving Communion.

for the piano, he locked it and put the key in his pocket.

'Don't spoil your present mood,' he said, 'you have the sweetest of all music in your soul just now.'

I was grateful for his words, and yet I was not quite pleased at his understanding too easily and clearly what ought to have been an exclusive secret in my heart. At dinner he said that he had come to congratulate me and also to say good-bye; for he must go to Moscow to-morrow. He looked at Kátya as he spoke; but then he stole a glance at me, and I saw that he was afraid he might detect signs of emotion on my face. But I was neither surprised nor agitated; I did not even ask whether he would be long away. I knew he would say this, and I knew that he would not go. How did I know? I cannot explain that to myself now; but on that memorable day it seemed that I knew everything that had been and that would be. It was like a delightful dream, when all that happens seems to have happened already and to be quite familiar, and it will all happen over again, and one knows that it will happen.

He meant to go away immediately after dinner; but, as Kátya was tired after church and went to lie down for a little, he had to wait until she woke up in order to say good-bye to her. The sun shone into the drawing-room, and we went out to the veranda. When we were seated, I began at once, quite calmly, the conversation that was bound to fix the fate of my heart. I began to speak, no sooner and no later, but at the very moment when we sat down, before our talk had taken any turn or colour that might have hindered me from saying what I meant to say. I cannot tell myself where it came from—my coolness and determination and preciseness of expression. It was as if something independent of my will was speaking through my lips. He sat opposite me with his elbows resting on the rails of the veranda; he pulled a lilac-branch towards him and stripped the leaves off it. When I began to speak, he let go the branch and leaned his head on one hand. His attitude might have shown either perfect calmness or strong emotion.

'Why are you going?' I asked, significantly, deliberately, and looking straight at him.

He did not answer at once.

'Business!' he muttered at last and dropped his eyes.

I realized how difficult he found it to lie to me, and in reply to such a frank question.

'Listen,' I said; 'you know what to-day is to me, how important for many reasons. If I question you, it is not to show an interest in your doings (you know that I have become intimate with you and fond of you)—I ask you this question, because I *must* know the answer. Why are you going?'

'It is very hard for me to tell you the true reason,' he said. 'During this week I have thought much about you and about myself, and have decided that I must go. You understand why; and if you care for me, you will ask no questions.' He put up a hand to rub his forehead and cover his eyes. 'I find it very difficult . . . But you will understand.'

My heart began to beat fast.

'I cannot understand you,' I said; 'I *cannot! you* must tell me; in God's name and for the sake of this day tell me what you please, and I shall hear it with calmness,' I said.

He changed his position, glanced at me, and again drew the lilac-twig towards him.

'Well!' he said, after a short silence in a voice that tried in vain to seem steady, 'it is a foolish business and impossible to put into words, and I feel the difficulty, but I will try to explain it to you,' he added, frowning as if in bodily pain.

'Well?' I said.

'Just imagine the existence of a man—let us call him A—who has left youth far behind, and of a woman whom we may call B, who is young and happy and has seen nothing as yet of life or of the world. Family circumstances of various kinds brought them together, and he grew to love her as a daughter, and had no fear that his love would change its nature.'

He stopped, but I did not interrupt him.

'But he forgot that B was so young, that life was still all a May-game to her,' he went on with a sudden swiftness and determination and without looking at me, 'and that it was easy to fall in love with her in a different way, and that this would amuse her. He made a mistake and was suddenly aware of another feeling, as heavy as remorse, making its way into his heart, and he was afraid. He was afraid that their old friendly relations would be destroyed, and he made up his mind to go away before that happened.' As he said this, he began again to rub his eyes, with a pretence of indifference, and to close them.

'Why was he afraid to love differently?' I asked very low; but I restrained my emotion and spoke in an even voice. He evidently thought that I was not serious; for he answered as if he were hurt.

'You are young, and I am not young. You want amusement, and I want something different. Amuse yourself, if you like, but not with me. If you do, I shall take it seriously; and then I shall be unhappy, and you will repent. That is what A said,' he added; 'however, this is all nonsense; but you understand why I am going. And don't let us continue this conversation. Please not!'

'No! no!' I said, 'we must continue it,' and tears began to tremble in my voice 'Did he love her, or not?'

He did not answer.

'If he did not love her, why did he treat her as a child and pretend to her?' I asked.

'Yes, A behaved badly,' he interrupted me quickly; 'but it all came to an end and they parted friends.'

'This is horrible! Is there no other ending?' I said with a great effort, and then felt afraid of what I had said.

'Yes, there is,' he said, showing a face full of emotion and looking straight at me. 'There are two different endings. But, for God's sake, listen to me quietly and don't interrupt. Some say'—here he stood up and smiled with a smile that was heavy with pain—'some say that A went off his head, fell passionately in love with B, and told her so. But she only laughed. To her it was all a jest, but to him a matter of life and death.'

I shuddered and tried to interrupt him—tried to say that he must not dare to speak for me; but he checked me, laying his hand on mine.

'Wait!' he said, and his voice shook. 'The other story is that she took pity on him, and fancied, poor child, from her ignorance of the world, that she really could love him, and so consented to be his wife. And he, in his madness, believed it—believed that his whole life could begin anew; but she saw herself that she had deceived him and that he had deceived her. . . . But let us drop the subject finally,' he ended, clearly unable to say more; and then he began to walk up and down in silence before me.

Though he had asked that the subject should be dropped, I saw that his whole soul was hanging on my answer. I tried to speak, but the pain at my heart kept me dumb. I glanced at him—he was pale and his lower lip trembled. I felt sorry for him. With a sudden effort I broke the bonds of silence which had held me fast, and began to speak in a low inward voice, which I feared would break every moment.

'There is a third ending to the story,' I said, and then paused, but he said nothing; 'the third ending is that he did not love her, but hurt her, hurt her, and thought that he was right; and he left her and was actually proud of himself. You have been pretending, not I; I have loved you since the first day we met, loved you,' I repeated, and at the word 'loved' my low inward voice changed, without intention of mine, to a wild cry which frightened me myself.

He stood pale before me, his lip trembled more and more violently, and two tears came out upon his cheeks.

'It is wrong!' I almost screamed, feeling that I was choking with angry unshed tears. 'Why do you do it?' I cried, and got up to leave him.

But he would not let me go. His head was resting on my knees, his lips were kissing my still trembling hands, and his tears were wetting them. 'My God! if I had only known!' he whispered.

'Why? why?' I kept on repeating, but in my heart there was happiness, happiness which had now come back, after so nearly departing for ever.

Five minutes later Sónya was rushing upstairs to Kátya and proclaiming all over the house that Másha intended to marry Sergéy Mikháylych.

CHAPTER V

There were no reasons for putting off our wedding, and neither he nor I wished for delay. Kátya, it is true, thought we ought to go to Moscow, to buy and order wedding-clothes; and his mother tried to insist that, before the wedding, he must set up a new carriage, buy new furniture, and re-paper the whole house. But we two together carried our point, that all these things, if they were really indispensable, should be done afterwards, and that we should be married within a fortnight after my birthday, quietly, without wedding-clothes, without a party, without best men and supper and champagne, and all the other conventional features of a wedding. He told me how dissatisfied his mother was that there should be no band, no mountain of luggage, no renovation of the whole house—so unlike her own marriage which had cost thirty thousand roubles; and he told of the solemn and secret confabulations which she held in her store-room with her housekeeper, Maryúshka, rummaging the chests and discussing carpets, curtains, and salvers as indispensable conditions of our happiness. At our house Kátya did just the same with my old nurse, Kuzmínichna. It was impossible to treat the matter lightly with Kátya. She was firmly convinced that he and I, when discussing our future, were merely talking the sentimental nonsense natural to people in our position; and that our real future happiness depended on the hemming of table-cloths and napkins and the proper cutting-out and stitching of under-clothing. Several times a day secret information passed between the two houses, to communicate what was going forward in each; and though the external relations between Kátya and his mother were most affectionate, yet a slightly hostile though very subtle diplomacy was already perceptible in their dealings. I now became more intimate with Tatyána Semënovna, the mother of Sergéy Mikháylych, an old-fashioned lady, strict and formal in the management of her household. Her son loved her, and not merely because she was his mother: he thought her the best, cleverest, kindest, and most affectionate woman in the world. She was always kind to us and to me especially, and was glad that her son should be getting married; but when I was with her after our engagement, I always felt that she wished me to understand that, in her opinion, her son might have looked higher, and that it would be as well for me to keep that in mind. I understood her meaning perfectly and thought her quite right.

During that fortnight he and I met every day. He came to dinner regularly and stayed on till midnight. But though he said—and I knew he was speaking the truth—that he had no life apart from me, yet he never spent the whole day with me, and tried to go on with his ordinary occupations. Our outward relations remained unchanged to the very day of our marriage: we went on saying 'you' and not 'thou' to each other; he did not even kiss my hand; he did not seek, but even avoided, opportunities of being alone with me. It was as if he feared to yield to the harmful excess of tenderness he felt. I don't know which of us had changed; but I now felt myself entirely his equal; I no longer found in him the pretence of simplicity which had displeased me earlier; and I often delighted to see in him, not a grown man inspiring respect and awe but a loving and wildly happy child. 'How mistaken I was about him!' I often thought; 'he is just such another human being as myself!' It seemed to me now, that his whole character was before me and that I thoroughly understood it. And how simple was every feature of his character, and how congenial to my own! Even his plans for our future life together were just my plans, only more clearly and better expressed in his words.

The weather was bad just then, and we spent most of our time indoors. The corner between the piano and the window was the scene of our best intimate talks. The candle-light was reflected on the blackness of the window near us; from time to time drops struck the glistening pane and rolled down. The rain pattered on the roof; the water splashed in a puddle under the spout; it felt damp near the window; but our corner seemed all the brighter and warmer and happier for that.

'Do you know, there is something I have long wished to say to you,' he began one night when we were sitting up late in our corner; 'I was thinking of it all the time you were playing.'

'Don't say it, I know all about it,' I replied.

'All right! mum's the word!'

'No! what is it?' I asked.

'Well, it is this. You remember the story I told you about A and B?'

'I should just think I did! What a stupid story! Lucky that it ended as it did!'

'Yes, I was very near destroying my happiness by my own act. You saved me. But the main thing is that I was always telling lies then, and I'm ashamed of it, and I want to have my say out now.'

'Please don't! you really mustn't!'

'Don't be frightened,' he said, smiling. 'I only want to justify myself. When I began then, I meant to argue.'

'It is always a mistake to argue,' I said.

'Yes, I argued wrong. After all my disappointments and mistakes in life, I told myself firmly when I came to the country this year, that love was no more for me, and that all I had to do was to grow old decently. So for a long time, I was unable to clear up my feeling towards you, or to make out where it might lead me. I hoped, and I didn't hope: at one time I thought you were trifling with me; at another I felt sure of you but could not decide what to do. But after that evening, you remember, when we walked in the garden at night, I got alarmed: the present happiness seemed too great to be real. What if I allowed myself to hope and then failed? But of course I was thinking only of myself, for I am disgustingly selfish.'

He stopped and looked at me.

'But it was not all nonsense that I said then. It was possible and right for me to have fears. I take so much from you and can give so little. You are still a child, a bud that has yet to open; you have never been in love before, and I . . .'

'Yes, do tell me the truth . . .,' I began, and then stopped, afraid of his answer. 'No, never mind,' I added.

'Have I been in love before? is that it?' he said, guessing my thoughts at once. 'That I can tell you. No, never before—nothing at all like what I feel now.' But a sudden painful recollection seemed to flash across his mind. 'No,' he said sadly; 'in this too I need your compassion, in order to have the right to love you. Well, was I not bound to think twice before saying that I loved you? What do I give you? love, no doubt.'

'And is that little?' I asked, looking him in the face.

'Yes, my dear, it is little to give *you*,' he continued; 'you have youth and beauty. I often lie awake at night from happiness, and all the time I think of our future life together. I have lived through much, and now I think I have found what is needed for happiness. A quiet secluded life in the country, with the possibility of being useful to people to whom it is easy to do good, and who are not accustomed to have it done to them; then work which one hopes may be of some use; then rest, nature, books, music, love for one's neighbour—such is my idea of happiness. And then, on the top of all that, you for a mate, and children, perhaps—what more can the heart of man desire?'

'It should be enough,' I said.

'Enough for me whose youth is over,' he went on, 'but not for you. Life is still before you, and you will perhaps seek happiness, and perhaps find it, in something different. You think now that this is happiness, because you love me.'

'You are wrong,' I said; 'I have always desired just that quiet domestic life and prized it. And you only say just what I have thought.'

He smiled.

'So you think, my dear; but that is not enough for you. You have youth and beauty,' he repeated thoughtfully.

But I was angry because he disbelieved me and seemed to cast my youth and beauty in my teeth.

'Why do you love me then?' I asked angrily; 'for my youth or for myself?'

'I don't know, but I love you,' he answered, looking at me with his attentive and attractive gaze.

I did not reply and involuntarily looked into his eyes. Suddenly a strange thing happened to me: first I ceased to see what was around me; then his face seemed to vanish till only the eyes were left, shining over against mine; next the eyes seemed to be in my own head, and then all became confused—I could see nothing and was forced to shut my eyes, in order to break loose from the feeling of pleasure and fear which his gaze was producing in me . . .

The day before our wedding-day, the weather cleared up towards evening. The rains which had begun in summer gave place to clear weather, and we had our first autumn evening, bright and cold. It was a wet, cold, shining world, and the garden showed for the first time the spaciousness and colour and bareness of autumn. The sky was clear, cold, and pale. I went to bed happy in the thought that to-morrow, our wedding-day, would be fine. I awoke with the sun, and the thought that this very day . . . seemed alarming and surprising. I went out into the garden. The sun had just risen and shone fitfully through the meagre yellow leaves of the lime avenue. The path was strewn with rustling leaves, clusters of mountain-ash berries hung red and wrinkled on the boughs, with a sprinkling of frost-bitten crumpled leaves; the dahlias were black and wrinkled. The first rime lay like silver on the pale green of the grass and on the broken burdock plants round the house. In the clear cold sky there was not, and could not be, a single cloud.

'Can it possibly be to-day?' I asked myself, incredulous of my own happiness. 'Is it possible that I shall wake to-morrow, not here but in that strange house with the pillars? Is it possible that I shall never again wait for his coming and meet him, and sit up late with Kátya to talk about him? Shall I never sit with him beside the piano in our drawing-room? never see him off and feel uneasy about him on dark nights?' But I remembered that he promised yesterday to pay a last visit, and that Kátya had insisted on my trying on my wedding-dress, and had said 'For to-morrow'. I believed for a moment that it was all real, and then doubted again. 'Can it be that after to-day I shall be living there with a mother-in-law, without Nadëzha or old Grigóri or Kátya? Shall I go to bed without kissing my old nurse good-night and hearing her say, while she signs me with the cross from old custom, "Good-night, Miss"? Shall I never again teach Sónya and play with her and knock through the wall to her in the morning and hear her hearty laugh? Shall I become from to-day someone that I myself do not know? and is a new world, that will realize my hopes and desires, opening before me? and will that new world last for ever?' Alone with these thoughts I was depressed and impatient for his arrival. He came early, and it required his presence to convince me that I should really be his wife that very day, and the prospect ceased to frighten me.

Before dinner we walked to our church, to attend a memorial service for my father.

'If only he were living now!' I thought as we were returning and I leant silently on the arm of him who had been the dearest friend of the object of my thoughts. During the service, while I pressed my forehead against the cold stone of the chapel floor, I called up my father so vividly; I was so convinced that he understood me and approved my choice, that I felt as if his spirit were still hovering over us and blessing me. And my recollections and hopes, my joy and sadness, made up one solemn and satisfied feeling which was in harmony with the fresh still air, the silence, the bare fields and pale sky, from which the bright but powerless rays, trying in vain to burn my cheek, fell over all the landscape. My companion seemed to understand and share my feeling. He walked slowly and silently; and his face, at which I glanced from time to time, expressed the same serious mood between joy and sorrow which I shared with nature.

Suddenly he turned to me, and I saw that he intended to speak. 'Suppose he starts some other subject than that which is in my mind?' I thought. But he began to speak of my father and did not even name him.

'He once said to me in jest, "you should marry my Másha",' he began.

'He would have been happy now,' I answered, pressing closer the arm which held mine.

'You were a child then,' he went on, looking into my eyes; 'I loved those eyes then and used to kiss them only because they were like his, never thinking they would be so dear to me for their own sake. I used to call you Másha then.'

'I want you to say "thou" to me,' I said.

'I was just going to,' he answered; 'I feel for the first time that *thou art* entirely mine;' and his calm happy gaze that drew me to him rested on me.

We went on along the footpath over the beaten and trampled stubble; our voices and footsteps were the only sounds. On one side the brownish stubble stretched over a hollow to a distant leafless wood; across it at some distance a peasant was noiselessly ploughing a black strip which grew wider and wider. A drove of horses scattered under the hill seemed close to us. On the other side, as far as the garden and our house peeping through the trees, a field of winter corn, thawed by the sun, showed black with occasional patches of green. The winter sun shone over everything, and everything was covered with long gossamer spider's webs, which floated in the air round us, lay on the frost-dried stubble, and got into our eyes and hair and clothes. When we spoke, the sound of our voices hung in the motionless air above us, as if we two were alone in the whole world—alone under that azure vault, in which the beams of the winter sun played and flashed without scorching.

I too wished to say 'thou' to him, but I felt ashamed.

'Why *dost thou* walk so fast?' I said quickly and almost in a whisper; I could not help blushing.

He slackened his pace, and the gaze he turned on me was even more affectionate, gay, and happy.

At home we found that his mother and the inevitable guests had arrived already, and I was never alone with him again till we came out of church to drive to Nikólskoe.

The church was nearly empty: I just caught a glimpse of his mother standing up straight on a mat by the choir and of Kátya wearing a cap with purple ribbons and with tears on her cheeks, and of two or three of our servants looking curiously at me. I did not look at him, but felt his presence there beside me. I attended to the words of the prayers and repeated them, but they found no echo in my heart. Unable to pray, I looked listlessly at the icons, the candles, the embroidered cross on the priest's cope, the screen, and the window, and took nothing in. I only felt that something strange was being done to me. At last the priest turned to us with the cross in his hand, congratulated us, and said, 'I christened you and by God's mercy have lived to marry you.' Kátya and his mother kissed us, and Grigóri's voice was heard, calling up the carriage. But I was only frightened and disappointed: all was over, but nothing extraordinary, nothing worthy of the Sacrament I had just received, had taken place in myself. He and I exchanged kisses, but the kiss seemed strange and not expressive of our feeling. 'Is this all?' I thought. We went out of church, the sound of wheels reverberated under the vaulted roof, the fresh air blew on my face, he put on his hat and handed me into the carriage. Through the window I could see a frosty moon with a halo round it. He sat down beside me and shut the door after him. I felt a sudden pang. The assurance of his proceedings seemed to me insulting. Kátya called out that I should put something on my head; the wheels rumbled on the stone and then moved along the soft road, and we were off. Huddling in a corner, I looked out at the distant fields and the road flying past in the cold glitter of the moon. Without looking at him, I felt his presence beside me. 'Is this all I have got from the moment, of which I expected so much?' I thought; and still it seemed humiliating and insulting to be sitting alone with him, and so close. I turned to him, intending to speak; but the words would not come, as if my love had vanished, giving place to a feeling of mortification and alarm.

'Till this moment I did not believe it was possible,' he said in a low voice in answer to my look.

'But I am afraid somehow,' I said.

'Afraid of me, my dear?' he said, taking my hand and bending over it.

My hand lay lifeless in his, and the cold at my heart was painful.

'Yes,' I whispered.

But at that moment my heart began to beat faster, my hand trembled and pressed his, I grew hot, my eyes sought his in the half-darkness, and all at once I felt that I did not fear him, that this fear was love—a new love still more tender and stronger than the old. I felt that I was wholly his, and that I was happy in his power over me.

PART II

CHAPTER I

DAYS, weeks, two whole months, of seclusion in the country slipped by unnoticed, as we thought then; and yet those two months comprised feelings, emotions, and happiness, sufficient for a lifetime. Our plans for the regulation of our life in the country were not carried out at all in the way that we expected; but the reality was not inferior to our ideal. There was none of that hard work, performance of duty, self-sacrifice, and life for others, which I had pictured to myself before our marriage; there was, on the contrary, merely a selfish feeling of love for one another, a wish to be loved, a constant causeless gaiety and entire oblivion of all the world. It is true that my husband sometimes went to his study to work, or drove to town on business, or walked about attending to the management of the estate; but I saw what it cost him to tear himself away from me. He confessed later that every occupation, in my absence, seemed to him mere nonsense in which it was impossible to take any interest. It was just the same with me. If I read, or played the piano, or passed my time with his mother, or taught in the school, I did so only because each of these occupations was connected with him and won his approval; but whenever the thought of him was not associated with any duty, my hands fell by my sides and it seemed to me absurd to think that anything existed apart from him. Perhaps it was a wrong and selfish feeling, but it gave me happiness and lifted me high above all the world. He alone existed on earth for me, and I considered him the best and most faultless man in the world; so that I could not live for anything else than for him, and my one object was to realize his conception of me. And in his eyes I was the first and most excellent woman in the world, the possessor of all possible virtues; and I strove to be that woman in the opinion of the first and best of men.

He came to my room one day while I was praying. I looked round at him and went on with my prayers. Not wishing to interrupt me, he sat down at a table and opened a book. But I thought he was looking at me and looked round myself. He smiled, I laughed, and had to stop my prayers.

'Have you prayed already?' I asked.

'Yes. But you go on; I'll go away.'

'You do say your prayers, I hope?'

He made no answer and was about to leave the room when I stopped him.

'Darling, for my sake, please repeat the prayers with me!' He stood up beside me, dropped his arms awkwardly, and began, with a serious face and some hesitation. Occasionally he turned towards me, seeking signs of approval and aid in my face.

When he came to an end, I laughed and embraced him.

'I feel just as if I were ten! And you do it all!' he said, blushing and kissing my hands.

Our house was one of those old-fashioned country houses in which several generations have passed their lives together under one roof, respecting and loving one another. It was all redolent of good sound family traditions, which as soon as I entered it seemed to become mine too. The management of the household was carried on by Tatyána Semënovna, my mother-in-law, on old-fashioned lines. Of grace and beauty there was not much; but, from the servants down to the furniture and food, there was abundance of everything, and a general cleanliness, solidity, and order, which inspired respect. The drawing-room furniture was arranged symmetrically; there were portraits on the walls, and the floor was covered with home-made carpets and mats. In the morning-room there was an old piano, with chiffoniers of two different patterns, sofas, and little carved tables with bronze ornaments. My sitting-room, specially arranged by Tatyána Semënovna, contained the best furniture in the house, of many styles and periods, including an old pier-glass, which I was frightened to look into at first, but came to value as an old friend. Though Tatyána Semënovna's voice was never heard, the whole household went like a clock. The number of servants was far too large (they all wore soft boots with no heels, because Tatyána Semēnovna had an intense dislike for stamping heels and creaking soles); but they all seemed proud of their calling, trembled before their old mistress, treated my husband and me with an affectionate air of patronage, and performed their duties, to all appearance, with extreme satisfaction. Every Saturday the floors were scoured and the carpets beaten without fail; on the first of every month there was a religious service in the house and holy water was sprinkled; on Tatyána Semënovna's name-day and on her son's (and on mine too, beginning from that autumn) an entertainment was regularly provided for the whole neighbourhood. And all this had gone on without a break ever since the beginning of Tatyána Semënovna's life.

My husband took no part in the household management, he attended only to the farm-work and the labourers, and gave much time to this. Even in winter he got up so early that I often woke to find him gone. He generally came back for early tea, which we drank alone together; and at that time, when the worries and vexations of the farm were over, he was almost always in that state of high spirits which we called 'wild ecstasy'. I often made him tell me what he had been doing in the morning, and he gave such absurd accounts that we both laughed till we cried. Sometimes I insisted on a serious account, and he gave it, restraining a smile. I watched his eyes and moving lips and took nothing in: the sight of him and the sound of his voice was pleasure enough.

'Well, what have I been saying? repeat it,' he would sometimes say. But I could repeat nothing. It seemed so absurd that *he* should talk to *me* of any other subject than ourselves. As if it mattered in the least what went on in the world outside! It was at a much later time that I began to some extent to understand and take an interest in his occupations. Tatyána Semënovna never appeared before dinner: she breakfasted alone and said good-morning to us by deputy. In our exclusive little world of frantic happiness a voice from the staid orderly region in which she dwelt was quite startling: I often lost self-control and could only laugh without speaking, when the maid stood before me with folded hands and made her formal report: 'The mistress bade me inquire how you slept after your walk yesterday evening; and about her I was to report that she had pain in her side all night, and a stupid dog barked in the village and kept her awake: and also I was to ask how you liked the bread this morning, and to tell you that it was not Tarás who baked to-day, but Nikoláshka who was trying his hand for the first time; and she says his baking is not at all bad, especially the cracknels: but the tea-rusks were over-baked.' Before dinner we saw little of each other: he wrote or went out again while I played the piano or read; but at four o'clock we all met in the drawing-room before dinner. Tatyána Semënovna sailed out of her own room, and certain poor and pious maiden ladies, of whom there were always two or three living in the house, made their appearance also. Every day without fail my husband by old habit offered his arm to his mother, to take her in to dinner; but she insisted that I should take the other, so that every day, without fail, we stuck in the doors and got in each other's way. She also presided at dinner, where the conversation, if rather solemn, was polite and sensible. The commonplace talk between my husband and me was a pleasant interruption to the formality of those entertainments. Sometimes there were squabbles between mother and son and they bantered one another; and I especially enjoyed those scenes, because they were the best proof of the strong and tender love which united the two. After dinner Tatyána Semënovna went to the parlour, where she sat in an armchair and ground her snuff or cut the leaves of new books, while we read aloud or went off to the piano in the morning-room. We read much together at this time, but music was our favourite and best enjoyment, always evoking fresh chords in our hearts and as it were revealing each afresh to the other. While I played his favourite pieces, he sat on a distant sofa where I could hardly see him. He was ashamed to betray the impression produced on him by the music; but often, when he was not expecting it, I rose from the piano, went up to him, and tried to detect on his face signs of emotion—the unnatural brightness and moistness of the eyes, which he tried in vain to conceal. Tatyána Semënovna, though she often wanted to take a look at us there, was also anxious to put no constraint upon us. So she always passed through the room with an air of indifference and a pretence of being busy; but I knew that she had no real reason for going to her room and returning so soon. In the evening I poured out tea in the large drawing-room, and all the household met again. This solemn ceremony of distributing cups and glasses before the solemnly shining samovar made me nervous for a long time. I felt myself still unworthy of such a distinction, too young and frivolous to turn the tap of such a big samovar, to put glasses on Nikíta's salver, saying 'For Peter Ivánovich', 'For Márya Mínichna', to ask 'Is it sweet enough?' and to leave out lumps of sugar for Nurse and other deserving persons. 'Capital! capital! Just like a grown-up person!' was a frequent comment from my husband, which only increased my confusion.

After tea Tatyána Semënovna played patience or listened to Márya Mínichna telling fortunes by the cards. Then she kissed us both and signed us with the cross, and we went off to our own rooms. But we generally sat up together till midnight, and that was our best and pleasantest time. He told me stories of his past life; we made plans and sometimes even talked philosophy; but we tried always to speak low, for fear we should be heard upstairs and reported to Tatyána Semënovna, who insisted on our going to bed early. Sometimes we grew hungry; and then we stole off to the pantry, secured a cold supper by the good offices of Nikíta, and ate it in my sitting-room by the light of one candle. He and I lived like strangers in that big old house, where the uncompromising spirit of the past and of Tatyána Semënovna ruled supreme. Not she only, but the servants, the old ladies, the furniture, even the pictures, inspired me with respect and a little alarm, and made me feel that he and I were a little out of place in that house and must always be very careful and cautious in our doings. Thinking it over now, I see that many things—the pressure of that unvarying routine, and that crowd of idle and inquisitive servants—were uncomfortable and oppressive; but at the time that very constraint made our love for one another still keener. Not I only, but he also, never grumbled openly at anything; on the contrary he shut his eyes to what was amiss. Dmítri Sídorov, one of the footmen, was a great smoker; and regularly every day, when we two were in the morning-room after dinner, he went to my husband's study to take tobacco from the jar; and it was a sight to see Sergéy Mikháylych creeping on tiptoe to me with a face between delight and terror, and a wink and a warning forefinger, while he pointed at Dmítri Sídorov, who was quite unconscious of being watched. Then, when Dmítri Sídorov had gone away without having seen us, in his joy that all had passed off successfully, he declared (as he did on every other occasion) that I was a darling, and kissed me. At times his calm connivance and apparent indifference to everything annoyed me, and I took it for weakness, never noticing that I acted in the same way myself. 'It's like a child who dares not show his will,' I thought.

'My dear! my dear!' he said once when I told him that his weakness surprised me; 'how can a man, as happy as I am, be dissatisfied with anything? Better to give way myself than to put compulsion on others; of that I have long been convinced. There is no condition in which one cannot be happy; but our life is such bliss! I simply cannot be angry; to me now nothing seems bad, but only pitiful and amusing. Above all—*le mieux est l'ennemi du bien.** Will you believe it, when I hear a ring at the bell, or receive a letter, or even wake

* The better is the enemy of the good.

up in the morning, I'm frightened. Life must go on, something may change; and nothing can be better than the present.'

I believed him but did not understand him. I was happy; but I took that as a matter of course, the invariable experience of people in our position, and believed that there was somewhere, I knew not where, a different happiness, not greater but different.

So two months went by and winter came with its cold and snow; and, in spite of his company, I began to feel lonely, that life was repeating itself, that there was nothing new either in him or in myself, and that we were merely going back to what had been before. He began to give more time to business which kept him away from me, and my old feeling returned, that there was a special department of his mind into which he was unwilling to admit me. His unbroken calmness provoked me. I loved him as much as ever and was as happy as ever in his love; but my love, instead of increasing, stood still; and another new and disquieting sensation began to creep into my heart. To love him was not enough for me after the happiness I had felt in falling in love. I wanted movement and not a calm course of existence. I wanted excitement and danger and the chance to sacrifice myself for my love. I felt in myself a superabundance of energy which found no outlet in our quiet life. I had fits of depression which I was ashamed of and tried to conceal from him, and fits of excessive tenderness and high spirits which alarmed him. He realized my state of mind before I did, and proposed a visit to Petersburg; but I begged him to give this up and not to change our manner of life or spoil our happiness. Happy indeed I was; but I was tormented by the thought that this happiness cost me no effort and no sacrifice, though I was even painfully conscious of my power to face both. I loved him and saw that I was all in all to him; but I wanted everyone to see our love; I wanted to love him in spite of obstacles. My mind, and even my senses, were fully occupied; but there was another feeling of youth and craving for movement, which found no satisfaction in our quiet life. What made him say that, whenever I liked, we could go to town? Had he not said so I might have realized that my uncomfortable feelings were my own fault and dangerous nonsense, and that the sacrifice I desired was there before me, in the task of overcoming these feelings. I was haunted by the thought that I could escape from depression by a mere change from the country; and at the same time I felt ashamed and sorry to tear him away, out of selfish motives, from all he cared for. So time went on, the snow grew deeper, and there we remained together, all alone and just the same as before, while outside I knew there was noise and glitter and excitement, and hosts of people suffering or rejoicing without one thought of us and our remote existence. I suffered most from the feeling that custom was daily petrifying our lives into one fixed shape, that our minds were losing their freedom and becoming enslaved to the steady passionless course of time. The morning always found us cheerful; we were polite at dinner, and affectionate in the evening. 'It is all right,' I thought, 'to do good to others and lead upright lives, as he says; but there is time for that later; and there are other things, for which the time is now or never.' I wanted, not what I had got, but a life of struggle; I wanted feeling to be the guide of life, and not life to guide feeling. If only I could go with him to the edge of a precipice and say, 'One step, and I shall fall over—one movement, and I shall be lost!' then, pale with fear, he would catch me in his strong arms and hold me over the edge till my blood froze, and then carry me off whither he pleased.

This state of feeling even affected my health, and I began to suffer from nerves. One morning I was worse than usual. He had come back from the estate-office out of sorts, which was a rare thing with him. I noticed it at once and asked what was the matter. He would not tell me and said it was of no importance. I found out afterwards that the police-inspector, out of spite against my husband, was summoning our peasants, making illegal demands on them, and using threats to them. My husband could not swallow this at once; he could not feel it merely 'pitiful and amusing'. He was provoked, and therefore unwilling to speak of it to me. But it seemed to me that he did not wish to speak to me about it because he considered me a mere child, incapable of understanding his concerns. I turned from him and said no more. I then told the servant to ask Márya Mínichna, who was staying in the house, to join us at breakfast. I ate my breakfast very fast and took her to the morning-room, where I began to talk loudly to her about some trifle which did not interest me in the least. He walked about the room, glancing at us from time to time. This made me more and more inclined to talk and even to laugh; all that I said myself, and all that Márya Mínichna said, seemed to me laughable. Without a word to me he went off to his study and shut the door behind him. When I ceased to hear him, all my high spirits vanished at once: indeed Márya Mínichna was surprised and asked what was the matter. I sat down on a sofa without answering, and felt ready to cry. 'What has he got on his mind?' I wondered; 'some trifle which he thinks important; but, if he tried to tell it me, I should soon show him it was mere nonsense. But he must needs think that I won't understand, must humiliate me by his majestic composure, and always be in the right as against me. But I too am in the right when I find things tiresome and trivial,' I reflected; 'and I do well to want an active life rather than to stagnate in one spot and feel life flowing past me. I want to move forward, to have some new experience every day and every hour, whereas he wants to stand still and to keep me standing beside him. And how easy it would be for him to gratify me! He need not take me to town; he need only be like me and not put compulsion on himself and regulate his feelings, but live simply. That is the advice he gives me, but he is not simple himself. That is what is the matter.'

I felt the tears rising and knew that I was irritated with him. My irritation frightened me, and I went to his study. He was sitting at the table, writing. Hearing my step, he looked up for a moment and then went on writing; he seemed calm and unconcerned. His look vexed me: instead of going up to him, I stood beside his writing-table, opened a book, and began to look at it. He broke off his writing again and looked at me.

'Másha, are you out of sorts?' he asked.

I replied with a cold look, as much as to say, 'You are very polite, but what is the use of asking?' He shook his head and smiled with a tender timid air; but his smile, for the first time, drew no answering smile from me.

'What happened to you to-day?' I asked; 'why did you not tell me?'

'Nothing much—a trifling nuisance,' he said. 'But I might tell you now. Two of our serfs went off to the town . . .'

But I would not let him go on.

'Why would you not tell me, when I asked you at breakfast?'

'I was angry then and should have said something foolish.'

'I wished to know then.'

'Why?'

'Why do you suppose that I can never help you in anything?'

'Not help me!' he said, dropping his pen. 'Why, I believe that without you I could not live. You not only help me in everything I do, but you do it yourself. You are very wide of the mark,' he said, and laughed. 'My life depends on you. I am pleased with things, only because you are there, because I need you . . .'

'Yes, I know; I am a delightful child who must be humoured and kept quiet,' I said in a voice that astonished him, so that he looked up as if this was a new experience; 'but I don't want to be quiet and calm; that is more in your line, and too much in your line,' I added.

'Well,' he began quickly, interrupting me and evidently afraid to let me continue, 'when I tell you the facts, I should like to know your opinion.'

'I don't want to hear them now,' I answered. I did want to hear the story, but I found it so pleasant to break down his composure. 'I don't want to play at life,' I said, 'but to live, as you do yourself.'

His face, which reflected every feeling so quickly and so vividly, now expressed pain and intense attention.

'I want to share your life, to . . .,' but I could not go on—his face showed such deep distress. He was silent for a moment.

'But what part of my life do you not share?' he

asked; 'is it because I, and not you, have to bother with the inspector and with tipsy labourers?'

'That's not the only thing,' I said.

'For God's sake try to understand me, my dear!' he cried. 'I know that excitement is always painful; I have learnt that from the experience of life. I love you, and I can't but wish to save you from excitement. My life consists of my love for you; so you should not make life impossible for me.'

'You are always in the right,' I said without looking at him.

I was vexed again by his calmness and coolness while I was conscious of annoyance and some feeling akin to penitence.

'Másha, what is the matter?' he asked. 'The question is not, which of us is in the right—not at all; but rather, what grievance have you against me? Take time before you answer, and tell me all that is in your mind. You are dissatisfied with me: and you are, no doubt, right; but let me understand what I have done wrong.'

But how could I put my feeling into words? That he understood me at once, that I again stood before him like a child, that I could do nothing without his understanding and foreseeing it—all this only increased my agitation.

'I have no complaint to make of you,' I said; 'I am merely bored and want not to be bored. But you say that it can't be helped, and, as always, you are right.'

I looked at him as I spoke. I had gained my object: his calmness had disappeared, and I read fear and pain in his face.

'Másha,' he began in a low troubled voice, 'this is no mere trifle: the happiness of our lives is at stake. Please hear me out without answering. Why do you wish to torment me?'

But I interrupted him.

'Oh, I know you will turn out to be right. Words are useless; of course you are right.' I spoke coldly, as if some evil spirit were speaking with my voice.

'If you only knew what you are doing!' he said, and his voice shook.

I burst out crying and felt relieved. He sat down beside me and said nothing. I felt sorry for him, ashamed of myself, and annoyed at what I had done. I avoided looking at him. I felt that any look from him at that moment must express severity or perplexity. At last I looked up and saw his eyes: they were fixed on me with a tender gentle expression that seemed to ask for pardon. I caught his hand and said,

'Forgive me! I don't know myself what I have been saying.'

'But I do; and you spoke the truth.'

'What do you mean?' I asked.

'That we must go to Petersburg,' he said; 'there is nothing for us to do here just now.'

'As you please,' I said.

He took me in his arms and kissed me.

'You must forgive me,' he said; 'for I am to blame.'

That evening I played to him for a long time, while he walked about the room. He had a habit of muttering to himself; and when I asked him what he was muttering, he always thought for a moment and then told me exactly what it was. It was generally verse, and sometimes mere nonsense, but I could always judge of his mood by it. When I asked him now, he stood still, thought an instant, and then repeated two lines from Lérmontov:

He in his madness prays for storms,
And dreams that storms will bring him peace.

'He is really more than human,' I thought;

'he knows everything. How can one help loving him?'

I got up, took his arm, and began to walk up and down with him, trying to keep step.

'Well?' he asked, smiling and looking at me.

'All right,' I whispered. And then a sudden fit of merriment came over us both: our eyes laughed, we took longer and longer steps, and rose higher and higher on tiptoe. Prancing in this manner, to the profound dissatisfaction of the butler and astonishment of my mother-in-law, who was playing patience in the parlour, we proceeded through the house till we reached the dining-room; there we stopped, looked at one another, and burst out laughing.

A fortnight later, before Christmas, we were in Petersburg.

CHAPTER II

THE journey to Petersburg, a week in Moscow, visits to my own relations and my husband's, settling down in our new quarters, travel, new towns and new faces—all this passed before me like a dream. It was all so new, various, and delightful, so warmly and brightly lighted up by his presence and his love, that our quiet life in the country seemed to me something very remote and unimportant. I had expected to find people in society proud and cold; but to my great surprise, I was received everywhere with unfeigned cordiality and pleasure, not only by relations, but also by strangers. I seemed to be the one object of their thoughts, and my arrival the one thing they wanted, to complete their happiness. I was surprised too to discover in what seemed to me the very best society a number of people acquainted with my husband, though he had never spoken of them to me; and I often felt it odd and disagreeable to hear him now speak disapprovingly of some of these people who seemed to me so kind. I could not understand his coolness towards them or his endeavours to avoid many acquaintances that seemed to me flattering. Surely, the more kind people one knows, the better; and here everyone was kind.

'This is how we must manage, you see,' he said to me before we left the country; 'here we are little Croesuses, but in town we shall not be at all rich. So we must not stay after Easter, or go into society, or we shall get into difficulties. For your sake too I should not wish it.'

'Why should we go into society?' I asked; 'we shall have a look at the theatres, see our relations, go to the opera, hear some good music, and be ready to come home before Easter.'

But these plans were forgotten the moment we got to Petersburg. I found myself at once in such a new and delightful world, surrounded by so many pleasures and confronted by such novel interests, that I instantly, though unconsciously, turned my back on my past life and its plans. 'All that was preparatory, a mere playing at life; but here is the real thing! And there is the future too!' Such were my thoughts. The restlessness and symptoms of depression which had troubled me at home vanished at once and entirely, as if by magic. My love for my husband grew calmer, and I ceased to wonder whether he loved me less. Indeed I could not doubt his love: every thought of mine was understood at once, every feeling shared, and every wish gratified by him. His composure, if it still existed, no longer provoked me. I also began to realize that he not only loved me but was proud of me. If we paid a call, or made some new acquaintance, or gave an evening party at which I, trembling inwardly from fear of disgracing myself, acted as hostess, he often said when it was over: 'Bravo, young woman! capital! you needn't be frightened; a real success!' And his praise gave me great pleasure. Soon after our arrival he wrote to his mother and asked me to add a postscript, but refused to let me see his letter; of course I insisted on reading it; and he had said: 'You would not know Másha again, I don't myself. Where does she get that charming graceful self-confidence and ease, such social gifts with such simplicity and charm and kindliness? Everybody is delighted with her. I can't admire her enough myself, and should be more in love with her than ever, if that were possible.'

'Now I know what I am like,' I thought. In my joy and pride I felt that I loved him more than before. My success with all our new acquaintances was a complete surprise to me. I heard on all sides, how this uncle had taken a special fancy for me, and that aunt was raving about me; I was told by one admirer that I had no rival among the Petersburg ladies, and assured by another, a lady, that I might, if I cared, lead the fashion in society. A cousin of my husband's, in particular, a Princess D., middle-aged and very much at home in society, fell in love with me at first sight and paid me compliments which turned my head. The first time that she invited me to a ball and spoke to my husband about it, he turned to me and asked if I wished to go; I could just detect a sly smile on his face. I nodded assent and felt that I was blushing.

'She looks like a criminal when confessing what she wishes,' he said with a good-natured laugh.

'But you said that we must not go into society,

and you don't care for it yourself,' I answered, smiling and looking imploringly at him.

'Let us go, if you want to very much,' he said.

'Really, we had better not.'

'Do you want to? very badly?' he asked again.

I said nothing.

'Society in itself is no great harm,' he went on; 'but unsatisfied social aspirations are a bad and ugly business. We must certainly accept, and we will.'

'To tell you the truth,' I said, 'I never in my life longed for anything as much as I do for this ball.'

So we went, and my delight exceeded all my expectations. It seemed to me, more than ever, that I was the centre round which everything revolved, that for my sake alone this great room was lighted up and the band played, and that this crowd of people had assembled to admire me. From the hairdresser and the lady's maid to my partners and the old gentlemen promenading the ball-room, all alike seemed to make it plain that they were in love with me. The general verdict formed at the ball about me and reported by my cousin, came to this: I was quite unlike the other women and had a rural simplicity and charm of my own. I was so flattered by my success that I frankly told my husband I should like to attend two or three more balls during the season, and 'so get thoroughly sick of them', I added; but I did not mean what I said.

He agreed readily; and he went with me at first with obvious satisfaction. He took pleasure in my success, and seemed to have quite forgotten his former warning or to have changed his opinion.

But a time came when he was evidently bored and wearied by the life we were leading. I was too busy, however, to think about that. Even if I sometimes noticed his eyes fixed questioningly on me with a serious attentive gaze, I did not realize its meaning. I was utterly blinded by this sudden affection which I seemed to evoke in all our new acquaintances, and confused by the unfamiliar atmosphere of luxury, refinement, and novelty. It pleased me so much to find myself in these surroundings not merely his equal but his superior, and yet to love him better and more independently than before, that I could not understand what he could object to for me in society life. I had a new sense of pride and self-satisfaction when my entry at a ball attracted all eyes, while he, as if ashamed to confess his ownership of me in public, made haste to leave my side and efface himself in the crowd of black coats. 'Wait a little!' I often said in my heart, when I identified his obscure and sometimes woebegone figure at the end of the room—'Wait till we get home! Then you will see and understand for whose sake I try to be beautiful and brilliant, and what it is I love in all that surrounds me this evening!' I really believed that my success pleased me only because it enabled me to give it up for his sake. One danger I recognized as possible—that I might be carried away by a fancy for some new acquaintance, and that my husband might grow jealous. But he trusted me so absolutely, and seemed so undisturbed and indifferent, and all the young men were so inferior to him, that I was not alarmed by this one danger. Yet the attention of so many people in society gave me satisfaction, flattered my vanity, and made me think that there was some merit in my love for my husband. Thus I became more offhand and self-confident in my behaviour to him.

'Oh, I saw you this evening carrying on a most animated conversation with Mme N.,' I said one night on returning from a ball, shaking my finger at him. He had really been talking to this lady, who was a well-known figure in Petersburg society. He was more silent and depressed than usual, and I said this to rouse him up.

'What is the good of talking like that, for *you* especially, Másha?' he said with half-closed teeth and frowning as if in pain. 'Leave that to others; it does not suit you and me. Pretence of that sort may spoil the true relation between us, which I still hope may come back.'

I was ashamed and said nothing.

'Will it ever come back, Másha, do you think?' he asked.

'It never was spoilt and never will be,' I said; and I really believed this then.

'God grant that you are right!' he said; 'if not, we ought to be going home.'

But he only spoke like this once—in general he seemed as satisfied as I was, and I was so gay and so happy! I comforted myself too by thinking, 'If he is bored sometimes, I endured the same thing for his sake in the country. If the relation between us has become a little different, everything will be the same again in summer, when we shall be alone in our house at Nikólskoe with Tatyána Semënovna.'

So the winter slipped by, and we stayed on, in spite of our plans, over Easter in Petersburg. A week later we were preparing to start; our packing was all done; my husband, who had bought things—plants for the garden and presents for people at Nikólskoe, was in a specially cheerful and affectionate mood. Just then Princess D. came and begged us to stay till the Saturday, in order to be present at a reception to be given by Countess R. The Countess was very anxious to secure me, because a foreign prince, who was visiting Petersburg and had seen me already at a ball, wished to make my acquaintance; indeed this was his motive for attending the reception, and he declared that I was the most beautiful woman in Russia. All the world was to be there; and, in a word, it would really be too bad, if I did not go too.

My husband was talking to someone at the other end of the drawing-room.

'So you will go, won't you, Mary?' said the Princess.

'We meant to start for the country the day after to-morrow,' I answered undecidedly, glancing at my husband. Our eyes met, and he turned away at once.

'I must persuade him to stay,' she said, 'and then we can go on Saturday and turn all heads. All right?'

'It would upset our plans; and we have packed,' I answered, beginning to give way.

'She had better go this evening and make her curtsey to the Prince,' my husband called out from the other end of the room; and he spoke in a tone of suppressed irritation which I had never heard from him before.

'I declare he's jealous, for the first time in his life,' said the lady, laughing. 'But it's not for the sake of the Prince I urge it, Sergéy Mikháylych, but for all our sakes. The Countess was so anxious to have her.'

'It rests with her entirely,' my husband said coldly, and then left the room.

I saw that he was much disturbed, and this pained me. I gave no positive promise. As soon as our visitor left, I went to my husband. He was walking up and down his room, thinking, and neither saw nor heard me when I came in on tiptoe.

Looking at him I said to myself: 'He is dreaming

already of his dear Nikólskoe, our morning coffee in the bright drawing-room, the land and the labourers, our evenings in the music-room, and our secret midnight suppers.' Then I decided in my own heart: 'Not for all the balls and all the flattering princes in the world will I give up his glad confusion and tender cares.' I was just about to say that I did not wish to go to the ball and would refuse, when he looked round, saw me, and frowned. His face, which had been gentle and thoughtful, changed at once to its old expression of sagacity, penetration, and patronizing composure. He would not show himself to me as a mere man, but had to be a demigod on a pedestal.

'Well, my dear?' he asked, turning towards me with an unconcerned air.

I said nothing. I was provoked, because he was hiding his real self from me, and would not continue to be the man I loved.

'Do you want to go to this reception on Saturday?' he asked.

'I did, but you disapprove. Besides, our things are all packed,' I said.

Never before had I heard such coldness in his tone to me, and never before seen such coldness in his eye.

'I shall order the things to be unpacked,' he said, 'and I shall stay till Tuesday. So you can go to the party, if you like. I hope you will; but I shall not go.'

Without looking at me, he began to walk about the room jerkily, as his habit was when perturbed.

'I simply can't understand you,' I said, following him with my eyes from where I stood. 'You say that you never lose self-control' (he had never really said so); 'then why do you talk to me so strangely? I am ready on your account to sacrifice this pleasure, and then you, in a sarcastic tone which is new from you to me, insist that I should go.'

'So you make a *sacrifice*!' he threw special emphasis on the last word. 'Well, so do I. What could be better? We compete in generosity—what an example of family happiness!'

Such harsh and contemptuous language I had never heard from his lips before. I was not abashed, but mortified by his contempt; and his harshness did not frighten me but made me harsh too. How could *he* speak thus, he who was always so frank and simple and dreaded insincerity in our speech to one another? And what had I done that he should speak so? I really intended to sacrifice for his sake a pleasure in which I could see no harm; and a moment ago I loved him and understood his feelings as well as ever. We had changed parts: now he avoided direct and plain words, and I desired them.

'You are much changed,' I said, with a sigh. 'How am I guilty before you? It is not this party—you have something else, some old count against me. Why this insincerity? You used to be so afraid of it yourself. Tell me plainly what you complain of.' 'What will he say?' thought I, and reflected with some complacency that I had done nothing all winter which he could find fault with.

I went into the middle of the room, so that he had to pass close to me, and looked at him. I thought, 'He will come and clasp me in his arms, and there will be an end of it.' I was even sorry that I should not have the chance of proving him wrong. But he stopped at the far end of the room and looked at me.

'Do you not understand yet?' he asked.

'No, I don't.'

'Then I must explain. What I feel, and cannot

help feeling, positively sickens me for the first time in my life.' He stopped, evidently startled by the harsh sound of his own voice.

'What do you mean?' I asked, with tears of indignation in my eyes.

'It sickens me that the Prince admired you, and you therefore run to meet him, forgetting your husband and yourself and womanly dignity; and you wilfully misunderstand what your want of self-respect makes your husband feel for you: you actually come to your husband and speak of the "sacrifice" you are making, by which you mean—"To show myself to His Highness is a great pleasure to me, but I 'sacrifice' it."'

The longer he spoke, the more he was excited by the sound of his own voice, which was hard and rough and cruel. I had never seen him, had never thought of seeing him, like that. The blood rushed to my heart and I was frightened; but I felt that I had nothing to be ashamed of, and the excitement of wounded vanity made me eager to punish him.

'I have long been expecting this,' I said. 'Go on. Go on!'

'What you expected, I don't know,' he went on; 'but I might well expect the worst, when I saw you day after day sharing the dirtiness and idleness and luxury of this foolish society, and it has come at last. Never have I felt such shame and pain as now—pain for myself, when your friend thrusts her unclean fingers into my heart and speaks of my jealousy!—jealousy of a man whom neither you nor I know; and you refuse to understand me and offer to make a sacrifice for me—and what sacrifice? I am ashamed for you, for your degradation! . . . Sacrifice!' he repeated again.

'Ah, so this is a husband's power,' thought I: 'to insult and humiliate a perfectly innocent woman.

Such may be a husband's rights, but I will not submit to them.' I felt the blood leave my face and a strange distension of my nostrils, as I said, 'No! I make no sacrifice on your account. I shall go to the party on Saturday without fail.'

'And I hope you may enjoy it. But all is over between us two!' he cried out in a fit of unrestrained fury. 'But you shall not torture me any longer! I was a fool, when I . . .', but his lips quivered, and he refrained with a visible effort from ending the sentence.

I feared and hated him at that moment. I wished to say a great deal to him and punish him for all his insults; but if I had opened my mouth, I should have lost my dignity by bursting into tears. I said nothing and left the room. But as soon as I ceased to hear his footsteps, I was horrified at what we had done. I feared that the tie which had made all my happiness might really be snapped for ever; and I thought of going back. But then I wondered: 'Is he calm enough now to understand me, if I mutely stretch out my hand and look at him? Will he realize my generosity? What if he calls my grief a mere pretence? Or he may feel sure that he is right and accept my repentance and forgive me with unruffled pride. And why, oh why, did he whom I loved so well insult me so cruelly?'

I went not to him but to my own room, where I sat for a long time and cried. I recalled with horror each word of our conversation, and substituted different words, kind words, for those that we had spoken, and added others; and then again I remembered the reality with horror and a feeling of injury. In the evening I went down for tea and met my husband in the presence of a friend who was staying with us; and it seemed to me that a wide gulf had opened between us from that day.

Our friend asked me when we were to start; and before I could speak, my husband answered:

'On Tuesday,' he said; 'we have to stay for Countess R.'s reception.' He turned to me: 'I believe you intend to go?' he asked.

His matter-of-fact tone frightened me, and I looked at him timidly. His eyes were directed straight at me with an unkind and scornful expression; his voice was cold and even.

'Yes,' I answered.

When we were alone that evening, he came up to me and held out his hand.

'Please forget what I said to you to-day,' he began.

As I took his hand, a smile quivered on my lips and the tears were ready to flow; but he took his hand away and sat down on an armchair at some distance, as if fearing a sentimental scene. 'Is it possible that he still thinks himself in the right?' I wondered; and, though I was quite ready to explain and to beg that we might not go to the party, the words died on my lips.

'I must write to my mother that we have put off our departure,' he said; 'otherwise she will be uneasy.'

'When do you think of going?' I asked.

'On Tuesday, after the reception,' he replied.

'I hope it is not on my account,' I said, looking into his eyes; but those eyes merely looked—they said nothing, and a veil seemed to cover them from me. His face seemed to me to have grown suddenly old and disagreeable.

We went to the reception, and good friendly relations between us seemed to have been restored, but these relations were quite different from what they had been.

At the party I was sitting with other ladies when

the Prince came up to me, so that I had to stand up in order to speak to him. As I rose, my eyes involuntarily sought my husband. He was looking at me from the other end of the room, and now turned away. I was seized by a sudden sense of shame and pain; in my confusion I blushed all over my face and neck under the Prince's eye. But I was forced to stand and listen, while he spoke, eyeing me from his superior height. Our conversation was soon over: there was no room for him beside me, and he, no doubt, felt that I was uncomfortable with him. We talked of the last ball, of where I should spend the summer, and so on. As he left me, he expressed a wish to make the acquaintance of my husband, and I saw them meet and begin a conversation at the far end of the room. The Prince evidently said something about me; for he smiled in the middle of their talk and looked in my direction.

My husband suddenly flushed up. He made a low bow and turned away from the Prince without being dismissed. I blushed too: I was ashamed of the impression which I and, still more, my husband must have made on the Prince. Everyone, I thought, must have noticed my awkward shyness when I was presented, and my husband's eccentric behaviour. 'Heaven knows how they will interpret such conduct? Perhaps they know already about my scene with my husband!'

Princess D. drove me home, and on the way I spoke to her about my husband. My patience was at an end, and I told her the whole story of what had taken place between us owing to this unlucky party. To calm me, she said that such differences were very common and quite unimportant, and that our quarrel would leave no trace behind. She explained to me her view of my husband's character

—that he had become very stiff and unsociable. I agreed, and believed that I had learned to judge him myself more calmly and more truly.

But when I was alone with my husband later, the thought that I had sat in judgement upon him weighed like a crime upon my conscience; and I felt that the gulf which divided us had grown still greater.

CHAPTER III

FROM that day there was a complete change in our life and our relations to each other. We were no longer as happy when we were alone together as before. To certain subjects we gave a wide berth, and conversation flowed more easily in the presence of a third person. When the talk turned on life in the country, or on a ball, we were uneasy and shrank from looking at one another. Both of us knew where the gulf between us lay, and seemed afraid to approach it. I was convinced that he was proud and irascible, and that I must be careful not to touch him on his weak point. He was equally sure that I disliked the country and was dying for social distraction, and that he must put up with this unfortunate taste of mine. We both avoided frank conversation on these topics, and each misjudged the other. We had long ceased to think each other the most perfect people in the world; each now judged the other in secret, and measured the offender by the standard of other people. I fell ill before we left Petersburg, and we went from there to a house near town, from which my husband went on alone, to join his mother at Nikólskoe. By that time I was well enough to have gone with him, but he urged me to stay on the pretext of my health. I knew, however, that he was really afraid we should be uncomfortable together in the country; so I did not insist much, and he went off alone. I felt it dull and solitary in his absence; but when he came back, I saw that he did not add to my life what he had added formerly. In the old days every thought and experience weighed on me like a crime till I had imparted it to him; every action and word of his seemed to me a model of perfection; we often laughed for joy at the mere sight of each other. But these relations had changed, so imperceptibly that we had not even noticed their disappearance. Separate interests and cares, which we no longer tried to share, made their appearance, and even the fact of our estrangement ceased to trouble us. The idea became familiar, and, before a year had passed, each could look at the other without confusion. His fits of boyish merriment with me had quite vanished; his mood of calm indulgence to all that passed, which used to provoke me, had disappeared; there was an end of those penetrating looks which used to confuse and delight me, an end of the ecstasies and prayers which we once shared in common. We did not even meet often: he was continually absent, with no fears or regrets for leaving me alone; and I was constantly in society, where I did not need him.

There were no further scenes or quarrels between us. I tried to satisfy him, he carried out all my wishes, and we seemed to love each other.

When we were by ourselves, which we seldom were, I felt neither joy nor excitement nor embarrassment in his company: it seemed like being alone. I realized that he was my husband and no mere stranger, a good man, and as familiar to me as my own self. I was convinced that I knew just what he would say and do, and how he would look; and if anything he did surprised me, I concluded that he had made a mistake. I expected nothing from him. In a word, he was my husband—and that was all. It seemed to me that things must be so, as a matter of course, and that no other relations between us had ever existed. When he left home, especially at first, I was lonely and frightened and felt keenly my need of support; when he came back, I ran to his arms with joy, though two hours later my joy was quite forgotten, and I found nothing to say to him. Only at moments which sometimes occurred between us of quiet undemonstrative affection, I felt something wrong and some pain at my heart, and I seemed to read the same story in his eyes. I was conscious of a limit to tenderness, which he seemingly would not, and I could not, overstep. This saddened me sometimes; but I had no leisure to reflect on anything, and my regret for a change which I vaguely realized I tried to drown in the distractions which were always within my reach. Fashionable life, which had dazzled me at first by its glitter and flattery of my self-love, now took entire command of my nature, became a habit, laid its fetters upon me, and monopolized my capacity for feeling. I could not bear solitude, and was afraid to reflect on my position. My whole day, from late in the morning till late at night, was taken up by the claims of society; even if I stayed at home, my time was not my own. This no longer seemed to me either gay or dull, but it seemed that so, and not otherwise, it always, had to be.

So three years passed, during which our relations to one another remained unchanged and seemed to have taken a fixed shape which could not become either better or worse. Though two events of importance in our family life took place during that time, neither of them changed my own life. These were the birth of my first child and the death of

Tatyána Semënovna. At first the feeling of motherhood did take hold of me with such power, and produce in me such a passion of unanticipated joy, that I believed this would prove the beginning of a new life for me. But, in the course of two months, when I began to go out again, my feeling grew weaker and weaker, till it passed into mere habit and the lifeless performance of a duty. My husband, on the contrary, from the birth of our first boy, became his old self again—gentle, composed, and home-loving, and transferred to the child his old tenderness and gaiety. Many a night when I went, dressed for a ball, to the nursery, to sign the child with the cross before he slept, I found my husband there and felt his eyes fixed on me with something of reproof in their serious gaze. Then I was ashamed and even shocked by my own callousness, and asked myself if I was worse than other women. 'But it can't be helped,' I said to myself; 'I love my child, but to sit beside him all day long would bore me; and nothing will make me pretend what I do not really feel.'

His mother's death was a great sorrow to my husband; he said that he found it painful to go on living at Nikólskoe. For myself, although I mourned for her and sympathized with my husband's sorrow, yet I found life in that house easier and pleasanter after her death. Most of those three years we spent in town: I went only once to Nikólskoe for two months; and the third year we went abroad and spent the summer at Baden.

I was then twenty-one; our financial position was, I believed, satisfactory; my domestic life gave me all that I asked of it; everyone I knew, it seemed to me, loved me; my health was good; I was the best-dressed woman in Baden; I knew that I was good-looking; the weather was fine; I enjoyed the atmosphere of beauty and refinement; and, in short, I was in excellent spirits. They had once been even higher at Nikólskoe, when my happiness was in myself and came from the feeling that I deserved to be happy, and from the anticipation of still greater happiness to come. That was a different state of things; but I did very well this summer also. I had no special wishes or hopes or fears; it seemed to me that my life was full and my conscience easy. Among all the visitors at Baden that season there was no one man whom I preferred to the rest, or even to our old ambassador, Prince K., who was assiduous in his attentions to me. One was young, and another old; one was English and fair, another French and wore a beard—to me they were all alike, but all indispensable. Indistinguishable as they were, they together made up the atmosphere which I found so pleasant. But there was one, an Italian marquis, who stood out from the rest by reason of the boldness with which he expressed his admiration. He seized every opportunity of being with me—danced with me, rode with me, and met me at the casino; and everywhere he spoke to me of my charms. Several times I saw him from my windows loitering round our hotel, and the fixed gaze of his bright eyes often troubled me, and made me blush and turn away. He was young, handsome, and well-mannered; and, above all, by his smile and the expression of his brow, he resembled my husband, though much handsomer than he. He struck me by this likeness, though in general, in his lips, eyes, and long chin, there was something coarse and animal which contrasted with my husband's charming expression of kindness and noble serenity. I supposed him to be passionately in love with me, and thought of him sometimes with proud commiseration. When I tried at times to soothe him and change his tone to one of easy, half-friendly confidence, he resented the suggestion with vehemence, and continued to disquiet me by a smouldering passion which was ready at any moment to burst forth. Though I would not own it even to myself, I feared him and often thought of him against my will. My husband knew him, and treated him—even more than other acquaintances of ours who regarded him only as my husband—with coldness and disdain.

Towards the end of the season I fell ill and stayed indoors for a fortnight. The first evening that I went out again to hear the band, I learnt that Lady S., an Englishwoman famous for her beauty, who had long been expected, had arrived in my absence. My return was welcomed, and a group gathered round me; but a more distinguished group attended the beautiful stranger. She and her beauty were the one subject of conversation around me. When I saw her, she was really beautiful, but her self-satisfied expression struck me as disagreeable, and I said so. That day everything that had formerly seemed amusing, seemed dull. Lady S. arranged an expedition to the ruined castle for the next day; but I declined to be of the party. Almost everyone else went; and my opinion of Baden underwent a complete change. Everything and everybody seemed to me stupid and tiresome; I wanted to cry, to break off my cure, to return to Russia. There was some evil feeling in my soul, but I did not yet acknowledge it to myself. Pretending that I was not strong, I ceased to appear at crowded parties; if I went out, it was only in the morning by myself, to drink the waters; and my only companion was Mme M., a Russian lady, with whom I sometimes took drives in the surrounding country. My husband was absent: he had gone to Heidelberg for a time, intending to return to Russia when my cure was over, and only paid me occasional visits at Baden.

One day when Lady S. had carried off all the company on a hunting-expedition, Mme M. and I drove in the afternoon to the castle. While our carriage moved slowly along the winding road, bordered by ancient chestnut-trees and commanding a vista of the pretty and pleasant country round Baden, with the setting sun lighting it up, our conversation took a more serious turn than had ever happened to us before. I had known my companion for a long time; but she appeared to me now in a new light, as a well-principled and intelligent woman, to whom it was possible to speak without reserve, and whose friendship was worth having. We spoke of our private concerns, of our children, of the emptiness of life at Baden, till we felt a longing for Russia and the Russian countryside. When we entered the castle we were still under the impression of this serious feeling. Within the walls there was shade and coolness; the sunlight played from above upon the ruins. Steps and voices were audible. The landscape, charming enough but cold to a Russian eye, lay before us in the frame made by a doorway. We sat down to rest and watched the sunset in silence. The voices now sounded louder, and I thought I heard my own name. I listened and could not help overhearing every word. I recognized the voices: the speakers were the Italian marquis and a French friend of his whom I knew also. They were talking of me and of Lady S., and the Frenchman was comparing us as rival beauties. Though he said nothing insulting, his words made my pulse quicken. He explained in detail the good points of us both. I was already a mother, while Lady S. was only nineteen; though

I had the advantage in hair, my rival had a better figure. 'Besides,' he added, 'Lady S. is a real *grande dame*, and the other is nothing in particular, only one of those obscure Russian princesses who turn up here nowadays in such numbers.' He ended by saying that I was wise in not attempting to compete with Lady S., and that I was completely buried as far as Baden was concerned.

'I am sorry for her—unless indeed she takes a fancy to console herself with you,' he added with a hard ringing laugh.

'If she goes away, I follow her'—the words were blurted out in an Italian accent.

'Happy man! he is still capable of a passion!' laughed the Frenchman.

'Passion!' said the other voice and then was still for a moment. 'It is a necessity to me: I cannot live without it. To make life a romance is the one thing worth doing. And with me romance never breaks off in the middle, and this affair I shall carry through to the end.'

'*Bonne chance, mon ami!*'* said the Frenchman.

They now turned a corner, and the voices stopped. Then we heard them coming down the steps, and a few minutes later they came out upon us by a side-door. They were much surprised to see us. I blushed when the marquis approached me, and felt afraid when we left the castle and he offered me his arm. I could not refuse, and we set off for the carriage, walking behind Mme M. and his friend. I was mortified by what the Frenchman had said of me, though I secretly admitted that he had only put in words what I felt myself; but the plain speaking of the Italian had surprised and upset me by its coarseness. I was tormented by the thought that, though I had overheard him, he

* Good luck, my friend!

showed no fear of me. It was hateful to have him so close to me; and I walked fast after the other couple, not looking at him or answering him and trying to hold his arm in such a way as not to hear him. He spoke of the fine view, of the unexpected pleasure of our meeting, and so on; but I was not listening. My thoughts were with my husband, my child, my country; I felt ashamed, distressed, anxious; I was in a hurry to get back to my solitary room in the Hôtel de Bade, there to think at leisure of the storm of feeling that had just risen in my heart. But Mme M. walked slowly, it was still a long way to the carriage, and my escort seemed to loiter on purpose as if he wished to detain me. 'None of that!' I thought, and resolutely quickened my pace. But it soon became unmistakable that he was detaining me and even pressing my arm. Mme M. turned a corner, and we were quite alone. I was afraid.

'Excuse me,' I said coldly and tried to free my arm; but the lace of my sleeve caught on a button of his coat. Bending towards me, he began to unfasten it, and his ungloved fingers touched my arm. A feeling new to me, half horror and half pleasure, sent an icy shiver down my back. I looked at him, intending by my coldness to convey all the contempt I felt for him; but my look expressed nothing but fear and excitement. His liquid blazing eyes, right up against my face, stared strangely at me, at my neck and breast; both his hands fingered my arm above the wrist; his parted lips were saying that he loved me, and that I was all the world to him; and those lips were coming nearer and nearer, and those hands were squeezing mine harder and harder and burning me. A fever ran through my veins, my sight grew dim, I trembled, and the words intended to check him died in my throat.

Suddenly I felt a kiss on my cheek. Trembling all over and turning cold, I stood still and stared at him. Unable to speak or move, I stood there, horrified, expectant, even desirous. It was over in a moment, but the moment was horrible! In that short time I saw him exactly as he was—the low straight forehead (that forehead so like my husband's!) under the straw hat; the handsome regular nose and dilated nostrils; the long waxed moustache and short beard; the close-shaved cheeks and sunburnt neck. I hated and feared him; he was utterly repugnant and alien to me. And yet the excitement and passion of this hateful strange man raised a powerful echo in my own heart; I felt an irresistible longing to surrender myself to the kisses of that coarse handsome mouth, and to the pressure of those white hands with their delicate veins and jewelled fingers; I was tempted to throw myself headlong into the abyss of forbidden delights that had suddenly opened up before me.

'I am so unhappy already,' I thought; 'let more and more storms of unhappiness burst over my head!'

He put one arm round me and bent towards my face. 'Better so!' I thought: 'let sin and shame cover me ever deeper and deeper!'

'*Je vous aime!*'* he whispered in the voice which was so like my husband's. At once I thought of my husband and child, as creatures once precious to me who had now passed altogether out of my life. At that moment I heard Mme M.'s voice; she called to me from round the corner. I came to myself, tore my hand away without looking at him, and almost ran after her: I only looked at him after she and I were already seated in the carriage. Then I saw him raise his hat and ask some

* I love you.

commonplace question with a smile. He little knew the inexpressible aversion I felt for him at that moment.

My life seemed so wretched, the future so hopeless, the past so black! When Mme M. spoke, her words meant nothing to me. I thought that she talked only out of pity, and to hide the contempt I aroused in her. In every word and every look I seemed to detect this contempt and insulting pity. The shame of that kiss burnt my cheek, and the thought of my husband and child was more than I could bear. When I was alone in my own room, I tried to think over my position; but I was afraid to be alone. Without drinking the tea which was brought me, and uncertain of my own motives, I got ready with feverish haste to catch the evening train and join my husband at Heidelberg.

I found seats for myself and my maid in an empty carriage. When the train started and the fresh air blew through the window on my face, I grew more composed and pictured my past and future to myself more clearly. The course of our married life from the time of our first visit to Petersburg now presented itself to me in a new light, and lay like a reproach on my conscience. For the first time I clearly recalled our start at Nikólskoe and our plans for the future; and for the first time I asked myself what happiness had my husband had since then. I felt that I had behaved badly to him. 'But why', I asked myself, 'did he not stop me? Why did he make pretences? Why did he always avoid explanations? Why did he insult me? Why did he not use the power of his love to influence me? Or did he not love me?' But whether he was to blame or not, I still felt the kiss of that strange man upon my cheek. The nearer we got to Heidelberg, the clearer grew my picture of my husband, and the more I dreaded our meeting. 'I shall tell him all,' I thought, 'and wipe out everything with tears of repentance; and he will forgive me.' But I did not know myself what I meant by 'everything'; and I did not believe in my heart that he would forgive me.

As soon as I entered my husband's room and saw his calm though surprised expression, I felt at once that I had nothing to tell him, no confession to make, and nothing to ask forgiveness for. I had to suppress my unspoken grief and penitence.

'What put this into your head?' he asked. 'I meant to go to Baden to-morrow.' Then he looked more closely at me and seemed to take alarm. 'What's the matter with you? What has happened?' he said.

'Nothing at all,' I replied, almost breaking down. 'I am not going back. Let us go home, to-morrow if you like, to Russia.'

For some time he said nothing but looked at me attentively. Then he said, 'But do tell me what has happened to you.'

I blushed involuntarily and looked down. There came into his eyes a flash of anger and displeasure. Afraid of what he might imagine, I said with a power of pretence that surprised myself:

'Nothing at all has happened. It was merely that I grew weary and sad by myself; and I have been thinking a great deal of our way of life and of you. I have long been to blame towards you. Why do you take me abroad, when you can't bear it yourself? I have long been to blame. Let us go back to Nikólskoe and settle there for ever.'

'Spare us these sentimental scenes, my dear,' he said coldly. 'To go back to Nikólskoe is a good idea, for our money is running short; but the notion of stopping there "for ever" is fanciful. I know you would not settle down. Have some tea, and you will feel better,' and he rose to ring for the waiter.

I imagined all he might be thinking about me; and I was offended by the horrible thoughts which I ascribed to him when I encountered the dubious and shame-faced look he directed at me. 'He will not and cannot understand me.' I said I would go and look at the child, and I left the room. I wished to be alone, and to cry and cry and cry . . .

CHAPTER IV

The house at Nikólskoe, so long unheated and uninhabited, came to life again; but much of the past was dead beyond recall. Tatyána Semënovna was no more, and we were now alone together. But far from desiring such close companionship, we even found it irksome. To me that winter was the more trying because I was in bad health, from which I only recovered after the birth of my second son. My husband and I were still on the same terms as during our life in Petersburg: we were coldly friendly to each other; but in the country each room and wall and sofa recalled what he had once been to me, and what I had lost. It was as if some unforgiven grievance held us apart, as if he were punishing me and pretending not to be aware of it. But there was nothing to ask pardon for, no penalty to deprecate; my punishment was merely this, that he did not give his whole heart and mind to me as he used to do; but he did not give it to anyone or to anything; as though he had no longer a heart to give. Sometimes it occurred to me that he was only pretending to be like that, in order to hurt me, and that the old feeling was still alive in his breast; and I tried to call it forth. But I always failed: he always seemed to avoid frankness, evidently suspecting me of insincerity, and dreading the folly of any emotional display. I could read in his face and the tone of his voice, 'What is the good of talking? I know all the facts already, and I know what is on the tip of your tongue, and I know that you will say one thing and do another.' At first I was mortified by his dread of frankness, but I came later to think that it was rather the absence, on his part, of any need of frankness. It would never have occurred to me now, to tell him of a sudden that I loved him, or to ask him to repeat the prayers with me or listen while I played the piano. Our intercourse came to be regulated by a fixed code of good manners. We lived our separate lives: he had his own occupations in which I was not needed, and which I no longer wished to share, while I continued my idle life which no longer vexed or grieved him. The children were still too young to form a bond between us.

But spring came round and brought Kátya and Sónya to spend the summer with us in the country. As the house at Nikólskoe was under repair, we went to live at my old home at Pokróvskoe. The old house was unchanged—the veranda, the folding table and the piano in the sunny drawing-room, and my old bedroom with its white curtains and the dreams of my girlhood which I seemed to have left behind me there. In that room there were two beds: one had been mine, and in it now my plump little Kokósha lay sprawling, when I went at night to sign him with the cross; the other was a crib, in which the little face of my baby, Ványa, peeped out from his swaddling-clothes. Often, when I had made the sign over them and remained standing in the middle of the quiet room, suddenly there rose up from all the corners, from the walls and curtains, old forgotten visions of youth. Old voices began to sing the songs of my girlhood. Where were those visions now? where were those dear old sweet songs? All that I had hardly dared to hope for had come to pass. My vague confused dreams had become a reality, and the reality had become an oppressive, difficult, and joyless life. All remained the same—the garden visible through the window, the grass, the path, the very same bench over there above the dell, the same song of the nightingale by the pond, the same lilacs in full bloom, the same moon shining above the house; and yet, in everything such a terrible inconceivable change! Such coldness in all that might have been near and dear! Just as in old times, Kátya and I sit quietly alone together in the parlour and talk, and talk of him. But Kátya has grown wrinkled and pale; and her eyes no longer shine with joy and hope, but express only sympathy, sorrow, and regret. We do not go into raptures as we used to, we judge him coolly; we do not wonder what we have done to deserve such happiness, or long to proclaim our thoughts to all the world. No! we whisper together like conspirators and ask each other for the hundredth time why all has changed so sadly. Yet he was still the same man, save for the deeper furrow between his eyebrows and the whiter hair on his temples; but his serious attentive look was constantly veiled from me by a cloud. And I am the same woman, but without love or desire for love, with no longing for work and no content with myself. My religious ecstasies, my love for my husband, the fullness of my former life—all these now seem utterly remote and visionary. Once it seemed so plain and right that to live for others was happiness; but now it has become unintelligible. Why live for others, when life had no attraction even for oneself?

I had given up my music altogether since the

time of our first visit to Petersburg; but now the old piano and the old music tempted me to begin again.

One day I was not well and stayed indoors alone. My husband had taken Kátya and Sónya to see the new buildings at Nikólskoe. Tea was laid; I went downstairs and while waiting for them sat down at the piano. I opened the 'Moonlight Sonata' and began to play. There was no one within sight or sound, the windows were open over the garden, and the familiar sounds floated through the room with a solemn sadness. At the end of the first movement I looked round instinctively to the corner where he used once to sit and listen to my playing. He was not there; his chair, long unmoved, was still in its place; through the window I could see a lilac-bush against the light of the setting sun; the freshness of evening streamed in through the open windows. I rested my elbows on the piano and covered my face with both hands; and so I sat for a long time, thinking. I recalled with pain the irrevocable past, and timidly imagined the future. But for me there seemed to be no future, no desires at all and no hopes. 'Can life be over for me?' I thought with horror; then I looked up, and, trying to forget and not to think, I began playing the same movement over again. 'O God!' I prayed, 'forgive me if I have sinned, or restore to me all that once blossomed in my heart, or teach me what to do and how to live now.' There was a sound of wheels on the grass and before the steps of the house; then I heard cautious and familiar footsteps pass along the veranda and cease; but my heart no longer replied to the sound. When I stopped playing the footsteps were behind me and a hand was laid on my shoulder.

'How clever of you to think of playing that!' he said.

I said nothing.

'Have you had tea?' he asked.

I shook my head without looking at him—I was unwilling to let him see the signs of emotion on my face.

'They'll be here immediately,' he said; 'the horse gave trouble, and they got out on the high road to walk home.'

'Let us wait for them,' I said, and went out to the veranda, hoping that he would follow; but he asked about the children and went upstairs to see them. Once more his presence and simple kindly voice made me doubt if I had really lost anything. What more could I wish? 'He is kind and gentle, a good husband, a good father; I don't know myself what more I want.' I sat down under the veranda awning on the very bench on which I had sat when we became engaged. The sun had set, it was growing dark, and a little spring rain-cloud hung over the house and garden, and only behind the trees the horizon was clear, with the fading glow of twilight, in which one star had just begun to twinkle. The landscape, covered by the shadow of the cloud, seemed waiting for the light spring shower. There was not a breath of wind; not a single leaf or blade of grass stirred; the scent of lilac and bird-cherry was so strong in the garden and veranda that it seemed as if all the air was in flower; it came in wafts, now stronger and now weaker, till one longed to shut both eyes and ears and drink in that fragrance only. The dahlias and rose-bushes, not yet in flower, stood motionless on the black mould of the border, looking as if they were growing slowly upwards on their white-shaved props; beyond the dell, the frogs were making the most of their time before the rain drove them to the pond, croaking busily and loudly. Only the high continuous note of water falling at some distance rose above their croaking. From time to time the nightingales called to one another, and I could hear them flitting restlessly from bush to bush. Again this spring a nightingale had tried to build in a bush under the window, and I heard her fly off across the avenue when I went into the veranda. From there she whistled once and then stopped; she, too, was expecting the rain.

I tried in vain to calm my feelings: I had a sense of anticipation and regret.

He came downstairs again and sat down beside me.

'I am afraid they will get wet,' he said.

'Yes,' I answered; and we sat for long without speaking.

The cloud came down lower and lower with no wind. The air grew stiller and more fragrant. Suddenly a drop fell on the canvas awning and seemed to rebound from it; then another broke on the gravel path; soon there was a splash on the burdock leaves, and a fresh shower of big drops came down faster and faster. Nightingales and frogs were both dumb; only the high note of the falling water, though the rain made it seem more distant, still went on; and a bird, which must have sheltered among the dry leaves near the veranda, steadily repeated its two unvarying notes. My husband got up to go in.

'Where are you going?' I asked, trying to keep him; 'it is so pleasant here.'

'We must send them an umbrella and goloshes,' he replied.

'Don't trouble—it will soon be over.'

He thought I was right, and we remained together in the veranda. I rested one hand upon the wet slippery rail and put my head out. The fresh rain wetted my hair and neck in places. The cloud, growing lighter and thinner, was passing overhead; the steady patter of the rain gave place to occasional drops that fell from the sky or dripped from the trees. The frogs began to croak again in the dell; the nightingales woke up and began to call from the dripping bushes from one side and then from another. The whole prospect before us grew clear.

'How delightful!' he said, seating himself on the veranda rail and passing a hand over my wet hair.

This simple caress had on me the effect of a reproach: I felt inclined to cry.

'What more can a man need?' he said; 'I am so content now that I want nothing; I am perfectly happy!'

He told me a different story once, I thought. He had said that, however great his happiness might be, he always wanted more and more. Now he is calm and contented; while my heart is full of unspoken repentance and unshed tears.

'I think it delightful too,' I said; 'but I am sad just because of the beauty of it all. All is so fair and lovely outside me, while my own heart is confused and baffled and full of vague unsatisfied longing. Is it possible that there is no element of pain, no yearning for the past, in your enjoyment of nature?'

He took his hand off my head and was silent for a little.

'I used to feel that too,' he said, as though recalling it, 'especially in spring. I used to sit up all night too, with my hopes and fears for company, and good company they were! But life was all before me then. Now it is all behind me, and I am content with what I have. I find life capital,' he added with such careless confidence, that I believed, whatever pain it gave me to hear it, that it was the truth.

'But is there nothing you wish for?' I asked.

'I don't ask for impossibilities,' he said, guessing my thoughts. 'You go and get your head wet,' he added, stroking my head like a child's and again passing his hand over the wet hair; 'you envy the leaves and the grass their wetting from the rain, and you would like yourself to be the grass and the leaves and the rain. But I am content to enjoy them and everything else that is good and young and happy.'

'And do you regret nothing of the past?' I asked, while my heart grew heavier and heavier.

Again he thought for a time before replying. I saw that he wished to reply with perfect frankness.

'Nothing,' he said shortly.

'Not true! not true!' I said, turning towards him and looking into his eyes. 'Do you really not regret the past?'

'No!' he repeated; 'I am grateful for it, but I don't regret it.'

'But would you not like to have it back?' I asked.

He turned away and looked out over the garden.

'No; I might as well wish to have wings. It is impossible.'

'And would you not alter the past? do you not reproach yourself or me?'

'No, never! It was all for the best.'

'Listen to me!' I said, touching his arm to make him look round. 'Why did you never tell me that you wished me to live as you really wished me to? Why did you give me a freedom for which I was unfit? Why did you stop teaching me? If you had wished it, if you had guided me differently, none of all this would have happened!' said I in a voice that increasingly expressed cold displeasure and reproach, in place of the love of former days.

'What would not have happened?' he asked, turning to me in surprise. 'As it is, there is nothing wrong. Things are all right, quite all right,' he added with a smile.

'Does he really not understand?' I thought; 'or, still worse, does he not wish to understand?'

Then I suddenly broke out. 'Had you acted differently, I should not now be punished, for no fault at all, by your indifference and even contempt, and you would not have taken from me unjustly all that I valued in life!'

'What do you mean, my dear one?' he asked—he seemed not to understand me.

'No! don't interrupt me! You have taken from me your confidence, your love, even your respect; for I cannot believe, when I think of the past, that you still love me. No! don't speak! I must once for all say out what has long been torturing me. Is it my fault that I knew nothing of life, and that you left me to learn experience for myself? Is it my fault that now, when I have gained the knowledge and have been struggling for nearly a year to come back to you, you push me away and pretend not to understand what I want? And you always do it so that it is impossible to reproach you, while I am guilty and unhappy. Yes, you wish to drive me out again to that life which might rob us both of happiness.'

'How did I show that?' he asked in evident alarm and surprise.

'No later than yesterday you said, and you constantly say, that I can never settle down here, and that we must spend this winter too at Petersburg; and I hate Petersburg!' I went on. 'Instead of supporting me, you avoid all plain speaking, you never say a single frank affectionate word to me. And then, when I fall utterly, you will reproach me and rejoice in my fall.'

'Stop!' he said with cold severity. 'You have no right to say that. It only proves that you are ill-disposed towards me, that you don't . . .'

'That I don't love you? Don't hesitate to say it!' I cried, and the tears began to flow. I sat down on the bench and covered my face with my handkerchief.

'So that is how he understood me!' I thought, trying to restrain the sobs which choked me. 'Gone, gone is our former love!' said a voice at my heart. He did not come close or try to comfort me. He was hurt by what I had said. When he spoke, his tone was cool and dry.

'I don't know what you reproach me with,' he began. 'If you mean that I don't love you as I once did . . .'

'Did love!' I said, with my face buried in the handkerchief, while the bitter tears fell still more abundantly.

'If so, time is to blame for that, and we ourselves. Each time of life has its own kind of love.' He was silent for a moment. 'Shall I tell you the whole truth, if you really wish for frankness? In that summer when I first knew you, I used to lie awake all night, thinking about you, and I made that love myself, and it grew and grew in my heart. So again, in Petersburg and abroad, in the course of horrible sleepless nights, I strove to shatter and destroy that love, which had come to torture me. I did not destroy it, but I destroyed that part of it which gave me pain. Then I grew calm; and I feel love still, but it is a different kind of love.'

'You call it love, but I call it torture!' I said. 'Why did you allow me to go into society, if you thought so badly of it that you ceased to love me on that account?'

'No, it was not society, my dear,' he said.

'Why did you not exercise your authority?' I went on; 'why did you not lock me up or kill me? That would have been better than the loss of all that formed my happiness. I should have been happy, instead of being ashamed.'

I began to sob again and hid my face.

Just then Kátya and Sónya, wet and cheerful, came out to the veranda, laughing and talking loudly. They were silent as soon as they saw us, and went in again immediately.

We remained silent for a long time. I had had my cry out and felt relieved. I glanced at him. He was sitting with his head resting on his hand; he intended to make some reply to my glance, but only sighed deeply and resumed his former position.

I went up to him and removed his hand. His eyes turned thoughtfully to my face.

'Yes,' he began, as if continuing his thoughts aloud, 'all of us, and especially you women, must have personal experience of all the nonsense of life, in order to get back to life itself; the evidence of other people is no good. At that time you had not got near the end of that charming nonsense which I admired in you. So I let you go through it alone, feeling that I had no right to put pressure on you, though my own time for that sort of thing was long past.'

'If you loved me,' I said, 'how could you stand beside me and suffer me to go through it?'

'Because it was impossible for you to take my word for it, though you would have tried to. Personal experience was necessary, and now you have had it.'

'There was much calculation in all that,' I said, 'but little love.'

Again we were silent.

'What you said just now is severe, but it is true,' he began, rising suddenly and beginning to walk about the veranda. 'Yes, it is true. I was to blame,' he added, stopping opposite me; 'I ought either to have kept myself from loving you at all, or to have loved you in a simpler way.'

'Let us forget it all,' I said timidly.

'No,' he said; 'the past can never come back, never;' and his voice softened as he spoke.

'It is restored already,' I said, laying a hand on his shoulder.

He took my hand away and pressed it.

'I was wrong when I said that I did not regret the past. I do regret it; I weep for that past love which can never return. Who is to blame, I do not know. Love remains, but not the old love; its place remains, but it is all wasted away and has lost all strength and substance; recollections are still left, and gratitude; but . . .'

'Do not say that!' I broke in. 'Let all be as it was before! Surely that is possible?' I asked, looking into his eyes; but their gaze was clear and calm, and did not look deeply into mine.

Even while I spoke, I knew that my wishes and my petition were impossible. He smiled calmly and gently; and I thought it the smile of an old man.

'How young you are still!' he said, 'and I am so old. What you seek in me is no longer there. Why deceive ourselves?' he added, still smiling.

I stood silent opposite to him, and my heart grew calmer.

'Don't let us try to repeat life,' he went on. 'Don't let us make pretences to ourselves. Let us be thankful that there is an end of the old emotions and excitements. The excitement of searching is over for us; our quest is done, and happiness enough has fallen to our lot. Now we must stand aside and make room—for him, if you like,' he said, pointing to the nurse who was carrying Ványa out and had stopped at the veranda door. 'That's the truth, my dear one,' he said, drawing down my head and kissing it, not a lover any longer but an old friend.

The fragrant freshness of the night rose ever stronger and sweeter from the garden; the sounds and the silence grew more solemn; star after star began to twinkle overhead. I looked at him, and suddenly my heart grew light; it seemed that the cause of my suffering had been removed like an aching nerve. Suddenly I realized clearly and calmly that the past feeling, like the past time itself, was gone beyond recall, and that it would be not only impossible but painful and uncomfortable to bring it back. And after all, was that time so good which seemed to me so happy? And it was all so long, long ago!

'Time for tea!' he said, and we went together to the parlour. At the door we met the nurse with the baby. I took him in my arms, covered his bare little red legs, pressed him to me, and kissed him with the lightest touch of my lips. Half asleep, he moved the parted fingers of one creased little hand and opened dim little eyes, as if he was looking for something or recalling something. All at once his eyes rested on me, a spark of consciousness shone in them, the little pouting lips, parted before, now met and opened in a smile. 'Mine, mine, mine!' I thought, pressing him to my breast with such an impulse of joy in every limb that I found it hard to restrain myself from hurting him. I fell to kissing the cold little feet, his stomach and hand and head with its thin covering of down. My husband came up to me, and I quickly covered the child's face and uncovered it again.

'Iván Sergéich!' said my husband, tickling him under the chin. But I made haste to cover Iván Sergéich up again. None but I had any business to look long at him. I glanced at my husband. His eyes smiled as he looked at me; and I looked into them with an ease and happiness which I had not felt for a long time.

That day ended the romance of our marriage; the old feeling became a precious irrecoverable remembrance; but a new feeling of love for my children and the father of my children laid the foundation of a new life and a quite different happiness; and that life and happiness have lasted to the present time.

THE KREUTZER SONATA

The figures in the text refer to the Appendix of readings contained in the lithographed version circulated in Russia. See pp. xviii, 210–31.

THE KREUTZER SONATA

But I say unto you, that every one that looketh on a woman to lust after her hath committed adultery with her already in his heart. Matt. v. 28.

The disciples say unto him, If the case of the man is so with his wife, it is not expedient to marry. But he said unto them, All men cannot receive this saying, but they to whom it is given. Ibid. xix. 10, 11.

I

It was early spring, and the second day of our journey. Passengers going short distances entered and left our carriage, but three others, like myself, had come all the way with the train. One was a lady, plain and no longer young, who smoked, had a harassed look, and wore a mannish coat and cap; another was an acquaintance of hers, a talkative man of about forty, whose things looked neat and new; the third was a rather short man[1] who kept himself apart. He was not old, but his curly hair had gone prematurely grey. His movements were abrupt and his unusually glittering eyes moved rapidly from one object to another. He wore an old overcoat, evidently from a first-rate tailor, with an astrakhan collar, and a tall astrakhan cap. When he unbuttoned his overcoat a sleeveless Russian coat and embroidered shirt showed beneath it. A peculiarity of this man was a strange sound he emitted, something like a clearing of his throat, or a laugh begun and sharply broken off.

All the way this man had carefully avoided making acquaintance or having any intercourse with his fellow passengers. When spoken to by those near him he gave short and abrupt answers, and at other times read, looked out of the window, smoked, or drank tea and ate something he took out of an old bag.

It seemed to me that his loneliness depressed him, and I made several attempts to converse with him, but whenever our eyes met, which happened often as he sat nearly opposite me, he turned away and took up his book or looked out of the window.

Towards the second evening, when our train stopped at a large station, this nervous man fetched himself some boiling water and made tea. The man with the neat new things—a lawyer as I found out later—and his neighbour, the smoking lady with the mannish coat, went to the refreshment-room to drink tea.

During their absence several new passengers entered the carriage, among them a tall, shaven, wrinkled old man, evidently a tradesman, in a coat lined with skunk fur, and a cloth cap with an enormous peak. The tradesman sat down opposite the seats of the lady and the lawyer, and immediately started a conversation with a young man who had also entered at that station and, judging by his appearance, was a tradesman's clerk.[2]

I was sitting the other side of the gangway and as the train was standing still I could hear snatches of their conversation when nobody was passing between us. The tradesman began by saying that he was going to his estate which was only one station farther on; then as usual the conversation turned to prices and trade, and they spoke of the state of business in Moscow and then of the Nízhni-Nóvgorod Fair. The clerk began to relate how a wealthy merchant, known to both of them, had gone on the spree at the fair, but the old man interrupted him by telling of the orgies he had been at in former times at Kunávin Fair. He evidently prided himself on the part he had played in them, and[3] recounted with pleasure how he and some acquaintances, together with the merchant they had been speaking of, had once got drunk at Kunávin and played such a trick that he had to tell of it in a whisper. The clerk's roar of laughter filled the whole carriage; the old man laughed also, exposing two yellow teeth.

Not expecting to hear anything interesting, I got up to stroll about the platform till the train should start. At the carriage door I met the lawyer and the lady who were talking with animation as they approached.

'You won't have time,' said the sociable lawyer, 'the second bell will ring in a moment.'*

And the bell did ring before I had gone the length of the train. When I returned, the animated conversation between the lady and the lawyer was proceeding. The old tradesman sat silent opposite to them, looking sternly before him, and occasionally mumbled disapprovingly as if chewing something.

'Then she plainly informed her husband,' the lawyer was smilingly saying as I passed him, 'that she was not able, and did not wish, to live with him since . . .'

He went on to say something I could not hear. Several other passengers came in after me. The guard passed, a porter hurried in, and for some time the noise made their voices inaudible. When all was quiet again the conversation had evidently turned from the particular case to general considerations.

The lawyer was saying that public opinion in Europe was occupied with the question of divorce, and that cases of 'that kind' were occurring more and more often in Russia. Noticing that his was the only voice audible, he stopped his discourse and turned to the old man.

* It was customary in Russia for a first, second, and third bell to ring before a train left a station.—A. M.

'Those things did not happen in the old days, did they?' he said, smiling pleasantly.

The old man was about to reply, but the train moved and he took off his cap, crossed himself, and whispered a prayer. The lawyer turned away his eyes and waited politely. Having finished his prayer and crossed himself three times the old man set his cap straight, pulled it well down over his forehead, changed his position, and began to speak.

'They used to happen even then, sir, but less often,' he said. 'As times are now they can't help happening. People have got too educated.'

The train moved faster and faster and jolted over the joints of the rails, making it difficult to hear, but being interested I moved nearer. The nervous man with the glittering eyes opposite me, evidently also interested, listened without changing his place.

'What is wrong with education?' said the lady, with a scarcely perceptible smile. 'Surely it can't be better to marry as they used to in the old days when the bride and bridegroom did not even see one another before the wedding,' she continued, answering not what her interlocutor had said but what she thought he would say, in the way many ladies have. 'Without knowing whether they loved, or whether they could love, they married just anybody, and were wretched all their lives. And you think that was better?' she said, evidently addressing me and the lawyer chiefly and least of all the old man with whom she was talking.

'They've got so very educated,' the tradesman reiterated, looking contemptuously at the lady and leaving her question unanswered.

'It would be interesting to know how you explain the connexion between education and matrimonial discord,' said the lawyer, with a scarcely perceptible smile.

The tradesman was about to speak, but the lady interrupted him.

'No,' she said, 'those times have passed.' But the lawyer stopped her.

'Yes, but allow the gentleman to express his views.'

'Foolishness comes from education,' the old man said categorically.

'They make people who don't love one another marry, and then wonder that they live in discord,' the lady hastened to say, turning to look at the lawyer, at me, and even at the clerk, who had got up and, leaning on the back of the seat, was smilingly listening to the conversation. 'It's only animals, you know, that can be paired off as their master likes; but human beings have their own inclinations and attachments,' said the lady, with an evident desire to annoy the tradesman.

'You should not talk like that, madam,' said the old man, 'animals are cattle, but human beings have a law given them.'

'Yes, but how is one to live with a man when there is no love?' the lady again hastened to express her argument, which probably seemed very new to her.[5]

'They used not to go into that,' said the old man in an impressive tone, 'it is only now that all this has sprung up. The least thing makes them say: "I will leave you!" The fashion has spread even to the peasants. "Here you are!" she says, "Here, take your shirts and trousers and I will go with Ványka; his head is curlier than yours." What can you say? The first thing that should be required of a woman is fear!'

The clerk glanced at the lawyer, at the lady, and at me, apparently suppressing a smile and prepared to ridicule or to approve of the tradesman's words according to the reception they met with.

'Fear of what?' asked the lady.

'Why this: Let her fear her husband! That fear!'

'Oh, the time for that, sir, has passed,' said the lady with a certain viciousness.

'No, madam, that time cannot pass. As she, Eve, was made from the rib of a man, so it will remain to the end of time,' said the old man, jerking his head with such sternness and such a victorious look that the clerk at once concluded that victory was on his side, and laughed loudly.

'Ah yes, that's the way you men argue,' said the lady unyieldingly, and turned to us. 'You have given yourselves freedom but want to shut women up in a tower.* You no doubt permit yourselves everything.'

'[6]No one is permitting anything, but a man does not bring offspring into the home; while a woman —a wife—is a leaky vessel,' the tradesman continued insistently. His tone was so impressive that it evidently vanquished his hearers, and even the lady felt crushed but still did not give in.

'Yes, but I think you will agree that a woman is a human being and has feelings as a man has. What is she to do then, if she does not love her husband?'

'Does not love!' said the tradesman severely, moving his brows and lips. 'She'll love, no fear!' This unexpected argument particularly pleased the clerk, and he emitted a sound of approval.

'Oh, no, she won't!' the lady began, 'and when there is no love you can't enforce it.'

'Well, and supposing the wife is unfaithful, what then?' asked the lawyer.

* Literally 'in the *terem*', the *terem* being the woman's quarter where in olden times the women of a Russian family used to be secluded in oriental fashion.—A. M.

'That is not admissible,' said the old man. 'One has to see to that.'

'But if it happens, what then? You know it does occur.'

'It happens among some, but not among us,' said the old man.[7]

All were silent. The clerk moved, came still nearer, and, evidently unwilling to be behindhand, began with a smile.

'Yes, a young fellow of ours had a scandal. It was a difficult case to deal with. It too was a case of a woman who was a bad lot. She began to play the devil, and the young fellow is respectable and cultured. At first it was with one of the office-clerks. The husband tried to persuade her with kindness. She would not stop, but played all sorts of dirty tricks. Then she began to steal his money. He beat her, but she only grew worse. Carried on intrigues, if I may mention it, with an unchristened Jew. What was he to do? He turned her out altogether and lives as a bachelor, while she gads about.'

'Because he is a fool,' said the old man. 'If he'd pulled her up properly from the first and not let her have her way, she'd be living with him, no fear! It's giving way at first that counts. Don't trust your horse in the field, or your wife in the house.'

At that moment the guard entered to collect the tickets for the next station. The old man gave up his.

'Yes, the female sex must be curbed in time or else all is lost!'

'Yes, but you yourself just now were speaking about the way married men amuse themselves at the Kunávin Fair,' I could not help saying.[8]

'That's a different matter,' said the old man and relapsed into silence.

When the whistle sounded the tradesman rose,

got out his bag from under the seat, buttoned up his coat, and slightly lifting his cap went out of the carriage.

II

As soon as the old man had gone several voices were raised.

'A daddy of the old style!' remarked the clerk.

'A living Domostróy!'* said the lady. 'What barbarous views of women and marriage!'

'Yes, we are far from the European understanding of marriage,' said the lawyer.†

'The chief thing such people do not understand,' continued the lady, 'is that marriage without love is not marriage; that love alone sanctifies marriage, and that real marriage is only such as is sanctified by love.'

The clerk listened smilingly, trying to store up for future use all he could of the clever conversation.

In the midst of the lady's remarks we heard, behind me, a sound like that of a broken laugh or sob; and on turning round we saw my neighbour, the lonely grey-haired man with the glittering eyes, who had approached unnoticed during our conversation, which evidently interested him. He stood with his arms on the back of the seat, evidently much excited; his face was red[9] and a muscle twitched in his cheek.

'What kind of love . . . love . . . is it that sanctifies marriage?' he asked hesitatingly.[10]

Noticing the speaker's agitation, the lady tried to answer him as gently and fully as possible.

'True love . . . When such love exists between

* *The Housebuilder*, a sixteenth-century manual, by the monk Silvester, on religion and household management.—A. M.

† One Russian edition adds: 'First woman's rights, then civil marriage, and then divorce, come as unsettled questions.' —A. M.

a man and a woman, then marriage is possible,' she said.

'Yes, but how is one to understand what is meant by "true love"?' said the gentleman with the glittering eyes timidly and with an awkward smile.

'Everybody knows what love is,' replied the lady, evidently wishing to break off her conversation with him.

'But I don't,' said the man. 'You must define what you understand . . .'

'Why? It's very simple,' she said, but stopped to consider. 'Love? Love is an exclusive preference for one above everybody else,' said the lady.

'Preference for how long? A month, two days, or half an hour?' said the grey-haired man and began to laugh.

'Excuse me, we are evidently not speaking of the same thing.'

'Oh, yes! Exactly the same.'

'She means,' interposed the lawyer, pointing to the lady, 'that in the first place marriage must be the outcome of attachment—or love, if you please—and only where that exists is marriage sacred, so to speak. Secondly, that marriage when not based on natural attachment—love, if you prefer the word—lacks the element that makes it morally binding. Do I understand you rightly?' he added, addressing the lady.

The lady indicated her approval of his explanation by a nod of her head.

'It follows . . .' the lawyer continued—but the nervous man whose eyes now glowed as if aflame and who had evidently restrained himself with difficulty, began without letting the lawyer finish:

'Yes, I mean exactly the same thing, a preference for one person over everybody else, and I am only asking: a preference for how long?'

'For how long? For a long time; for life sometimes,' replied the lady, shrugging her shoulders.

'Oh, but that happens only in novels and never in real life. In real life this preference for one may last for years (that happens very rarely), more often for months, or perhaps for weeks, days, or hours,' he said, evidently aware that he was astonishing everybody by his views and pleased that it was so.

'Oh, what are you saying?' 'But no . . .' 'No, allow me . . .' we all three began at once. Even the clerk uttered an indefinite sound of disapproval.

'Yes, I know,' the grey-haired man shouted above our voices, 'you are talking about what is supposed to be, but I am speaking of what is. Every man experiences what you call love for every pretty woman.'[11]

'Oh, what you say is awful! But the feeling that is called love does exist among people, and is given not for months or years, but for a lifetime!'

'No, it does not! Even if we should grant that a man might prefer a certain woman all his life, the woman in all probability would prefer someone else;[12] and so it always has been and still is in the world,' he said, and taking out his cigarette-case he began to smoke.

'But the feeling may be reciprocal,' said the lawyer.

'No, sir, it can't!' rejoined the other. 'Just as it cannot be that in a cartload of peas, two marked peas will lie side by side. Besides, it is not merely this impossibility, but the inevitable satiety.[13] To love one person for a whole lifetime is like saying that one candle will burn a whole life,' he said, greedily inhaling the smoke.

'But you are talking all the time about physical love. Don't you acknowledge love based on identity of ideals, on spiritual affinity?' asked the lady.

'Spiritual affinity! Identity of ideals!' he repeated, emitting his peculiar sound. 'But in that case why go to bed together? (Excuse my coarseness!) Or do people go to bed together because of the identity of their ideals?' he said, bursting into a nervous laugh.[14]

'But permit me,' said the lawyer. 'Facts contradict you. We do see that matrimony exists, that all mankind, or the greater part of it, lives in wedlock, and many people honourably live long married lives.'

The grey-haired man again laughed.

'First you say that marriage is based on love, and when I express a doubt as to the existence of a love other than sensual, you prove the existence of love by the fact that marriages exist. But marriages in our days are mere deception!'

'No, allow me!' said the lawyer. 'I only say that marriages have existed and do exist.'

'They do! But why? They have existed and do exist among people who see in marriage something sacramental, a mystery binding them in the sight of God. Among them marriages do exist. Among us, people marry regarding marriage as nothing but copulation, and the result is either deception or coercion.[15] When it is deception it is easier to bear. The husband and wife merely deceive people by pretending to be monogamists, while living polygamously. That is bad, but still bearable. But when, as most frequently happens, the husband and wife have undertaken the external duty of living together all their lives,[16] and begin to hate each other after a month, and wish to part but still continue to live together, it leads to that terrible hell which makes people take to drink, shoot themselves, and kill or poison themselves or one another,' he went on, speaking more and more rapidly, not allowing anyone to put in a word and becoming more and more excited. We all felt embarrassed.

'Yes, undoubtedly there are critical episodes in married life,' said the lawyer, wishing to end this disturbingly heated conversation.

'I see you have found out who I am!' said the grey-haired man softly, and with apparent calm.

'No, I have not that pleasure.'

'It is no great pleasure. I am that Pózdnyshev in whose life that critical episode occurred to which you alluded; the episode when he killed his wife,' he said, rapidly glancing at each of us.

No one knew what to say and all remained silent.

'Well, never mind,' he said with that peculiar sound of his. 'However, pardon me. Ah! . . . I won't intrude on you.'

'Oh, no, if you please . . .' said the lawyer, himself not knowing 'if you please' what.

But Pózdnyshev, without listening to him, rapidly turned away and went back to his seat. The lawyer and the lady whispered together. I sat down beside Pózdnyshev in silence, unable to think of anything to say. It was too dark to read, so I shut my eyes pretending that I wished to go to sleep. So we travelled in silence to the next station.

At that station the lawyer and the lady moved into another car, having some time previously consulted the guard about it. The clerk lay down on the seat and fell asleep. Pózdnyshev kept smoking and drinking tea which he had made at the last station.

When I opened my eyes and looked at him he suddenly addressed me resolutely and irritably:

'Perhaps it is unpleasant for you to sit with me, knowing who I am? In that case I will go away.'

'Oh no, not at all.'

'Well then, won't you have some? Only it's very strong.'

He poured out some tea for me.

'They talk . . . and they always lie . . .' he remarked.

'What are you speaking about?' I asked.

'Always about the same thing. About that love of theirs and what it is! Don't you want to sleep?'

'Not at all.'

'Then would you like me to tell you how that love led to what happened to me?'

'Yes, if it will not be painful for you.'

'No, it is painful for me to be silent. Drink the tea . . . or is it too strong?'

The tea was really like beer, but I drank a glass of it.* Just then the guard entered. Pózdnyshev followed him with angry eyes, and only began to speak after he had left.[17]

III

'WELL then, I'll tell you.[18] But do you really want to hear it?'

I repeated that I wished it very much. He paused, rubbed his face with his hands, and began:

'If I am to tell it, I must tell everything from the beginning: I must tell how and why I married, and the kind of man I was before my marriage.[19]

'Till my marriage I lived as everybody does, that is, everybody in our class. I am a landowner and a graduate of the university, and was a marshal of the gentry. Before my marriage I lived as everyone does, that is, dissolutely; and while living dissolutely I was convinced, like everybody in our class, that I was living as one has to. I thought I was a charming fellow and quite a moral man.[20] I was not a

* Tea in Russia is usually drunk out of tumblers.—A. M.

seducer, had no unnatural tastes, did not make that the chief purpose of my life as many of my associates did, but I practised debauchery in a steady, decent way for health's sake.[21] I avoided women who might tie my hands by having a child or by attachment for me. However, there may have been children and attachments, but I acted as if there were not. And this I not only considered moral, but I was even proud of it.'

He paused and gave vent to his peculiar sound, as he evidently did whenever a new idea occurred to him.

'And you know, that is the chief abomination!' he exclaimed. 'Dissoluteness does not lie in anything physical—no kind of physical misconduct is debauchery; real debauchery lies precisely in freeing oneself from moral relations with a woman with whom you have physical intimacy. And such emancipation I regarded as a merit. I remember how I once worried because I had not had an opportunity to pay a woman who gave herself to me (having probably taken a fancy to me) and how I only became tranquil after having sent her some money—thereby intimating that I did not consider myself in any way morally bound to her . . . Don't nod as if you agreed with me,' he suddenly shouted at me. 'Don't I know these things? We all, and you too unless you are a rare exception, hold those same views, just as I used to. Never mind, I beg your pardon, but the fact is that it's terrible, terrible, terrible!'

'What is terrible?' I asked.

'That abyss of error in which we live[22] regarding women and our relations with them. No, I can't speak calmly about it, not because of that "episode", as he called it, in my life, but because since that "episode" occurred my eyes have been opened and I have seen everything in quite a different light. Everything reversed, everything reversed!'

He lit a cigarette and began to speak, leaning his elbows on his knees.

It was too dark to see his face, but, above the jolting of the train, I could hear his impressive and pleasant voice.

IV

'Yes, only after such torments as I have endured, only by their means, have I understood where the root of the matter lies—understood what ought to be, and therefore seen all the horror of what is.[23]

'So you will see how and when that which led up to my "episode" began. It began when I was not quite sixteen. It happened when I still went to the grammar school and my elder brother was a first-year student at the university. I had not yet known any woman, but, like all the unfortunate children of our class, I was no longer an innocent boy. I had been depraved two years before that by other boys. Already woman, not some particular woman but woman as something to be desired, woman, every woman, woman's nudity, tormented me. My solitude was not pure. I was tormented, as ninety-nine per cent. of our boys are. I was horrified, I suffered, I prayed, and I fell. I was already depraved in imagination and in fact, but I had not yet taken the last step. I was perishing, but I had not yet laid hands on another human being. But one day a comrade of my brother's, a jolly student, a so-called good fellow, that is, the worst kind of good-for-nothing, who had taught us to drink and to play cards, persuaded us after a carousal to go *there*. We went. My brother was also still innocent, and he fell that same night. And I, a fifteen-year-old boy, defiled myself and took part in defiling a woman, without at all understanding what I was doing. I had never heard from any of my elders that what I was doing was wrong, you know. And indeed no one hears it now. It is true it is in the Commandments, but then the Commandments are only needed to answer the priest at Scripture examination, and even then they are not very necessary, not nearly as necessary as the commandment about the use of *ut* in conditional sentences in Latin.

'And so I never heard those older persons whose opinions I respected say that it was an evil. On the contrary, I heard people I respected say it was good. I had heard that my struggles and sufferings would be eased after that. I heard this and read it, and heard my elders say it would be good for my health, while from my comrades I heard that it was rather a fine, spirited thing to do. So in general I expected nothing but good from it. The risk of disease? But that too had been foreseen. A paternal government saw to that. It sees to the correct working of the brothels,* and makes profligacy safe for schoolboys. Doctors too deal with it for a consideration. That is proper. They assert that debauchery is good for the health, and they organize proper well-regulated debauchery. I know some mothers who attend to their sons' health in that sense. And science sends them to the brothels.'

'Why do you say "science"?' I asked.

'Why, who are the doctors? The priests of science. Who deprave youths[24] by maintaining that this is necessary for their health? They do.

'Yet if a one-hundredth part of the efforts devoted

* In Russia, as in other continental countries and formerly in England, the *maisons de tolérance* were under the supervision of the government; doctors were employed to examine the women, and, as far as possible, see they did not continue their trade when diseased.—A. M.

to the cure of syphilis were devoted to the eradication of debauchery, there would long ago not have been a trace of syphilis left. But as it is, efforts are made not to eradicate debauchery but to encourage it and to make debauchery safe. That is not the point however. The point is that with me—and with nine-tenths, if not more, not of our class only but of all classes, even the peasants—this terrible thing happens that happened to me; I fell not because I succumbed to the natural temptation of a particular woman's charm—no, I was not seduced by a woman—but I fell because, in the set around me, what was really a fall was regarded by some as a most legitimate function good for one's health, and by others as a very natural and not only excusable but even innocent amusement for a young man. I did not understand that it was a fall, but simply indulged in that half-pleasure, half-need, which, as was suggested to me, was natural at a certain age. I began to indulge in debauchery as I began to drink and to smoke. Yet in that first fall there was something special and pathetic. I remember that at once, on the spot before I left the room, I felt sad, so sad that I wanted to cry—to cry for the loss of my innocence and for my relationship with women, now sullied for ever. Yes, my natural, simple relationship with women was spoilt for ever. From that time I have not had, and could not have, pure relations with women. I had become what is called a libertine. To be a libertine is a physical condition like that of a morphinist, a drunkard, or a smoker. As a morphinist, a drunkard, or a smoker is no longer normal, so too a man who has known several women for his pleasure is not normal but is a man perverted for ever, a libertine. As a drunkard or a morphinist can be recognized at once by his face and manner, so it is with a libertine.

A libertine may restrain himself, may struggle, but he will never have those pure, simple, clear, brotherly relations with a woman. By the way he looks at a young woman and examines her, a libertine can always be recognized. And I had become and I remained a libertine, and it was this that brought me to ruin.'

V

'Ah, yes! After that things went from bad to worse, and there were all sorts of deviations. Oh, God! When I recall the abominations I committed in this respect I am seized with horror! And that is true of me, whom my companions, I remember, ridiculed for my so-called innocence. And when one hears of the "gilded youths", of officers, of the Parisians . . .! And when all these gentlemen, and I—who have on our souls hundreds of the most varied and horrible crimes against women—when we thirty-year-old profligates, very carefully washed, shaved, perfumed, in clean linen and in evening dress or uniform, enter a drawing-room or ball-room, we are emblems of purity, charming!

'Only think of what ought to be, and of what is! When in society such a gentleman comes up to my sister or daughter, I, knowing his life, ought to go up to him, take him aside, and say quietly, "My dear fellow, I know the life you lead, and how and with whom you pass your nights. This is no place for you. There are pure, innocent girls here. Be off!" That is what ought to be; but what happens is that when such a gentleman comes and dances, embracing our sister or daughter, we are jubilant, if he is rich and well-connected. Maybe after Rigulboche* he will honour my daughter! Even if traces

* A notorious Parisian *cancanière*.—A. M.

of disease remain, no matter! They are clever at curing that nowadays. Oh, yes, I know several girls in the best society whom their parents enthusiastically gave in marriage to men suffering from a certain disease. Oh, oh . . . the abomination of it! But a time will come when this abomination and falsehood will be exposed!'

He made his strange noise several times and again drank tea. It was fearfully strong and there was no water with which to dilute it. I felt that I was much excited by the two glasses I had drunk. Probably the tea affected him too, for he became more and more excited. His voice grew increasingly mellow and expressive. He continually changed his position, now taking off his cap and now putting it on again, and his face changed strangely in the semi-darkness in which we were sitting.

'Well, so I lived till I was thirty, not abandoning for a moment the intention of marrying and arranging for myself a most elevated and pure family life. With that purpose I observed the girls suitable for that end,' he continued. 'I weltered in a mire of debauchery and at the same time was on the look-out for a girl pure enough to be worthy of me.

'I rejected many just because they were not pure enough to suit me, but at last I found one whom I considered worthy. She was one of two daughters of a once-wealthy Pénza landowner who had been ruined.

'[25]One evening after we had been out in a boat and had returned by moonlight, and I was sitting beside her admiring her curls and her shapely figure in a tight-fitting jersey, I suddenly decided that it was she! It seemed to me that evening that she understood all that I felt and thought, and that what I felt and thought was very lofty. In reality it was only that the jersey and the curls were particularly becoming to her and that after a day spent near her I wanted to be still closer.

'It is amazing how complete is the delusion that beauty is goodness. A handsome woman talks nonsense, you listen and hear not nonsense but cleverness. She says and does horrid things, and you see only charm. And if a handsome woman does not say stupid or horrid things, you at once persuade yourself that she is wonderfully clever and moral.

'I returned home in rapture, decided that she was the acme of moral perfection, and that therefore she was worthy to be my wife, and I proposed to her next day.

'[26]What a muddle it is! Out of a thousand men who marry (not only among us but unfortunately also among the masses) there is hardly one who has not already been married ten, a hundred, or even, like Don Juan, a thousand times, before his wedding.

'It is true as I have heard and have myself observed that there are nowadays some chaste young men who feel and know that this thing is not a joke but an important matter.

'God help them! But in my time there was not one such in ten thousand. And everybody knows this and pretends not to know it. In all the novels they describe in detail the heroes' feelings and the ponds and bushes beside which they walk, but when their great love for some maiden is described, nothing is said about what has happened to these interesting heroes before: not a word about their frequenting certain houses, or about the servant-girls, cooks, and other people's wives! If there are such improper novels they are not put into the hands of those who most need this information—the unmarried girls.

'We first pretend to these girls that the profligacy

which fills half the life of our towns, and even of the villages, does not exist at all.

'Then we get so accustomed to this pretence that at last, like the English, we ourselves really begin to believe that we are all moral people and live in a moral world. The girls, poor things, believe this quite seriously. So too did my unfortunate wife. I remember how, when we were engaged, I showed her my diary, from which she could learn something, if but a little, of my past, especially about my last *liaison*, of which she might hear from others, and about which I therefore felt it necessary to inform her. I remember her horror, despair, and confusion, when she learnt of it and understood it. I saw that she then wanted to give me up. And why did she not do so? . . .'[27]

He again made that sound, swallowed another mouthful of tea, and remained silent for a while.

VI

'No, after all, it is better, better so!' he exclaimed. 'It serves me right! But that's not to the point—I meant to say that it is only the unfortunate girls who are deceived.

'The mothers know it, especially mothers educated by their own husbands—they know it very well. While pretending to believe in the purity of men, they act quite differently. They know with what sort of bait to catch men for themselves and for their daughters.

'You see it is only we men who don't know (because we don't wish to know) what women know very well, that the most exalted poetic love, as we call it, depends not on moral qualities but on physical nearness and on the *coiffure*, and the colour and cut of the dress. Ask an expert coquette who has set herself the task of captivating a man, which she would prefer to risk: to be convicted in his presence of lying, of cruelty, or even of dissoluteness, or to appear before him in an ugly and badly made dress —she will always prefer the first. She knows that we are continually lying about high sentiments, but really only want her body and will therefore forgive any abomination except an ugly tasteless costume that is in bad style.

'A coquette knows that consciously, and every innocent girl knows it unconsciously just as animals do.

'That is why there are those detestable jerseys, bustles, and naked shoulders, arms, almost breasts. A woman, especially if she has passed the male school, knows very well that all the talk about elevated subjects is just talk, but that what a man wants is her body and all that presents it in the most deceptive but alluring light; and she acts accordingly.[28] If we only throw aside our familiarity with this indecency, which has become a second nature to us, and look at the life of our upper classes as it is, in all its shamelessness—why, it is simply a brothel . . . You don't agree? Allow me, I'll prove it,' he said, interrupting me. 'You say that the women of our society have other interests in life than prostitutes have, but I say no, and will prove it. If people differ in the aims of their lives, by the inner content of their lives, this difference will necessarily be reflected in externals and their externals will be different. But look at those unfortunate despised women and at the highest society ladies: the same costumes, the same fashions, the same perfumes, the same exposure of arms, shoulders, and breasts, the same tight skirts over prominent bustles, the same passion for little stones, for costly, glittering objects, the same amusements, dances, music, and singing. As the former employ all means to allure, so do these others.[29]

VII

'WELL, so these jerseys and curls and bustles caught me!

'It was very easy to catch me for I was brought up in the conditions in which amorous young people are forced like cucumbers in a hot-bed. You see our stimulating super-abundance of food, together with complete physical idleness, is nothing but a systematic excitement of desire.[30] Whether this astonishes you or not, it is so. Why, till quite recently I did not see anything of this myself, but now I have seen it. That is why it torments me that nobody knows this, and people talk such nonsense as that lady did.

'Yes, last spring some peasants were working in our neighbourhood on a railway embankment. The usual food of a young peasant is rye-bread, kvas, and onions; he keeps alive and is vigorous and healthy; his work is light agricultural work. When he goes to railway-work his rations are buckwheat porridge and a pound of meat a day. But he works off that pound of meat during his sixteen hours' work wheeling barrow-loads of half-a-ton weight, so it is just enough for him. But we who every day consume two pounds of meat, and game, and fish and all sorts of heating foods and drinks—where does that go to? Into excesses of sensuality. And if it goes there and the safety-valve is open, all is well; but try and close the safety-valve, as I closed it temporarily, and at once a stimulus arises which, passing[31] through the prism of our artificial life, expresses itself in utter infatuation, sometimes even platonic. And I fell in love as they all do.

'Everything was there to hand: raptures, tenderness, and poetry. In reality that love of mine was the result, on the one hand of her mamma's and the dressmakers' activity, and on the other of the super-abundance of food consumed by me while living an idle life. If on the one hand there had been no boating, no dressmaker with her waists and so forth, and had my wife been sitting at home in a shapeless dressing-gown, and had I on the other hand been in circumstances normal to man—consuming just enough food to suffice for the work I did, and had the safety-valve been open—it happened to be closed at the time—I should not have fallen in love and nothing of all this would have happened.

VIII

'Well, and now it so chanced that everything combined—my condition, her becoming dress, and the satisfactory boating. It had failed twenty times but now it succeeded. Just like a trap! I am not joking. You see nowadays marriages are arranged that way—like traps. What is the natural way? The lass is ripe, she must be given in marriage. It seems very simple if the girl is not a fright and there are men wanting to marry. That is how it was done in olden times. The lass was grown up and her parents arranged the marriage.[32] So it was done, and is done, among all mankind—Chinese, Hindus, Mohammedans, and among our own working classes; so it is done among at least ninety-nine per cent. of the human race. Only among one per cent. or less, among us libertines, has it been discovered that that is not right, and something new has been invented. And what is this novelty? It is that the maidens sit round and the men walk about, as at a bazaar, choosing. And the maidens wait and think, but dare not say: "Me, please!"

"No, me!" "Not her, but me!" "Look what shoulders and other things I have!" And we men stroll around and look,[33] and are very pleased. "Yes, I know! I won't be caught!" They stroll about and look, and are very pleased that everything is arranged like that for them. And then in an unguarded moment—snap! He is caught!'

'Then how ought it to be done?' I asked. 'Should the woman propose?'

'Oh, I don't know how; only if there's to be equality, let it be equality. If they have discovered that pre-arranged matches are degrading, why this is a thousand times worse! Then the rights and chances were equal, but here the woman is a slave in a bazaar[34] or the bait in a trap. Tell any mother, or the girl herself, the truth, that she is only occupied in catching a husband . . . oh dear! what an insult! Yet they all do it and have nothing else to do. What is so terrible is to see sometimes quite innocent poor young girls engaged on it. And again, if it were but done openly—but it is always done deceitfully. "Ah, the origin of species, how interesting!" "Oh, Lily takes such an interest in painting! And will you be going to the exhibition? How instructive!" And the troyka-drives, and shows, and symphonies! "Oh! how remarkable! My Lily is mad on music." "And why don't you share these convictions?" And boating . . . But their one thought is: "Take me, take me!" "Take my Lily!" "Or try—at least!" Oh, what an abomination! What falsehood!' he concluded, finishing his tea and beginning to put away the tea-things.

IX

'You know,' he began while packing the tea and sugar into his bag. 'The domination of women from which the world suffers all arises from this.'

'What "domination of women"?' I asked.[35] 'The rights, the legal privileges, are on the man's side.'

'Yes, yes! That's just it,' he interrupted me. 'That's just what I want to say. It explains the extraordinary phenomenon that on the one hand woman is reduced to the lowest stage of humiliation, while on the other she dominates. Just like the Jews: as they pay us back for their oppression by a financial domination, so it is with women. "Ah, you want us to be traders only,—all right, as traders we will dominate you!" say the Jews. "Ah, you want us to be merely objects of sensuality—all right, as objects of sensuality we will enslave you," say the women. Woman's lack of rights arises not from the fact that she must not vote or be a judge—to be occupied with such affairs is no privilege—but from the fact that she is not man's equal in sexual intercourse and has not the right to use a man or abstain from him as she likes—is not allowed to choose a man at her pleasure instead of being chosen by him. You say that is monstrous. Very well! Then a man must not have those rights either. As it is at present, a woman is deprived of that right while a man has it. And to make up for that right she acts on man's sensuality, and through his sensuality subdues him so that he only chooses formally, while in reality it is she who chooses. And once she has obtained these means she abuses them and acquires a terrible power over people.'

'But where is this special power?' I inquired.

'Where is it? Why everywhere, in everything! Go round the shops in any big town. There are goods worth millions and you cannot estimate the human labour expended on them, and look whether in nine-tenths of these shops there is anything for the use of men. All the luxuries of life are demanded and maintained by women.

'Count all the factories. An enormous proportion of them produce useless ornaments, carriages, furniture, and trinkets, for women. Millions of people, generations of slaves, perish at hard labour in factories merely to satisfy woman's caprice. Women, like queens, keep nine-tenths of mankind in bondage to heavy labour. And all because they have been abased and deprived of equal rights with men. And they revenge themselves by acting on our sensuality and catch us in their nets. Yes, it all comes of that.

'Women have made of themselves such an instrument for acting upon our sensuality that a man cannot quietly consort with a woman.[36] As soon as a man approaches a woman he succumbs to her stupefying influence and becomes intoxicated and crazy. I used formerly to feel uncomfortable and uneasy when I saw a lady dressed up for a ball, but now I am simply frightened and plainly see her as something dangerous and illicit. I want to call a policeman and ask for protection from the peril, and demand that the dangerous object be removed and put away.

'Ah, you are laughing!' he shouted at me, 'but it is not at all a joke. I am sure a time will come, and perhaps very soon, when people will understand this and will wonder how a society could exist in which actions were permitted which so disturb social tranquillity as those adornments of the body directly evoking sensuality, which we tolerate for women in our society. Why, it's like setting all sorts of traps along the paths and promenades—it is even worse! Why is gambling forbidden while women in costumes which evoke sensuality are not forbidden? They are a thousand times more dangerous!

X

'WELL, you see, I was caught that way. I was what is called in love. I not only imagined her to be the height of perfection, but during the time of our engagement I regarded myself also as the height of perfection. You know there is no rascal who cannot, if he tries, find rascals in some respects worse than himself, and who consequently cannot find reasons for pride and self-satisfaction. So it was with me: I was not marrying for money—covetousness had nothing to do with it—unlike the majority of my acquaintances who married for money or connexions—I was rich, she was poor. That was one thing. Another thing I prided myself on was that while others married intending to continue in future the same polygamous life they had lived before marriage, I was firmly resolved to be monogamous after marriage, and there was no limit to my pride on that score. Yes, I was a dreadful pig and imagined myself to be an angel.

'Our engagement did not last long. I cannot now think of that time without shame! What nastiness! Love is supposed to be spiritual and not sensual. Well, if the love is spiritual, a spiritual communion, then that spiritual communion should find expression in words, in conversations, in discourse. There was nothing of the kind. It used to be dreadfully difficult to talk when we were left alone. It was the labour of Sisyphus. As soon as we thought of something to say and said it, we had again to be silent, devising something else. There was nothing to talk about. All that could be said about the life that awaited us, our arrangements and plans, had been said, and what was there more? Now if we had been animals we should have known that speech was unnecessary; but here on the contrary it was necessary to speak, and there was nothing to say, because we were not occupied with what finds vent in speech. And moreover there was that ridiculous custom of giving sweets, of coarse gormandizing on sweets, and all those abominable preparations for the wedding: remarks about the house, the bedroom, beds, wraps, dressing-gowns, underclothing, costumes. You must remember that if one married according to the injunctions of Domostróy, as that old fellow was saying, then the feather-beds, the trousseau, and the bedstead—are all but details appropriate to the sacrament. But among us, when of ten who marry there are certainly nine who not only do not believe in the sacrament,[37] but do not even believe that what they are doing entails certain obligations—where scarcely one man out of a hundred has not been married before, and of fifty scarcely one is not preparing in advance to be unfaithful to his wife at every convenient opportunity—when the majority regard the going to church as only a special condition for obtaining possession of a certain woman—think what a dreadful significance all these details acquire. They show that the whole business is only that; they show that it is a kind of sale. An innocent girl is sold to a profligate, and the sale is accompanied by certain formalities.

XI

'THAT is how everybody marries and that is how I married, and the much vaunted honeymoon began. Why, its very name is vile!' he hissed viciously. 'In Paris I once went to see the sights, and noticing a bearded woman and a water-dog on a sign-board, I entered the show. It turned out to be nothing but a man in a woman's low-necked dress, and a dog done up in walrus skin and swimming in a bath. It was very far from being interesting; but as I was leaving, the showman politely saw me out and, addressing the public at the entrance, pointed to me and said, "Ask the gentleman whether it is not worth seeing! Come in, come in, one franc apiece!" I felt ashamed to say it was not worth seeing, and the showman had probably counted on that. It must be the same with those who have experienced the abomination of a honeymoon and who do not disillusion others. Neither did I disillusion anyone, but I do not now see why I should not tell the truth. Indeed, I think it needful to tell the truth about it. One felt awkward, ashamed, repelled, sorry, and above all dull, intolerably dull! It was something like what I felt when I learnt to smoke—when I felt sick and the saliva gathered in my mouth and I swallowed it and pretended that it was very pleasant. Pleasure from smoking, just as from that, if it comes at all, comes later. The husband must cultivate that vice in his wife in order to derive pleasure from it.'

'Why vice?' I said. 'You are speaking of the most natural human functions.'

'Natural?' he said. 'Natural? No, I may tell you that I have come to the conclusion that it is, on the contrary, *un*natural. Yes, quite *un*natural. Ask a child, ask an unperverted girl.[38]

'Natural, you say!

'It is natural to eat. And to eat is, from the very beginning, enjoyable, easy, pleasant, and not shameful; but this is horrid, shameful, and painful. No, it is unnatural! And an unspoilt girl, as I have convinced myself, always hates it.'[39]

'But how,' I asked, 'would the human race continue?'

'Yes, would not the human race perish?' he said, irritably and ironically, as if he had expected this familiar and insincere objection. 'Teach abstention from child-bearing so that English lords may always gorge themselves—that is all right. Preach it for the sake of greater pleasure—that is all right; but just hint at abstention from child-bearing in the name of morality—and, my goodness, what a rumpus . . .! Isn't there a danger that the human race may die out because they want to cease to be swine? But forgive me! This light is unpleasant, may I shade it?' he said, pointing to the lamp. I said I did not mind; and with the haste with which he did everything, he got up on the seat and drew the woollen shade over the lamp.

'All the same,' I said, 'if everyone thought this the right thing to do, the human race would cease to exist.'

He did not reply at once.

'You ask how the human race will continue to exist,' he said, having again sat down in front of me, and spreading his legs far apart he leant his elbows on his knees. 'Why should it continue?'

'Why? If not, we should not exist.'

'And why should we exist?'

'Why? In order to live, of course.'

'But why live?[40] If life has no aim, if life is given us for life's sake, there is no reason for living. And if it is so, then the Schopenhauers, the Hartmanns, and all the Buddhists as well, are quite right. But if life has an aim, it is clear that it ought to come to an end when that aim is reached. And so it turns out,' he said with noticeable agitation, evidently prizing his thought very highly. 'So it turns out. Just think: if the aim of humanity is goodness, righteousness, love—call it what you will—if it is what the prophets have said, that all mankind should be united together in love, that the spears should be beaten into pruning-hooks and so forth, what is it that hinders the attainment of this aim? The passions hinder it. Of all the passions the strongest, cruellest, and most stubborn is the sex-passion, physical love; and therefore if the passions are destroyed, including the strongest of them—physical love—the prophecies will be fulfilled, mankind will be brought into a unity, the aim of human existence will be attained, and there will be nothing further to live for. As long as mankind exists the ideal is before it, and of course not the rabbits' and pigs' ideal of breeding as fast as possible, nor that of monkeys or Parisians—to enjoy sex-passion in the most refined manner, but the ideal of goodness attained by continence and purity. Towards that people have always striven and still strive. You see what follows.

'It follows that physical love is a safety-valve. If the present generation has not attained its aim, it has not done so because of its passions, of which the sex-passion is the strongest. And if the sex-passion endures there will be a new generation and consequently the possibility of attaining the aim in the next generation. If the next one does not attain it, then the next after that may, and so on, till the aim is attained, the prophecies fulfilled, and mankind attains unity. If not, what would result? If one admits that God created men for the attainment of a certain aim, and created them mortal but sexless, or created them immortal, what would be the result? Why, if they were mortal but without the sex-passion, and died without attaining the aim, God would have had to create new people to attain his aim. If they were immortal, let us grant that (though it would be more difficult for the same people to correct their mistakes and approach perfection than for those of another generation) they might attain that aim after many thousands of years, but then what use would they be afterwards? What could be done with them? It is best as it is. . . . But perhaps you don't like that way of putting it? Perhaps you are an evolutionist? It comes to the same thing. The highest race of animals, the human race, in order to maintain itself in the struggle with other animals ought to unite into one whole like a swarm of bees, and not breed continually; it should bring up sexless members as the bees do; that is, again, it should strive towards continence and not towards inflaming desire—to which the whole system of our life is now directed.' He paused. 'The human race will cease? But can anyone doubt it, whatever his outlook on life may be? Why, it is as certain as death. According to all the teaching of the Church the end of the world will come, and according to all the teaching of science the same result is inevitable.

XII[41]

'In our world it is just the reverse: even if a man does think of continence while he is a bachelor, once married he is sure to think continence no longer necessary. You know those wedding tours—the seclusion into which, with their parents' consent, the young couple go—are nothing but licensed debauchery. But a moral law avenges itself when it is violated. Hard as I tried to make a success of my honeymoon, nothing came of it. It was horrid, shameful, and dull, the whole time. And very soon I began also to experience a painful, oppressive feeling. That began very quickly. I think it was on the third or fourth day that I found my wife depressed. I began asking her the reason and embracing her, which in my view was all she could want, but she removed my arm and began to cry. What about? She could not say. But she felt sad and distressed. Probably her exhausted nerves suggested to her the truth as to the vileness of our relation but she did not know how to express it. I began to question her, and she said something about feeling sad without her mother. It seemed to me that this was untrue, and I began comforting her without alluding to her mother. I did not understand that she was simply depressed and her mother was merely an excuse. But she immediately took offence because I had not mentioned her mother, as though I did not believe her. She told me she saw that I did not love her. I reproached her with being capricious, and suddenly her face changed entirely and instead of sadness it expressed irritation, and with the most venomous words she began accusing me of selfishness and cruelty. I gazed at her. Her whole face showed complete coldness and hostility, almost hatred. I remember how horror-struck I was when I saw this. 'How? What?' I thought. 'Love is a union of souls—and instead of that there is this! Impossible, this is not she!' I tried to soften her, but encountered such an insuperable wall of cold virulent hostility that before I had time to turn round I too was seized with irritation and we said a great many unpleasant things to one another. The impression of that first quarrel was dreadful. I call it a quarrel, but it was not a quarrel but only the disclosure of the abyss that really existed between us. Amorousness was exhausted by the satisfaction of sensuality and we were left confronting one another in our true relation: that is, as two egotists quite alien to each other who wished to get as much pleasure as possible each from the other. I call what took place between us a quarrel, but it was not a quarrel, only the consequence of the cessation of sensuality—revealing our real relations to one another. I did not understand that this cold and hostile relation was our normal state, I did not understand it because at first this hostile attitude was very soon concealed from us by a renewal of redistilled sensuality, that is by love-making.

'I thought we had quarrelled and made it up again, and that it would not recur. But during that same first month of honeymoon a period of satiety soon returned, we again ceased to need one another, and another quarrel supervened. This second quarrel struck me even more painfully than the first. "So the first one was not an accident but was bound to happen and will happen again," I thought. I was all the more staggered by that second quarrel because it arose from such an impossible pretext. It had something to do with money, which I never grudged and could certainly not have grudged to my wife. I only remember that she gave the matter such a twist that some remark of mine appeared to be an expression of a desire on my part to dominate over her by means of money, to which I was supposed to assert an exclusive right—it was something impossibly stupid, mean, and not natural either to me or to her. I became exasperated, and upbraided her with lack of consideration for me. She accused me of the same thing, and it all began again. In her words and in the expression of her face and eyes I again noticed the cruel cold hostility that had so staggered me before. I had formerly quarrelled with my brother, my friends, and my father, but there had never, I remember, been the special venomous malice which there was here. But after a while this mutual hatred was screened by amorousness, that is sensuality, and I still consoled myself with the thought that these two quarrels had been mistakes and could be remedied. But then a third and a fourth quarrel followed and I realized that it was not accidental, but that it was bound to happen and would happen so, and I was horrified at the prospect before me. At the same time I was tormented by the terrible thought that I alone lived on such bad terms with my wife, so unlike what I had expected, whereas this did not happen between other married couples. I did not know then that it is our common fate, but that everybody imagines, just as I did, that it is their peculiar misfortune, and everyone conceals this exceptional and shameful misfortune not only from others but even from himself and does not acknowledge it to himself.

'It began during the first days and continued all the time, ever increasing and growing more obdurate. In the depths of my soul I felt from the first weeks that I was lost, that things had not turned out as I expected, that marriage was not only no happiness but a very heavy burden; but like everybody else I did not wish to acknowledge this to myself (I should not have acknowledged it even now but for the end that followed) and I concealed it not only from others but from myself too. Now I am astonished that I failed to see my real position. It might have been seen from the fact that the quarrels began on pretexts it was impossible to remember when they were over. Our reason was not quick enough to *devise* sufficient excuses for the animosity that always existed between us.[42] But more striking still was the insufficiency of the excuses for our reconciliations. Sometimes there were words, explanations, even tears, but sometimes . . . oh! it is disgusting even now to think of it—after the most cruel words to one another, came sudden silent glances, smiles, kisses, embraces. . . . Faugh, how horrid! How is it I did not then see all the vileness of it?'

XIII

Two fresh passengers entered and settled down on the farthest seats. He was silent while they were seating themselves but as soon as they had settled down continued, evidently not for a moment losing the thread of his idea.

[43]'You know, what is vilest about it,' he began, 'is that in theory love is something ideal and exalted, but in practice it is something abominable, swinish, which it is horrid and shameful to mention or remember. It is not for nothing that nature has made it disgusting and shameful. And if it is disgusting and shameful one must understand that it is so. But here, on the contrary, people pretend that what is disgusting and shameful is beautiful and lofty. What were the first symptoms of my love? Why that I gave way to animal excesses, not only without shame but being somehow even proud of the possibility of these physical excesses, and without in the least considering either her spiritual or even her physical life. I wondered what embittered us against one another, yet it was perfectly simple: that animosity was nothing but the protest of our human nature against the animal nature that overpowered it.

'I was surprised at our enmity to one another; yet it could not have been otherwise. That hatred was nothing but the mutual hatred of accomplices in a crime—both for the incitement to the crime and for the part taken in it. What was it but a crime when she, poor thing, became pregnant in the first month and our *swinish* connexion continued? You think I am straying from my subject? Not at all! I am telling you *how* I killed my wife. They asked me at the trial with what and how I killed her. Fools! They thought I killed her with a knife, on the 5th of October. It was not then I killed her, but much earlier. Just as they are all now killing, all, all. . . .'

'But with what?' I asked.

'That is just what is so surprising, that nobody wants to see what is so clear and evident, what doctors ought to know and preach, but are silent about. Yet the matter is very simple. Men and women are created like the animals so that physical love is followed by pregnancy and then by suckling—conditions under which physical love is bad for the woman and for her child. There are an equal number of men and women. What follows from this? It seems clear, and no great wisdom is needed to draw the conclusion that animals do, namely, the need of continence. But no. Science has been able to discover some kind of leucocytes that run about in the blood, and all sorts of useless nonsense, but cannot understand that. At least one does not hear of science teaching it!

'And so a woman has only two ways out: one is to make a monster of herself, to destroy and go on destroying within herself to such degree as may be necessary the capacity of being a woman, that is, a mother, in order that a man may quietly and continuously get his enjoyment; the other way out—and it is not even a way out but a simple, coarse, and direct violation of the laws of nature—practised in all so-called decent families—is that, contrary to her nature, the woman must be her husband's mistress even while she is pregnant or nursing—must be what not even an animal descends to, and for which her strength is insufficient. That is what causes nerve troubles and hysteria in our class, and among the peasants causes what they call being 'possessed by the devil"—epilepsy. You will notice that no pure maidens are ever "possessed", but only married women living with their husbands That is so here, and it is just the same in Europe. All the hospitals for hysterical women are full of those who have violated nature's law. The epileptics and Charcot's patients are complete wrecks you know, but the world is full of half-crippled women. Just think of it, what a great work goes on within a woman when she conceives or when she is nursing an infant. That is growing which will continue us and replace us. And this sacred work is violated—by what? It is terrible to think of it! And they prate about the freedom and the rights of women! It is as if cannibals fattened their captives to be eaten, and at the same time declared that they were concerned about their prisoners' rights and freedom.'

All this was new to me and startled me.

'What is one to do? If that is so,' I said, 'it means that one may love one's wife once in two years, yet men . . .'

'Men must!' he interrupted me. 'It is again those precious priests of science who have persuaded everybody of that.[44] Imbue a man with the idea that he requires vodka, tobacco, or opium, and all these things will be indispensable to him. It seems that God did not understand what was necessary and therefore, omitting to consult those wizards, arranged things badly. You see matters do not tally. They have decided that it is essential for a man to satisfy his desires, and the bearing and nursing of children comes and interferes with it and hinders the satisfaction of that need. What is one to do then? Consult the wizards! They will arrange it. And they have devised something. Oh! when will those wizards with their deceptions be dethroned? It is high time! It has come to such a point that people go mad and shoot themselves and all because of this. How could it be otherwise?

The animals seem to know that their progeny continue their race, and they keep to a certain law in this matter. Man alone neither knows it nor wishes to know, but is concerned only to get all the pleasure he can. And who is doing that? The lord of nature —man! Animals, you see, only come together at times when they are capable of producing progeny, but the filthy lord of nature is at it any time if only it pleases him! And as if that were not sufficient, he exalts this apish occupation into the most precious pearl of creation, into love. In the name of this love, that is, this filth, he destroys—what? Why, half the human race! All the women who might help the progress of mankind towards truth and goodness he converts, for the sake of his pleasure, into enemies instead of helpmates. See what it is that everywhere impedes the forward movement of mankind. Women! And why are they what they are? Only because of that. Yes, yes . . .' he repeated several times, and began to move about, and to get out his cigarettes and to smoke, evidently trying to calm himself.

XIV

'I TOO lived like a pig of that sort,' he continued in his former tone. 'The worst thing about it was that while living that horrid life I imagined that, because I did not go after other women, I was living an honest family life, that I was a moral man and in no way blameworthy, and if quarrels occurred it was her fault and resulted from her character.

'Of course the fault was not hers. She was like everybody else—like the majority of women. She had been brought up as the position of women in our society requires, and as therefore all women of the leisured classes without exception are brought up and cannot help being brought up. People talk about some new kind of education for women. It is all empty words: their education is exactly what it has to be in view of our unfeigned, real, general opinion about women.[45]

'The education of women will always correspond to men's opinion about them. Don't we know how men regard women:[46] *Wein, Weib, und Gesang*, and what the poets say in their verses? Take all poetry, all pictures and sculpture, beginning with love poems[47] and the nude Venuses and Phrynes, and you will see that woman is an instrument of enjoyment; she is so on the Trubá and the Grachévka,* and also at the Court† balls. And note the devil's cunning: if they are here for enjoyment and pleasure, let it be known that it is pleasure and that woman is a sweet morsel. But no, first the knights-errant declare that they worship women (worship her, and yet regard her as an instrument of enjoyment), and now people assure us that they respect women. Some give up their places to her, pick up her handkerchief; others acknowledge her right to occupy all positions and to take part in the government, and so on. They do all that, but their outlook on her remains the same. She is a means of enjoyment. Her body is a means of enjoyment. And she knows this. It is just as it is with slavery. Slavery, you know, is nothing else than the exploitation by some of the unwilling labour of many. Therefore to get rid of slavery it is necessary that people should not wish to profit by the forced labour of others and should consider it a sin and a shame. But they go and abolish the external form of slavery

* Streets in Moscow in which brothels were numerous.—A. M.

† In the printed and censored Russian edition the word 'Court' was changed to 'most refined'.—A. M.

and arrange so that one can no longer buy and sell slaves, and they imagine and assure themselves that slavery no longer exists, and do not see or wish to see that it does, because people still want and consider it good and right to exploit the labour of others. And as long as they consider that good, there will always be people stronger or more cunning than others who will succeed in doing it. So it is with the emancipation of woman: the enslavement of woman lies simply in the fact that people desire, and think it good, to avail themselves of her as a tool of enjoyment. Well, and they liberate woman, give her all sorts of rights equal to man, but continue to regard her as an instrument of enjoyment, and so educate her in childhood and afterwards by public opinion. And there she is, still the same humiliated and depraved slave, and the man still a depraved slave-owner.

[48]'They emancipate women in universities and in law courts, but continue to regard her as an object of enjoyment. Teach her, as she is taught among us, to regard herself as such, and she will always remain an inferior being. Either with the help of those scoundrels the doctors she will prevent the conception of offspring—that is, will be a complete prostitute, lowering herself not to the level of an animal but to the level of a thing—or she will be what the majority of women are, mentally diseased, hysterical, unhappy, and lacking capacity for spiritual development. High schools and universities cannot alter that. It can only be changed by a change in men's outlook on women and women's way of regarding themselves. It will change only when woman regards virginity as the highest state, and does not, as at present, consider the highest state of a human being a shame and a disgrace. While that is not so, the ideal of every girl, whatever her

education may be, will continue to be to attract as many men as possible, as many males as possible, so as to have the possibility of choosing.

'But the fact that one of them knows more mathematics, and another can play the harp, makes no difference. A woman is happy and attains all she can desire when she has bewitched man. Therefore the chief aim of a woman is to be able to bewitch him. So it has been and will be. So it is in her maiden life in our society, and so it continues to be in her married life. For a maiden this is necessary in order to have a choice, for the married woman in order to have power over her husband.

'The one thing that stops this or at any rate suppresses it for a time, is children, and then only if the mother is not a monster, that is, if she nurses them herself. But here the doctors again come in.

'My wife, who wanted to nurse, and did nurse the four later children herself, happened to be unwell after the birth of her first child. And those doctors, who cynically undressed her and felt her all over—for which I had to thank them and pay them money—those dear doctors considered that she must not nurse the child; and that first time she was deprived of the only means which might have kept her from coquetry. We engaged a wet nurse, that is, we took advantage of the poverty, the need, and the ignorance of a woman, tempted her away from her own baby to ours, and in return gave her a fine head-dress with gold lace.* But that is not the point. The point is that during that time when my wife was free from pregnancy and from suckling, the feminine coquetry which had lain dormant within her manifested itself with particular force. And coinciding with this the torments of jealousy

* In Russia wet-nurses were usually provided with an elaborate national costume by their employers.—A.M.

rose up in me with special force. They tortured me all my married life, as they cannot but torture all husbands who live with their wives as I did with mine, that is, immorally.

XV[49]

'DURING the whole of my married life I never ceased to be tormented by jealousy, but there were periods when I specially suffered from it. One of these periods was when, after the birth of our first child, the doctors forbade my wife to nurse it. I was particularly jealous at that time, in the first place because my wife was experiencing that unrest natural to a mother which is sure to be aroused when the natural course of life is needlessly violated; and secondly, because seeing how easily she abandoned her moral obligations as a mother, I rightly though unconsciously concluded that it would be equally easy for her to disregard her duty as a wife, especially as she was quite well and in spite of the precious doctors' prohibition was able to nurse her later children admirably.'

'I see you don't like doctors,' I said, noticing a peculiarly malevolent tone in his voice whenever he alluded to them.

'It is not a case of liking or disliking. They have ruined my life as they have ruined and are ruining the lives of thousands and hundreds of thousands of human beings, and I cannot help connecting the effect with the cause. I understand that they want to earn money like lawyers and others, and I would willingly give them half my income, and all who realize what they are doing would willingly give them half of their possessions, if only they would not interfere with our family life and would never come near us. I have not collected evidence, but I know dozens of cases (there are any number of them!) where they have killed a child in its mother's womb asserting that she could not give it birth, though she has had children quite safely later on; or they have killed the mother on the pretext of performing some operation. No one reckons these murders any more than they reckoned the murders of the Inquisition, because it is supposed that it is done for the good of mankind. It is impossible to number all the crimes they commit. But all those crimes are as nothing compared to the moral corruption of materialism they introduce into the world, especially through women.

'I don't lay stress on the fact that if one is to follow their instructions, then on account of the infection which exists everywhere and in everything, people would not progress towards greater unity but towards separation; for according to their teaching we ought all to sit apart and not remove the carbolic atomizer from our mouths (though now they have discovered that even that is of no avail). But that does not matter either. The principal poison lies in the demoralization of the world, especially of women.

'To-day one can no longer say: "You are not living rightly, live better." One can't say that, either to oneself or to anyone else. If you live a bad life it is caused by the abnormal functioning of your nerves, &c. So you must go to them, and they will prescribe eight penn'orth of medicine from a chemist, which you must take!

'You get still worse: then more medicine and the doctor again. An excellent trick!

'That however is not the point. All I wish to say is that she nursed her babies perfectly well and that only her pregnancy and the nursing of her babies saved me from the torments of jealousy. Had it not been for that it would all have happened sooner. The children saved me and her. In eight years she had five children and nursed all except the first herself.'

'And where are your children now?' I asked.

'The children?' he repeated in a frightened voice.

'Forgive me, perhaps it is painful for you to be reminded of them.'

'No, it does not matter. My wife's sister and brother have taken them. They would not let me have them. I gave them my estate, but they did not give them up to me. You know I am a sort of lunatic. I have left them now and am going away. I have seen them, but they won't let me have them because I might bring them up so that they would not be like their parents, and they have to be just like them. Oh well, what is to be done? Of course they won't let me have them and won't trust me. Besides, I do not know whether I should be able to bring them up. I think not. I am a ruin, a cripple. Still I have one thing in me. I know! Yes, that is true, I know what others are far from knowing.

'Yes, my children are living and growing up just such savages as everybody around them. I saw them, saw them three times. I can do nothing for them, nothing. I am now going to my place in the south. I have a little house and a small garden there.

'Yes, it will be a long time before people learn what I know. How much of iron and other metal there is in the sun and the stars is easy to find out, but anything that exposes our swinishness is difficult, terribly difficult!

'You at least listen to me, and I am grateful for that.

XVI

'You mentioned my children. There again, what terrible lies are told about children! Children a blessing from God, a joy! That is all a lie. It was so once upon a time, but now it is not so at all. Children are a torment and nothing else. Most mothers feel this quite plainly, and sometimes inadvertently say so. Ask most mothers of our propertied classes and they will tell you that they do not want to have children for fear of their falling ill and dying. [50]They don't want to nurse* them if they do have them, for fear of becoming too much attached to them and having to suffer. The pleasure a baby gives them by its loveliness, its little hands and feet, and its whole body, is not as great as the suffering caused by the very fear of its possibly falling ill and dying, not to speak of its actual illness or death. After weighing the advantages and disadvantages it seems disadvantageous, and therefore undesirable, to have children. They say this quite frankly and boldly, imagining that these feelings of theirs arise from their love of children, a good and laudable feeling of which they are proud. They do not notice that by this reflection they plainly repudiate love, and only affirm their own selfishness. They get less pleasure from a baby's loveliness than suffering from fear on its account, and therefore the baby they would love is not wanted. They do not sacrifice themselves for a beloved being, but sacrifice a being whom they might love, for their own sakes.

'It is clear that this is not love but selfishness. But one has not the heart to blame them—the mothers

* The practice of employing wet-nurses was very much more general in Russia than in the English-speaking countries. —A. M.

in well-to-do families—for that selfishness, when one remembers how dreadfully they suffer on account of their children's health, again thanks to the influence of those same doctors among our well-to-do classes. Even now, when I do but remember my wife's life and the condition she was in during the first years when we had three or four children and she was absorbed in them, I am seized with horror! We led no life at all, but were in a state of constant danger, of escape from it, recurring danger, again followed by a desperate struggle and another escape—always as if we were on a sinking ship. Sometimes it seemed to me that this was done on purpose and that she pretended to be anxious about the children in order to subdue me. It solved all questions in her favour with such tempting simplicity. It sometimes seemed as if all she did and said on these occasions was pretence. But no! She herself suffered terribly, and continually tormented herself about the children and their health and illnesses. It was torture for her and for me too;[51] and it was impossible for her not to suffer. After all, the attachment to her children, the animal need of feeding, caressing, and protecting them, was there as with most women, but there was not the lack of imagination and reason that there is in animals. A hen is not afraid of what may happen to her chick, does not know all the diseases that may befall it, and does not know all those remedies with which people imagine that they can save from illness and death. And for a hen her young are not a source of torment. She does for them what it is natural and pleasurable for her to do; her young ones are a pleasure to her. When a chick falls ill her duties are quite definite: she warms and feeds it. And doing this she knows that she is doing all that is necessary. If her chick dies she does not ask herself why it died, or where it has gone to; she cackles for a while, and then leaves off and goes on living as before. But for our unfortunate women, my wife among them, it was not so. Not to mention illnesses and how to cure them, she was always hearing and reading from all sides endless rules for the rearing and educating of children, which were continually being superseded by others. This is the way to feed a child: feed it in this way, on such a thing; no, not on such a thing, but in this way; clothes, drinks, baths, putting to bed, walking, fresh air,—for all these things we, especially she, heard of new rules every week, just as if children had only begun to be born into the world since yesterday. And if a child that had not been fed or bathed in the right way or at the right time fell ill, it appeared that we were to blame for not having done what we ought.

'That was so while they were well. It was a torment even then. But if one of them happened to fall ill, it was all up: a regular hell! It is supposed that illness can be cured and that there is a science about it, and people—doctors—who know about it. Ah, but not all of them know—only the very best. When a child is ill one must get hold of the very best one, the one who saves, and then the child is saved; but if you don't get that doctor, or if you don't live in the place where that doctor lives, the child is lost. This was not a creed peculiar to her, it is the creed of all the women of our class, and she heard nothing else from all sides. Catherine Semënovna lost two children because Iván Zakhárych was not called in in time, but Iván Zakhárych saved Mary Ivánovna's eldest girl, and the Petróvs moved in time to various hotels by the doctor's advice, and the children remained alive; but if they had not been segregated the children would have died.[52] Another who had a delicate child moved south by the doctor's advice and saved the child. How can she help being tortured and agitated all the time, when the lives of the children for whom she has an animal attachment depend on her finding out in time what Iván Zakhárych will say! But what Iván Zakhárych will say nobody knows, and he himself least of all, for he is well aware that he knows nothing and therefore cannot be of any use, but just shuffles about at random so that people should not cease to believe that he knows something or other. You see, had she been wholly an animal she would not have suffered so, and if she had been quite a human being she would have had faith in God and would have said and thought, as a believer does: "The Lord gave and the Lord hath taken away. One can't escape from God."

'Our whole life with the children, for my wife and consequently for me, was not a joy but a torment. How could she help torturing herself? She tortured herself incessantly. Sometimes when we had just made peace after some scene of jealousy, or simply after a quarrel, and thought we should be able to live, to read, and to think a little, we had no sooner settled down to some occupation than the news came that Vásya was being sick, or Másha showed symptoms of dysentery, or Andrúsha had a rash, and there was an end to peace, it was not life any more. Where was one to drive to? For what doctor? How isolate the child? And then it's a case of enemas, temperatures, medicines, and doctors. Hardly is that over before something else begins. We had no regular settled family life but only, as I have already said, continual escapes from imaginary and real dangers. It is like that in most families nowadays you know, but in my family it was especially acute. My wife was a child-loving and a credulous woman.

'So the presence of children not only failed to improve our life but poisoned it. Besides, the children were a new cause of dissension. As soon as we had children they became the means and the object of our discord, and more often the older they grew. They were not only the object of discord but the weapons of our strife. We used our children, as it were, to fight one another with. Each of us had a favourite weapon among them for our strife. I used to fight her chiefly through Vásya, the eldest boy, and she me through Lisa. Besides that, as they grew older and their characters became defined, it came about that they grew into allies whom each of us tried to draw to his or her side. They, poor things, suffered terribly from this, but we, with our incessant warfare, had no time to think of that. The girl was my ally, and the eldest boy, who resembled his mother and was her favourite, was often hateful to me.

XVII

'Well, and so we lived.[53] Our relations to one another grew more and more hostile and at last reached a stage where it was not disagreement that caused hostility but hostility that caused disagreement. Whatever she might say I disagreed with beforehand, and it was just the same with her.

'In the fourth year we both, it seemed, came to the conclusion that we could not understand one another or agree with one another. We no longer tried to bring any dispute to a conclusion. We invariably kept to our own opinions even about the most trivial questions,[54] but especially about the children. As I now recall them the views I maintained were not at all so dear to me that I could not have given them up; but she was of the opposite opinion and to yield meant yielding to her, and that I could not do. It was the same with her. She probably considered herself quite in the right towards me, and as for me I always thought myself a saint towards her. When we were alone together we were doomed almost to silence, or to conversations such as I am convinced animals can carry on with one another: "What is the time? Time to go to bed. What is to-day's dinner? Where shall we go? What is there in the papers? Send for the doctor; Másha has a sore throat." We only needed to go a hairbreadth beyond this impossibly limited circle of conversation for irritation to flare up.[55] We had collisions and acrimonious words about the coffee, a tablecloth, a trap, a lead at bridge,* all of them things that could not be of any importance to either of us. In me at any rate there often raged a terrible hatred of her. Sometimes I watched her pouring out tea, swinging her leg, lifting a spoon to her mouth, smacking her lips and drawing in some liquid, and I hated her for these things as though they were the worst possible actions. I did not then notice that the periods of anger corresponded quite regularly and exactly to the periods of what we called love. A period of love—then a period of animosity; an energetic period of love, then a long period of animosity; a weaker manifestation of love, and a shorter period of animosity. We did not then understand that this love and animosity were one and the same animal feeling only at opposite poles. To live like that would have been awful had we understood our position; but we neither understood nor saw it. Both salvation and punishment for man lie in the fact that if he lives wrongly he can befog himself so as not to see the misery of his position. And this we did. She tried to forget herself in

* The card-game named in the original, and then much played in Russia, was *vint*, which resembles bridge.—A. M.

intense and always hurried occupation with household affairs, busying herself with the arrangements of the house, her own and the children's clothes, their lessons, and their health;[56] while I had my own occupations: wine, my office duties, shooting, and cards. We were both continually occupied, and we both felt that the busier we were the nastier we might be to each other. "It's all very well for you to grimace," I thought, "but you have harassed me all night with your scenes, and I have a meeting on." "It's all very well for you," she not only thought but said, "but I have been awake all night with the baby." Those new theories of hypnotism, psychic diseases, and hysterics are not a simple folly, but a dangerous and repulsive one. Charcot would certainly have said that my wife was hysterical, and that I was abnormal, and he would no doubt have tried to cure me. But there was nothing to cure.[57]

'Thus we lived in a perpetual fog, not seeing the condition we were in. And if what did happen had not happened, I should have gone on living so to old age and should have thought, when dying, that I had led a good life. I should not have realized the abyss of misery and the horrible falsehood in which I wallowed.

'We were like two convicts hating each other and chained together, poisoning one another's lives and trying not to see it. I did not then know that ninety-nine per cent. of married people live in a similar hell to the one I was in and that it cannot be otherwise. I did not then know this either about others or about myself.

'It is strange what coincidences there are in regular, or even in irregular, lives! Just when the parents find life together unendurable, it becomes necessary to move to town for the children's education.'

He stopped, and once or twice gave vent to his strange sounds, which were now quite like suppressed sobs. We were approaching a station.

'What is the time?' he asked.

I looked at my watch. It was two o'clock.

'You are not tired?' he asked.

'No, but you are?'

'I am suffocating. Excuse me, I will walk up and down and drink some water.'

He went unsteadily through the carriage. I remained alone thinking over what he had said, and I was so engrossed in thought that I did not notice when he re-entered by the door at the other end of the carriage.

XVIII

'Yes, I keep diverging,' he began. 'I have thought much over it. I now see many things differently and I want to express it.

'Well, so we lived in town.[58] In town a man can live for a hundred years without noticing that he has long been dead and has rotted away. He has no time to take account of himself, he is always occupied. Business affairs, social intercourse, health, art, the children's health and their education. Now one has to receive so-and-so and so-and-so, go to see so-and-so and so-and-so; now one has to go and look at this, and hear this man or that woman. In town, you know, there are at any given moment one or two, or even three, celebrities whom one must on no account miss seeing. Then one has to undergo a treatment oneself or get someone else attended to, then there are teachers, tutors, and governesses, but one's own life is quite empty. Well, so we lived and felt less the painfulness of living together.

Besides at first we had splendid occupations, arranging things in a new place, in new quarters; and we were also occupied in going from the town to the country and back to town again.

'We lived so through one winter, and the next there occurred, unnoticed by anyone, an apparently unimportant thing, but the cause of all that happened later.

'She was not well and the doctors told her not to have children, and taught her how to avoid it. To me it was disgusting. I struggled against it, but she with frivolous obstinacy insisted on having her own way and I submitted. The last excuse for our swinish life—children—was then taken away, and life became viler than ever.

'To a peasant, a labouring man, children are necessary; though it is hard for him to feed them, still he needs them, and therefore his marital relations have a justification. But to us who have children, more children are unnecessary; they are an additional care and expense, a further division of property, and a burden. So our swinish life has no justification. We either artificially deprive ourselves of children or regard them as a misfortune, the consequences of carelessness, and that is still worse.

'We have no justification. But we have fallen morally so low that we do not even feel the need of any justification.

'The majority of the present educated world devote themselves to this kind of debauchery without the least qualm of conscience.

'There is indeed nothing that can feel qualms, for conscience in our society is non-existent, unless one can call public opinion and the criminal law a "conscience". In this case neither the one nor the other is infringed: there is no reason to be ashamed of public opinion for everybody acts in the same way—Mary Pávlovna, Iván Zakhárych, and the rest. Why breed paupers or deprive oneself of the possibility of social life? There is no need to fear or be ashamed in face of the criminal law either. Those shameless hussies, or soldiers' wives, throw their babies into ponds or wells, and they of course must be put in prison, but we do it all at the proper time and in a clean way.

'We lived like that for another two years. The means employed by those scoundrel-doctors evidently began to bear fruit; she became physically stouter and handsomer, like the late beauty of summer's end. She felt this and paid attention to her appearance. She developed a provocative kind of beauty which made people restless. She was in the full vigour of a well-fed and excited woman of thirty who is not bearing children. Her appearance disturbed people. When she passed men she attracted their notice. She was like a fresh, well-fed, harnessed horse, whose bridle has been removed. There was no bridle, as is the case with ninety-nine hundredths of our women. And I felt this—and was frightened.'

XIX

He suddenly rose and sat down close to the window.

'Pardon me,' he muttered and, with his eyes fixed on the window, he remained silent for about three minutes. Then he sighed deeply and moved back to the seat opposite mine. His face was quite changed, his eyes looked pathetic, and his lips puckered strangely, almost as if he were smiling. 'I am rather tired but I will go on with it. We have still plenty of time, it is not dawn yet. Ah, yes,' he began after lighting a cigarette, 'she grew plumper after she stopped having babies, and her malady—that everlasting worry about the children—began to pass . . .

at least not actually to pass, but she as it were woke up from an intoxication, came to herself, and saw that there was a whole divine world with its joys which she had forgotten, but a divine world she did not know how to live in and did not at all understand. "I must not miss it! Time is passing and won't come back!" So, I imagine, she thought, or rather felt, nor could she have thought or felt differently: she had been brought up in the belief that there was only one thing in the world worthy of attention—love. She had married and received something of that love, but not nearly what had been promised and was expected. Even that had been accompanied by many disappointments and sufferings, and then this unexpected torment: so many children! The torments exhausted her. And then, thanks to the obliging doctors, she learnt that it is possible to avoid having children. She was very glad, tried it, and became alive again for the one thing she knew—for love. But love with a husband, befouled by jealousy and all kinds of anger, was no longer the thing she wanted. She had visions of some other, clean, new love; at least I thought she had. And she began to look about her as if expecting something. I saw this and could not help feeling anxious. It happened again and again that while talking to me, as usual through other people—that is, telling a third person what she meant for me—she boldly, without remembering that she had expressed the opposite opinion an hour before, declared, though half-jokingly, that a mother's cares are a fraud, and that it is not worth while to devote one's life to children when one is young and can enjoy life. She gave less attention to the children, and less frenziedly than before, but gave more and more attention to herself, to her appearance (though she tried to conceal this), and to her pleasures, even to her accomplishments. She again enthusiastically took to the piano which she had quite abandoned, and it all began from that.'

He turned his weary eyes to the window again but, evidently making an effort, immediately continued once more.

'Yes, that man made his appearance . . .' he became confused and once or twice made that peculiar sound with his nose.

I could see that it was painful for him to name that man, to recall him, or speak about him. But he made an effort and, as if he had broken the obstacle that hindered him, continued resolutely.

'He was a worthless man in my opinion and according to my estimate. And not because of the significance he acquired in my life but because he really was so. However, the fact that he was a poor sort of fellow only served to show how irresponsible she was. If it had not been he then it would have been another. It had to be!'

Again he paused. 'Yes, he was a musician, a violinist; not a professional, but a semi-professional semi-society man.

'His father, a landowner, was a neighbour of my father's. He had been ruined, and his children—there were three boys—had obtained settled positions; only this one, the youngest, had been handed over to his godmother in Paris. There he was sent to the *Conservatoire* because he had a talent for music, and he came out as a violinist and played at concerts. He was a man . . .' Having evidently intended to say something bad about him, Pózdnyshev restrained himself and rapidly said: 'Well, I don't really know how he lived, I only know that he returned to Russia that year and appeared in my house.

'With moist almond-shaped eyes, red smiling lips,

a small waxed moustache, hair done in the latest fashion, and an insipidly pretty face, he was what women call "not bad looking". His figure was weak though not misshapen, and he had a specially developed posterior, like a woman's, or such as Hottentots are said to have. They too are reported to be musical. Pushing himself as far as possible into familiarity, but sensitive and always ready to yield at the slightest resistance, he maintained his dignity in externals, wore buttoned boots of a special Parisian fashion, bright-coloured ties, and other things foreigners acquire in Paris, which by their noticeable novelty always attract women. There was an affected external gaiety in his manner. That manner, you know, of speaking about everything in allusions and unfinished sentences, as if you knew it all, remembered it, and could complete it yourself.

'It was he with his music who was the cause of it all. You know at the trial the case was put as if it was all caused by jealousy. No such thing, that is, I don't mean "no such thing", it was and yet it was not. At the trial it was decided that I was a wronged husband and that I had killed her while defending my outraged honour (that is the phrase they employ, you know). That is why I was acquitted. I tried to explain matters at the trial but they took it that I was trying to rehabilitate my wife's honour.

'What my wife's relations with that musician may have been has no meaning for me, or for her either. What has a meaning is what I have told you about—my swinishness. The whole thing was an outcome of the terrible abyss between us of which I have told you—that dreadful tension of mutual hatred which made the first excuse sufficient to produce a crisis, The quarrels between us had for some time past become frightful, and were all the more startling because they alternated with similarly intense animal passion.

'If he had not appeared there would have been someone else. If the occasion had not been jealousy it would have been something else. I maintain that all husbands who live as I did, must either live dissolutely, separate, or kill themselves or their wives as I have done. If there is anybody who has not done so, he is a rare exception. Before I ended as I did, I had several times been on the verge of suicide, and she too had repeatedly tried to poison herself.

XX

'Well, that is how things were going not long before it happened. We seemed to be living in a state of truce and had no reason to infringe it. Then we chanced to speak about a dog which I said had been awarded a medal at an exhibition. She remarked "Not a medal, but an honourable mention." A dispute ensues. We jump from one subject to another, reproach one another, "Oh, that's nothing new, it's always been like that." "You said . . ." "No, I didn't say so." "Then I am telling lies! . . ." You feel that at any moment that dreadful quarrelling which makes you wish to kill yourself or her will begin. You know it will begin immediately, and fear it like fire and therefore wish to restrain yourself, but your whole being is seized with fury. She being in the same or even a worse condition purposely misinterprets every word you say, giving it a wrong meaning. Her every word is venomous; where she alone knows that I am most sensitive, she stabs. It gets worse and worse. I shout: "Be quiet!" or something of that kind.

'She rushes out of the room and into the nursery.

I try to hold her back in order to finish what I was saying, to prove my point, and I seize her by the arm. She pretends that I have hurt her and screams: "Children, your father is striking me!" I shout: "Don't lie!" "But it's not the first time!" she screams, or something like that. The children rush to her. She calms them down. I say, "Don't sham!" She says, "Everything is sham in your eyes, you would kill any one and say they were shamming. Now I have understood you. That's just what you want!" "Oh, I wish you were dead as a dog!" I shout. I remember how those dreadful words horrified me. I never thought I could utter such dreadful, coarse words, and am surprised that they escaped me. I shout them and rush away into my study and sit down and smoke. I hear her go out into the hall preparing to go away. I ask, "Where are you going to?" She does not reply. "Well, devil take her," I say to myself, and go back to my study and lie down and smoke. A thousand different plans of how to revenge myself on her and get rid of her, and how to improve matters and go on as if nothing had happened, come into my head. I think all that and go on smoking and smoking. I think of running away from her, hiding myself, going to America. I get as far as dreaming of how I shall get rid of her, how splendid that will be, and how I shall unite with another, an admirable woman—quite different. I shall get rid of her either by her dying or by a divorce, and I plan how it is to be done. I notice that I am getting confused and not thinking of what is necessary, and to prevent myself from perceiving that my thoughts are not to the point I go on smoking.

'Life in the house goes on. The governess comes in and asks: "Where is madame? When will she be back?" The footman asks whether he is to serve tea. I go to the dining-room. The children, especially Lisa who already understands, gaze inquiringly and disapprovingly at me. We drink tea in silence. She has still not come back. The evening passes, she has not returned, and two different feelings alternate within me. Anger because she torments me and all the children by her absence which will end by her returning; and fear that she will not return but will do something to herself. I would go to fetch her, but where am I to look for her? At her sister's? But it would be so stupid to go and ask. And it's all the better: if she is bent on tormenting someone, let her torment herself. Besides that is what she is waiting for; and next time it would be worse still. But suppose she is not with her sister but is doing something to herself, or has already done it! It's past ten, past eleven! I don't go to the bedroom—it would be stupid to lie there alone waiting—but I'll not lie down here either. I wish to occupy my mind, to write a letter or to read, but I can't do anything. I sit alone in my study, tortured, angry, and listening. It's three o'clock, four o'clock, and she is not back. Towards morning I fall asleep. I wake up, she has still not come!

'Everything in the house goes on in the usual way, but all are perplexed and look at me inquiringly and reproachfully, considering me to be the cause of it all. And in me the same struggle still continues: anger that she is torturing me, and anxiety for her.

'At about eleven in the morning her sister arrives as her envoy. And the usual talk begins. "She is in a terrible state. What does it all mean?" "After all, nothing has happened." I speak of her impossible character and say that I have not done anything.

' "But, you know, it can't go on like this," says her sister.

' "It's all her doing and not mine," I say. "I won't take the first step.[59] If it means separation, let it be separation."

'My sister-in-law goes away having achieved nothing. I had boldly said that I would not take the first step; but after her departure, when I came out of my study and saw the children piteous and frightened, I was prepared to take the first step. I should be glad to do it, but[60] I don't know how. Again I pace up and down and smoke; at lunch I drink vodka and wine and attain what I unconsciously desire—I no longer see the stupidity and humiliation of my position.

'At about three she comes. When she meets me she does not speak. I imagine that she has submitted, and begin to say that I had been provoked by her reproaches. She, with the same stern expression on her terribly harassed face, says that she has not come for explanations but to fetch the children, because we cannot live together. I begin telling her that the fault is not mine and that she provoked me beyond endurance. She looks severely and solemnly at me and says: "Do not say any more, you will repent it." I tell her that I cannot stand comedies. Then she cries out something I don't catch, and rushes into her room. The key clicks behind her,—she has locked herself in. I try the door, but getting no answer, go away angrily. Half-an-hour later Lisa runs in crying. "What is it? Has anything happened?" "We can't hear mama." We go. I pull at the double doors with all my might. The bolt had not been firmly secured, and the two halves both open. I approach the bed, on which she is lying awkwardly in her petticoats and with a pair of high boots on. An empty opium bottle is on the table. She is brought to herself. Tears follow, and a reconciliation. No, not a reconciliation: in the heart of each there is still the old animosity, with the additional irritation produced by the pain of this quarrel which each attributes to the other. But one must of course finish it all somehow, and life goes on in the old way. And so the same kind of quarrel, and even worse ones, occurred continually: once a week, once a month, or at times every day. It was always the same. Once I had already procured a passport to go abroad—the quarrel had continued for two days. But there was again a partial explanation, a partial reconciliation, and I did not go.

XXI

'So those were our relations when that man appeared. He arrived in Moscow—his name is Trukhachévski—and came to my house. It was in the morning. I received him. We had once been on familiar terms and he tried to maintain a familiar tone by using non-committal expressions, but I definitely adopted a conventional tone and he at once submitted to it. I disliked him from the first glance.[61] But curiously enough a strange and fatal force led me not to repulse him, not to keep him away, but on the contrary to invite him to the house. After all, what could have been simpler than to converse with him coldly, and say good-bye without introducing him to my wife? But no, as if purposely, I began talking about his playing, and said I had been told he had given up the violin. He replied that, on the contrary, he now played more than ever. He referred to the fact that there had been a time when I myself played. I said I had given it up but that my wife played well. It is an astonishing thing[62] that from the first day, from the first hour of my meeting him, my relations with him were such as they might have been only after all that subsequently happened.[63] There was something strained in them: I noticed every word, every expression he or I used, and attributed importance to them.

'I introduced him to my wife. The conversation immediately turned to music, and he offered to be of use to her by playing with her. My wife was, as usual of late, very elegant, attractive, and disquietingly beautiful. He evidently pleased her at first sight. Besides she was glad that she would have someone to accompany her on a violin, which she was so fond of that she used to engage a violinist from the theatre for the purpose; and her face reflected her pleasure. But catching sight of me she at once understood my feeling and changed her expression, and a game of mutual deception began. I smiled pleasantly to appear as if I liked it. He, looking at my wife as all immoral men look at pretty women, pretended that he was only interested in the subject of the conversation—which no longer interested him at all; while she tried to seem indifferent, though my false smile of jealousy with which she was familiar, and his lustful gaze, evidently excited her. I saw that from their first encounter her eyes were particularly bright and, probably as a result of my jealousy, it seemed as if an electric current had been established between them, evoking as it were an identity of expressions, looks, and smiles. She blushed and he blushed. She smiled and he smiled. We spoke about music, Paris, and all sorts of trifles. Then he rose to go, and stood smilingly, holding his hat against his twitching thigh and looking now at her and now at me, as if in expectation of what we would do.

I remember that instant just because at that moment I might not have invited him, and then nothing would have happened. But I glanced at him and at her and said silently to myself, "Don't suppose that I am jealous," "or that I am afraid of you," I added mentally addressing him, and I invited him to come some evening and bring his violin to play with my wife. She glanced at me with surprise, flushed, and as if frightened began to decline, saying that she did not play well enough. This refusal irritated me still more, and I insisted the more on his coming. I remember the curious feeling with which I looked at the back of his head, with the black hair parted in the middle contrasting with the white nape of his neck, as he went out with his peculiar springing gait suggestive of some kind of a bird. I could not conceal from myself that that man's presence tormented me. "It depends on me," I reflected, "to act so as to see nothing more of him. But that would be to admit that I am afraid of him. No, I am not afraid of him; it would be too humiliating," I said to myself. And there in the ante-room, knowing that my wife heard me, I insisted that he should come that evening with his violin. He promised to do so, and left.

'In the evening he brought his violin and they played. But it took a long time to arrange matters —they had not the music they wanted, and my wife could not without preparation play what they had. I was very fond of music and sympathized with their playing, arranging a music-stand for him and turning over the pages. They played a few things, some songs without words, and a little sonata by Mozart. They played splendidly,[64] and he had an exceptionally fine tone. Besides that, he had a refined and elevated taste not at all in correspondence with his character.

'He was of course a much better player than my wife, and he helped her, while at the same time politely praising her playing. He behaved himself very well. My wife seemed interested only in music and was very simple and natural.[65] But though I pretended to be interested in the music I was tormented by jealousy all the evening.

'From the first moment his eyes met my wife's I saw that the animal in each of them, regardless of all conditions of their position and of society, asked, "May I?" and answered, "Oh, yes, certainly." I saw that he had not at all expected to find my wife, a Moscow lady, so attractive, and that he was very pleased. For he had no doubt whatever that she was *willing*. The only crux was whether that unendurable husband could hinder them. Had I been pure I should not have understood this, but, like the majority of men, I had myself regarded women in that way before I married and therefore could read his mind like a manuscript. I was particularly tormented because I saw without doubt that she had no other feeling towards me than a continual irritation only occasionally interrupted by the habitual sensuality; but that this man—by his external refinement and novelty and still more by his undoubtedly great talent for music, by the nearness that comes of playing together, and by the influence music, especially the violin, exercises on impressionable natures—was sure not only to please but certainly and without the least hesitation to conquer, crush, bind her, twist her round his little finger and do whatever he liked with her. I could not help seeing this and I suffered terribly. But for all that, or perhaps on account of it, some force obliged me against my will to be not merely polite but amiable to him. Whether I did it for my wife or for him, to show that I was not afraid of him, or whether I did it to deceive myself—I don't know, but I know that from the first I could not behave naturally with him. In order not to yield to my wish to kill him there and then, I had to make much of him. I gave him expensive wines at supper, went into raptures over his playing, spoke to him with a particularly amiable smile, and invited him to dine and play with my wife again the next Sunday. I told him I would ask a few friends who were fond of music to hear him. And so it ended.'

Greatly agitated, Pózdnyshev changed his position and emitted his peculiar sound.

'It is strange how the presence of that man acted on me,' he began again, with an evident effort to keep calm. 'I come home from the Exhibition a day or two later, enter the ante-room, and suddenly feel something heavy, as if a stone had fallen on my heart, and I cannot understand what it is. It was that passing through the ante-room I noticed something which reminded me of him. I realized what it was only in my study, and went back to the ante-room to make sure. Yes, I was not mistaken, there was his overcoat. A fashionable coat, you know. (Though I did not realize it, I observed everything connected with him with extraordinary attention.) I inquire: sure enough he is there. I pass on to the dancing-room, not through the drawing-room but through the schoolroom. My daughter, Lisa, sits reading a book and the nurse sits with the youngest boy at the table, making a lid of some kind spin round. The door to the dancing-room is shut but I hear the sound of a rhythmic arpeggio and his[66] and her voices. I listen, but cannot make out anything.

'Evidently the sound of the piano is purposely made to drown the sound of their voices, their kisses . . . perhaps. My God! What was aroused in me! Even to think of the beast that then lived in me fills me with horror! My heart suddenly contracted, stopped, and then began to beat like a hammer. My chief feeling, as usual whenever I was enraged, was one of self-pity. "In the presence of the children! of their nurse!"[67] thought I. Probably I looked awful, for Lisa gazed at me with strange eyes. "What am I to do?" I asked myself. "Go in? I can't: heaven only knows what I should do. But neither can I go away." The nurse looked at me as if she understood my position.[68] "But it is impossible not to go in," I said to myself, and I quickly opened the door. He was sitting at the piano playing those arpeggios with his large white upturned fingers. She was standing in the curve of the piano, bending over some open music. She was the first to see or hear, and glanced at me. Whether she was frightened and pretended not to be, or whether she was really not frightened, anyway she did not start or move but only blushed, and that not at once.

' "How glad I am that you have come: we have not decided what to play on Sunday," she said in a tone she would not have used to me had we been alone. This and her using the word "we" of herself and him, filled me with indignation. I greeted him silently.

'He pressed my hand, and at once, with a smile which I thought distinctly ironic, began to explain that he had brought some music to practise for Sunday, but that they disagreed about what to play: a classical but more difficult piece, namely Beethoven's sonata for the violin, or a few little pieces. It was all so simple and natural that there was nothing one could cavil at, yet I felt certain that it was all untrue and that they had agreed how to deceive me.

'One of the most distressing conditions of life for

a jealous man (and everyone is jealous in our world) are certain society conventions which allow a man and woman the greatest and most dangerous proximity. You would become a laughing-stock to others if you tried to prevent such nearness at balls, or the nearness of doctors to their women-patients, or of people occupied with art, sculpture, and especially music. A couple are occupied with the noblest of arts, music; this demands a certain nearness, and there is nothing reprehensible in that and only a stupid jealous husband can see anything undesirable in it.[69] Yet everybody knows that it is by means of those very pursuits, especially of music, that the greater part of the adulteries in our society occur. I evidently confused them by the confusion I betrayed: for a long time I could not speak. I was like a bottle held upside down from which the water does not flow because it is too full. I wanted to abuse him and to turn him out, but again felt that I must treat him courteously and amiably. And I did so. I acted as though I approved of it all, and again because of the strange feeling which made me behave to him the more amiably the more his presence distressed me. I told him that I trusted his taste and advised her to do the same. He stayed as long as was necessary to efface the unpleasant impression caused by my sudden entrance—looking frightened and remaining silent—and then left, pretending that it was now decided what to play next day. I was however fully convinced that compared to what interested them the question of what to play was quite indifferent.

'I saw him out to the ante-room with special politeness. (How could one do less than accompany a man who had come to disturb the peace and destroy the happiness of a whole family?) And I pressed his soft white hand with particular warmth.

XXII

'I DID not speak to her all that day—I could not. Nearness to her aroused in me such hatred of her that I was afraid of myself. At dinner in the presence of the children she asked me when I was going away. I had to go next week to the District Meetings of the Zémstvo. I told her the date. She asked whether I did not want anything for the journey. I did not answer but sat silent at table and then went in silence to my study. Latterly she used never to come to my room, especially not at that time of day. I lay in my study filled with anger. Suddenly I heard her familiar step, and the terrible, monstrous idea entered my head that she, like Uriah's wife, wished to conceal the sin she had already committed and that that was why she was coming to me at such an unusual time. "Can she be coming to me?" thought I, listening to her approaching footsteps. "If she is coming here, then I am right," and an inexpressible hatred of her took possession of me. Nearer and nearer came the steps. Is it possible that she won't pass on to the dancing-room? No, the door creaks and in the doorway appears her tall[70] handsome figure, on her face and in her eyes a timid ingratiating look which she tries to hide, but which I see and the meaning of which I know. I almost choked, so long did I hold my breath, and still looking at her I grasped my cigarette-case and began to smoke.

' "Now how can you? One comes to sit with you for a bit, and you begin smoking"—and she sat down close to me on the sofa, leaning against me. I moved away so as not to touch her.

' "I see you are dissatisfied at my wanting to play on Sunday," she said.

' "I am not at all dissatisfied," I said.

' "As if I don't see!"

' "Well, I congratulate you on seeing. But I only see that you behave like a coquette. . . . You always find pleasure in all kinds of vileness, but to me it is terrible!"

' "Oh, well, if you are going to scold like a cabman I'll go away."

' "Do, but remember that if you don't value the family honour, I value not you (devil take you) but the honour of the family!"

' "But what is the matter? What?"

' "Go away, for God's sake be off!"

'Whether she pretended not to understand what it was about or really did not understand, at any rate she took offence, grew angry, and did not go away but stood in the middle of the room.

' "You have really become impossible," she began.[71] "You have a character that even an angel could not put up with." And as usual trying to sting me as painfully as possible, she reminded me of my conduct to my sister (an incident when, being exasperated, I said rude things to my sister); she knew I was distressed about it and she stung me just on that spot. "After that, nothing from you will surprise me," she said.

' "Yes! Insult me, humiliate me, disgrace me, and then put the blame on me," I said to myself, and suddenly I was seized by such terrible rage as I had never before experienced.

'For the first time I wished to give physical expression to that rage. I jumped up and went towards her; but just as I jumped up I remember becoming conscious of my rage and asking myself: "Is it right to give way to this feeling?" and at once I answered that it was right, that it would frighten her, and instead of restraining my fury I immediately began inflaming it still further, and was glad it burnt yet more fiercely within me.

'"Be off, or I'll kill you!" I shouted,[72] going up to her and seizing her by the arm. I consciously intensified the anger in my voice as I said this. And I suppose I was terrible, for she was so frightened that she had not even the strength to go away, but only said: "Vásya, what is it? What is the matter with you?"

'"Go!" I roared louder still.[73] "No one but you can drive me to fury. I do not answer for myself!"

'Having given reins to my rage, I revelled in it and wished to do something still more unusual to show the extreme degree of my anger. I felt a terrible desire to beat her, to kill her, but knew that this would not do, and so[74] to give vent to my fury I seized a paper-weight from my table, again shouting "Go!" and hurled it to the floor near her. I aimed it very exactly past her. Then she left the room, but stopped at the doorway, and immediately, while she still saw it (I did it so that she might see), I began snatching things from the table—candlesticks and ink-stand—and hurling them on the floor still shouting "Go! Get out! I don't answer for myself!" She went away—and I immediately stopped.

'An hour later the nurse came to tell me that my wife was in hysterics. I went to her; she sobbed, laughed, could not speak, and her whole body was convulsed. She was not pretending, but was really ill.[75]

'Towards morning she grew quiet, and we made peace under the influence of the feeling we called love.

'In the morning when, after our reconciliation, I confessed to her that I was jealous of Trukhachévski, she was not at all confused, but laughed most naturally; so strange did the very possibility of an infatuation for such a man seem to her, she said.

' "Could a decent woman have any other feeling for such a man than the pleasure of his music? Why, if you like I am ready never to see him again . . . not even on Sunday, though everybody has been invited. Write and tell him that I am ill, and there's an end of it! Only it is unpleasant that anyone, especially he himself, should imagine that he is dangerous. I am too proud to allow anyone to think that of me!"

'And you know, she was not lying, she believed what she was saying; she hoped by those words to evoke in herself contempt for him and so to defend herself from him, but she did not succeed in doing so. Everything was against her, especially that accursed music. So it all ended, and on the Sunday the guests assembled and they again played together.

XXIII

'I SUPPOSE it is hardly necessary to say that I was very vain: if one is not vain there is nothing to live for in our usual way of life. So on that Sunday I arranged the dinner and the musical evening with much care. I bought the provisions myself and invited the guests.

'Towards six the visitors assembled. He came in evening dress with diamond studs that showed bad taste. He behaved in a free and easy manner, answered everything hurriedly with a smile of agreement and understanding, you know, with that peculiar expression which seems to say that all you may do or say is just what he expected. Everything that was not in good taste about him I noticed with particular pleasure, because it ought all to have had the effect of tranquillizing me and showing that he was so far beneath my wife that, as she had said, she could not lower herself to his level. I did not now allow myself to be jealous.[76] In the first place I had worried through that torment and needed rest, and secondly I wanted to believe my wife's assurances and did believe them. But though I was not jealous I was nevertheless not natural with either of them, and at dinner and during the first half of the evening before the music began I still followed their movements and looks.

'The dinner was, as dinners are, dull and pretentious. The music began pretty early.[77] Oh, how I remember every detail of that evening! I remember how he brought in his violin, unlocked the case, took off the cover a lady had embroidered for him, drew out the violin, and began tuning it. I remember how my wife sat down at the piano with pretended unconcern, under which I saw that she was trying to conceal great timidity—chiefly as to her own ability—and then the usual A on the piano began, the pizzicato of the violin, and the arrangement of the music. Then I remember how they glanced at one another, turned to look at the audience who were seating themselves, said something to one another, and began. He took the first chords. His face grew serious, stern, and sympathetic, and listening to the sounds he produced, he touched the strings with careful fingers. The piano answered him. The music began. . . .'

Pózdnyshev paused and produced his strange sound several times in succession. He tried to speak, but sniffed, and stopped.

'They played Beethoven's Kreutzer Sonata,' he continued. 'Do you know the first presto? You do?' he cried.[78] 'Ugh! Ugh! It is a terrible thing, that sonata. And especially that part. And in general music is a dreadful thing! What is it? I don't understand it. What is music? What does it do? And why does it do what it does? They say music exalts the soul. Nonsense, it is not true! It has an effect, an awful effect—I am speaking of myself—but not of an exalting kind. It has neither an exalting nor a debasing effect but it produces agitation. How can I put it? Music makes me forget myself, my real position; it transports me to some other position not my own. Under the influence of music it seems to me that I feel what I do not really feel, that I understand what I do not understand, that I can do what I cannot do. I explain it by the fact that music acts like yawning, like laughter: I am not sleepy, but I yawn when I see someone yawning; there is nothing for me to laugh at, but I laugh when I hear people laughing.

'Music carries me immediately and directly into the mental condition in which the man was who composed it. My soul merges with his and together with him I pass from one condition into another, but why this happens I don't know. You see, he who wrote, let us say, the Kreutzer Sonata—Beethoven—knew of course why he was in that condition; that condition caused him to do certain actions and therefore that condition had a meaning for him, but for me—none at all. That is why music only agitates and doesn't lead to a conclusion. Well, when a military march is played the soldiers march to the music and the music has achieved its object. A dance is played, I dance and the music has achieved its object. Mass has been sung, I receive Communion, and that music too has reached a conclusion. Otherwise it is only agitating, and what ought to be done in that agitation is lacking. That is why music sometimes acts so dreadfully, so terribly. In China, music is a State affair. And that is as it should be. How can one allow anyone who pleases to hypnotize another, or many others, and do what he likes with them? And especially that this hypnotist should be the first immoral man who turns up?

'It is a terrible instrument in the hands of any chance user! Take that Kreutzer Sonata for instance, how can that first presto be played in a drawing-room among ladies in low-necked dresses? To hear that played, to clap a little, and then to eat ices and talk of the latest scandal? Such things should only be played on certain important significant occasions, and then only when certain actions answering to such music are wanted; play it then and do what the music has moved you to. Otherwise an awakening of energy and feeling unsuited both to the time and the place, to which no outlet is given, cannot but act harmfully. At any rate that piece had a terrible effect on me; it was as if quite new feelings, new possibilities, of which I had till then been unaware, had been revealed to me. "That's how it is: not at all as I used to think and live, but that way," something seemed to say within me. What this new thing was that had been revealed to me I could not explain to myself, but the consciousness of this new condition was very joyous.[79] All those same people, including my wife and him, appeared in a new light.[80]

'After that allegro they played the beautiful, but common and unoriginal, andante with trite variations, and the very weak finale. Then, at the request of the visitors, they played Ernst's Elegy and a few small pieces. They were all good, but they did not produce on me a one-hundredth part of the impression the first piece had. The effect of the first piece formed the background for them all.

'I felt light-hearted and cheerful the whole

evening. I had never seen my wife as she was that evening. Those shining eyes, that severe, significant expression while she played, and her melting languor and feeble, pathetic, and blissful smile after they had finished. I saw all that but did not attribute any meaning to it except that she was feeling what I felt, and that to her as to me new feelings, never before experienced, were revealed or, as it were, recalled.[81] The evening ended satisfactorily and the visitors departed.

'Knowing that I had to go away to attend the Zémstvo Meetings two days later, Trukhachévski on leaving said he hoped to repeat the pleasure of that evening when he next came to Moscow. From this I concluded that he did not consider it possible to come to my house during my absence, and this pleased me.

'It turned out that as I should not be back before he left town, we should not see one another again.

'For the first time I pressed his hand with real pleasure, and thanked him for the enjoyment he had given us. In the same way he bade a final farewell to my wife. Their leave-taking seemed to be most natural and proper. Everything was splendid. My wife and I were both very well satisfied with our evening party.[82]

XXIV

'Two days later I left for the Meetings, parting from my wife in the best and most tranquil of moods.

'In the district there was always an enormous amount to do and a quite special life, a special little world of its own. I spent two ten-hour days at the Council. A letter from my wife was brought me on the second day and I read it there and then.

'She wrote about the children, about uncle, about the nurse, about shopping, and among other things she mentioned, as a most natural occurrence, that Trukhachévski had called, brought some music he had promised, and had offered to play again, but that she had refused.

'I did not remember his having promised any music, but thought he had taken leave for good, and I was therefore unpleasantly struck by this. I was however so busy that I had no time to think of it, and it was only in the evening when I had returned to my lodgings that I re-read her letter.

'Besides the fact that Trukhachévski had called at my house during my absence, the whole tone of the letter seemed to me unnatural. The mad beast of jealousy began to growl in its kennel and wanted to leap out, but I was afraid of that beast and quickly fastened him in. "What an abominable feeling this jealousy is!" I said to myself. "What could be more natural than what she writes?"

'I went to bed and began thinking about the affairs awaiting me next day. During those Meetings, sleeping in a new place, I usually slept badly, but now I fell asleep very quickly. And as sometimes happens, you know, you feel a kind of electric shock and wake up. So I awoke thinking of her, of my physical love for her, and of Trukhachévski, and of everything being accomplished between them. Horror and rage compressed my heart. But I began to reason with myself. "What nonsense!" said I to myself. "There are no grounds to go on, there is nothing and there has been nothing. How can I so degrade her and myself as to imagine such horrors? He is a sort of hired violinist, known as a worthless fellow, and suddenly an honourable woman, the respected mother of a family, *my* wife. . . . What absurdity!" So it seemed to me on the one hand. "How could it help being so?" it seemed on the other. "How could that simplest and most intelligible thing help happening—that for the sake of which I married her, for the sake of which I have been living with her, what alone I wanted of her, and which others including this musician must therefore also want? He is an unmarried man, healthy (I remember how he crunched the gristle of a cutlet and how greedily his red lips clung to the glass of wine), well-fed, plump, and not merely unprincipled but evidently making it a principle to accept the pleasures that present themselves. And they have music, that most exquisite voluptuousness of the senses, as a link between them. What then could make him refrain? She? But who is she? She was, and still is, a mystery. I don't know her. I only know her as an animal. And nothing can or should restrain an animal."

'Only then did I remember their faces that evening when, after the Kreutzer Sonata, they played some impassioned little piece, I don't remember by whom, impassioned to the point of obscenity. "How dared I go away?" I asked myself, remembering their faces. Was it not clear that everything had happened between them that evening? Was it not evident already then that there was not only no barrier between them, but that they both, and she chiefly, felt a certain measure of shame after what had happened? I remember her weak, piteous, and beatific smile as she wiped the perspiration from her flushed face when I came up to the piano. Already then they avoided looking at one another, and only at supper when he was pouring out some water for her, they glanced at each other with the vestige of a smile. I now recalled with horror the glance and scarcely perceptible smile I had then caught. "Yes, it is all over," said one voice, and immediately the other voice said something entirely different. "Something has come over you, it can't be that it is so," said that other voice. It felt uncanny lying in the dark and I struck a light, and felt a kind of terror in that little room with its yellow wall-paper. I lit a cigarette and, as always happens when one's thoughts go round and round in a circle of insoluble contradictions, I smoked, taking one cigarette after another in order to befog myself so as not to see those contradictions.

'I did not sleep all night, and at five in the morning,[83] having decided that I could not continue in such a state of tension, I rose, woke the caretaker who attended me and sent him to get horses. I sent a note to the Council saying that I had been recalled to Moscow on urgent business and asking that one of the members should take my place. At eight o'clock I got into my trap and started.'

XXV

THE conductor entered and seeing that our candle had burnt down put it out, without supplying a fresh one. The day was dawning. Pózdnyshev was silent, but sighed deeply all the time the conductor was in the carriage. He continued his story only after the conductor had gone out, and in the semi-darkness of the carriage only the rattle of the windows of the moving carriage and the rhythmic snoring of the clerk could be heard. In the half-light of dawn I could not see Pózdnyshev's face at all, but only heard his voice becoming ever more and more excited and full of suffering.

'I had to travel twenty-four miles by road and eight hours by rail. It was splendid driving. It was frosty autumn weather, bright and sunny. The roads were in that condition when the tyres leave their dark imprint on them, you know. They were smooth, the light brilliant, and the air invigorating. It was pleasant driving in the tarantas. When it grew lighter and I had started I felt easier. Looking at the houses, the fields, and the passers-by, I forgot where I was going. Sometimes I felt that I was simply taking a drive,[84] and that nothing of what was calling me back had taken place. This oblivion was peculiarly enjoyable. When I remembered where I was going to, I said to myself, "We shall see when the time comes; I must not think about it." When we were half-way an incident occurred which detained me and still further distracted my thoughts. The tarantas[85] broke down and had to be repaired. That break-down had a very important effect, for it caused me to arrive in Moscow at midnight, instead of at seven o'clock as I had expected, and to reach home between twelve and one, as I missed the express and had to travel by an ordinary train. Going to fetch a cart, having the tarantas mended, settling up, tea at the inn, a talk with the innkeeper—all this still further diverted my attention. It was twilight before all was ready and I started again. By night it was even pleasanter driving than during the day. There was a new moon, a slight frost, still good roads, good horses, and a jolly driver, and as I went on I enjoyed it, hardly thinking at all of what lay before me; or perhaps I enjoyed it just because I knew what awaited me and was saying good-bye to the joys of life. But that tranquil mood, that ability to suppress my feelings, ended with my drive. As soon as I entered the train something entirely different began. That eight-hour journey in a railway carriage was something dreadful, which I shall never forget all my life. Whether it was that having taken my seat in the carriage I vividly imagined myself as having already arrived, or that railway travelling has such an exciting effect on people, at any rate from the moment I sat down in the train I could no longer control my imagination, and with extraordinary vividness which inflamed my jealousy it painted incessantly, one after another, pictures[86] of what had gone on in my absence, of how she had been false to me. I burnt with indignation, anger, and a peculiar feeling of intoxication with my own humiliation, as I gazed at those pictures, and I could not tear myself away from them; I could not help looking at them, could not efface them, and could not help evoking them.

'That was not all. The more I gazed at those imaginary pictures the stronger grew my belief in their reality.[87] The vividness with which they presented themselves to me seemed to serve as proof that what I imagined was real. It was as if some devil against my will invented and suggested to me the most terrible reflections. An old conversation I had had with Trukhachévski's brother came to my mind, and in a kind of ecstasy I rent my heart with that conversation, making it refer to Trukhachévski and my wife.

'That had occurred long before, but I recalled it. Trukhachévski's brother, I remember, in reply to a question whether he frequented houses of ill-fame, had said that a decent man would not go to places where there was danger of infection and it was dirty and nasty, since he could always find a decent woman. And now his brother had found my wife! "True, she is not in her first youth, has lost a side-tooth, and there is a slight puffiness about her; but it can't be helped, one has to take advantage of what one can get," I imagined him to be thinking. "Yes, it is condescending of him to take her for his mistress!" I said to myself. "And she is safe. . . ." "No, it is impossible!" I thought horror-struck. "There is nothing of the kind, nothing! There are not even any grounds for suspecting such things. Didn't she tell me that the very thought that I could be jealous of him was degrading to her? Yes, but she is lying, she is always lying!"[88] I exclaimed, and everything began anew. . . . There were only two other people in the carriage; an old woman and her husband, both very taciturn, and even they got out at one of the stations and I was quite alone. I was like a caged animal: now I jumped up and went to the window, now I began to walk up and down trying to speed the carriage up; but the carriage with all its seats and windows went jolting on in the same way, just as ours does. . . .'

Pózdnyshev jumped up, took a few steps, and sat down again.

'Oh, I am afraid, afraid of railway carriages, I am seized with horror. Yes, it is awful!' he continued. 'I said to myself, "I will think of something else. Suppose I think of the innkeeper where I had tea," and there in my mind's eye appears the innkeeper with his long beard and his grandson, a boy of the age of my Vásya. "My Vásya! He will see how the musician kisses his mother. What will happen in his poor soul? But what does she care? She loves"[89] . . . and again the same thing rose up in me. "No, no . . . I will think about the inspection of the District Hospital. Oh, yes, about the patient who complained of the doctor yesterday. The doctor has a moustache like Trukhachévski's. And how impudent he is . . . they both deceived me when he said he was leaving Moscow," and it began afresh. Everything I thought of had some connexion with them. I suffered dreadfully. The chief cause of the suffering was my ignorance, my doubt, and the contradictions within me: my not knowing whether I ought to love or hate her. My suffering was of a strange kind. I felt a hateful consciousness of my humiliation and of his victory, but a terrible hatred for her. "It will not do to put an end to myself and leave her; she must at least suffer to some extent, and at least understand that I have suffered," I said to myself. I got out at every station to divert my mind. At one station I saw some people drinking, and I immediately drank some vodka. Beside me stood a Jew who was also drinking. He began to talk, and to avoid being alone in my carriage I went with him into his dirty third-class carriage reeking with smoke and bespattered with shells of sunflower seeds. There I sat down beside him and he chattered a great deal and told anecdotes. I listened to him, but could not take in what he was saying because I continued to think about my own affairs. He noticed this and demanded my attention. Then I rose and went back to my carriage. "I must think it over," I said to myself. "Is what I suspect true, and is there any reason for me to suffer?" I sat down, wishing to think it over calmly, but immediately, instead of calm reflection, the same thing began again: instead of reflection, pictures and fancies. "How often I have suffered like this," I said to myself (recalling former similar attacks of jealousy), "and afterwards it all ended in nothing. So it will be now perhaps, yes certainly it will. I shall find her calmly asleep, she will wake up, be pleased to see me, and by her words and looks I shall know that there has been nothing and that this is all nonsense. Oh, how good that would be! But no, that has happened too often and won't happen again now," some voice seemed to say; and it began again. Yes, that was where the punishment lay! I wouldn't take a young man to a lock-hospital to knock the hankering after women out of him, but into my soul, to see the devils that were rending it! What was terrible, you know, was that I considered myself to have a complete right to her body as if it were my own, and yet at the same time I felt I could not control that body, that it was not mine and she could dispose of it as she pleased, and that she wanted to dispose of it not as I wished her to. And I could do nothing either to her or to him. He, like Vánka the Steward,* could sing a song before the gallows of how he kissed the sugared lips and so forth. And he would triumph. If she has not yet done it but wishes to—and I know that she does wish to—it is still worse; it would be better if she had done it and I knew it, so that there would be an end to this uncertainty. I could not have said what it was I wanted. I wanted her not to desire that which she was bound to desire. It was utter insanity.

XXVI

'At the last station but one, when the conductor had been to collect the tickets, I gathered my things together and went out onto the brake-platform, and the consciousness that the crisis was at hand still further increased my agitation. I felt cold, and my jaw trembled so that my teeth chattered. I automatically left the terminus with the crowd, took a cab, got in, and drove off. I rode looking at the few passers-by, the night-watchmen,[90] and the shadows of my trap thrown by the street lamps, now in front and now behind me, and did not think of anything. When we had gone about half a mile my feet felt cold, and I remembered that I had taken off my woollen stockings in the train and put

* *Vánka the Steward* is the subject and name of some old Russian poems. Vánka seduces his master's wife, boasts of having done so, and is hanged.—A. M.

them in my satchel. "Where is the satchel? Is it here? Yes." And my wicker trunk? I remembered that I had entirely forgotten about my luggage, but finding that I had the luggage-ticket I decided that it was not worth while going back for it, and so continued my way.

[91]"Try now as I will, I cannot recall my state of mind at the time. What did I think? What did I want? I don't know at all. All I remember is a consciousness that something dreadful and very important in my life was imminent. Whether that important event occurred because I thought it would, or whether I had a presentiment of what was to happen, I don't know. It may even be that after what has happened all the foregoing moments have acquired a certain gloom in my mind. I drove up to the front porch. It was past midnight. Some cabmen were waiting in front of the porch expecting, from the fact that there were lights in the windows, to get fares. (The lights were in our flat, in the dancing-room and drawing-room.) Without considering why it was still light in our windows so late, I went upstairs in the same state of expectation of something dreadful, and rang. Egór, a kind, willing, but very stupid footman, opened the door. The first thing my eyes fell on in the hall was a man's cloak hanging on the stand with other outdoor coats. I ought to have been surprised but was not, for I had expected it. "That's it!" I said to myself. When I asked Egór who the visitor was and he named Trukhachévski, I inquired whether there was anyone else. He replied, "Nobody, sir." I remember that he replied in a tone as if he wanted to cheer me and dissipate my doubts of there being anybody else there. "So it is, so it is," I seemed to be saying to myself. "And the children?" "All well. heaven be praised. In bed, long ago."

'I could not breathe, and could not check the trembling of my jaw. "Yes, so it is not as I thought: I used to expect a misfortune but things used to turn out all right and in the usual way. Now it is not as usual, but is all as I pictured to myself. I thought it was only fancy, but here it is, all real. Here it all is . . .!"

'I almost began to sob, but the devil immediately suggested to me: "Cry, be sentimental, and they will get away quietly. You will have no proof and will continue to suffer and doubt all your life." And my self-pity immediately vanished, and[92] a strange sense of joy arose in me, that my torture would now be over, that now I could punish her, could get rid of her, and could vent my anger. And I gave vent to it—I became a beast, a cruel and cunning beast.

' "Don't!" I said to Egór, who was about to go to the drawing-room. "Here is my luggage-ticket, take a cab as quick as you can and go and get my luggage. Go!" He went down the passage to fetch his overcoat. Afraid that he might alarm them, I went as far as his little room and waited while he put on his overcoat. From the drawing-room, beyond another room, one could hear voices and the clatter of knives and plates. They were eating and had not heard the bell. "If only they don't come out now," thought I. Egór put on his overcoat, which had an astrakhan collar, and went out. I locked the door after him and felt creepy when I knew I was alone and must act at once. How, I did not yet know. I only knew that all was now over, that there could be no doubt as to her guilt, and that I should punish her immediately and end my relations with her.

'Previously I had doubted and had thought: "Perhaps after all it's not true, perhaps I am mistaken." But now it was so no longer. It was all irrevocably decided. "Without my knowledge she is alone with him at night! That is a complete disregard of everything! Or worse still: it is intentional boldness and impudence in crime, that the boldness may serve as a sign of innocence. All is clear. There is no doubt." I only feared one thing—their parting hastily, inventing some fresh lie, and thus depriving me of clear evidence[93] and of the possibility of proving the fact. So as to catch them more quickly I went on tiptoe to the dancing-room where they were, not through the drawing-room but through the passage and nurseries.

'In the first nursery slept the boys. In the second nursery the nurse moved and was about to wake, and I imagined to myself what she would think when she knew all; and such pity for myself seized me at that thought that I could not restrain my tears, and not to wake the children I ran on tiptoe into the passage and on into my study, where I fell sobbing on the sofa.

' "I, an honest man, I, the son of my parents, I, who have all my life dreamt of the happiness of married life; I, a man who was never unfaithful to her. . . . And now! Five children, and she is embracing a musician because he has red lips!

' "No, she is not a human being. She is a bitch, an abominable bitch! In the next room to her children whom she has all her life pretended to love. And writing to me as she did! Throwing herself so barefacedly on his neck! But what do I know? Perhaps she long ago carried on with the footmen, and so got the children who are considered mine!

' "To-morrow I should have come back and she would have met me with her fine coiffure, with her elegant waist and her indolent, graceful movements" (I saw all her attractive, hateful face), "and that beast of jealousy would for ever have sat in my heart lacerating it. What will the nurse think? . . . And Egór? And poor little Lisa! She already understands something. Ah, that impudence, those lies! And that animal sensuality which I know so well," I said to myself.

'I tried to get up but could not. My heart was beating so that I could not stand on my feet. "Yes, I shall die of a stroke. She will kill me. That is just what she wants. What is killing to her? But no, that would be too advantageous for her and I will not give her that pleasure. Yes, here I sit while they eat and laugh and . . . Yes, though she was no longer in her first freshness he did not disdain her. For in spite of that she is not bad looking, and above all she is at any rate not dangerous to his precious health. And why did I not throttle her then?" I said to myself, recalling the moment when, the week before, I drove her out of my study and hurled things about. I vividly recalled the state I had then been in; I not only recalled it, but again felt the need to strike and destroy that I had felt then. I remember how I wished to act, and how all considerations except those necessary for action went out of my head. I entered into that condition when an animal or a man, under the influence of physical excitement at a time of danger, acts with precision and deliberation but without losing a moment and always with a single definite aim in view.

'The first thing I did was to take off my boots and, in my socks, approach the sofa, on the wall above which guns and daggers were hung. I took down a curved Damascus dagger that had never been used and was very sharp. I drew it out of its scabbard. I remember the scabbard fell behind the sofa, and I remember thinking "I must find it afterwards or it will get lost". Then I took off my overcoat which I was still wearing, and stepping softly in my socks I went there.[94]

XXVII

'HAVING crept up stealthily to the door, I suddenly opened it.[95] I remember the expression of their faces. I remember that expression because it gave me a painful pleasure—it was an expression of terror. That was just what I wanted. I shall never forget the look of desperate terror that appeared on both their faces the first instant they saw me. He I think was sitting at the table, but on seeing or hearing me he jumped to his feet and stood with his back to the cupboard. His face expressed nothing but quite unmistakable terror. Her face too expressed terror but there was something else besides. If it had expressed only terror, perhaps what happened might not have happened; but on her face there was, or at any rate so it seemed to me at the first moment, also an expression of regret and annoyance that love's raptures and her happiness with him had been disturbed. It was as if she wanted nothing but that her present happiness should not be interfered with. These expressions remained on their faces but an instant. The look of terror on his changed immediately to one of inquiry: might he, or might he not, begin lying? If he might, he must begin at once; if not, something else would happen. But what? . . . He looked inquiringly at her face. On her face the look of vexation and regret changed as she looked at him (so it seemed to me) to one of solicitude for him.

'For an instant I stood in the doorway holding the dagger behind my back.

'At that moment he smiled, and in a ridiculously indifferent tone remarked: "And we have been having some music."

' "What a surprise!" she began, falling into his tone. But neither of them finished; the same fury I had experienced the week before overcame me. Again I felt that need of destruction, violence, and a transport of rage, and yielded to it. Neither finished what they were saying. That something else began which he had feared and which immediately destroyed all they were saying. I rushed towards her, still hiding the dagger that he might not prevent my striking her in the side under her breast. I selected that spot from the first. Just as I rushed at her he saw it, and—a thing I never expected of him—seized me by the arm and shouted: "Think what you are doing! . . . Help, someone! . . ."

'I snatched my arm away and rushed at him in silence. His eyes met mine and he suddenly grew as pale as a sheet to his very lips. His eyes flashed in a peculiar way, and—what again I had not expected—he darted under the piano and out at the door. I was going to rush after him, but a weight hung on my left arm. It was she. I tried to free myself, but she hung on yet more heavily and would not let me go. This unexpected hindrance, the weight, and her touch which was loathsome to me, inflamed me still more. I felt that I was quite mad and that I must look frightful, and this delighted me. I swung my left arm with all my might, and my elbow hit her straight in the face. She cried out and let go my arm. I wanted to run after him, but remembered that it is ridiculous to run after one's wife's lover in one's socks; and I did not wish to be ridiculous but terrible. In spite of the fearful frenzy I was in, I was all the time aware of the impression I might produce on others, and was even partly guided by that impression. I turned towards her. She fell on the couch, and holding her hand to her bruised eyes, looked at me. Her face showed fear and hatred of me, the enemy, as a rat's does when one lifts the trap in which it has been caught. At any rate I saw nothing in her expression but this fear and hatred of me. It was just the fear and hatred of me which would be evoked by love for another. But still I might perhaps have restrained myself and not done what I did had she remained silent. But she suddenly began to speak and to catch hold of the hand in which I held the dagger.

' "Come to yourself! What are you doing? What is the matter? There has been nothing, nothing, nothing. . . . I swear it!"

'I might still have hesitated, but those last words of hers, from which I concluded just the opposite—that everything had happened—called forth a reply. And the reply had to correspond to the temper to which I had brought myself, which continued to increase and had to go on increasing. Fury, too, has its laws.

' "Don't lie, you wretch!" I howled, and seized her arm with my left hand, but she wrenched herself away. Then, still without letting go of the dagger, I seized her by the throat with my left hand, threw her backwards, and began throttling her. What a firm neck it was . . .! She seized my hand with both hers trying to pull it away from her throat, and as if I had only waited for that, I struck her with all my might with the dagger in the side below the ribs.

'When people say they don't remember what they do in a fit of fury, it is rubbish, falsehood. I remembered everything and did not for a moment lose consciousness of what I was doing. The more frenzied I became the more brightly the light of consciousness burnt in me, so that I could not help knowing everything I did. I knew what I was doing every second. I cannot say that I knew beforehand what I was going to do; but I knew what I was doing when I did it, and even I think a little before, as if to make repentance possible and to be able to tell myself that I could stop. I knew I was hitting below the ribs and that the dagger would enter. At the moment I did it I knew I was doing an awful thing such as I had never done before, which would have terrible consequences. But that consciousness passed like a flash of lightning and the deed immediately followed the consciousness. I realized the action with extraordinary clearness. I felt, and remember, the momentary resistance of her corset and of something else, and then the plunging of the dagger into something soft. She seized the dagger with her hands, and cut them, but could not hold it back.

'For a long time afterwards, in prison when the moral change had taken place in me, I thought of that moment, recalled what I could of it, and considered it. I remembered that for an instant, only an instant, before the action I had a terrible consciousness that I was killing, had killed, a defenceless woman, my wife! I remember the horror of that consciousness and conclude from that, and even dimly remember, that having plunged the dagger in I pulled it out immediately, trying to remedy what had been done and to stop it. I stood for a second motionless waiting to see what would happen, and whether it could be remedied.

'She jumped to her feet and screamed: "Nurse! He has killed me."

'Having heard the noise the nurse was standing by the door. I continued to stand waiting, and not believing the truth. But the blood rushed from under her corset.[96] Only then did I understand that it could not be remedied, and I immediately decided that it was not necessary it should be, that I had done what I wanted and had to do. I waited till she fell down, and the nurse, crying "Good God!" ran to her, and only then did I throw away the dagger and leave the room.

' "I must not be excited; I must know what I am doing," I said to myself without looking at her and at the nurse. The nurse was screaming—calling for the maid. I went down the passage, sent the maid, and went into my study. "What am I to do now?" I asked myself, and immediately realized what it must be. On entering the study I went straight to the wall, took down a revolver and examined it—it was loaded—I put it on the table. Then I picked up the scabbard from behind the sofa and sat down there.

'I sat thus for a long time. I did not think of anything or call anything to mind. I heard the sounds of bustling outside. I heard someone drive up, then someone else. Then I heard and saw Egór bring into the room my wicker trunk he had fetched. As if anyone wanted that!

' "Have you heard what has happened?" I asked. "Tell the yard-porter to inform the police." He did not reply, and went away. I rose, locked the door, got out my cigarettes and matches and began to smoke. I had not finished the cigarette before sleep overpowered me. I must have slept for a couple of hours. I remember dreaming that she and I were friendly together, that we had quarrelled but were making it up, there was something rather in the way, but we were friends. I was awakened by someone knocking at the door. "That is the police!" I thought, waking up. "I have committed murder, I think. But perhaps it is *she*, and nothing has happened." There was again a knock at the door. I did not answer, but was trying to solve the question whether it had happened or not. Yes, it had! I remembered the resistance of the corset and the plunging in of the dagger, and a cold shiver ran down my back. "Yes, it has. Yes, and now I must do away with myself too," I thought. But I thought this knowing that I should *not* kill myself. Still I got up and took the revolver in my hand. But it is strange: I remember how I had many times been near suicide, how even that day on the railway it had seemed easy, easy just because I thought how it would stagger her—now I was not only unable to kill myself but even to think of it. "Why should I do it?" I asked myself, and there was no reply. There was more knocking at the door. "First I must find out who is knocking. There will still be time for this." I put down the revolver and covered it with a newspaper. I went to the door and unlatched it. It was my wife's sister, a kindly, stupid widow. "Vásya, what is this?" and her ever ready tears began to flow.

' "What do you want?" I asked rudely. I knew I ought not to be rude to her and had no reason to be, but I could think of no other tone to adopt.

' "Vásya, she is dying! Iván Zakhárych says so." Iván Zakhárych was her doctor and adviser.

' "Is he here?" I asked, and all my animosity against her surged up again. "Well, what of it?"

' "Vásya, go to her. Oh, how terrible it is!" said she.

' "Shall I go to her?" I asked myself, and immediately decided that I must go to her. Probably it is always done, when a husband has killed his wife, as I had—he must certainly go to her. "If that is what is done, then I must go," I said to myself. "If necessary I shall always have time," I reflected, referring to the shooting of myself, and

I went to her. "Now we shall have phrases, grimaces, but I will not yield to them," I thought. "Wait," I said to her sister, "it is silly without boots, let me at least put on slippers."

XXVIII

'WONDERFUL to say, when I left my study and went through the familiar rooms, the hope that nothing had happened again awoke in me; but the smell of that doctor's nastiness—iodoform and carbolic—took me aback. "No, it had happened." Going down the passage past the nursery I saw little Lisa. She looked at me with frightened eyes. It even seemed to me that all the five children were there and all looked at me. I approached the door, and the maid opened it from inside for me and passed out. The first thing that caught my eye was her light-grey dress thrown on a chair and all stained black with blood. She was lying on one of the twin beds (on mine because it was easier to get at), with her knees raised. She lay in a very sloping position supported by pillows, with her dressing jacket unfastened. Something had been put on the wound. There was a heavy smell of iodoform in the room. What struck me first and most of all was her swollen and bruised face, blue on part of the nose and under the eyes. This was the result of the blow with my elbow when she had tried to hold me back. There was nothing beautiful about her, but something repulsive as it seemed to me. I stopped on the threshold. "Go up to her, do," said her sister. "Yes, no doubt she wants to confess," I thought. "Shall I forgive her? Yes, she is dying and may be forgiven," I thought, trying to be magnanimous. I went up close to her. She raised her eyes to me with difficulty, one of them was black, and with an effort said falteringly:

' "You've got your way, killed . . ." and through the look of suffering and even the nearness of death her face had the old expression of cold animal hatred that I knew so well. "I shan't . . . let you have . . . the children, all the same. . . . She (her sister) will take . . ."

'Of what to me was the most important matter, her guilt, her faithlessness, she seemed to consider it beneath her to speak.

' "Yes, look and admire what you have done," she said looking towards the door, and she sobbed. In the doorway stood her sister with the children. "Yes, see what you have done."

'I looked at the children and at her bruised disfigured face, and for the first time I forgot myself, my rights, my pride, and for the first time saw a human being in her.[97] And so insignificant did all that had offended me, all my jealousy, appear, and so important what I had done, that I wished to fall with my face to her hand, and say: "Forgive me," but dared not do so.

'She lay silent with her eyes closed, evidently too weak to say more. Then her disfigured face trembled and puckered. She pushed me feebly away.

' "Why did it all happen? Why?"

' "Forgive me," I said.

[98]' "Forgive! That's all rubbish! . . . Only not to die! . . ." she cried, raising herself, and her glittering eyes were bent on me. "Yes, you have had your way! . . . I hate you! Ah! Ah!" she cried, evidently already in delirium and frightened at something. "Shoot! I'm not afraid! . . . Only kill everyone . . .! He has gone . . .! Gone . . .!"

'After that the delirium continued all the time. She did not recognize[99] anyone. She died towards noon that same day. Before that they had taken me to the police-station and from there to prison. There, during the eleven months I remained awaiting trial, I examined myself and my past, and understood it. I began to understand it on the third day: on the third day they took me *there* . . .'

He was going on but, unable to repress his sobs, he stopped. When he recovered himself he continued:

'I only began to understand when I saw her in her coffin . . .'

He gave a sob, but immediately continued hurriedly:

'Only when I saw her dead face did I understand all that I had done. I realized that I, I, had killed her; that it was my doing that she, living, moving, warm, had now become motionless, waxen, and cold, and that this could never, anywhere, or by any means, be remedied. He who has not lived through it cannot understand. . . . Ugh! Ugh! Ugh! . . .' he cried several times and then was silent.

We sat in silence a long while. He kept sobbing and trembling as he sat opposite me without speaking. His face had grown narrow and elongated and his mouth seemed to stretch right across it.

'Yes,' he suddenly said. 'Had I then known what I know now, everything would have been different. Nothing would have induced me to marry her. . . . I should not have married at all.'

Again we remained silent for a long time.

[100]'Well, forgive me. . . .'* He turned away from me and lay down on the seat, covering himself up with his plaid. At the station where I had to get out (it was at eight o'clock in the morning)

* In Russian the word for 'forgive me' is very similar to that for 'good-bye', and is sometimes used in place of the latter.—A. M.

I went up to him to say good-bye. Whether he was asleep or only pretended to be, at any rate he did not move. I touched him with my hand. He uncovered his face, and I could see he had not been asleep.

'Good-bye,' I said, holding out my hand. He gave me his and smiled slightly, but so piteously that I felt ready to weep.

'Yes, forgive me . . .' he said, repeating the same words with which he had concluded his story.

APPENDIX

The following are the readings of the lithograph:

[1] *Add*: with remarkable glittering eyes of an indefinite colour, which attracted attention. *Some of the description that follows is omitted.*

[2] *Read*: At first the clerk said that the place opposite was engaged; to which the old man replied that he was only going as far as the next station.

[3] *Read*: considering probably that this did not at all infringe the dignity his figure and manner denoted, . . .

[4] *For the above paragraph read*: 'And then come discord, financial troubles, mutual recrimination, and the married couple separate,' said the lawyer.

[5] *In place of the two preceding lines, read*: said the lady, evidently encouraged by the general attention and approval.

[6] *The old man here replies*: 'Men are a different matter.' *And the lady says*: 'Then to a man, in your opinion, everything is permitted.'

[7] *Add*: 'Or if some stupid man cannot control his wife—it serves him right. But all the same one must not create a scandal about it. Love or don't love, but don't break up the home. Every husband can keep his wife in order, he has the right to do it. Only a fool can't manage it.'

[8] *In place of this paragraph read*: 'But you yourself may go on the spree with the girls at Kunávin,' said the lawyer with a smile.

[9] *Add*: a vein on his forehead stood out,

[10] *The lithograph here reads differently, and the words that follow are*: 'How do you mean "what kind of love"?' said the lady. 'The ordinary love of married couples.'

'But how can ordinary love sanctify marriage?' continued the nervous gentleman. He was as agitated as though he were angry and wished to speak unpleasantly to the lady. She felt this and was also agitated.

'How? Very simply,' said she. The nervous gentleman at once seized on the word.

'No, not simply!'

[11] *Add*: and least of all for his wife. That is what the proverb says, and it is a true one. "Another's wife is a swan, but one's own is bitter wormwood." '

[12] *Read*: Even if one admits that Menelaus might prefer Helen for his whole lifetime, Helen would prefer Paris.

[13] *Add*: . . . of Helen with Menelaus or vice versa. The only difference is that with one it comes sooner and with another later. It is only written in stupid novels that they loved one another all their lives, and only children can believe that.

[14] *Add*: 'This identity of ideals does not occur among old people, but always between handsome and young ones. And I assert that love, real love, does not sanctify marriage as we are accustomed to suppose for one's whole life, but on the contrary destroys it.'

[15] *Add*: 'And we feel this, and to avoid it we preach "love". In reality the preaching of free love is only a call to return to the mingling of the sexes—excuse me,' said he, turning to the lady, 'to fornication. The old basis has worn out, and we must find a new one, but not preach depravity!' He had become so excited that we all remained silent and looked at him.

'And at present the transition stage is terrible. People feel that it will not do to allow adultery, and that sexual relations must in some way be defined; but bases for this are lacking, except the old ones in which no one any longer believes. And people go on getting married in the old way without believing in what they are doing, and the result is either deception or coercion.

[16] *Add*: and do not themselves know why or what for,

[17] *Add*: In the course of his story he did not once stop after that, and not even the entry of fresh passengers interrupted him. During his narration his face completely changed several times so that nothing resembling the former face remained: his eyes, his mouth, his moustache and even his beard were all different—it was a beautiful, touching, new face. These changes occurred suddenly in the dim light, and for some five minutes there was one face and it was impossible to see the former face, and then, one did not know how, another face appeared and again it was impossible to see it otherwise.

[18] *Add*: . . . my life and all my terrible story. Terrible, really terrible. The whole story is more terrible than the end.

[19] *Add*: In the first place let me tell you who I am. I am the son of a rich landowner in the steppes, and I took a degree in law at the university. I married when I was rather over thirty, but before telling of my marriage I must say how I lived previously and how I regarded family life.

[20] *Add*: This—the fact that I considered myself moral—came about because in our family there was not any of that particular specialized vice which was so common in our landowning class, and therefore, being brought up in a family where neither my father nor my mother was unfaithful, I nursed the dream of a most elevated and poetic family life from my early years. My wife had to be the height of perfection. Our mutual love had to be most elevated. The purity of our family life was to be dove-like. So I thought, and I praised myself all the time for having such elevated thoughts. And at the same time, for ten years, I lived as an adult, in no haste to get married, and led what I called a respectable, reasonable, bachelor life.

[21] *Add*: and I was naïvely confident that I was quite a moral man. The women I was intimate with were not mine, and I had nothing to do with them except for the pleasure they afforded me. And I saw nothing disgraceful in this.

[22] *Add*: . . . in regard to the real woman-question . . .'

'That is to say . . . what do you understand to be the real woman-question?'

'The question of what this organic creature that is distinct from man is, and how she herself and men also should regard her.

[23] *For this paragraph read*: 'Yes, for ten years I lived in most disgraceful debauchery, dreaming of a pure, elevated love—and even in the name of that love. Yes, I want to tell of how I killed my wife, and to tell that I must tell how I became depraved.

'I killed her before I met her; I killed a woman the first time I knew one without loving her, and it was already then that I killed my wife.

[24] *Read*: Who deprave youths? They do! Who deprave women by devising means for them and teaching them not to bear children? Who treat syphilis with enthusiasm? They.'

'But why not treat syphilis?'

'Because to cure syphilis is the same as to safeguard vice; it is the same as the Foundlings Hospital for discarded babies.

'No, not the same . . . *Then omit to end of paragraph.*

[25] *Insert here*: To tell the truth without false shame, I was trapped and caught. Her mamma—her papa was dead—arranged all sorts of traps and one of them—namely boating—succeeded.

[26] *Insert*: No, say what you will, we live up to our ears in such a swamp of lies that unless we have our heads bumped, as I did, we cannot come to our senses.

[27] *Add*: How fortunate that would have been for us!

[28] *Add*: If we only reject the conventional explanations of why and for what reason these things are done, if we . . .'

[29] *Add*: There is no difference. Strictly defining the matter, one must say that prostitutes for short terms are usually despised, while prostitutes for long terms are respected.

[30] *Add*: The men of our circle are kept and fed like breeding stallions. It is only necessary, you know, to close the safety-valve—that is, for a vicious young man to live a continent life for a little while—and immediately

a terrible restlessness and excitement is caused, which passing through the prism of the artificial conditions of our social life shows itself in the guise of falling in love. Our love affairs and marriages, for the most part, are conditioned by our food. You are surprised: one ought to be surprised that we have not noticed it sooner.

31 *Read*: through the prism of novels, stories, verses, music—through the idle, luxurious setting of our life—and there will be amorousness of the purest water.

32 *Read*: . . . her parents, knowing more of life and not distracted by a momentary infatuation, but yet loving her not less than they loved themselves—arranged the marriage.

33 *Instead of the following lines, read*: And we talk of woman's rights, of "freedom" which is somehow obtainable at university lectures.'

34 *Add*: and as she cannot consent to be a slave and cannot herself propose, there begins that other abominable lie which is sometimes called "coming out into society", and sometimes "amusing themselves", and which is nothing but husband-hunting.

35 *Add*: 'They all complain that they are deprived of rights and are oppressed.

36 *Add*: Look at the people's fêtes, and at our balls and parties. Woman knows how she acts, you can see that by her triumphant smile.

37 *Add*: whether they believe in that or not—is unimportant.

38 *Add*: My sister, when very young, married a man twice her age and a debauchee. I remember how astonished we were the night of the wedding, when she ran out of her bedroom in tears and, shaking all over, said that she could on no account, on no account, even tell us what he had wanted to do to her.

39 *Add*: A pure girl only wants children. Children,—yes, but not a husband.'

'How then,' I said with astonishment, 'how is the human race to be continued?'

'And why should it be continued?' was his unexpected rejoinder.

40 *Add*: You know that Schopenhauer, Hartmann, and

all the Buddhists too, declare that it is a blessing not to live. And they are so far right that welfare for humanity coincides with self-annihilation, only they have not expressed themselves rightly: they say that the human race should destroy itself to escape from suffering—that its aim should be self-destruction. That is wrong. The aim of humanity cannot be to escape from suffering by self-destruction, because sufferings are the result of activity, and the aim of an activity cannot be to destroy its consequences. The aim both of men and of humanity is blessedness. For the attainment of blessedness a law has been given to humanity which it should fulfil. The law is that of the union of mankind.

[41] *In the lithographed version there are a number of small differences in the last paragraphs of Chapter XI, and Chapter XII commences with the words*: 'It is a strange story,' said I.

'What is there strange about it? According to all Church teaching the end of the world is coming, and according to all that science teaches the same thing is inevitable. So what is there strange in the fact that moral teaching reaches the same result? "He that is able to receive it, let him receive it," said Christ. And I understand that just as he said it. For morality to exist between people in sexual relations it is necessary that the aim they set themselves should be complete chastity. In striving towards chastity, man falls; he falls, and the result is a moral marriage; but if, as in our society, man aims directly at physical love, then though it may clothe itself in the pseudo-moral form of marriage, that will merely be permitted debauchery with one woman—and will none the less be an immoral life, such as that in which I perished and destroyed her, and such as among us is called moral family life. Note what a perverse conception exists among us, when the happiest position for a man—that of freedom, celibacy—is considered pitiable and ridiculous. And the highest ideal, the best position, for a woman—that of being pure, a vestal, a virgin—is a thing to be afraid of and a subject for ridicule in our society. How many and many young girls have offered up their purity to that Moloch of opinion by marrying good-for-nothing fellows, merely to avoid remaining virgin, which is the highest state. For fear that she may remain in that highest state she ruins herself! But I did not then understand that the words in the Gospel—that he who looks upon a woman with desire has already committed adultery with her in his heart—refer not to other wives only, but specially and chiefly to one's own. I did not understand that, and thought that this honeymoon and my behaviour on this honeymoon were most excellent, and that to satisfy desire with my own wife was a perfectly right thing. *Then follow in the lithographed version the words*: You know those wedding tours, &c.

42 *Read*: As happens with mirthful young people who, unable to devise funny things to laugh at quickly enough, laugh at their own laughter, so we had not time to devise excuses for our hatred.

43 *Read*: 'We all—men and women—are brought up to a kind of veneration for that feeling which we are accustomed to call love. From childhood I prepared to fall in love, and I fell in love; all my youth I was in love and was glad to be so. It was instilled into me that there was no nobler and more exalted business in the world than to be in love. Well at last the expected feeling comes, and a man devotes himself to it. But that is where the deception appears. In theory love is something ideal . . .

44 *Add*: I would order them—those wizards—to perform the office of those women who, in their opinion, are necessary to men—and then let them talk!

45 *Add*: According to the view existing in our society a woman's vocation is to afford pleasure to man, and the education given her corresponds with this view. From childhood she learns only how to be more attractive. Girls are all taught to think entirely of that. As serfs were brought up to satisfy their masters and it could not be otherwise, so also all our women are educated to attract men and this too cannot be otherwise. But you will perhaps say that this is true only of badly brought-up girls—those who among us are contemptuously called "young ladies"—you will say there is another, a serious education, supplied in high-schools—even classical ones—in midwifery, and in medical and university courses. That

is not true. All female education of whatever kind has in view only the capture of men. Some girls captivate men by music and curls; others by learning and by political services. But the aim is always the same and cannot be other, because there is no other than that of charming a man so as to capture him. Can you imagine courses for women, and scholarship for women, without men: that is to say, that they should be educated but that men should not know about it? I cannot! No bringing up, no education, can alter this as long as woman's highest ideal remains marriage, and not virginity and freedom from sensuality. Till then she will be a slave. You know one need only think—forgetting how customary they are —of the conditions in which our young ladies are brought up, and we shall be surprised not at the vice which rules among the women of our propertied classes, but on the contrary that there is so little vice. Only think of the finery from early childhood, the adorning of herself, the cleanliness, the grace, the music, the reading of verses and novels, the songs and theatres and concerts for external and internal application, that is those they hear and those in which they perform. And with it all their complete physical idleness and the food they eat, with so much sweetness and so much fat in it. You see, it is only because it is all wrapped up and concealed that we do not know what those unfortunate girls suffer from the excitation of their sensuality: nine out of ten suffer and are unendurably tormented at the period of adolescence and later, if they do not get married by twenty. You know it is only that we do not want to see it, but anyone who has eyes sees that the majority of these unfortunates are so excited by this concealed sensuality (it is well if it is concealed) that they can do nothing, they only begin to live in the presence of a man. Their whole life is passed in preparations for coquetry and in coquetting. In the presence of men they overflow with life and become animated with sensual energy, but as soon as the man goes away their energy all droops and they cease to live. And this is not with some particular man but with any man, if only he is not quite repulsive. You will say, that is exceptional. No, this is the rule. Only it shows itself more strongly in some girls and less in others; none of them however lives a full life of her own, but only in dependence on man. When he is absent they are all alike and cannot help being alike, because for them all to attract to themselves as many men as possible is the highest ideal both of their girlhood and of their married life. And from this arises a feeling stronger than that one which I will not call their feminine vanity—the animal need of every female animal to attract to herself as many males as possible in order to have a chance of choosing. So it is in their girlhood and so it continues to be after marriage.

[46] *Insert*: You must understand that in our world an opinion exists, shared by everyone, that woman is there to afford man enjoyment (and vice versa probably, but I don't know about that, I know my own part).

[47] *Add*: from Pushkin's lines about "little feet".

[48] *Read*: 'The emancipation of woman lies not in universities and law-courts but in the bedroom. Yes, and the struggle against prostitution lies not in the brothels but in the families.'

The arrangement of this chapter differs in the two versions, and the following passage occurs in the lithographed but is omitted in the printed version:

'But why so?' I asked.

'That is what is surprising—that no one wishes to know what is so clear and evident, and what the doctors ought to know and to preach, but about which they are silent. Man desires the law of nature—children; but the coming of children presents an obstacle to continuous enjoyment, and people who only desire continuous enjoyment have to devise means to evade that obstacle. And they have devised three such means. One is, by the receipt the rascals give, to cripple the woman by making her barren—which has always been, and must be, a misfortune for a woman—then man can quietly and constantly enjoy himself; the second way is polygamy, not honourable polygamy as among the Mohammedans but our base European polygamy, replete with falsehood and hypocrisy; and there is the third evasion—which is not even an evasion, but a simple, coarse, direct infringement of the laws of nature, and which is committed by all the husbands among the peasants and by most husbands in our so-called honourable families. I too lived in that way. We have not even reached the level of Europe, of Paris, of the *Zwei Kinder System*, or of the Mohammedans, and we have devised nothing of our own because we have not thought at all about the matter. We feel that there is something nasty in the one plan and in the other, and we wish to have families, but our barbarous view of woman remains the same and the result is yet worse. A woman with us must at one and the same time be pregnant and be her husband's mistress—must be a nursing mother and his mistress. But her strength cannot stand it.'

49 *The lithographed version of Chapter XV begins with a long section on jealousy, omitted in the printed version:*

'Yes, jealousy is one of the secrets of marriage that are known to all and hidden from everybody. Besides the general reason for married couples' hatred of one another—which is their co-operation in defiling a human being—mutual jealousy is continually gnawing at them. But by mutual agreement it is generally decided to conceal this from everyone, and it is so concealed. Knowing that this is so, each assumes that it is an unhappy peculiarity of his own and not the common lot. So it was with me. So it must be. Jealousy must exist between married couples who live immorally with one another. If they are both unable to sacrifice their own pleasure for the welfare of their child, each rightly concludes that the other will certainly not sacrifice pleasure—I will not say for welfare or tranquillity (for one may sin so as not to be found out), but—merely for conscience' sake. Each knows that no strong moral obstacle to unfaithfulness exists in the other. They know this because they infringe the demands of morality with one another, and therefore they distrust and watch each other. Oh, what an awful feeling jealousy is! I am not speaking of that real jealousy which at any rate has some basis. That real jealousy is tormenting but it has, and promises, a result; but I am speaking of the unconscious jealousy which inevitably accompanies every immoral marriage, and which, having no definite cause, has also no end. The other is an abscess on a tooth, but this is a tooth aching with its bone—unchanging pain day and night, and again day and night, and unendingly. This jealousy is dreadful, really dreadful! It is like this: a young man is pleasantly talking to my wife and looking at her, as it seems to me, examining her body. How dare he think about her, or dream of a romance with her! But she not merely tolerates it, she is apparently quite pleased. I even see that she is behaving in the same way to him as he is doing to her. And in my soul there arises such a hatred of her that every word of hers and every gesture becomes repulsive. She notices this, and does not know what she is to do, and she puts on an air of animated indifference. "Ah! I suffer and she finds it amusing, she is well satisfied!" And the hatred increases tenfold but I dare not give it vent, for in the depth of my soul I know that there is no real ground for it. And I sit, pretending to be indifferent, and put on an air of special regard and politeness towards him. Then I become angry with myself and wish to get out of the room and leave them alone, and I really go out. But as soon as I am out I am seized with horror at what is going on in my absence. I go back—inventing some excuse for doing so; or sometimes I do not re-enter the room but stop at the door and listen. How can she humiliate herself and me, putting me—me—in such a mean position of suspicion and eaves-dropping! What meanness! Oh, the nasty beast! And he, he! What about him? He is what all men are, what I was when a bachelor. For him it is a pleasure. He even smiles when he looks at me as though saying: "What can you say about it? It is my turn now!" Oh, that feeling is terrible! The sting of that feeling is terrible: I had only to let loose that feeling on anyone if but once—it was enough if once I suspected a man of having designs on my wife—and that man was for ever spoilt for me, as if vitriol had been poured over him. It was enough for me to be jealous of a man once and I could never afterwards renew simple human relations with him. For ever after that, our eyes flashed when we looked at one another. As for my wife, whom I deluged with quantities of this vitriol of jealous hatred, I entirely disfigured her. During this period of unfounded hatred, I quite dethroned and shamed her in my imagination. I imagined the most impossible tricks on her part. I suspected her, I am ashamed to say, of behaving like the queen in the *Arabian Nights*: being unfaithful to me with a slave almost before my very eyes, and then laughing at me. So that with each fresh access of jealousy (I am still speaking of groundless jealousy) I fell into an already prepared rut of filthy suspicions about her and I made the rut deeper and deeper. She did the same. If I had reasons for jealousy, she, knowing my past, had a thousand times more. And she was even more jealous of me. And the sufferings I experienced from her jealousy were quite different and were also very severe. They occurred like this: we are living more or less quietly; I am even merry and tranquil, when we happen to begin a most ordinary conversation and all at once she does not agree with things she had always agreed with. More than that, I notice that she is becoming irritable without a cause. I think she is upset or that what we are saying is really unpleasant to her. But we turn to something else and the same thing happens, she again attacks me and is again irritable. I am astonished and seek the cause of this. What is it all about? She becomes silent, replies in monosyllables, or when she speaks is evidently hinting at something. I begin to guess that the reason of it is that I have taken a walk in the garden with her cousin, with whom I never even thought of anything wrong, or there is some cause of that kind. I begin to guess at it but cannot mention it. Were I to do so I should confirm her suspicions. I begin to investigate and to interrogate her. She does not reply but guesses that I have understood what it is, and she feels still more strongly confirmed in her suspicions. "What is the matter with you?" I ask. "Nothing, I am the same as usual," she says; but like a lunatic she utters meaningless, inexplicable, and bitter words. Sometimes I endure it, but sometimes I burst out and become irritable myself, and then a flood of abuse pours forth and I am convicted of some imaginary offence. And all this is carried to an extreme with sobs and tears, and she rushes out of the house to most unusual places. I begin to search for her.

I am uneasy as to what the servants and children will think but there is nothing for it. She is in such a state that I feel she may do anything. I run after her and look for her. I spend tormenting nights. And finally, with exhausted nerves, after most cruel words and accusations, we both become tranquillized again.'

[50] *The lithographed version varies here considerably from the printed version, though in some passages the one repeats the other. The lithograph runs as follows:*

That is why they do not wish to suckle them: "If I suckle him," they say, "I shall love him too much—and what shall I do then if he dies?" It seems that they would prefer it if their children were gutta-percha, so that they could not be ill or die but could always be mended. Think what a muddle goes on in the heads and hearts of these unfortunate women. That is why they do nasty things to prevent births: so as not to love! Love—the most joyful condition of the soul—seems to them a danger. And why is this so? Because when a man or woman does not live as a human being should, he or she is much worse than a beast. You see, our women are unable to regard a child otherwise than as a pleasure. It is true that the birth is painful, but its little hands. . . . Ah, its little feet! Ah, it smiles! Ah, what a darling little body it has! Ah, and it smacks its lips and hiccups! In a word, the animal maternal instinct is sensual. There is in it no thought at all of the mysterious meaning of the arrival of a new human being who will replace us. There is nothing of what is said and done in baptism. You know, nobody believes in baptism, and yet that was really a reminder of the human importance of the baby. People have given that up, they do not believe in it, but they have not replaced it in any way, and only the ribbons and lace and little hands and feet have remained. The animal part has remained. But the thing is that an animal does not possess imagination or foresight or reflections or doctors—yes—again those doctors! Take a hen or a cow: when a chicken gets the pip or a calf dies she cackles a bit or lows a little, and goes on living as before. When among us a child falls ill—what happens? How is it to be treated? Where is it to be nursed? What doctor must we call in?

Where is one to drive to? And if it should die—where will the little hands and little feet be then? Why has it all happened so? Why do we have this suffering? A cow does not ask this, and this is why our children are a torment. A cow has no imagination, and therefore cannot think of how she might have saved her offspring by doing so-and-so and so-and-so; and therefore her grief, mingling with her physical condition and continuing for a certain limited time, is not a condition of grief which is augmented by physical idleness and satiation till it becomes despair. She has not a reason which asks, "Why has this happened? Why were all these sufferings endured, why did I love the babies—if they had to die?" The cow has no reason which could say that in future it will be better not to bear offspring or if that happens accidentally then not to suckle it and in general not to love it, or things will be worse for her. But that is how our women reason. And it shows that when a human being does not live humanly, it is worse for him or her than for a beast.'

'Then what, in your opinion, is the human way in which one should treat children?' I asked.

'How? Love them humanly.'

'Well, don't mothers love their children?'

'Not like human beings, they hardly ever do that, and therefore they do not even love them in dog-fashion. Just notice: a hen, a goose, a she-wolf, are always unattainable models of animal love for our women. Few women would at the risk of their lives rush at an elephant to take their baby from him, but no hen, and no she-crow even, would fail to fly at a dog; and each of them would sacrifice itself for its children, while few women would do so. Notice that a human mother can refrain from physical love of her children while an animal cannot do so. Well, is that because a woman is inferior to an animal? No, but because she is superior (though "superior" is incorrect; she is not "superior", but is a different creature). She has other obligations—human ones; she can refrain from animal love and can transfer her love to the child's soul. That is becoming to a human mother, and that is what never is done in our society.

We read of the heroism of mothers who sacrifice their children for the sake of something higher, and it seems to us that these cases are merely stories of ancient times, which have no relation to us. But yet I think that if a mother has nothing for the sake of which she can sacrifice her animal feelings for her child, and if she transfers the spiritual force, which has been left unapplied, to attempting the impossible—the physical preservation of her child—in which attempt the doctors will assist her, it will be much worse for her, and she will suffer, as she actually does suffer! So it was with my wife. Whether there was one child or five—it was always the same. It was even a little better when we had five of them. Our whole life was continually poisoned by fear on the children's account—fear of their real or imaginary illnesses—and even by their very presence. I at any rate, during my whole married life, always felt that my life and all my interests continually hung by a hair, and depended on the children's health and condition and lessons. Children are of course an important matter, but then we all have to live! In our times the grown-ups are not allowed to live. They have no proper life: the life of the whole family hangs every second by a hair; and family life, life for the married couple, is lacking. No matter what important affair you may have, if you suddenly hear that Vásya has vomited, or Lisa's motion shows signs of blood, everything has instantly to be left, forgotten, thrown away. Everything else is insignificant. . . . The only important things are the doctors, the enemas, the temperatures: not to mention the fact that you can never begin a conversation without it happening at the most interesting part that Pétya runs in with a troubled face to ask whether he is to eat an apple or which jacket he is to put on, or without the nurse bringing in a shrieking baby. There is no regular firm family life. How you are to live, where to live, and therefore what your occupation is to be, all depends on the children's health; while their health does not depend on anyone, but, thanks to the doctors who say that they can preserve their health, your whole life may be disturbed at any moment. There is no life; it is a constant peril.'

[51] *Add*: But besides this, the children were for her also a means of forgetting herself—an intoxication. I often noticed that when she was upset about anything she felt better if one of the children fell ill and she could revert to that state of intoxication. But it was an involuntary intoxication; there was nothing evil about it.

[52] *Add*: Of course the doctors confirmed all this with an air of importance and encouraged her in the belief. She would have been glad not to be afraid, but the doctor dropped a word or two about "blood-poisoning", "scarlatina", or (God forbid) "dysentery"—and it was all up! Nor could it be otherwise. You see, if among us women had, as in olden times, a belief that "The Lord gave, and the Lord hath taken away", that a young child's angel-soul goes to God and it is better for him—the dead child—to die in innocence than to die later on in sin, and so forth, which is what people did believe, you know—if they had any faith of that sort, they could bear the children's illnesses more quietly; but now there is nothing of that sort left—not a trace of it. There is no belief of that kind. But one must have faith in something, and they have faith—a senseless faith—in medicine—and not even in medicine but in doctors. One woman in I. I., and another in P. P.; and like religious believers they do not see the absurdity of their faith but believe *quia absurdum*. You know, if they did not believe irrationally, they would see the absurdity of what those brigands prescribe—the whole of it. Scarlatina is an infectious disease; on account of it, in a large town, half the family has to move into an hotel (they twice made us move in that way). But, you see, everyone in a town is a centre of innumerable diameters which carry the threads of all kinds of infection, and there is no possibility of avoiding them: the baker, the tailor, the laundress, and the cabman. So that for everyone who moves out of his own house to another place to escape an infection he knows of, I will undertake to find, in that other place, another infection—if not the very same infection—as near at hand. But that is not enough. We all know of rich people who after diphtheria have had everything in their house destroyed, and in that house when freshly done up, have

themselves fallen ill; and we all know of dozens of people who have remained with the sick ones and have not been infected. And so it is with everything; one only need keep one's ears open. One woman tells another that her doctor is a good one. The other replies: "What are you saying? Why, he killed so-and-so." And vice versa. Well, bring a country doctor to a lady and she won't trust him; but bring another doctor in a carriage, who knows precisely as much and who treats his patients on the basis of the same books and the same experiments, and tell her that he must be paid £10 for each visit, and she will believe in him. The root of the matter is that our women are savages. They have no faith in God, and so some of them believe in an evil eye cast by wicked people and others in Doctor I. P. because he charges high fees. If they had faith they would know that scarlatina and so forth is not at all so terrible, for it cannot injure what one can and should love—namely, the soul, and that sickness and death which none of us can avoid may occur. But as there is no faith in God they only love physically and all their energy is directed towards preserving life, which cannot be done, and which only the doctors assure fools, and especially she-fools, that they can save. And so they have to be called in. Therefore having children, far from improving our relations to one another, did not unite us but on the contrary divided us.

53 *In the lithographed version the chapter continues*: At first we lived in the country, and later on in town. What I chiefly felt was that I was a man, and that a man, as I understood it, ought to be master, but that I had fallen under my wife's slipper, as the saying is, and could not manage to escape from under it. What chiefly kept me under her slipper was the children. I wished to get up and assert my authority, but it never came off. She had the children and, supporting herself on them, she ruled. I did not then understand that she was sure to rule, chiefly because when she married she was morally immeasurably superior to me as all maidens always are to man, because they are immeasurably purer than he. Notice this surprising fact, that a woman, an average woman of our circle, is usually a very poor creature, lack-

ing moral bases, an egotist, a chatterbox, and wrong-headed, but a maiden, an ordinary maiden, a girl up to twenty years of age, is for the most part a charming creature ready for everything noble and good. Why is that so? Clearly it is because the husbands pervert their wives and bring them morally down to their own lower level. In fact if boys and girls are born equal the advantage on the girls' side is still enormous. In the first place a girl is not exposed to those vicious conditions to which we are exposed; she has not the smoking, the wine, the cards, the schools, the comrades, or the state-service we have, and secondly and chiefly she is physically virgin. And so a maiden when she marries is always superior to her husband. She is superior to him while she is a maiden, and when she becomes a married woman, in our circle where the men are under no direct compulsion to earn their own maintenance, she usually becomes superior to him also by the greater importance of her occupation when she begins to bear children and to feed them. A woman when bearing and nursing, clearly sees that her occupation is more important than the man's—who sits on the County Council,* in Courts of Justice, or in the Senate. She knows that in all such affairs the one important thing is to get money. But money can be got in various other ways, and therefore the getting of it is not so indubitably necessary as the feeding of a child. So that the woman is certainly superior to the man and ought to rule him. But a man of our circle not only does not acknowledge this, but on the contrary always looks down on woman from the height of his grandeur, and despises her activity. So my wife despised me and my County activities, on the ground that she bore and nursed children. While I, supported by the established masculine view, considered that a woman's fussing: "swaddlings, teats, and teething," as I jokingly called it, is a most contemptible activity which one may and should jest about. "The women know how to attend to that." So besides all other causes we were also separated by mutual contempt.

54 *Instead of the next nine lines, read:* To people who were

* The *Zémskoe Sobránie*, work in the administration of which was paid for.—A. M.

quite strangers to us she and I spoke of various subjects, but not with one another. Sometimes hearing how she spoke to other people in my presence, I said to myself: "What lies she is telling!" And I was surprised that the person she was speaking to did not see that she was pretending.

[55] *Add*: The periods of what we called love occurred as often as before, but were barer, coarser, and lacked any cover. But they did not last long and were immediately followed by periods of quite causeless anger springing up on most unintelligible grounds.

[56] *Add*: All these were occupations that were not directly necessary, but she always behaved as if her life and that of the children depended on the pies with the soup not being burnt, on the curtain being hung up, the dress finished, the lesson learnt, and some medicine or other taken. It was clear to me that all this was for her mainly a means of forgetting herself, an intoxication, such as was for me the intoxication of my service, shooting, or cards. It is true that besides these I also had intoxication in its direct meaning—drunkenness: with tobacco, of which I smoked an enormous quantity, and alcohol with which I did not actually get drunk, but of which I took some vodka before meals and a couple of tumblers of wine during meals, so that a continual fog screened from us the discord of our life.

[57] *Add*: All this mental illness of ours occurred simply because we lived immorally. We suffered from our immoral life, and to smother our suffering we committed various abnormal acts—just what those doctors call "indications of mental disease"—hysterics. The cure for these illnesses does not lie with Charcot, nor with them. It cannot be cured by any suggestions or bromides, but it is necessary to recognize what the pain comes from. It is like sitting down on a nail: if you notice the nail, or see what is wrong in your life and cease to do it, the pain will cease and there will be nothing to smother. The wrongness of our life caused the pain, caused my torments of jealousy and my need of going out shooting, of cards, and above all of wine and tobacco to keep myself in a constant state of intoxication. From that wrongness of life arose also her

passionate relation to all her occupations, her instability of mood—now gloomy, now terribly gay,—and her volubility—it all came from the constant need of diverting her attention from herself and her life. It was a constant intoxication with this or that work, which always had to be done in a hurry.

58 *Add*: Unhappy people can get on better in town.

59 *Instead of the following line, read*: Divorce, well then divorce!" My sister-in-law would not admit that idea.

60 *Read*: but I have bound myself by my own words.

61 *Read*: disliked him and understood that he was a dirty adulterer, and I began to be jealous of him even before he saw my wife.

62 *Read*: why, in the important events of our life, in those which decide a man's fate—as mine was decided then—why, there is no distinction between past and future.

63 *Instead of the following three lines, read*: I had a consciousness of some terrible calamity connected with that man. But for all that I could not help being affable with him.

64 *Read*: He played excellently, with a strong and tender tone; difficulties did not exist for him. As soon as he began to play his face altered, became serious and far more sympathetic; he was of course a much better player than my wife and helped her simply and naturally.

65 *Read*: . . . simple and pleasant. During the whole evening I seemed not only to the others, but to myself, to be solely interested in the music, while in reality I was unceasingly tormented by jealousy. From the first moment that his eyes met my wife's I saw that he looked at her as at a woman who was not unpleasant and with whom on occasion it would not be unpleasant to have a liaison. Had I been pure I should not have thought about what he might think of her, but like most men I also thought about women, and therefore understood him and was tormented by it.

66 *Read*: his restrained voice and her refusal. She seemed to say "but no", and something more. It was as if someone was intentionally smothering the words. My God, what then arose in me! What I imagined!

[67] *Add*: She will disgrace me! I will go away—but I can't.

[68] *Add*: and advised me to see it out.

[69] *Add*: A husband ought not to think so, and still less should he shove his nose in and hinder things.

[70] *Read*: graceful, indolent, subtle figure,

[71] *Add*: or something of that kind about my character.

[72] *Instead of the next six lines, read*: and I turned her round and gave her a violent push. "What is the matter with you? Recollect yourself!" said she.

[73] *Add*: rolling my eyes.

[74] *Read*: I restrained myself and

[75] *Add*: We sent for the doctor. and I attended her all night.

[76] *Add*: . . . not so much on account of my wife's assurances, as on account of the tormenting suffering I had experienced from my jealousy.

[77] *Add*: He went to fetch his violin. My wife went to the piano and began selecting the music.

[78] *Add*: and long remained silent.

[79] *Add*: In this new condition jealousy had no place.

[80] *Add*: That music drew me into some world in which jealousy no longer had place. Jealousy and the feeling that evoked it seemed trifles not worth considering.

[81] *Instead of the next eleven lines, read*: I hardly felt jealous all the evening. I had to go to the Meetings in two days' time, and he, when leaving, collected all his music and inquired when I should be back, as he wished to say good-bye before his own departure. . . . It appeared that I should hardly be back before he left Moscow, so we bade one another a definite good-bye.

[82] *Add*: We spoke in very general terms of the impressions produced by the music, but we were nearer and more friendly to one another that evening, in a way we had seldom been of late.

[83] *Read*: while it was still dark,

[84] *Add*: and as if I should drive on like tnat to the end of my life and of the world.

[85] *Add*: which was quite a new one,

[86] *Add*: one more cynical than another,

[87] *Add*: forgetting that there was no ground for this.

88 *Instead of the next line, read*: I cried out, and began to groan.

89 *Add*: And the same thing began again within me. I suffered as I never had suffered before. I did not know what to do with myself, and the thought occurred to me —and it pleased me very much—of getting out onto the line, lying down under the train, and finishing everything. The one thing that hindered my doing this was my self-pity, which immediately evoked hatred of her and of him. Of him not so much. Regarding him I had a strange feeling of my own humiliation and of his victory, but of her I felt terrible hatred. It will not do to finish myself off and to leave her, it is necessary that she should suffer.

90 *Instead of the following words, read*: and read the shop sign-boards,

91 *Instead of the next sentence, read*: I cannot at all explain to myself now why I was in such a hurry.

92 *Read*: there arose in me an animal craving for physical, agile, cunning, and decisive action.

93 *Read*: and of the tormenting pleasure of punishing, and executing.

94 *In the lithograph the chapter ends with the words*: I do not know how I went, with what steps, whether I ran or only walked, through which rooms I went on my way to the drawing-room, how I opened the door or how I entered the room—I remember nothing of all that.

95 *In the lithograph this first sentence is omitted.*

96 *Add*: as from a spring.

97 *Add*: —a sister.

98 *Read*: ' "Yes, if you had not killed me!" she suddenly exclaimed, and her eyes glittered feverishly.

99 *The sentence ends*: the children, not even Lisa who rushed up to her.

100 *In the lithograph the conclusion is different, the last paragraph being as follows*: Yes, that is what I have done, and what I have gone through. Yes, a man should understand that the real meaning of the words in the Gospel—Matthew v. 28—where it says that everyone that looketh on a woman to lust after her commits adultery, relates to woman, his fellow human being—not merely to casual women or strangers, but above all to his own wife.

THE DEVIL

THE DEVIL

But I say unto you, that every one that looketh on a woman to lust after her hath committed adultery with her already in his heart.

And if thy right eye causeth thee to stumble, pluck it out, and cast it from thee: for it is profitable for thee that one of thy members should perish, and not thy whole body be cast into hell.

And if thy right hand causeth thee to stumble, cut it off, and cast it from thee: for it is profitable for thee that one of thy members should perish, and not thy whole body go into hell. Matthew v. 28, 29, 30.

I

A BRILLIANT career lay before Eugène Irténev. He had everything necessary to attain it: an admirable education at home, high honours when he graduated in law at Petersburg University, and connexions in the highest society through his recently deceased father; he had also already begun service in one of the Ministries under the protection of the Minister. Moreover he had a fortune; even a large one, though insecure. His father had lived abroad and in Petersburg, allowing his sons, Eugène and Andrew (who was older than Eugène and in the Horse Guards), six thousand rubles a year each, while he himself and his wife spent a great deal. He only used to visit his estate for a couple of months in summer and did not concern himself with its direction, entrusting it all to an unscrupulous manager who also failed to attend to it, but in whom he had complete confidence.

After the father's death, when the brothers began to divide the property, so many debts were discovered that their lawyer even advised them to refuse the inheritance and retain only an estate left them by their grandmother, which was valued at a hundred thousand rubles. But a neighbouring landed-proprietor who had done business with old

Irténev, that is to say, who had promissory notes from him and had come to Petersburg on that account, said that in spite of the debts they could straighten out affairs so as to retain a large fortune (it would only be necessary to sell the forest and some outlying land, retaining the rich Semënov estate with four thousand desyatins of black earth, the sugar factory, and two hundred desyatins of water-meadows) if one devoted oneself to the management of the estate, settled there, and farmed it wisely and economically.

And so, having visited the estate in spring (his father had died in Lent), Eugène looked into everything, resolved to retire from the Civil Service, settle in the country with his mother, and undertake the management with the object of preserving the main estate. He arranged with his brother, with whom he was very friendly, that he would pay him either four thousand rubles a year, or a lump sum of eighty thousand, for which Andrew would hand over to him his share of the inheritance.

So he arranged matters and, having settled down with his mother in the big house, began managing the estate eagerly, yet cautiously.

It is generally supposed that Conservatives are usually old people, and that those in favour of change are the young. That is not quite correct. Usually Conservatives are young people: those who want to live but who do not think about how to live, and have not time to think, and therefore take as a model for themselves a way of life that they have seen.

Thus it was with Eugène. Having settled in the village, his aim and ideal was to restore the form of life that had existed, not in his father's time—his father had been a bad manager—but in his grandfather's. And now he tried to resurrect the general spirit of his grandfather's life—in the house, the garden, and in the estate management—of course with changes suited to the times—everything on a large scale—good order, method, and everybody satisfied. But to do this entailed much work. It was necessary to meet the demands of the creditors and the banks, and for that purpose to sell some land and arrange renewals of credit. It was also necessary to get money to carry on (partly by farming out land, and partly by hiring labour) the immense operations on the Semënov estate, with its four hundred desyatins of ploughland and its sugar factory, and to deal with the garden so that it should not seem to be neglected or in decay.

There was much work to do, but Eugène had plenty of strength—physical and mental. He was twenty-six, of medium height, strongly built, with muscles developed by gymnastics. He was full-blooded and his whole neck was very red, his teeth and lips were bright, and his hair soft and curly though not thick. His only physical defect was short-sightedness, which he had himself developed by using spectacles, so that he could not now do without a pince-nez, which had already formed a line on the bridge of his nose.

Such he was physically. For his spiritual portrait it might be said that the better people knew him the better they liked him. His mother had always loved him more than anyone else, and now after her husband's death she concentrated on him not only her whole affection but her whole life. Nor was it only his mother who so loved him. All his comrades at the high school and the university not merely liked him very much, but respected him. He had this effect on all who met him. It was impossible not to believe what he said, impossible to suspect any deception or falseness in one who had such an open, honest face and in particular such eyes.

In general his personality helped him much in his affairs. A creditor who would have refused another trusted him. The clerk, the village Elder, or a peasant, who would have played a dirty trick and cheated someone else, forgot to deceive under the pleasant impression of intercourse with this kindly, agreeable, and above all candid man.

It was the end of May. Eugène had somehow managed in town to get the vacant land freed from the mortgage, so as to sell it to a merchant, and had borrowed money from that same merchant to replenish his stock, that is to say, to procure horses, bulls, and carts, and in particular to begin to build a necessary farm-house. The matter had been arranged. The timber was being carted, the carpenters were already at work, and manure for the estate was being brought on eighty carts, but everything still hung by a thread.

II

Amid these cares something came about which though unimportant tormented Eugène at the time. As a young man he had lived as all healthy young men live, that is, he had had relations with women of various kinds. He was not a libertine but neither, as he himself said, was he a monk. He only turned to this, however, in so far as was necessary for physical health and to have his mind free, as he used to say. This had begun when he was sixteen and had gone on satisfactorily—in the sense that he had never given himself up to debauchery, never once been infatuated, and had never contracted a disease. At first he had had a seamstress in Petersburg, then she got spoilt and he made other arrangements, and that side of his affairs was so well secured that it did not trouble him.

But now he was living in the country for the second month and did not at all know what he was to do. Compulsory self-restraint was beginning to have a bad effect on him.

Must he really go to town for that purpose? And where to? How? That was the only thing that disturbed him; but as he was convinced that the thing was necessary and that he needed it, it really became a necessity, and he felt that he was not free and that his eyes involuntarily followed every young woman.

He did not approve of having relations with a married woman or a maid in his own village. He knew by report that both his father and grandfather had been quite different in this matter from other landowners of that time. At home they had never had any entanglements with peasant-women, and he had decided that he would not do so either; but afterwards, feeling himself ever more and more under compulsion and imagining with horror what might happen to him in the neighbouring country town, and reflecting on the fact that the days of serfdom were now over, he decided that it might be done on the spot. Only it must be done so that no one should know of it, and not for the sake of debauchery but merely for health's sake—as he said to himself. And when he had decided this he became still more restless. When talking to the village Elder, the peasants, or the carpenters, he involuntarily brought the conversation round to women, and when it turned to women he kept it on that theme. He noticed the women more and more.

III

To settle the matter in his own mind was one thing but to carry it out was another. To approach a woman himself was impossible. Which one? Where? It must be done through someone else, but to whom should he speak about it?

He happened to go into a watchman's hut in the forest to get a drink of water. The watchman had been his father's huntsman, and Eugène Ivánich chatted with him, and the man began telling some strange tales of hunting sprees. It occurred to Eugène Ivánich that it would be convenient to arrange matters in this hut, or in the wood, only he did not know how to manage it and whether old Daniel would undertake the arrangement. 'Perhaps he will be horrified at such a proposal and I shall have disgraced myself, but perhaps he will agree to it quite simply.' So he thought while listening to Daniel's stories. Daniel was telling how once when they had been stopping at the hut of the sexton's wife in an outlying field, he had brought a woman for Fëdor Zakhárich Pryánishnikov.

'It will be all right,' thought Eugène.

'Your father, may the kingdom of heaven be his, did not go in for nonsense of that kind.'

'It won't do,' thought Eugène. But to test the matter he said: 'How was it you engaged on such bad things?'

'But what was there bad in it? She was glad, and Fëdor Zakhárich was satisfied, very satisfied. I got a ruble. Why, what was he to do? He too is a lively limb apparently, and drinks wine.'

'Yes, I may speak,' thought Eugène, and at once proceeded to do so.

'And do you know, Daniel, I don't know how to endure it,'—he felt himself going scarlet.

Daniel smiled.

'I am not a monk—I have been accustomed to it.'

He felt that what he was saying was stupid, but was glad to see that Daniel approved.

'Why of course, you should have told me long ago. It can all be arranged,' said he: 'only tell me which one you want.'

'Oh, it is really all the same to me. Of course not an ugly one, and she must be healthy.'

'I understand!' said Daniel briefly. He reflected.

'Ah! There is a tasty morsel,' he began. Again Eugène went red. 'A tasty morsel. See here, she was married last autumn.' Daniel whispered,—'and he hasn't been able to do anything. Think what that is worth to one who wants it!'

Eugène even frowned with shame.

'No, no,' he said. 'I don't want that at all. I want, on the contrary (what could the contrary be?), on the contrary I only want that she should be healthy and that there should be as little fuss as possible—a woman whose husband is away in the army or something of that kind.'

'I know. It's Stepanída I must bring you. Her husband is away in town, just the same as a soldier. And she is a fine woman, and clean. You will be satisfied. As it is I was saying to her the other day—you should go, but she . . .'

'Well then, when is it to be?'

'To-morrow if you like. I shall be going to get some tobacco and I will call in, and at the dinner-hour come here, or to the bath-house behind the kitchen garden. There will be nobody about. Besides after dinner everybody takes a nap.'

'All right then.'

A terrible excitement seized Eugène as he rode home. 'What will happen? What is a peasant woman like? Suppose it turns out that she is hideous, horrible? No, she is handsome,' he told himself, remembering some he had been noticing. 'But what shall I say? What shall I do?'

He was not himself all that day. Next day at

noon he went to the forester's hut. Daniel stood at the door and silently and significantly nodded towards the wood. The blood rushed to Eugène's heart, he was conscious of it and went to the kitchen-garden. No one was there. He went to the bath-house—there was no one about, he looked in, come out, and suddenly heard the crackling of a breaking twig. He looked round—and she was standing in the thicket beyond the little ravine. He rushed there across the ravine. There were nettles in it which he had not noticed. They stung him and, losing the pince-nez from his nose, he ran up the slope on the farther side. She stood there, in a white embroidered apron, a red-brown skirt, and a bright red kerchief, barefoot, fresh, firm, and handsome, and smiling shyly.

'There is a path leading round—you should have gone round,' she said. 'I came long ago, ever so long.'

He went up to her and, looking her over, touched her.

A quarter of an hour later they separated; he found his pince-nez, called in to see Daniel, and in reply to his question: 'Are you satisfied, master?' gave him a ruble and went home.

He was satisfied. Only at first had he felt ashamed, then it had passed off. And everything had gone well. The best thing was that he now felt at ease, tranquil and vigorous. As for her, he had not even seen her thoroughly. He remembered that she was clean, fresh, not bad-looking, and simple, without any pretence. 'Whose wife is she?' said he to himself. 'Péchnikov's, Daniel said. What Péchnikov is that? There are two households of that name. Probably she is old Michael's daughter-in-law. Yes, that must be it. His son does live in Moscow. I'll ask Daniel about it some time.'

From then onward that previously important drawback to country life—enforced self-restraint—was eliminated. Eugène's freedom of mind was no longer disturbed and he was able to attend freely to his affairs.

And the matter Eugène had undertaken was far from easy: before he had time to stop up one hole a new one would unexpectedly show itself, and it sometimes seemed to him that he would not be able to go through with it and that it would end in his having to sell the estate after all, which would mean that all his efforts would be wasted and that he had failed to accomplish what he had undertaken. That prospect disturbed him most of all.

All this time more and more debts of his father's unexpectedly came to light. It was evident that towards the end of his life he had borrowed right and left. At the time of the settlement in May, Eugène had thought he at last knew everything, but in the middle of the summer he suddenly received a letter from which it appeared that there was still a debt of twelve thousand rubles to the widow Esípova. There was no promissory note, but only an ordinary receipt which his lawyer told him could be disputed. But it did not enter Eugène's head to refuse to pay a debt of his father's merely because the document could be challenged. He only wanted to know for certain whether there had been such a debt.

'Mamma! Who is Kalériya Vladímirovna Esípova?' he asked his mother when they met as usual for dinner.

'Esípova? She was brought up by your grandfather. Why?'

Eugène told his mother about the letter.

'I wonder she is not ashamed to ask for it. Your father gave her so much!'

'But do we owe her this?'

'Well now, how shall I put it? It is not a debt. Papa, out of his unbounded kindness . . .'

'Yes, but did Papa consider it a debt?'

'I cannot say. I don't know. I only know it is hard enough for you without that.'

Eugène saw that Mary Pávlovna did not know what to say, and was as it were sounding him.

'I see from what you say that it must be paid,' said he. 'I will go to see her to-morrow and have a chat, and see if it cannot be deferred.'

'Ah, how sorry I am for you, but you know that will be best. Tell her she must wait,' said Mary Pávlovna, evidently tranquillized and proud of her son's decision.

Eugène's position was particularly hard because his mother, who was living with him, did not at all realize his position. She had been so accustomed all her life long to live extravagantly that she could not even imagine to herself the position her son was in, that is to say, that to-day or to-morrow matters might shape themselves so that they would have nothing left and he would have to sell everything and live and support his mother on what salary he could earn, which at the very most would be two thousand rubles. She did not understand that they could only save themselves from that position by cutting down expense in everything, and so she could not understand why Eugène was so careful about trifles, in expenditure on gardeners, coachmen, servants—even on food. Also, like most widows, she nourished feelings of devotion to the memory of her departed spouse quite different from those she had felt for him while he lived, and she did not admit the thought that anything the departed had done or arranged could be wrong or could be altered.

Eugène by great efforts managed to keep up the garden and the conservatory with two gardeners, and the stables with two coachmen. And Mary Pávlovna naïvely thought that she was sacrificing herself for her son and doing all a mother could do, by not complaining of the food which the old man-cook prepared, of the fact that the paths in the park were not all swept clean, and that instead of footmen they had only a boy.

So, too, concerning this new debt, in which Eugène saw an almost crushing blow to all his undertakings, Mary Pávlovna only saw an incident displaying Eugène's noble nature. Moreover she did not feel much anxiety about Eugène's position, because she was confident that he would make a brilliant marriage which would put everything right. And he could make a very brilliant marriage: she knew a dozen families who would be glad to give their daughters to him. And she wished to arrange the matter as soon as possible.

IV

Eugène himself dreamt of marriage, but not in the same way as his mother. The idea of using marriage as a means of putting his affairs in order was repulsive to him. He wished to marry honourably, for love. He observed the girls whom he met and those he knew, and compared himself with them, but no decision had yet been taken. Meanwhile, contrary to his expectations, his relations with Stepanída continued, and even acquired the character of a settled affair. Eugène was so far from debauchery, it was so hard for him secretly to do this thing which he felt to be bad, that he could not arrange these meetings himself and even after the first one hoped not to see Stepanída again; but it turned out that after some time the same restlessness (due he believed to that cause) again overcame him. And his restlessness this time was no longer impersonal, but suggested just those same bright, black eyes, and that deep voice, saying, 'ever so long,' that same scent of something fresh and strong, and that same full breast lifting the bib of her apron, and all this in that hazel and maple thicket, bathed in bright sunlight.

Though he felt ashamed he again approached Daniel. And again a rendezvous was fixed for midday in the wood. This time Eugène looked her over more carefully and everything about her seemed attractive. He tried talking to her and asked about her husband. He really was Michael's son and lived as a coachman in Moscow.

'Well, then, how is it you . . .' Eugène wanted to ask how it was she was untrue to him.

'What about "how is it"?' asked she. Evidently she was clever and quick-witted.

'Well, how is it you come to me?'

'There now,' said she merrily. 'I bet he goes on the spree there. Why shouldn't I?'

Evidently she was putting on an air of sauciness and assurance, and this seemed charming to Eugène. But all the same he did not himself fix a rendezvous with her. Even when she proposed that they should meet without the aid of Daniel, to whom she seemed not very well disposed, he did not consent. He hoped that this meeting would be the last. He liked her. He thought such intercourse was necessary for him and that there was nothing bad about it, but in the depth of his soul there was a stricter judge who did not approve of it and hoped that this would be the last time, or if he did not hope that, at any rate did not wish to participate in arrangements to repeat it another time.

So the whole summer passed, during which they met a dozen times and always by Daniel's help. It happened once that she could not be there because her husband had come home, and Daniel proposed another woman, but Eugène refused with disgust. Then the husband went away and the meetings continued as before, at first through Daniel, but afterwards he simply fixed the time and she came with another woman, Prókhorova—as it would not do for a peasant-woman to go about alone.

Once at the very time fixed for the rendezvous a family came to call on Mary Pávlovna, with the very girl she wished Eugène to marry, and it was impossible for Eugène to get away. As soon as he could do so, he went out as though to the thrashing-floor, and round by the path to their meeting-place in the wood. She was not there, but at the accustomed spot everything within reach had been broken—the black alder, the hazel-twigs, and even a young maple the thickness of a stake. She had waited, had become excited and angry, and had skittishly left him a remembrance. He waited and waited, and then went to Daniel to ask him to call her for to-morrow. She came and was just as usual.

So the summer passed. The meetings were always arranged in the wood, and only once, when it grew towards autumn, in the shed that stood in her backyard.

It did not enter Eugène's head that these relations of his had any importance for him. About her he did not even think. He gave her money and nothing more. At first he did not know and did not think that the affair was known and that she was envied throughout the village, or that her relations took money from her and encouraged her, and that her conception of any sin in the matter had been quite obliterated by the influence of the money and her family's approval. It seemed to her that if people envied her, then what she was doing was good.

'It is simply necessary for my health,' thought Eugène. 'I grant it is not right, and though no one says anything, everybody, or many people, know of it. The woman who comes with her knows. And once she knows she is sure to have told others. But what's to be done? I am acting badly,' thought Eugène, 'but what's one to do? Anyhow it is not for long.'

What chiefly disturbed Eugène was the thought of the husband. At first for some reason it seemed to him that the husband must be a poor sort, and this as it were partly justified his conduct. But he saw the husband and was struck by his appearance: he was a fine fellow and smartly dressed, in no way a worse man than himself, but surely better. At their next meeting he told her he had seen her husband and had been surprised to see that he was such a fine fellow.

'There's not another man like him in the village,' said she proudly.

This surprised Eugène, and the thought of the husband tormented him still more after that. He happened to be at Daniel's one day and Daniel, having begun chatting, said to him quite openly:

'And Michael asked me the other day: "Is it true that the master is living with my wife?" I said I did not know. Anyway, I said, better with the master than with a peasant.'

'Well, and what did he say?'

'He said: "Wait a bit. I'll get to know and I'll give it her all the same."'

'Yes, if the husband returned to live here I would give her up,' thought Eugène.

But the husband lived in town and for the present their intercourse continued.

'When necessary I will break it off, and there will be nothing left of it,' thought he.

And this seemed to him certain, especially as during the whole summer many different things occupied him very fully: the erection of the new farm-house, and the harvest, and building, and above all meeting the debts and selling the waste land. All these were affairs that completely absorbed him and on which he spent his thoughts when he lay down and when he got up. All that was real life. His intercourse—he did not even call it connexion—with Stepanída he paid no attention to. It is true that when the wish to see her arose it came with such strength that he could think of nothing else. But this did not last long. A meeting was arranged, and he again forgot her for a week or even for a month.

In autumn Eugène often rode to town, and there became friendly with the Ánnenskis. They had a daughter who had just finished the Institute.* And then, to Mary Pávlovna's great grief, it happened that Eugène 'cheapened himself,' as she expressed it, by falling in love with Liza Ánnenskaya and proposing to her.

From that time his relations with Stepanída ceased.

V

It is impossible to explain why Eugène chose Liza Ánnenskaya, as it is always impossible to explain why a man chooses this and not that woman. There were many reasons—positive and negative. One

* The Institute was a boarding-school for the daughters of the nobility and gentry, in which great attention was paid to the manners and accomplishments of the pupils.—A. M.

reason was that she was not a very rich heiress such as his mother sought for him, another that she was naïve and to be pitied in her relations with her mother, another that she was not a beauty who attracted general attention to herself, and yet she was not bad-looking. But the chief reason was that his acquaintance with her began at the time when he was ripe for marriage. He fell in love because he knew that he would marry.

Liza Ánnenskaya was at first merely pleasing to Eugène, but when he decided to make her his wife his feelings for her became much stronger. He felt that he was in love.

Liza was tall, slender, and long. Everything about her was long; her face, and her nose (not prominently but downwards), and her fingers, and her feet. The colour of her face was very delicate, creamy white and delicately pink; she had long, soft, and curly, light-brown hair, and beautiful eyes, clear, mild, and confiding. Those eyes especially struck Eugène, and when he thought of Liza he always saw those clear, mild, confiding eyes.

Such was she physically; he knew nothing of her spiritually, but only saw those eyes. And those eyes seemed to tell him all he needed to know. The meaning of their expression was this:

While still in the Institute, when she was fifteen, Liza used continually to fall in love with all the attractive men she met and was animated and happy only when she was in love. After leaving the Institute she continued to fall in love in just the same way with all the young men she met, and of course fell in love with Eugène as soon as she made his acquaintance. It was this being in love which gave her eyes that particular expression which so captivated Eugène. Already that winter she had been in love with two young men at one and the same time, and blushed and became excited not only when they entered the room but whenever their names were mentioned. But afterwards, when her mother hinted to her that Irténev seemed to have serious intentions, her love for him increased so that she became almost indifferent to the two previous attractions, and when Irténev began to come to their balls and parties and danced with her more than with others and evidently only wished to know whether she loved him, her love for him became painful. She dreamed of him in her sleep and seemed to see him when she was awake in a dark room, and everyone else vanished from her mind. But when he proposed and they were formally engaged, and when they had kissed one another and were a betrothed couple, then she had no thoughts but of him, no desire but to be with him, to love him, and to be loved by him. She was also proud of him and felt emotional about him and herself and her love, and quite melted and felt faint from love of him.

The more he got to know her the more he loved her. He had not at all expected to find such love, and it strengthened his own feeling still more.

VI

TOWARDS spring he went to his estate at Semënovskoe to have a look at it and to give directions about the management, and especially about the house which was being done up for his wedding.

Mary Pávlovna was dissatisfied with her son's choice, not only because the match was not as brilliant as it might have been, but also because she did not like Varvára Alexéevna, his future mother-in-law. Whether she was good-natured or not she did not know and could not decide, but that she was not well-bred, not *comme il faut*—'not a lady' as Mary Pávlovna said to herself—she saw from their first acquaintance, and this distressed her; distressed her because she was accustomed to value breeding and knew that Eugène was sensitive to it, and she foresaw that he would suffer much annoyance on this account. But she liked the girl. Liked her chiefly because Eugène did. One could not help loving her, and Mary Pávlovna was quite sincerely ready to do so.

Eugène found his mother contented and in good spirits. She was getting everything straight in the house and preparing to go away herself as soon as he brought his young wife. Eugène persuaded her to stay for the time being, and the future remained undecided.

In the evening after tea Mary Pávlovna played patience as usual. Eugène sat by, helping her. This was the hour of their most intimate talks. Having finished one game and while preparing to begin another, she looked up at him and, with a little hesitation, began thus:

'I wanted to tell you, Jénya—of course I do not know, but in general I wanted to suggest to you—that before your wedding it is absolutely necessary to have finished with all your bachelor affairs so that nothing may disturb either you or your wife. God forbid that it should. You understand me?'

And indeed Eugène at once understood that Mary Pávlovna was hinting at his relations with Stepanída which had ended in the previous autumn, and that she attributed much more importance to those relations than they deserved, as solitary women always do. Eugène blushed, not from shame so much as from vexation that good-natured Mary Pávlovna was bothering—out of affection no doubt, but still was bothering—about matters that were not her business and that she did not and could not understand. He answered that there was nothing that needed concealment, and that he had always conducted himself so that there should be nothing to hinder his marrying.

'Well, dear, that is excellent. Only, Jénya . . . don't be vexed with me,' said Mary Pávlovna, and broke off in confusion.

Eugène saw that she had not finished and had not said what she wanted to. And this was confirmed when a little later she began to tell him how, in his absence, she had been asked to stand godmother at . . . the Péchnikovs.

Eugène flushed again, not with vexation or shame this time, but with some strange consciousness of the importance of what was about to be told him—an involuntary consciousness quite at variance with his conclusions. And what he expected happened. Mary Pávlovna, as if merely by way of conversation, mentioned that this year only boys were being born—evidently a sign of a coming war. Both at the Vásins and the Péchnikovs the young wife had a first child—at each house a boy. Mary Pávlovna wanted to say this casually, but she herself felt ashamed when she saw the colour mount to her son's face and saw him nervously removing, tapping, and replacing his pince-nez and hurriedly lighting a cigarette. She became silent. He too was silent and could not think how to break that silence. So they both understood that they had understood one another.

'Yes, the chief thing is that there should be justice and no favouritism in the village—as under your grandfather.'

'Mamma,' said Eugène suddenly, 'I know why you are saying this. You have no need to be disturbed. My future family-life is so sacred to me that I should not infringe it in any case. And as to what occurred in my bachelor days, that is quite ended. I never formed any union and no one has any claims on me.'

'Well, I am glad,' said his mother. 'I know how noble your feelings are.'

Eugène accepted his mother's words as a tribute due to him, and did not reply.

Next day he drove to town thinking of his fiancée and of anything in the world except of Stepanída. But, as if purposely to remind him, on approaching the church he met people walking and driving back from it. He met old Matvéy with Simon, some lads and girls, and then two women, one elderly, the other, who seemed familiar, smartly dressed and wearing a bright-red kerchief. This woman was walking lightly and boldly, carrying a child in her arms. He came up to them, and the elder woman bowed, stopping in the old-fashioned way, but the young woman with the child only bent her head, and from under the kerchief gleamed familiar, merry, smiling eyes.

Yes, this was she, but all that was over and it was no use looking at her: 'and the child may be mine,' flashed through his mind. No, what nonsense! There was her husband, she used to see him. He did not even consider the matter further, so settled in his mind was it that it had been necessary for his health—he had paid her money and there was no more to be said; there was, there had been, and there could be, no question of any union between them. It was not that he stifled the voice of conscience, no—his conscience simply said nothing to him. And he thought no more about her after the conversation with his mother and this meeting. Nor did he meet her again.

Eugène was married in town the week after

Easter, and left at once with his young wife for his country estate. The house had been arranged as usual for a young couple. Mary Pávlovna wished to leave, but Eugène begged her to remain, and Liza still more strongly, and she only moved into a detached wing of the house.

And so a new life began for Eugène.

VII

The first year of his marriage was a hard one for Eugène. It was hard because affairs he had managed to put off during the time of his courtship now, after his marriage, all came upon him at once.

To escape from debts was impossible. An outlying part of the estate was sold and the most pressing obligations met, but others remained, and he had no money. The estate yielded a good revenue, but he had had to send payments to his brother and to spend on his own marriage, so that there was no ready money and the factory could not carry on and would have to be closed down. The only way of escape was to use his wife's money; and Liza, having realized her husband's position, insisted on this herself. Eugène agreed, but only on condition that he should give her a mortgage on half his estate, which he did. Of course this was done not for his wife's sake, who felt offended at it, but to appease his mother-in-law.

These affairs with various fluctuations of success and failure helped to poison Eugène's life that first year. Another thing was his wife's ill-health. That same first year in autumn, seven months after their marriage, a misfortune befell Liza. She was driving out to meet her husband on his return from town, and the quiet horse became rather playful and she was frightened and jumped out. Her jump was comparatively fortunate—she might have been caught by the wheel—but she was pregnant, and that same night the pains began and she had a miscarriage from which she was long in recovering. The loss of the expected child and his wife's illness, together with the disorder in his affairs, and above all the presence of his mother-in-law, who arrived as soon as Liza fell ill—all this together made the year still harder for Eugène.

But notwithstanding these difficult circumstances, towards the end of the first year Eugène felt very well. First of all his cherished hope of restoring his fallen fortune and renewing his grandfather's way of life in a new form, was approaching accomplishment, though slowly and with difficulty. There was no longer any question of having to sell the whole estate to meet the debts. The chief estate, though transferred to his wife's name, was saved, and if only the beet crop succeeded and the price kept up, by next year his position of want and stress might be replaced by one of complete prosperity. That was one thing.

Another was that however much he had expected from his wife, he had never expected to find in her what he actually found. He found not what he had expected, but something much better. Raptures of love—though he tried to produce them—did not take place or were very slight, but he discovered something quite different, namely, that he was not merely more cheerful and happier but that it had become easier to live. He did not know why this should be so, but it was.

And it was so because immediately after marriage his wife decided that Eugène Irténev was superior to anyone else in the world: wiser, purer, and nobler than they, and that therefore it was right for everyone to serve him and please him; but that as it was impossible to make everyone do this, she must do it herself to the limit of her strength. And she did; directing all her strength of mind towards learning and guessing what he liked, and then doing just that thing, whatever it was and however difficult it might be.

She had the gift which furnishes the chief delight of intercourse with a loving woman: thanks to her love of her husband she penetrated into his soul. She knew his every state and his every shade of feeling—better it seemed to him than he himself—and she behaved correspondingly and therefore never hurt his feelings, but always lessened his distresses and strengthened his joys. And she understood not only his feelings but also his joys. Things quite foreign to her—concerning the farming, the factory, or the appraisement of others—she immediately understood so that she could not merely converse with him, but could often, as he himself said, be a useful and irreplaceable counsellor. She regarded affairs and people and everything in the world only through his eyes. She loved her mother, but having seen that Eugène disliked his mother-in-law's interference in their life she immediately took her husband's side, and did so with such decision that he had to restrain her.

Besides all this she had very good taste, much tact, and above all she had repose. All that she did, she did unnoticed; only the results of what she did were observable, namely, that always and in everything there was cleanliness, order, and elegance. Liza had at once understood in what her husband's ideal of life consisted, and she tried to attain, and in the arrangement and order of the house did attain, what he wanted. Children it is true were lacking, but there was hope of that also. In winter she went to Petersburg to see a specialist and he assured them that she was quite well and could have children.

And this desire was accomplished. By the end of the year she was again pregnant.

The one thing that threatened, not to say poisoned, their happiness was her jealousy—a jealousy she restrained and did not exhibit, but from which she often suffered. Not only might Eugène not love any other woman—because there was not a woman on earth worthy of him (as to whether she herself was worthy or not she never asked herself),—but not a single woman might therefore dare to love him.

VIII

This was how they lived: he rose early, as he always had done, and went to see to the farm or the factory where work was going on, or sometimes to the fields. Towards ten o'clock he would come back for his coffee, which they had on the veranda: Mary Pávlovna, an uncle who lived with them, and Liza. After a conversation which was often very animated while they drank their coffee, they dispersed till dinner-time. At two o'clock they dined and then went for a walk or a drive. In the evening when he returned from his office they drank their evening tea and sometimes he read aloud while she worked, or when there were guests they had music or conversation. When he went away on business he wrote to his wife and received letters from her every day. Sometimes she accompanied him, and then they were particularly merry. On his name-day and on hers guests assembled, and it pleased him to see how well she managed to arrange things so that everybody enjoyed coming. He saw and heard that they all admired her—the young, agreeable hostess—and he loved her still more for this.

All went excellently. She bore her pregnancy easily and, though they were afraid, they both began making plans as to how they would bring the child up. The system of education and the arrangements were all decided by Eugène, and her only wish was to carry out his desires obediently. Eugène on his part read up medical works and intended to bring the child up according to all the precepts of science. She of course agreed to everything and made preparations, making warm and also cool 'envelopes',* and preparing a cradle. Thus the second year of their marriage arrived and the second spring.

IX

It was just before Trinity Sunday. Liza was in her fifth month, and though careful she was still brisk and active. Both his mother and hers were living in the house, but under pretext of watching and safeguarding her only upset her by their tiffs. Eugène was specially engrossed with a new experiment for the cultivation of sugar-beet on a large scale.

Just before Trinity Liza decided that it was necessary to have a thorough house-cleaning as it had not been done since Easter, and she hired two women by the day to help the servants wash the floors and windows, beat the furniture and the carpets, and put covers on them. These women came early in the morning, heated the coppers, and set to work. One of the two was Stepanída, who had just weaned her baby boy and had begged for the job of washing the floors through the office-clerk—whom she now carried on with. She wanted to

* An 'envelope' was a small mattress with a coverlet attached, on which babies were carried about.—A. M.

have a good look at the new mistress. Stepanída was living by herself as formerly, her husband being away, and she was up to tricks as she had formerly been first with old Daniel (who had once caught her taking some logs of firewood), afterwards with the master, and now with the young clerk. She was not concerning herself any longer about her master. 'He has a wife now,' she thought. But it would be good to have a look at the lady and at her establishment: folk said it was well arranged.

Eugène had not seen her since he had met her with the child. Having a baby to attend to she had not been going out to work, and he seldom walked through the village. That morning, on the eve of Trinity Sunday, he got up at five o'clock and rode to the fallow land which was to be sprinkled with phosphates, and had left the house before the women were about, and while they were still engaged lighting the copper fires.

He returned to breakfast merry, contented, and hungry; dismounting from his mare at the gate and handing her over to the gardener. Flicking the high grass with his whip and repeating a phrase he had just uttered, as one often does, he walked towards the house. The phrase was: 'phosphates justify'—what or to whom, he neither knew nor reflected.

They were beating a carpet on the grass. The furniture had been brought out.

'There now! What a house-cleaning Liza has undertaken! . . . Phosphates justify. . . . What a manageress she is! A manageress! Yes, a manageress,' said he to himself, vividly imagining her in her white wrapper and with her smiling joyful face, as it nearly always was when he looked at her. 'Yes, I must change my boots, or else "phosphates justify", that is, smell of manure, and the manageress is in such a condition. Why "in such a condition"? Because a new little Irténev is growing there inside her,' he thought. 'Yes, phosphates justify,' and smiling at his thoughts he put his hand to the door of his room.

But he had not time to push the door before it opened of itself and he came face to face with a woman coming towards him carrying a pail, barefoot and with sleeves turned up high. He stepped aside to let her pass and she too stepped aside, adjusting her kerchief with a wet hand.

'Go on, go on, I won't go in, if you . . .' began Eugène and suddenly stopped, recognizing her.

She glanced merrily at him with smiling eyes, and pulling down her skirt went out at the door.

'What nonsense! . . . It is impossible,' said Eugène to himself, frowning and waving his hand as though to get rid of a fly, displeased at having noticed her. He was vexed that he had noticed her and yet he could not take his eyes from her strong body, swayed by her agile strides, from her bare feet, or from her arms and shoulders, and the pleasing folds of her shirt and the handsome skirt tucked up high above her white calves.

'But why am I looking?' said he to himself, lowering his eyes so as not to see her. 'And anyhow I must go in to get some other boots.' And he turned back to go into his own room, but had not gone five steps before he again glanced round to have another look at her without knowing why or wherefore. She was just going round the corner and also glanced at him.

'Ah, what am I doing!' said he to himself. 'She may think . . . It is even certain that she already does think . . .'

He entered his damp room. Another woman, an old and skinny one, was there, and was still washing it. Eugène passed on tiptoe across the floor, wet with dirty water, to the wall where his boots stood, and he was about to leave the room when the woman herself went out.

'This one has gone and the other, Stepanída, will come here alone,' someone within him began to reflect.

'My God, what am I thinking of and what am I doing!' He seized his boots and ran out with them into the hall, put them on there, brushed himself, and went out onto the veranda where both the mammas were already drinking coffee. Liza had evidently been expecting him and came onto the veranda through another door at the same time.

'My God! If she, who considers me so honourable, pure, and innocent—if she only knew!'—thought he.

Liza as usual met him with shining face. But to-day somehow she seemed to him particularly pale, yellow, long, and weak.

X

DURING coffee, as often happened, a peculiarly feminine kind of conversation went on which had no logical sequence but which evidently was connected in some way for it went on uninterruptedly.

The two old ladies were pin-pricking one another, and Liza was skilfully manœuvring between them.

'I am so vexed that we had not finished washing your room before you got back,' she said to her husband. 'But I do so want to get everything arranged.'

'Well, did you sleep well after I got up?'

'Yes, I slept well and I feel well.'

'How can a woman be well in her condition

during this intolerable heat, when her windows face the sun,' said Varvára Alexéevna, her mother. 'And they have no venetian-blinds or awnings. I always had awnings.'

'But you know we are in the shade after ten o'clock,' said Mary Pávlovna.

'That's what causes fever; it comes of dampness,' said Varvára Alexéevna, not noticing that what she was saying did not agree with what she had just said. 'My doctor always says that it is impossible to diagnose an illness unless one knows the patient. And he certainly knows, for he is the leading physician and we pay him a hundred rubles a visit. My late husband did not believe in doctors, but he did not grudge me anything.'

'How can a man grudge anything to a woman when perhaps her life and the child's depend . . .'

'Yes, when she has means a wife need not depend on her husband. A good wife submits to her husband,' said Varvára Alexéevna—'only Liza is too weak after her illness.'

'Oh no, mamma, I feel quite well. But why have they not brought you any boiled cream?'

'I don't want any. I can do with raw cream.'

'I offered some to Varvára Alexéevna, but she declined,' said Mary Pávlovna, as if justifying herself.

'No, I don't want any to-day.' And as if to terminate an unpleasant conversation and yield magnanimously, Varvára Alexéevna turned to Eugène and said: 'Well, and have you sprinkled the phosphates?'

Liza ran to fetch the cream.

'But I don't want it. I don't want it.'

'Liza, Liza, go gently,' said Mary Pávlovna. 'Such rapid movements do her harm.'

'Nothing does harm if one's mind is at peace,'

said Varvára Alexéevna as if referring to something, though she knew that there was nothing her words could refer to.

Liza returned with the cream and Eugène drank his coffee and listened morosely. He was accustomed to these conversations, but to-day he was particularly annoyed by its lack of sense. He wanted to think over what had happened to him but this chatter disturbed him. Having finished her coffee Varvára Alexéevna went away in a bad humour. Liza, Eugène, and Mary Pávlovna stayed behind, and their conversation was simple and pleasant. But Liza, being sensitive, at once noticed that something was tormenting Eugène, and she asked him whether anything unpleasant had happened. He was not prepared for this question and hesitated a little before replying that there had been nothing. This reply made Liza think all the more. That something was tormenting him, and greatly tormenting, was as evident to her as that a fly had fallen into the milk, yet he would not speak of it. What could it be?

XI

After breakfast they all dispersed. Eugène as usual went to his study, but instead of beginning to read or write his letters, he sat smoking one cigarette after another and thinking. He was terribly surprised and disturbed by the unexpected recrudescence within him of the bad feeling from which he had thought himself free since his marriage. Since then he had not once experienced that feeling, either for her—the woman he had known—or for any other woman except his wife. He had often felt glad of this emancipation, and now suddenly a chance meeting, seemingly so unimportant, revealed to him the fact that he was not free. What now tormented him was not that he was yielding to that feeling and desired her—he did not dream of so doing—but that the feeling was awake within him and he had to be on his guard against it. He had no doubt but that he would suppress it.

He had a letter to answer and a paper to write, and sat down at his writing-table and began to work. Having finished it and quite forgotten what had disturbed him, he went out to go to the stables. And again as ill-luck would have it, either by unfortunate chance or intentionally, as soon as he stepped from the porch a red skirt and red kerchief appeared from round the corner, and she went past him swinging her arms and swaying her body. She not only went past him, but on passing him ran, as if playfully, to overtake her fellow-servant.

Again the bright midday, the nettles, the back of Daniel's hut, and in the shade of the plane-trees her smiling face biting some leaves, rose in his imagination.

'No, it is impossible to let matters continue so,' he said to himself, and waiting till the women had passed out of sight he went to the office.

It was just the dinner-hour and he hoped to find the steward still there, and so it happened. The steward was just waking up from his after-dinner nap, and stretching himself and yawning was standing in the office, looking at the herdsman who was telling him something.

'Vasíli Nikoláich!' said Eugène to the steward.

'What is your pleasure?'

'I want to speak to you.'

'What is your pleasure?'

'Just finish what you are saying.'

'Aren't you going to bring it in?' said Vasíli Nikoláich to the herdsman.

'It's heavy, Vasíli Nikoláich.'

'What is it?' asked Eugène.

'Why, a cow has calved in the meadow. Well, all right, I'll order them to harness a horse at once. Tell Nicholas Lysúkh to get out the dray cart.'

The herdsman went out.

'Do you know,' began Eugène, flushing and conscious that he was doing so, 'do you know, Vasíli Nikoláich, while I was a bachelor I went off the track a bit. . . . You may have heard . . .'

Vasíli Nikoláich, evidently sorry for his master, said with smiling eyes: 'Is it about Stepanída?'

'Why, yes. Look here. Please, please do not engage her to help in the house. You understand, it is very awkward for me . . .'

'Yes, it must have been Ványa the clerk who arranged it.'

'Yes, please . . . and hadn't the rest of the phosphates better be strewn?' said Eugène, to hide his confusion.

'Yes, I am just going to see to it.'

So the matter ended, and Eugène calmed down, hoping that as he had lived for a year without seeing her, so things would go on now. 'Besides, Vasíli Nikoláich will speak to Iván the clerk; Iván will speak to her, and she will understand that I don't want it,' said Eugène to himself, and he was glad that he had forced himself to speak to Vasíli Nikoláich, hard as it had been to do so.

'Yes, it is better, much better, than that feeling of doubt, that feeling of shame.' He shuddered at the mere remembrance of his sin in thought.

XII

THE moral effort he had made to overcome his shame and speak to Vasíli Nikoláich tranquillized Eugène. It seemed to him that the matter was all over now. Liza at once noticed that he was quite calm, and even happier than usual. 'No doubt he was upset by our mothers pin-pricking one another. It really is disagreeable, especially for him who is so sensitive and noble, always to hear such unfriendly and ill-mannered insinuations,' thought she.

The next day was Trinity Sunday. It was a beautiful day, and the peasant-women, on their way into the woods to plait wreaths, came, according to custom, to the landowner's home and began to sing and dance. Mary Pávlovna and Varvára Alexéevna came out onto the porch in smart clothes, carrying sunshades, and went up to the ring of singers. With them, in a jacket of Chinese silk, came out the uncle, a flabby libertine and drunkard, who was living that summer with Eugène.

As usual there was a bright, many-coloured ring of young women and girls, the centre of everything, and around these from different sides like attendant planets that had detached themselves and were circling round, went girls hand in hand, rustling in their new print gowns; young lads giggling and running backwards and forwards after one another; full-grown lads in dark blue or black coats and caps and with red shirts, who unceasingly spat out sunflower-seed shells; and the domestic servants or other outsiders watching the dance-circle from aside. Both the old ladies went close up to the ring, and Liza accompanied them in a light blue dress, with light blue ribbons on her head, and with wide sleeves under which her long white arms and angular elbows were visible.

Eugène did not wish to come out, but it was ridiculous to hide, and he too came out onto the porch smoking a cigarette, bowed to the men and lads, and talked with one of them. The women meanwhile shouted a dance-song with all their might, snapping their fingers, clapping their hands, and dancing.

'They are calling for the master,' said a youngster coming up to Eugène's wife, who had not noticed the call. Liza called Eugène to look at the dance and at one of the women dancers who particularly pleased her. This was Stepanída. She wore a yellow skirt, a velveteen sleeveless jacket and a silk kerchief, and was broad, energetic, ruddy, and merry. No doubt she danced well. He saw nothing.

'Yes, yes,' he said, removing and replacing his pince-nez. 'Yes, yes,' he repeated. 'So it seems I cannot be rid of her,' he thought.

He did not look at her, fearing her attraction, and just on that account what his passing glance caught of her seemed to him especially attractive. Besides this he saw by her sparkling look that she saw him and saw that he admired her. He stood there as long as propriety demanded, and seeing that Varvára Alexéevna had called her 'my dear' senselessly and insincerely and was talking to her, he turned aside and went away.

He went into the house in order not to see her, but on reaching the upper story he approached the window, without knowing how or why, and as long as the women remained at the porch he stood there and looked and looked at her, feasting his eyes on her.

He ran, while there was no one to see him, and then went with quiet steps onto the veranda, and from there, smoking a cigarette, he passed through the garden as if going for a stroll, and followed the direction she had taken. He had not gone two steps along the alley before he noticed behind the trees a velveteen sleeveless jacket, with a pink and yellow skirt and a red kerchief. She was going somewhere with another woman. 'Where are they going?'

And suddenly a terrible desire scorched him as though a hand were seizing his heart. As if by someone else's wish he looked round and went towards her.

'Eugène Ivánich, Eugène Ivánich! I have come to see your honour,' said a voice behind him, and Eugène, seeing old Samókhin who was digging a well for him, roused himself and turning quickly round went to meet Samókhin. While speaking with him he turned sideways and saw that she and the woman who was with her went down the slope, evidently to the well or making an excuse of the well, and having stopped there a little while ran back to the dance-circle.

XIII

After talking to Samókhin, Eugène returned to the house as depressed as if he had committed a crime. In the first place she had understood him, believed that he wanted to see her, and desired it herself. Secondly that other woman, Anna Prókhorova, evidently knew of it.

Above all he felt that he was conquered, that he was not master of his own will but that there was another power moving him, that he had been saved only by good fortune, and that if not to-day then to-morrow or a day later, he would perish all the same.

'Yes, perish,' he did not understand it otherwise: to be unfaithful to his young and loving wife with a peasant-woman in the village, in the sight of everyone—what was it but to perish, perish utterly, so that it would be impossible to live? No, something must be done.

'My God, my God! What am I to do? Can it be that I shall perish like this?' said he to himself.

Is it not possible to do anything? Yet something must be done. Do not think about her'—he ordered himself. 'Do not think!' and immediately he began thinking and seeing her before him, and seeing also the shade of the plane tree.

He remembered having read of a hermit who, to avoid the temptation he felt for a woman on whom he had to lay his hand to heal her, thrust his other hand into a brazier and burnt his fingers. He called that to mind. 'Yes, I am ready to burn my fingers rather than to perish.' He looked round to make sure that there was no one in the room, lit a candle, and put a finger into the flame. 'There, now think about her,' he said to himself ironically. It hurt him and he withdrew his smoke-stained finger, threw away the match, and laughed at himself. What nonsense! That was not what had to be done. But it was necessary to do something, to avoid seeing her—either to go away himself or to send her away. Yes—send her away. Offer her husband money to remove to town or to another village. People would hear of it and would talk about it. Well, what of that? At any rate it was better than this danger. 'Yes, that must be done,' he said to himself, and at that very moment he was looking at her without moving his eyes. 'Where is she going?' he suddenly asked himself. She, it seemed to him, had seen him at the window and now, having glanced at him and taken another woman by the hand, was going towards the garden swinging her arm briskly. Without knowing why or wherefore, merely in accord with what he had been thinking, he went to the office.

Vasíli Nikoláich in holiday costume and with oiled hair was sitting at tea with his wife and a guest who was wearing an oriental kerchief.

'I want a word with you, Vasíli Nikoláich!'

'Please say what you want to. We have finished tea.'

'No. I'd rather you came out with me.'

'Directly; only let me get my cap. Tánya, put out the samovár,' said Vasíli Nikoláich, stepping outside cheerfully.

It seemed to Eugène that Vasíli had been drinking, but what was to be done? It might be all the better—he would sympathize with him in his difficulties the more readily.

'I have come again to speak about that same matter, Vasíli Nikoláich,' said Eugène—'about that woman.'

'Well, what of her? I told them not to take her again on any account.'

'No, I have been thinking in general, and this is what I wanted to take your advice about. Isn't it possible to get them away, to send the whole family away?'

'Where can they be sent?' said Vasíli, disapprovingly and ironically as it seemed to Eugène.

'Well, I thought of giving them money, or even some land in Koltóvski,—so that she should not be here.'

'But how can they be sent away? Where is he to go—torn up from his roots? And why should you do it? What harm can she do you?'

'Ah, Vasíli Nikoláich, you must understand that it would be dreadful for my wife to hear of it.'

'But who will tell her?'

'How can I live with this dread? The whole thing is very painful for me.'

'But really, why should you distress yourself? Whoever stirs up the past—out with his eye! Who is not a sinner before God and to blame before the Tsar, as the saying is?'

'All the same it would be better to get rid of them. Can't you speak to the husband?'

'But it is no use speaking! Eh, Eugène Ivánich, what is the matter with you? It is all past and forgotten. All sorts of things happen. Who is there that would now say anything bad of you? Everybody sees you.'

'But all the same go and have a talk with him.'

'All right, I will speak to him.'

Though he knew that nothing would come of it, this talk somewhat calmed Eugène. Above all, it made him feel that through excitement he had been exaggerating the danger.

Had he gone to meet her by appointment? It was impossible. He had simply gone to stroll in the garden and she had happened to run out at the same time.

XIV

After dinner that very Trinity Sunday Liza while walking from the garden to the meadow, where her husband wanted to show her the clover, took a false step and fell when crossing a little ditch. She fell gently, on her side; but she gave an exclamation, and her husband saw an expression in her face not only of fear but of pain. He was about to help her up, but she motioned him away with her hand.

'No, wait a bit, Eugène,' she said, with a weak smile, and looked up guiltily as it seemed to him. 'My foot only gave way under me.'

'There, I always say,' remarked Varvára Alexéevna, 'can anyone in her condition possibly jump over ditches?'

'But it is all right, mamma. I shall get up directly.' With her husband's help she did get up, but she immediately turned pale, and looked frightened.

'Yes, I am not well!' and she whispered something to her mother.

'Oh, my God, what have you done! I said you ought not to go there,' cried Varvára Alexéevna. 'Wait—I will call the servants. She must not walk. She must be carried!'

'Don't be afraid, Liza, I will carry you,' said Eugène, putting his left arm round her. 'Hold me by the neck. Like that.' And stooping down he put his right arm under her knees and lifted her. He could never afterwards forget the suffering and yet beatific expression of her face.

'I am too heavy for you, dear,' she said with a smile. 'Mamma is running, tell her!' And she bent towards him and kissed him. She evidently wanted her mother to see how he was carrying her.

Eugène shouted to Varvára Alexéevna not to hurry, and that he would carry Liza home. Varvára Alexéevna stopped and began to shout still louder.

'You will drop her, you'll be sure to drop her. You want to destroy her. You have no conscience!'

'But I am carrying her excellently.'

'I do not want to watch you killing my daughter, and I can't.' And she ran round the bend in the alley.

'Never mind, it will pass,' said Liza, smiling.

'Yes. If only it does not have consequences like last time.'

'No. I am not speaking of that. That is all right. I mean mamma. You are tired. Rest a bit.'

But though he found it heavy, Eugène carried his burden proudly and gladly to the house and did not hand her over to the housemaid and the man-cook whom Varvára Alexéevna had found and sent to meet them. He carried her to the bedroom and put her on the bed.

'Now go away,' she said, and drawing his hand to her she kissed it. 'Ánnushka and I will manage all right.'

Mary Pávlovna also ran in from her rooms in the wing. They undressed Liza and laid her on the bed. Eugène sat in the drawing-room with a book in his hand, waiting. Varvára Alexéevna went past him with such a reproachfully gloomy air that he felt alarmed.

'Well, how is it?' he asked.

'How is it? What's the good of asking? It is probably what you wanted when you made your wife jump over the ditch.'

'Varvára Alexéevna!' he cried. 'This is impossible. If you want to torment people and to poison their life' (he wanted to say, 'then go elsewhere to do it,' but restrained himself). 'How is it that it does not hurt you?'

'It is too late now.' And shaking her cap in a triumphant manner she passed out by the door.

The fall had really been a bad one; Liza's foot had twisted awkwardly and there was danger of her having another miscarriage. Everyone knew that there was nothing to be done but that she must just lie quietly, yet all the same they decided to send for a doctor.

'Dear Nikoláy Semënich,' wrote Eugène to the doctor, 'you have always been so kind to us that I hope you will not refuse to come to my wife's assistance. She . . .' and so on. Having written the letter he went to the stables to arrange about the horses and the carriage. Horses had to be got ready to bring the doctor and others to take him back. When an estate is not run on a large scale, such things cannot be quickly decided but have to be considered. Having arranged it all and dispatched the coachman, it was past nine before he got back to the house. His wife was lying down, and said that she felt perfectly well and had no pain. But Varvára Alexéevna was sitting with a lamp screened from Liza by some sheets of music and knitting a large red coverlet, with a mien that said that after what had happened peace was impossible, but that she at any rate would do her duty no matter what anyone else did.

Eugène noticed this, but, to appear as if he had not done so, tried to assume a cheerful and tranquil air and told how he had chosen the horses and how capitally the mare, Kabúshka, had galloped as left trace-horse in the troyka.

'Yes, of course, it is just the time to exercise the horses when help is needed. Probably the doctor will also be thrown into the ditch,' remarked Varvára Alexéevna, examining her knitting from under her pince-nez and moving it close up to the lamp.

'But you know we had to send one way or other, and I made the best arrangement I could.'

'Yes, I remember very well how your horses galloped with me under the arch of the gateway.' This was a long-standing fancy of hers, and Eugène now was injudicious enough to remark that that was not quite what had happened.

'It is not for nothing that I have always said, and have often remarked to the prince, that it is hardest of all to live with people who are untruthful and insincere. I can endure anything except that.'

'Well, if anyone has to suffer more than another, it is certainly I,' said Eugène. 'But you . . .'

'Yes, it is evident.'

'What?'

'Nothing, I am only counting my stitches.'

Eugène was standing at the time by the bed and Liza was looking at him, and one of her moist hands outside the coverlet caught his hand and pressed it.

'Bear with her for my sake. You know she cannot prevent our loving one another,' was what her look said.

'I won't do so again. It's nothing,' he whispered, and he kissed her damp, long hand and then her affectionate eyes, which closed while he kissed them.

'Can it be the same thing over again?' he asked. 'How are you feeling?'

'I am afraid to say for fear of being mistaken, but I feel that he is alive and will live,' said she, glancing at her stomach.

'Ah, it is dreadful, dreadful to think of.'

Notwithstanding Liza's insistence that he should go away, Eugène spent the night with her, hardly closing an eye and ready to attend on her.

But she passed the night well, and had they not sent for the doctor she would perhaps have got up.

By dinner-time the doctor arrived and of course said that though if the symptoms recurred there might be cause for apprehension, yet actually there were no positive symptoms, but as there were also no contrary indications one might suppose on the one hand that—and on the other hand that . . . And therefore she must lie still, and that 'though I do not like prescribing, yet all the same she should take this mixture and should lie quiet'. Besides this, the doctor gave Varvára Alexéevna a lecture on woman's anatomy, during which Varvára Alexéevna nodded her head significantly. Having received his fee, as usual into the backmost part of his palm, the doctor drove away and the patient was left to lie in bed for a week.

XV

Eugène spent most of his time by his wife's bedside, talking to her, reading to her, and what was hardest of all, enduring without murmur Vaevára

Alexéevna's attacks, and even contriving to turn these into jokes.

But he could not stay at home all the time. In the first place his wife sent him away, saying that he would fall ill if he always remained with her; and secondly the farming was progressing in a way that demanded his presence at every step. He could not stay at home, but had to be in the fields, in the wood, in the garden, at the thrashing-floor; and everywhere he was pursued not merely by the thought but by the vivid image of Stepanída, and he only occasionally forgot her. But that would not have mattered, he could perhaps have mastered his feeling; what was worst of all was that, whereas he had previously lived for months without seeing her, he now continually came across her. She evidently understood that he wished to renew relations with her and tried to come in his way. Nothing was said either by him or by her, and therefore neither he nor she went directly to a rendezvous, but only sought opportunities of meeting.

The most possible place for them to meet was in the forest, where peasant-women went with sacks to collect grass for their cows. Eugène knew this and therefore went there every day. Every day he told himself that he would not go, and every day it ended by his making his way to the forest and, on hearing the sound of voices, standing behind the bushes with sinking heart looking to see if she was there.

Why he wanted to know whether it was she who was there, he did not know. If it had been she and she had been alone, he would not have gone to her—so he believed—he would have run away; but he wanted to see her.

Once he met her. As he was entering the forest she came out of it with two other women, carrying a heavy sack-full of grass on her back. A little earlier he would perhaps have met her in the forest. Now, with the other women there, she could not go back to him. But though he realized this impossibility, he stood for a long time behind a hazel-bush, at the risk of attracting the other women's attention. Of course she did not return, but he stayed there a long time. And, great heavens, how delightful his imagination made her appear to him! And this not only once, but five or six times, and each time more intensely. Never had she seemed so attractive, and never had he been so completely in her power.

He felt that he had lost control of himself and had become almost insane. His strictness with himself had not weakened a jot; on the contrary he saw all the abomination of his desire and even of his action, for his going to the wood was an action. He knew that he only need come near her anywhere in the dark, and if possible touch her, and he would yield to his feelings. He knew that it was only shame before people, before her, and no doubt before himself also, that restrained him. And he knew too that he had sought conditions in which that shame would not be apparent—darkness or proximity—in which it would be stifled by animal passion. And therefore he knew that he was a wretched criminal, and despised and hated himself with all his soul. He hated himself because he still had not surrendered: every day he prayed God to strengthen him, to save him from perishing; every day he determined that from to-day onward he would not take a step to see her, and would forget her. Every day he devised means of delivering himself from this enticement, and he made use of those means.

But it was all in vain.

One of the means was continual occupation:

another was intense physical work and fasting; a third was imagining clearly to himself the shame that would fall upon him when everybody knew of it—his wife, his mother-in-law, and the folk around. He did all this and it seemed to him that he was conquering, but midday came—the hour of their former meetings and the hour when he had met her carrying the grass—and he went to the forest. Thus five days of torment passed. He only saw her from a distance, and did not once encounter her.

XVI

LIZA was gradually recovering, she could move about and was only uneasy at the change that had taken place in her husband, which she did not understand.

Varvára Alexéevna had gone away for a while, and the only visitor was Eugène's uncle. Mary Pávlovna was as usual at home.

Eugène was in his semi-insane condition when there came two days of pouring rain, as often happens after thunder in June. The rain stopped all work. They even ceased carting manure on account of the dampness and dirt. The peasants remained at home. The herdsmen wore themselves out with the cattle, and eventually drove them home. The cows and sheep wandered about in the pasture-land and ran loose in the grounds. The peasant-women, barefoot and wrapped in shawls, splashing through the mud, rushed about to seek the runaway cows. Streams flowed everywhere along the paths, all the leaves and all the grass were saturated with water, and streams flowed unceasingly from the spouts into the bubbling puddles.

Eugène sat at home with his wife, who was

particularly wearisome that day. She questioned Eugène several times as to the cause of his discontent, and he replied with vexation that nothing was the matter. She ceased questioning him but was still distressed.

They were sitting after breakfast in the drawing-room. His uncle for the hundredth time was recounting fabrications about his society acquaintances. Liza was knitting a jacket and sighed, complaining of the weather and of a pain in the small of her back. The uncle advised her to lie down, and asked for vodka for himself. It was terribly dull for Eugène in the house. Everything was weak and dull. He read a book and a magazine, but understood nothing of them.

'I must go out and look at the rasping-machine they brought yesterday,' said he, and got up and went out.

'Take an umbrella with you.'

'Oh, no, I have a leather coat. And I am only going as far as the boiling-room.'

He put on his boots and his leather coat and went to the factory; and he had not gone twenty steps before he met her coming towards him, with her skirts tucked up high above her white calves. She was walking, holding down the shawl in which her head and shoulders were wrapped.

'Where are you going?' said he, not recognizing her the first instant. When he recognized her it was already too late. She stopped, smiling, and looked long at him.

'I am looking for a calf. Where are you off to in such weather?' said she, as if she were seeing him every day.

'Come to the shed,' said he suddenly, without knowing how he said it. It was as if someone else had uttered the words.

She bit her shawl, winked, and ran in the direction which led from the garden to the shed, and he continued his path, intending to turn off beyond the lilac-bush and go there too.

'Master,' he heard a voice behind him. 'The mistress is calling you, and wants you to come back for a minute.'

This was Mísha, his man-servant.

'My God! This is the second time you have saved me,' thought Eugène, and immediately turned back. His wife reminded him that he had promised to take some medicine at the dinner-hour to a sick woman, and he had better take it with him.

While they were getting the medicine some five minutes elapsed, and then, going away with the medicine, he hesitated to go direct to the shed lest he should be seen from the house, but as soon as he was out of sight he promptly turned and made his way to it. He already saw her in imagination inside the shed smiling gaily. But she was not there, and there was nothing in the shed to show that she had been there.

He was already thinking that she had not come, had not heard or understood his words—he had muttered them through his nose as if afraid of her hearing them—or perhaps she had not wanted to come. 'And why did I imagine that she would rush to me? She has her own husband; it is only I who am such a wretch as to have a wife, and a good one, and to run after another.' Thus he thought sitting in the shed, the thatch of which had a leak and dripped from its straw. 'But how delightful it would be if she did come—alone here in this rain. If only I could embrace her once again, then let happen what may. But I could tell if she has been here by her footprints,' he reflected. He looked at the trodden ground near the shed and at the path overgrown by grass, and the fresh print of bare feet, and even of one that had slipped, was visible. 'Yes, she has been here. Well, now it is settled. Wherever I may see her I shall go straight to her. I will go to her at night.' He sat for a long time in the shed and left it exhausted and crushed. He delivered the medicine, returned home, and lay down in his room to wait for dinner.

XVII

Before dinner Liza came to him and, still wondering what could be the cause of his discontent, began to say that she was afraid he did not like the idea of her going to Moscow for her confinement, and that she had decided that she would remain at home and on no account go to Moscow. He knew how she feared both her confinement itself and the risk of not having a healthy child, and therefore he could not help being touched at seeing how ready she was to sacrifice everything for his sake. All was so nice, so pleasant, so clean, in the house; and in his soul it was so dirty, despicable, and foul. The whole evening Eugène was tormented by knowing that notwithstanding his sincere repulsion at his own weakness, notwithstanding his firm intention to break off,—the same thing would happen again to-morrow.

'No, this is impossible,' he said to himself, walking up and down in his room. 'There must be some remedy for it. My God! What am I to do?'

Someone knocked at the door as foreigners do. He knew this must be his uncle. 'Come in,' he said.

The uncle had come as a self-appointed ambassador from Liza.

'Do you know, I really do notice that there is a change in you,' he said,—'and Liza—I understand how it troubles her. I understand that it must be hard for you to leave all the business you have so excellently started, but *que veux-tu?** I should advise you to go away. It will be more satisfactory both for you and for her. And do you know, I should advise you to go to the Crimea. The climate is beautiful and there is an excellent *accoucheur* there, and you would be just in time for the best of the grape season.'

'Uncle,' Eugène suddenly exclaimed. 'Can you keep a secret? A secret that is terrible to me, a shameful secret.'

'Oh, come—do you really feel any doubt of me?'

'Uncle, you can help me. Not only help, but save me!' said Eugène. And the thought of disclosing his secret to his uncle whom he did not respect, the thought that he would show himself in the worst light and humiliate himself before him, was pleasant. He felt himself to be despicable and guilty, and wished to punish himself.

'Speak, my dear fellow, you know how fond I am of you,' said the uncle, evidently well content that there was a secret and that it was a shameful one, and that it would be communicated to him, and that he could be of use.

'First of all I must tell you that I am a wretch, a good-for-nothing, a scoundrel—a real scoundrel.'

'Now what are you saying . . .' began his uncle, as if he were offended.

'What! Not a wretch when I—Liza's husband, Liza's! One has only to know her purity, her love—and that I, her husband, want to be untrue to her with a peasant-woman!'

'What is this? Why do you want to—you have not been unfaithful to her?'

'Yes, at least just the same as being untrue, for

* What would you have?

it did not depend on me. I was ready to do so. I was hindered, or else I should . . . now. I do not know what I should have done . . .'

'But please, explain to me . . .'

'Well, it is like this. When I was a bachelor I was stupid enough to have relations with a woman here in our village. That is to say, I used to have meetings with her in the forest, in the field . . .'

'Was she pretty?' asked his uncle.

Eugène frowned at this question, but he was in such need of external help that he made as if he did not hear it, and continued:

'Well, I thought this was just casual and that I should break it off and have done with it. And I did break it off before my marriage. For nearly a year I did not see her or think about her.' It seemed strange to Eugène himself to hear the description of his own condition. 'Then suddenly, I don't myself know why—really one sometimes believes in witchcraft—I saw her, and a worm crept into my heart; and it gnaws. I reproach myself, I understand the full horror of my action, that is to say, of the act I may commit any moment, and yet I myself turn to it, and if I have not committed it, it is only because God preserved me. Yesterday I was on my way to see her when Liza sent for me.'

'What, in the rain?'

'Yes. I am worn out, Uncle, and have decided to confess to you and to ask your help.'

'Yes, of course, it's a bad thing on your own estate. People will get to know. I understand that Liza is weak and that it is necessary to spare her, but why on your own estate?'

Again Eugène tried not to hear what his uncle was saying, and hurried on to the core of the matter.

'Yes, save me from myself. That is what I ask of you. To-day I was hindered by chance. But to-morrow or next time no one will hinder me. And she knows now. Don't leave me alone.'

'Yes, all right,' said his uncle,—'but are you really so much in love?'

'Oh, it is not that at all. It is not that, it is some kind of power that has seized me and holds me. I do not know what to do. Perhaps I shall gain strength, and then . . .'

'Well, it turns out as I suggested,' said his uncle. 'Let us be off to the Crimea.'

'Yes, yes, let us go, and meanwhile you will be with me and will talk to me.'

XVIII

THE fact that Eugène had confided his secret to his uncle, and still more the sufferings of his conscience and the feeling of shame he experienced after that rainy day, sobered him. It was settled that they would start for Yálta in a week's time. During that week Eugène drove to town to get money for the journey, gave instructions from the house and from the office concerning the management of the estate, again became gay and friendly with his wife, and began to awaken morally.

So without having once seen Stepanída after that rainy day he left with his wife for the Crimea. There he spent an excellent two months. He received so many new impressions that it seemed to him that the past was obliterated from his memory. In the Crimea they met former acquaintances and became particularly friendly with them, and they also made new acquaintances. Life in the Crimea was a continual holiday for Eugène, besides being instructive and beneficial. They became friendly there with the former Marshal of the Nobility of their province, a clever and liberal-minded man who became fond of Eugène and coached him, and attracted him to his Party.

At the end of August Liza gave birth to a beautiful, healthy daughter, and her confinement was unexpectedly easy.

In September they returned home, the four of them, including the baby and its wet-nurse, as Liza was unable to nurse it herself. Eugène returned home entirely free from the former horrors and quite a new and happy man. Having gone through all that a husband goes through when his wife bears a child, he loved her more than ever. His feeling for the child when he took it in his arms was a funny, new, very pleasant and, as it were, a tickling feeling. Another new thing in his life now was that, besides his occupation with the estate, thanks to his acquaintance with Dúmchin (the ex-Marshal) a new interest occupied his mind, that of the Zémstvo—partly an ambitious interest, partly a feeling of duty. In October there was to be a special Assembly, at which he was to be elected. After arriving home he drove once to town and another time to Dúmchin.

Of the torments of his temptation and struggle he had forgotten even to think, and could with difficulty recall them to mind. It seemed to him something like an attack of insanity he had undergone.

To such an extent did he now feel free from it that he was not even afraid to make inquiries on the first occasion when he remained alone with the steward. As he had previously spoken to him about the matter he was not ashamed to ask.

'Well, and is Sídor Péchnikov still away from home?' he inquired.

'Yes, he is still in town.'

'And his wife?'

'Oh, she is a worthless woman. She is now carrying on with Zenóvi. She has gone quite on the loose.'

'Well, that is all right,' thought Eugène. 'How wonderfully indifferent to it I am! How I have changed.'

XIX

ALL that Eugène had wished had been realized. He had obtained the property, the factory was working successfully, the beet-crops were excellent, and he expected a large income; his wife had borne a child satisfactorily, his mother-in-law had left, and he had been unanimously elected to the Zémstvo.

He was returning home from town after the election. He had been congratulated and had had to return thanks. He had had dinner and had drunk some five glasses of champagne. Quite new plans of life now presented themselves to him, and he was thinking about these as he drove home. It was the Indian summer: an excellent road and a hot sun. As he approached his home Eugène was thinking of how, as a result of this election, he would occupy among the people the position he had always dreamed of; that is to say, one in which he would be able to serve them not only by production, which gave employment, but also by direct influence. He imagined what his own and the other peasants would think of him in three years' time. 'For instance this one,' he thought, driving just then through the village and glancing at a peasant who with a peasant-woman was crossing the street in front of him carrying a full water-tub. They stopped to let his carriage pass. The peasant was old Péchnikov, and the woman was Stepanída. Eugène looked at her, recognized her, and was glad to feel that he remained quite tranquil. She was still as good-looking as ever, but this did not touch him at all. He drove home.

'Well, may we congratulate you?' said his uncle.

'Yes, I was elected.'

'Capital! We must drink to it!'

Next day Eugène drove about to see to the farming which he had been neglecting. At the outlying farmstead a new thrashing machine was at work. While watching it Eugène stepped among the women, trying not to take notice of them; but try as he would he once or twice noticed the black eyes and red kerchief of Stepanída, who was carrying away the straw. Once or twice he glanced sideways at her and felt that something was happening, but could not account for it to himself. Only next day, when he again drove to the thrashing-floor and spent two hours there quite unnecessarily, without ceasing to caress with his eyes the familiar, handsome figure of the young woman, did he feel that he was lost, irremediably lost. Again those torments! Again all that horror and fear, and there was no saving himself.

What he expected happened to him. The evening of the next day, without knowing how, he found himself at her back-yard, by her hay-shed, where in autumn they had once had a meeting. As though having a stroll, he stopped there lighting a cigarette. A neighbouring peasant-woman saw him, and as he turned back he heard her say to someone: 'Go, he is waiting for you—on my dying word he is standing there. Go, you fool!'

He saw how a woman—she—ran to the hay-shed; but as a peasant had met him it was no longer possible for him to turn back, and so he went home.

XX

When he entered the drawing-room everything seemed strange and unnatural to him. He had risen that morning vigorous, determined to fling it all aside, to forget it and not allow himself to think about it. But without noticing how it occurred he had all the morning not merely not interested himself in the work, but tried to avoid it. What had formerly cheered him and been important was now insignificant. Unconsciously he tried to free himself from business. It seemed to him that he had to do so in order to think and to plan. And he freed himself and remained alone. But as soon as he was alone he began to wander about in the garden and the forest. And all those spots were besmirched in his recollection by memories that gripped him. He felt that he was walking in the garden and pretending to himself that he was thinking out something, but that really he was not thinking out anything, but insanely and unreasonably expecting her; expecting that by some miracle she would be aware that he was expecting her, and would come here at once and go somewhere where no one would see them, or would come at night when there would be no moon, and no one, not even she herself, would see—on such a night she would come and he would touch her body. . . .

'There now, talking of breaking off when I wish to,' said he to himself. 'Yes, and that is having a clean healthy woman for one's health's sake! No, it seems one can't play with her like that. I thought I had taken her, but it was she who took me; took me and does not let me go. Why, I thought I was free, but I was not free and was deceiving myself when I married. It was all nonsense—fraud. From the time I had her I experienced a new feeling, the real feeling of a husband. Yes, I ought to have lived with her.

'One of two lives is possible for me: that which I began with Liza: service, estate management, the child, and people's respect. If that is life, it is necessary that she, Stepanída, should not be there. She must be sent away, as I said, or destroyed so that she shall not exist. And the other life—is this: For me to take her away from her husband, pay him money, disregard the shame and disgrace, and live with her. But in that case it is necessary that Liza should not exist, nor Mimi (the baby). No, that is not so, the baby does not matter, but it is necessary that there should be no Liza—that she should go away—that she should know, curse me, and go away. That she should know that I have exchanged her for a peasant-woman, that I am a deceiver and a scoundrel!—No, that is too terrible! It is impossible. But it might happen,' he went on thinking,—'it might happen that Liza might fall ill and die. Die, and then everything would be capital.

'Capital! Oh, scoundrel! No, if someone must die it should be Stepanída. If she were to die, how good it would be.

'Yes, that is how men come to poison or kill their wives or lovers. Take a revolver and go and call her, and instead of embracing her, shoot her in the breast and have done with it.

'Really she is—a devil. Simply a devil. She has possessed herself of me against my own will.

'Kill? Yes. There are only two ways out: to kill my wife or her. For it is impossible to live like this.* It is impossible! I must consider the matter and look ahead. If things remain as they are what will happen? I shall again be saying to myself that

* At this place the alternative ending, printed at the end of the story, begins.

I do not wish it and that I will throw her off, but it will be merely words; in the evening I shall be at her back-yard, and she will know it and will come out. And if people know of it and tell my wife, or if I tell her myself—for I can't lie—I shall not be able to live so. I cannot! People will know. They will all know—Parásha and the blacksmith. Well, is it possible to live so?

'Impossible! There are only two ways out: to kill my wife, or to kill her. Yes, or else . . . Ah, yes, there is a third way: to kill myself,' said he softly, and suddenly a shudder ran over his skin. 'Yes, kill myself, then I shall not need to kill them.' He became frightened, for he felt that only that way was possible. He had a revolver. 'Shall I really kill myself? It is something I never thought of—how strange it will be . . .'

He returned to his study and at once opened the cupboard where the revolver lay, but before he had taken it out of its case his wife entered the room.

XXI

He threw a newspaper over the revolver.

'Again the same!' said she aghast when she had looked at him.

'What is the same?'

'The same terrible expression that you had before and would not explain to me. Jénya, dear one, tell me about it. I see that you are suffering. Tell me and you will feel easier. Whatever it may be, it will be better than for you to suffer so. Don't I know that it is nothing bad?'

'You know? While . . .'

'Tell me, tell me, tell me. I won't let you go.'

He smiled a piteous smile.

'Shall I?—No, it is impossible. And there is nothing to tell.'

Perhaps he might have told her, but at that moment the wet-nurse entered to ask if she should go for a walk. Liza went out to dress the baby.

'Then you will tell me? I will be back directly.'

'Yes, perhaps . . .'

She never could forget the piteous smile with which he said this. She went out.

Hurriedly, stealthily like a robber, he seized the revolver and took it out of its case. It was loaded, yes, but long ago, and one cartridge was missing.

'Well, how will it be?' He put it to his temple and hesitated a little, but as soon as he remembered Stepanída—his decision not to see her, his struggle, temptation, fall, and renewed struggle—he shuddered with horror. 'No, this is better,' and he pulled the trigger . . .

When Liza ran into the room—she had only had time to step down from the balcony—he was lying face downwards on the floor: black, warm blood was gushing from the wound, and his corpse was twitching.

There was an inquest. No one could understand or explain the suicide. It never even entered his uncle's head that its cause could be anything in common with the confession Eugène had made to him two months previously.

Varvára Alexéevna assured them that she had always foreseen it. It had been evident from his way of disputing. Neither Liza nor Mary Pávlovna could at all understand why it had happened, but still they did not believe what the doctors said, namely, that he was mentally deranged—a psychopath. They were quite unable to accept this, for they knew he was saner than hundreds of their acquaintances.

And indeed if Eugène Irténev was mentally deranged everyone is in the same case; the most mentally deranged people are certainly those who see in others indications of insanity they do not notice in themselves.

VARIATION OF THE CONCLUSION OF 'THE DEVIL'

'To kill, yes. There are only two ways out: to kill my wife, or to kill her. For it is impossible to live like this,' said he to himself, and going up to the table he took from it a revolver and, having examined it—one cartridge was wanting—he put it in his trouser pocket.

'My God! What am I doing?' he suddenly exclaimed, and folding his hands he began to pray.

'O God, help me and deliver me! Thou knowest that I do not desire evil, but by myself am powerless. Help me,' said he, making the sign of the cross on his breast before the icon.

'Yes, I can control myself. I will go out, walk about and think things over.'

He went to the entrance-hall, put on his overcoat and went out onto the porch. Unconsciously his steps took him past the garden along the field path to the outlying farmstead. There the thrashing machine was still droning and the cries of the driver-lads were heard. He entered the barn. She was there. He saw her at once. She was raking up the corn, and on seeing him she ran briskly and merrily about, with laughing eyes, raking up the scattered corn with agility. Eugène could not help watching her though he did not wish to do so. He only recollected himself when she was no longer in sight. The clerk informed him that they were now finishing thrashing the corn that had been beaten down—that was why it was going slower and the output was less. Eugène went up to the drum, which occasionally gave a knock as sheaves not evenly fed in passed under it, and he asked the clerk if there were many such sheaves of beaten-down corn.

'There will be five cartloads of it.'

'Then look here . . .' began Eugène, but he did not finish the sentence. She had gone close up to the drum and was raking the corn from under it, and she scorched him with her laughing eyes. That look spoke of a merry, careless love between them, of the fact that she knew he wanted her and had come to her shed, and that she as always was ready to live and be merry with him regardless of all conditions or consequences. Eugène felt himself to be in her power but did not wish to yield.

He remembered his prayer and tried to repeat it. He began saying it to himself, but at once felt that it was useless. A single thought now engrossed him entirely: how to arrange a meeting with her so that the others should not notice it.

'If we finish this lot to-day, are we to start on a fresh stack or leave it till to-morrow?' asked the clerk.

'Yes, yes,' replied Eugène, involuntarily following her to the heap to which with the other women she was raking the corn.

'But can I really not master myself?' said he to himself. 'Have I really perished? O God! But there is no God. There is only a devil. And it is she. She has possessed me. But I won't, I won't! A devil, yes, a devil.'

Again he went up to her, drew the revolver from his pocket and shot her, once, twice, thrice, in the back. She ran a few steps and fell on the heap of corn.

'My God, my God! What is that?' cried the women.

'No, it was not an accident. I killed her on purpose,' cried Eugène. 'Send for the police-officer.'

He went home and went to his study and locked himself in, without speaking to his wife.

'Do not come to me,' he cried to her through the door. 'You will know all about it.'

An hour later he rang, and bade the man-servant who answered the bell: 'Go and find out whether Stepanída is alive.'

The servant already knew all about it, and told him she had died an hour ago.

'Well, all right. Now leave me alone. When the police-officer or the magistrate comes, let me know.'

The police-officer and magistrate arrived next morning, and Eugène, having bidden his wife and baby farewell, was taken to prison.

He was tried. It was during the early days of trial by jury,* and the verdict was one of temporary insanity, and he was sentenced only to perform church penance.

He had been kept in prison for nine months and was then confined in a monastery for one month.

He had begun to drink while still in prison, continued to do so in the monastery, and returned home an enfeebled, irresponsible drunkard.

Varvára Alexéevna assured them that she had always predicted this. It was, she said, evident from the way he disputed. Neither Liza nor Mary Pávlovna could understand how the affair had happened, but for all that, they did not believe what the doctors said, namely, that he was mentally deranged—a psychopath. They could not accept that, for they knew that he was saner than hundreds of their acquaintances.

* Trial by jury was introduced in 1864, and at first the juries were inclined to be extremely lenient to the prisoners. —A. M.

And indeed, if Eugène Irténev was mentally deranged when he committed this crime, then everyone is similarly insane. The most mentally deranged people are certainly those who see in others indications of insanity they do not notice in themselves.

November 19, 1889.

FATHER SERGIUS

FATHER SERGIUS

I

In Petersburg in the eighteen-forties a surprising event occurred. An officer of the Cuirassier Life Guards, a handsome prince who everyone predicted would become aide-de-camp to the Emperor Nicholas I and have a brilliant career, left the service, broke off his engagement to a beautiful maid of honour, a favourite of the Empress's, gave his small estate to his sister, and retired to a monastery to become a monk.

This event appeared extraordinary and inexplicable to those who did not know his inner motives, but for Prince Stepán Kasátsky himself it all occurred so naturally that he could not imagine how he could have acted otherwise.

His father, a retired colonel of the Guards, had died when Stepán was twelve, and sorry as his mother was to part from her son, she entered him at the Military College as her deceased husband had intended.

The widow herself, with her daughter Varvára, moved to Petersburg to be near her son and have him with her for the holidays.

The boy was distinguished both by his brilliant ability and by his immense self-esteem. He was first both in his studies—especially in mathematics, of which he was particularly fond—and also in drill and in riding. Though of more than average height, he was handsome and agile, and he would have been an altogether exemplary cadet had it not been for his quick temper. He was remarkably truthful, and was neither dissipated nor addicted to drink. The only faults that marred his conduct were fits of fury to which he was subject and during which he lost control of himself and became like a wild animal. He once nearly threw out of the window another cadet who had begun to tease him about his collection of minerals. On another occasion he came almost completely to grief by flinging a whole dish of cutlets at an officer who was acting as steward, attacking him and, it was said, striking him for having broken his word and told a barefaced lie. He would certainly have been reduced to the ranks had not the Director of the College hushed up the whole matter and dismissed the steward.

By the time he was eighteen he had finished his College course and received a commission as lieutenant in an aristocratic regiment of the Guards.

The Emperor Nicholas Pávlovich (Nicholas I) had noticed him while he was still at the College, and continued to take notice of him in the regiment, and it was on this account that people predicted for him an appointment as aide-de-camp to the Emperor. Kasátsky himself strongly desired it, not from ambition only but chiefly because since his cadet days he had been passionately devoted to Nicholas Pávlovich. The Emperor had often visited the Military College and every time Kasátsky saw that tall erect figure, with breast expanded in its military overcoat, entering with brisk step, saw the cropped side-whiskers, the moustache, the aquiline nose, and heard the sonorous voice exchanging greetings with the cadets, he was seized by the same rapture that he experienced later on when he met the woman he loved. Indeed, his passionate adoration of the Emperor was even stronger: he wished to sacrifice something—everything, even himself—to prove his complete devotion. And the Emperor Nicholas was conscious of evoking this rapture and deliberately aroused it. He played with the cadets, surrounded himself with them, treating them sometimes with childish simplicity, sometimes as a friend, and then again with majestic solemnity. After that affair with the officer, Nicholas Pávlovich said nothing to Kasátsky, but when the latter approached he waved him away theatrically, frowned, shook his finger at him, and afterwards when leaving, said: 'Remember that I know everything. There are some things I would rather not know, but they remain here,' and he pointed to his heart.

When on leaving College the cadets were received by the Emperor, he did not again refer to Kasátsky's offence, but told them all, as was his custom, that they should serve him and the fatherland loyally, that he would always be their best friend, and that when necessary they might approach him direct. All the cadets were as usual greatly moved, and Kasátsky even shed tears, remembering the past, and vowed that he would serve his beloved Tsar with all his soul.

When Kasátsky took up his commission his mother moved with her daughter first to Moscow and then to their country estate. Kasátsky gave half his property to his sister and kept only enough to maintain himself in the expensive regiment he had joined.

To all appearance he was just an ordinary, brilliant young officer of the Guards making a career for himself; but intense and complex strivings went on within him. From early childhood his efforts had seemed to be very varied, but essentially they were all one and the same. He tried in everything he took up to attain such success and perfection as would evoke praise and surprise. Whether it was his studies or his military exercises, he took them up and worked at them till he was praised and held up as an example to others. Mastering one subject he took up another, and obtained first place in his studies. For example, while still at College he noticed in himself an awkwardness in French conversation, and contrived to master French till he spoke it as well as Russian, and then he took up chess and became an excellent player.

Apart from his main vocation, which was the service of his Tsar and the fatherland, he always set himself some particular aim, and however unimportant it was, devoted himself completely to it and lived for it until it was accomplished. And as soon as it was attained another aim would immediately present itself, replacing its predecessor. This passion for distinguishing himself, or for accomplishing something in order to distinguish himself, filled his life. On taking up his commission he set himself to acquire the utmost perfection in knowledge of the service, and very soon became a model officer, though still with the same fault of ungovernable irascibility, which here in the service again led him to commit actions inimical to his success. Then he took to reading, having once in conversation in society felt himself deficient in general education—and again achieved his purpose. Then, wishing to secure a brilliant position in high society, he learnt to dance excellently and very soon was invited to all the balls in the best circles, and to some of their evening gatherings. But this did not satisfy him: he was accustomed to being first, and in this society was far from being so.

The highest society then consisted, and I think always and everywhere does consist, of four sorts of people: rich people who are received at Court, people not wealthy but born and brought up in Court circles, rich people who ingratiate themselves into the Court set, and people neither rich nor belonging to the Court but who ingratiate themselves into the first and second sets.

Kasátsky did not belong to the first two sets, but was readily welcomed in the others. On entering society he determined to have relations with some society lady, and to his own surprise quickly accomplished this purpose. He soon realized, however, that the circles in which he moved were not the highest, and that though he was received in the highest spheres he did not belong to them. They were polite to him, but showed by their whole manner that they had their own set and that he was not of it. And Kasátsky wished to belong to that inner circle. To attain that end it would be necessary to be an aide-de-camp to the Emperor—which he expected to become—or to marry into that exclusive set, which he resolved to do. And his choice fell on a beauty belonging to the Court, who not merely belonged to the circle into which he wished to be accepted, but whose friendship was coveted by the very highest people and those most firmly established in that highest circle. This was Countess Korotkóva. Kasátsky began to pay court to her, and not merely for the sake of his career. She was extremely attractive and he soon fell in love with her. At first she was noticeably cool towards him, but then suddenly changed and became gracious, and her mother gave him pressing invitations to visit them. Kasátsky proposed and was accepted. He was surprised at the facility with which he attained such happiness. But though he noticed something strange and unusual in the behaviour towards him of both mother and daughter, he was blinded by being so deeply in love, and did not realize what almost the whole town knew—namely, that his fiancée had been the Emperor Nicholas's mistress the previous year.

Two weeks before the day arranged for the wedding, Kasátsky was at Tsárskoe Seló at his fiancée's country place. It was a hot day in May. He and his betrothed had walked about the garden and were sitting on a bench in a shady linden alley. Mary's white muslin dress suited her particularly well, and she seemed the personification of innocence and love as she sat, now bending her head, now gazing up at the very tall and handsome man who was speaking to her with particular tenderness and self-restraint, as if he feared by word or gesture to offend or sully her angelic purity.

Kasátsky belonged to those men of the eighteen-forties (they are now no longer to be found) who while deliberately and without any conscientious scruples condoning impurity in themselves, required ideal and angelic purity in their women, regarded all unmarried women of their circle as possessed of such purity, and treated them accordingly. There was much that was false and harmful in this outlook, as concerning the laxity the men permitted themselves, but in regard to the women that old-fashioned view (sharply differing from that held by young people to-day who see in every girl merely a female seeking a mate) was, I think, of value. The girls, perceiving such adoration, endeavoured with more or less success to be goddesses.

Such was the view Kasátsky held of women, and that was how he regarded his fiancée. He was particularly in love that day, but did not experience any sensual desire for her. On the contrary he regarded her with tender adoration as something unattainable.

He rose to his full height, standing before her with both hands on his sabre.

'I have only now realized what happiness a man can experience! And it is you, my darling, who have given me this happiness,' he said with a timid smile.

Endearments had not yet become usual between them, and feeling himself morally inferior he felt terrified at this stage to use them to such an angel.

'It is thanks to you that I have come to know myself. I have learnt that I am better than I thought.'

'I have known that for a long time. That was why I began to love you.'

Nightingales trilled near by and the fresh leafage rustled, moved by a passing breeze.

He took her hand and kissed it, and tears came into his eyes.

She understood that he was thanking her for having said she loved him. He silently took a few steps up and down, and then approached her again and sat down.

'You know . . . I have to tell you . . . I was not disinterested when I began to make love to you. I wanted to get into society; but later . . . how unimportant that became in comparison with you —when I got to know you. You are not angry with me for that?'

She did not reply but merely touched his hand. He understood that this meant: 'No, I am not angry.'

'You said . . .' He hesitated. It seemed too bold to say. 'You said that you began to love me. I believe it—but there is something that troubles you and checks your feeling. What is it?'

'Yes—now or never!' thought she. 'He is bound to know of it anyway. But now he will not forsake me. Ah, if he should, it would be terrible!' And she threw a loving glance at his tall, noble, powerful figure. She loved him now more than she had loved the Tsar, and apart from the Imperial dignity would not have preferred the Emperor to him.

'Listen! I cannot deceive you. I have to tell you. You ask what it is? It is that I have loved before.'

She again laid her hand on his with an imploring gesture. He was silent.

'You want to know who it was? It was—the Emperor.'

'We all love him. I can imagine you, a school-girl at the Institute . . .'

'No, it was later. I was infatuated, but it passed . . . I must tell you . . .'

'Well, what of it?'

'No, it was not simply—' She covered her face with her hands.

'What? You gave yourself to him?'

She was silent.

'His mistress?'

She did not answer.

He sprang up and stood before her with trembling jaws, pale as death. He now remembered how the Emperor, meeting him on the Névsky, had amiably congratulated him.

'O God, what have I done! Stíva!'

'Don't touch me! Don't touch me! Oh, how it pains!'

He turned away and went to the house. There he met her mother.

'What is the matter, Prince? I . . .' She became silent on seeing his face. The blood had suddenly rushed to his head.

'You knew it, and used me to shield them! If you weren't a woman . . .!' he cried, lifting his enormous fist, and turning aside he ran away.

Had his fiancée's lover been a private person he would have killed him, but it was his beloved Tsar.

Next day he applied both for furlough and his

discharge, and professing to be ill, so as to see no one, he went away to the country.

He spent the summer at his village arranging his affairs. When summer was over he did not return to Petersburg, but entered a monastery and there became a monk.

His mother wrote to try to dissuade him from this decisive step, but he replied that he felt God's call which transcended all other considerations. Only his sister, who was as proud and ambitious as he, understood him.

She understood that he had become a monk in order to be above those who considered themselves his superiors. And she understood him correctly. By becoming a monk he showed contempt for all that seemed most important to others and had seemed so to him while he was in the service, and he now ascended a height from which he could look down on those he had formerly envied. . . . But it was not this alone, as his sister Varvára supposed, that influenced him. There was also in him something else—a sincere religious feeling which Varvára did not know, which intertwined itself with the feeling of pride and the desire for pre-eminence, and guided him. His disillusionment with Mary, whom he had thought of angelic purity, and his sense of injury, were so strong that they brought him to despair, and the despair led him— to what? To God, to his childhood's faith which had never been destroyed in him.

II

KASÁTSKY entered the monastery on the feast of the Intercession of the Blessed Virgin.* The Abbot of that monastery was a gentleman by birth, a learned writer and a *stárets*, that is, he belonged to that

* 1st October o.s.—A. M.

succession of monks originating in Walachia who each choose a director and teacher whom they implicitly obey. This Superior had been a disciple of the *stárets* Ambrose, who was a disciple of Makarius, who was a disciple of the *stárets* Leonid, who was a disciple of Païssy Velichkóvsky.

To this Abbot Kasátsky submitted himself as to his chosen director. Here in the monastery, besides the feeling of ascendency over others that such a life gave him, he felt much as he had done in the world: he found satisfaction in attaining the greatest possible perfection outwardly as well as inwardly. As in the regiment he had been not merely an irreproachable officer but had even exceeded his duties and widened the borders of perfection, so also as a monk he tried to be perfect, and was always industrious, abstemious, submissive, and meek, as well as pure both in deed and in thought, and obedient. This last quality in particular made life far easier for him. If many of the demands of life in the monastery, which was near the capital and much frequented, did not please him and were temptations to him, they were all nullified by obedience: 'It is not for me to reason; my business is to do the task set me, whether it be standing beside the relics, singing in the choir, or making up accounts in the monastery guest-house.' All possibility of doubt about anything was silenced by obedience to the *stárets*. Had it not been for this, he would have been oppressed by the length and monotony of the church services, the bustle of the many visitors, and the bad qualities of the other monks. As it was, he not only bore it all joyfully but found in it solace and support. 'I don't know why it is necessary to hear the same prayers several times a day, but I know that it is necessary; and knowing this I find joy in them.' His director told him that as material food is necessary for the maintenance of the life of the body, so spiritual food—the church prayers—is necessary for the maintenance of the spiritual life. He believed this, and though the church services, for which he had to get up early in the morning, were a difficulty, they certainly calmed him and gave him joy. This was the result of his consciousness of humility, and the certainty that whatever he had to do, being fixed by the *stárets*, was right.

The interest of his life consisted not only in an ever greater and greater subjugation of his will, but in the attainment of all the Christian virtues, which at first seemed to him easily attainable. He had given his whole estate to his sister and did not regret it, he had no personal claims, humility towards his inferiors was not merely easy for him but afforded him pleasure. Even victory over the sins of the flesh, greed and lust, was easily attained. His director had specially warned him against the latter sin, but Kasátsky felt free from it and was glad.

One thing only tormented him—the remembrance of his fiancée; and not merely the remembrance but the vivid image of what might have been. Involuntarily he recalled a lady he knew who had been a favourite of the Emperor's, but had afterwards married and become an admirable wife and mother. The husband had a high position, influence and honour, and a good and penitent wife.

In his better hours Kasátsky was not disturbed by such thoughts, and when he recalled them at such times he was merely glad to feel that the temptation was past. But there were moments when all that made up his present life suddenly grew dim before him, moments when, if he did not cease to believe in the aims he had set himself, he ceased to see them and could evoke no confidence in them but was seized by a remembrance of, and—terrible to say—a regret for, the change of life he had made.

The only thing that saved him in that state of mind was obedience and work, and the fact that the whole day was occupied by prayer. He went through the usual forms of prayer, he bowed in prayer, he even prayed more than usual, but it was lip-service only and his soul was not in it. This condition would continue for a day, or sometimes for two days, and would then pass of itself. But those days were dreadful. Kasátsky felt that he was neither in his own hands nor in God's, but was subject to something else. All he could do then was to obey the *stárets*, to restrain himself, to undertake nothing, and simply to wait. In general all this time he lived not by his own will but by that of the *stárets*, and in this obedience he found a special tranquillity.

So he lived in his first monastery for seven years. At the end of the third year he received the tonsure and was ordained to the priesthood by the name of Sergius. The profession was an important event in his inner life. He had previously experienced a great consolation and spiritual exaltation when receiving communion, and now when he himself officiated, the performance of the preparation filled him with ecstatic and deep emotion. But subsequently that feeling became more and more deadened, and once when he was officiating in a depressed state of mind he felt that the influence produced on him by the service would not endure. And it did in fact weaken till only the habit remained.

In general in the seventh year of his life in the monastery Sergius grew weary. He had learnt all there was to learn and had attained all there was to attain, there was nothing more to do and his spiritual drowsiness increased. During this time he heard of his mother's death and his sister Varvára's marriage, but both events were matters of indifference to him. His whole attention and his whole interest were concentrated on his inner life.

In the fourth year of his priesthood, during which the Bishop had been particularly kind to him, the *stárets* told him that he ought not to decline it if he were offered an appointment to higher duties. Then monastic ambition, the very thing he had found so repulsive in other monks, arose within him. He was assigned to a monastery near the metropolis. He wished to refuse but the *stárets* ordered him to accept the appointment. He did so, and took leave of the *stárets* and moved to the other monastery.

The exchange into the metropolitan monastery was an important event in Sergius's life. There he encountered many temptations, and his whole will-power was concentrated on meeting them.

In the first monastery, women had not been a temptation to him, but here that temptation arose with terrible strength and even took definite shape. There was a lady known for her frivolous behaviour who began to seek his favour. She talked to him and asked him to visit her. Sergius sternly declined, but was horrified by the definiteness of his desire. He was so alarmed that he wrote about it to the *stárets*. And in addition, to keep himself in hand, he spoke to a young novice and, conquering his sense of shame, confessed his weakness to him, asking him to keep watch on him and not let him go anywhere except to service and to fulfil his duties.

Besides this, a great pitfall for Sergius lay in the fact of his extreme antipathy to his new Abbot, a cunning worldly man who was making a career for himself in the Church. Struggle with himself as he might, he could not master that feeling. He was submissive to the Abbot, but in the depths of his soul he never ceased to condemn him. And in the second year of his residence at the new monastery that ill-feeling broke out.

The Vigil service was being performed in the large church on the eve of the feast of the Intercession of the Blessed Virgin, and there were many visitors. The Abbot himself was conducting the service. Father Sergius was standing in his usual place and praying: that is, he was in that condition of struggle which always occupied him during the service, especially in the large church when he was not himself conducting the service. This conflict was occasioned by his irritation at the presence of fine folk, especially ladies. He tried not to see them or to notice all that went on: how a soldier conducted them, pushing the common people aside, how the ladies pointed out the monks to one another—especially himself and a monk noted for his good looks. He tried as it were to keep his mind in blinkers, to see nothing but the light of the candles on the altar-screen, the icons, and those conducting the service. He tried to hear nothing but the prayers that were being chanted or read, to feel nothing but self-oblivion in consciousness of the fulfilment of duty—a feeling he always experienced when hearing or reciting in advance the prayers he had so often heard.

So he stood, crossing and prostrating himself when necessary, and struggled with himself, now giving way to cold condemnation and now to a consciously evoked obliteration of thought and feeling. Then the sacristan, Father Nicodemus—also a great stumbling-block to Sergius who involuntarily reproached him for flattering and fawning on the Abbot—approached him and, bowing low, requested his presence behind the holy gates. Father Sergius straightened his mantle, put on his biretta, and went circumspectly through the crowd.

'*Lise, regarde à droite, c'est lui!*'* he heard a woman's voice say.

'*Où, où? Il n'est pas tellement beau.*'†

He knew that they were speaking of him. He heard them and, as always at moments of temptation, he repeated the words, 'Lead us not into temptation', and bowing his head and lowering his eyes went past the ambo and in by the north door, avoiding the canons in their cassocks who were just then passing the altar-screen. On entering the sanctuary he bowed, crossing himself as usual and bending double before the icons. Then, raising his head but without turning, he glanced out of the corner of his eye at the Abbot, whom he saw standing beside another glittering figure.

The Abbot was standing by the wall in his vestments. Having freed his short plump hands from beneath his chasuble he had folded them over his fat body and protruding stomach, and fingering the cords of his vestments was smilingly saying something to a military man in the uniform of a general of the Imperial suite, with its insignia and shoulder-knots which Father Sergius's experienced eye at once recognized. This general had been the commander of the regiment in which Sergius had served. He now evidently occupied an important position, and Father Sergius at once noticed that the Abbot was aware of this and that his red face and bald head beamed with satisfaction and pleasure. This vexed and disgusted Father Sergius,

* 'Lise, look to the right. That is he.'

† 'Where? Where? He is not so very handsome.'

the more so when he heard that the Abbot had only sent for him to satisfy the general's curiosity to see a man who had formerly served with him, as he expressed it.

'Very pleased to see you in your angelic guise,' said the general, holding out his hand. 'I hope you have not forgotten an old comrade.'

The whole thing—the Abbot's red, smiling face amid its fringe of grey, the general's words, his well-cared-for face with its self-satisfied smile and the smell of wine from his breath and of cigars from his whiskers—revolted Father Sergius. He bowed again to the Abbot and said:

'Your reverence deigned to send for me?'—and stopped, the whole expression of his face and eyes asking why.

'Yes, to meet the General,' replied the Abbot.

'Your reverence, I left the world to save myself from temptation,' said Father Sergius, turning pale and with quivering lips. 'Why do you expose me to it during prayers and in God's house?'

'You may go! Go!' said the Abbot, flaring up and frowning.

Next day Father Sergius asked pardon of the Abbot and of the brethren for his pride, but at the same time, after a night spent in prayer, he decided that he must leave this monastery, and he wrote to the *stárets* begging permission to return to him. He wrote that he felt his weakness and incapacity to struggle against temptation without his help, and penitently confessed his sin of pride. By return of post came a letter from the *stárets,* who wrote that Sergius's pride was the cause of all that had happened. The old man pointed out that his fits of anger were due to the fact that in refusing all clerical honours he humiliated himself not for the sake of God but for the sake of his pride. 'There now, am I not a splendid man not to want anything?' That was why he could not tolerate the Abbot's action. 'I have renounced everything for the glory of God, and here I am exhibited like a wild beast!' 'Had you renounced vanity for God's sake you would have borne it. Worldly pride is not yet dead in you. I have thought about you, Sergius my son, and prayed also, and this is what God has suggested to me. At the Tambóv hermitage the anchorite Hilary, a man of saintly life, has died. He had lived there eighteen years. The Tambóv Abbot is asking whether there is not a brother who would take his place. And here comes your letter. Go to Father Païssy of the Tambóv Monastery. I will write to him about you, and you must ask for Hilary's cell. Not that you can replace Hilary, but you need solitude to quell your pride. May God bless you!'

Sergius obeyed the *stárets*, showed his letter to the Abbot, and having obtained his permission, gave up his cell, handed all his possessions over to the monastery, and set out for the Tambóv hermitage.

There the Abbot, an excellent manager of merchant origin, received Sergius simply and quietly and placed him in Hilary's cell, at first assigning to him a lay brother but afterwards leaving him alone, at Sergius's own request. The cell was a dual cave, dug into the hillside, and in it Hilary had been buried. In the back part was Hilary's grave, while in the front was a niche for sleeping, with a straw mattress, a small table, and a shelf with icons and books. Outside the outer door, which fastened with a hook, was another shelf on which, once a day, a monk placed food from the monastery.

And so Sergius became a hermit.

III

At Carnival time, in the sixth year of Sergius's life at the hermitage, a merry company of rich people, men and women from a neighbouring town, made up a troyka-party, after a meal of carnival-pancakes and wine. The company consisted of two lawyers, a wealthy landowner, an officer, and four ladies. One lady was the officer's wife, another the wife of the landowner, the third his sister—a young girl—and the fourth a divorcée, beautiful, rich, and eccentric, who amazed and shocked the town by her escapades.

The weather was excellent and the snow-covered road smooth as a floor. They drove some seven miles out of town, and then stopped and consulted as to whether they should turn back or drive farther.

'But where does this road lead to?' asked Makóvkina, the beautiful divorcée.

'To Tambóv, eight miles from here,' replied one of the lawyers, who was having a flirtation with her.

'And then where?'

'Then on to L——, past the Monastery.'

'Where that Father Sergius lives?'

'Yes.'

'Kasátsky, the handsome hermit?'

'Yes.'

'*Mesdames and messieurs*, let us drive on and see Kasátsky! We can stop at Tambóv and have something to eat.'

'But we shouldn't get home to-night!'

'Never mind, we will stay at Kasátsky's.'

'Well, there is a very good hostelry at the Monastery. I stayed there when I was defending Mákhin.'

'No, I shall spend the night at Kasátsky's!'

'Impossible! Even your omnipotence could not accomplish that!'

'Impossible? Will you bet?'

'All right! If you spend the night with him, the stake shall be whatever you like.'

'*A discrétion!*'

'But on your side too!'

'Yes, of course. Let us drive on.'

Vodka was handed to the drivers, and the party got out a box of pies, wine, and sweets for themselves. The ladies wrapped up in their white dogskins. The drivers disputed as to whose troyka should go ahead, and the youngest, seating himself sideways with a dashing air, swung his long knout and shouted to the horses. The troyka-bells tinkled and the sledge-runners squeaked over the snow.

The sledges swayed hardly at all. The shaft-horse, with his tightly bound tail under his decorated breechband, galloped smoothly and briskly; the smooth road seemed to run rapidly backwards, while the driver dashingly shook the reins. One of the lawyers and the officer sitting opposite talked nonsense to Makóvkina's neighbour, but Makóvkina herself sat motionless and in thought, tightly wrapped in her fur. 'Always the same and always nasty! The same red shiny faces smelling of wine and cigars! The same talk, the same thoughts, and always about the same things! And they are all satisfied and confident that it should be so, and will go on living like that till they die. But I can't. It bores me. I want something that would upset it all and turn it upside down. Suppose it happened to us as to those people—at Sarátov was it?—who kept on driving and froze to death. . . . What would our people do? How would they behave? Basely, for certain. Each for himself. And I too should act badly. But I at any rate have beauty. They all know it. And how about that monk? Is it possible that he has become indifferent to it? No! That is the one thing they all care for—like that cadet last autumn. What a fool he was!'

'Iván Nikoláevich!' she said aloud.

'What are your commands?'

'How old is he?'

'Who?'

'Kasátsky.'

'Over forty, I should think.'

'And does he receive all visitors?'

'Yes, everybody, but not always.'

'Cover up my feet. Not like that—how clumsy you are! No! More, more—like that! But you need not squeeze them!'

So they came to the forest where the cell was.

Makóvkina got out of the sledge, and told them to drive on. They tried to dissuade her, but she grew irritable and ordered them to go on.

When the sledges had gone she went up the path in her white dogskin coat. The lawyer got out and stopped to watch her.

It was Father Sergius's sixth year as a recluse, and he was now forty-nine. His life in solitude was hard—not on account of the fasts and the prayers (they were no hardship to him) but on account of an inner conflict he had not at all anticipated. The sources of that conflict were two: doubts, and the lust of the flesh. And these two enemies always appeared together. It seemed to him that they were two foes, but in reality they were one and the same. As soon as doubt was gone so was the lustful desire. But thinking them to be two different fiends he fought them separately.

'O my God, my God!' thought he. 'Why dost thou not grant me faith? There is lust, of course: even the saints had to fight that—Saint Anthony and others. But they had faith, while I have moments, hours, and days, when it is absent. Why does the whole world, with all its delights, exist if it is sinful and must be renounced? Why hast Thou created this temptation? Temptation? Is it not rather a temptation that I wish to abandon all the joys of earth and prepare something for myself there where perhaps there is nothing?' And he became horrified and filled with disgust at himself. 'Vile creature! And it is you who wish to become a saint!' he upbraided himself, and he began to pray. But as soon as he started to pray he saw himself vividly as he had been at the Monastery, in a majestic post in biretta and mantle, and he shook his head. 'No, that is not right. It is deception. I may deceive others, but not myself or God. I am not a majestic man, but a pitiable and ridiculous one!' And he threw back the folds of his cassock and smiled as he looked at his thin legs in their underclothing.

Then he dropped the folds of the cassock again and began reading the prayers, making the sign of the cross and prostrating himself. 'Can it be that this couch will be my bier?' he read. And it seemed as if a devil whispered to him: 'A solitary couch is itself a bier. Falsehood!' And in imagination he saw the shoulders of a widow with whom he had lived. He shook himself, and went on reading. Having read the precepts he took up the Gospels, opened the book, and happened on a passage he often repeated and knew by heart: 'Lord, I believe. Help thou my unbelief!'—and he put away all the doubts that had arisen. As one replaces an object of insecure equilibrium, so he carefully replaced his belief on its shaky pedestal and carefully stepped back from it so as not to shake or upset it. The blinkers were adjusted again and he felt tranquillized, and repeating his childhood's prayer: 'Lord, receive me, receive me!' he felt not merely at ease, but thrilled and joyful. He crossed himself and lay down on the bedding on his narrow bench, tucking his summer cassock under his head. He fell asleep at once, and in his light slumber he seemed to hear the tinkling of sledge bells. He did not know whether he was dreaming or awake, but a knock at the door aroused him. He sat up, distrusting his senses, but the knock was repeated. Yes, it was a knock close at hand, at his door, and with it the sound of a woman's voice.

'My God! Can it be true, as I have read in the *Lives of the Saints*, that the devil takes on the form of a woman? Yes—it is a woman's voice. And a tender, timid, pleasant voice. Phui!' And he spat to exorcise the devil. 'No, it was only my imagination,' he assured himself, and he went to the corner where his lectern stood, falling on his knees in the regular and habitual manner which of itself gave him consolation and satisfaction. He sank down, his hair hanging over his face, and pressed his head, already going bald in front, to the cold damp strip of drugget on the draughty floor. He read the psalm old Father Pímon had told him warded off temptation. He easily raised his light and emaciated body on his strong sinewy legs and tried to continue saying his prayers, but instead of doing so he involuntarily strained his hearing. He wished to hear more. All was quiet. From the corner of the roof regular drops continued to fall into the tub below. Outside was a mist and fog eating into the snow that lay on the ground. It was still, very still. And suddenly there was a rustling at the window and a voice—that same tender, timid voice, which could only belong to an attractive woman—said:

'Let me in, for Christ's sake!'

It seemed as though his blood had all rushed to his heart and settled there. He could hardly breathe. 'Let God arise and let his enemies be scattered . . .'

'But I am not a devil!' It was obvious that the lips that uttered this were smiling. 'I am not a devil, but only a sinful woman who has lost her way, not figuratively but literally!' She laughed. 'I am frozen and beg for shelter.'

He pressed his face to the window, but the little icon-lamp was reflected by it and shone on the whole pane. He put his hands to both sides of his face and peered between them. Fog, mist, a tree, and—just opposite him—she herself. Yes, there, a few inches from him, was the sweet, kindly frightened face of a woman in a cap and a coat of long white fur, leaning towards him. Their eyes met with instant recognition: not that they had ever known one another, they had never met before, but by the look they exchanged they—and he particularly—felt that they knew and understood one another. After that glance to imagine her to be a devil and not a simple, kindly, sweet, timid woman, was impossible.

'Who are you? Why have you come?' he asked.

'Do please open the door!' she replied, with capricious authority. 'I am frozen. I tell you I have lost my way.'

'But I am a monk—a hermit.'

'Oh, do please open the door—or do you wish me to freeze under your window while you say your prayers?'

'But how have you . . .'

'I shan't eat you. For God's sake let me in! I am quite frozen.'

She really did feel afraid, and said this in an almost tearful voice.

He stepped back from the window and looked at an icon of the Saviour in His crown of thorns.

'Lord, help me! Lord, help me!' he exclaimed, crossing himself and bowing low. Then he went to the door, and opening it into the tiny porch, felt for the hook that fastened the outer door and began to lift it. He heard steps outside. She was coming from the window to the door. 'Ah!' she suddenly exclaimed, and he understood that she had stepped into the puddle that the dripping from the roof had formed at the threshold. His hands trembled, and he could not raise the hook of the tightly closed door.

'Oh, what are you doing? Let me in! I am all wet. I am frozen! You are thinking about saving your soul and are letting me freeze to death . . .'

He jerked the door towards him, raised the hook, and without considering what he was doing, pushed it open with such force that it struck her.

'Oh—*pardon!*' he suddenly exclaimed, reverting completely to his old manner with ladies.

She smiled on hearing that *pardon*. 'He is not quite so terrible, after all,' she thought. 'It's all right. It is you who must pardon me,' she said, stepping past him. 'I should never have ventured, but such an extraordinary circumstance . . .'

'If you please!' he uttered, and stood aside to let her pass him. A strong smell of fine scent, which he had long not encountered, struck him. She went through the little porch into the cell where he lived. He closed the outer door without fastening the hook, and stepped in after her.

'Lord Jesus Christ, Son of God, have mercy on me a sinner! Lord, have mercy on me a sinner!' he prayed unceasingly, not merely to himself but involuntarily moving his lips. 'If you please!' he said to her again. She stood in the middle of the room, moisture dripping from her to the floor as she looked him over. Her eyes were laughing.

'Forgive me for having disturbed your solitude. But you see what a position I am in. It all came about from our starting from town for a sledge-drive, and my making a bet that I would walk back by myself from the Vorobëvka to the town. But then I lost my way, and if I had not happened to come upon your cell . . .' She began lying, but his face confused her so that she could not continue, but became silent. She had not expected him to be at all such as he was. He was not as handsome as she had imagined, but was nevertheless beautiful in her eyes: his greyish hair and beard, slightly curling, his fine, regular nose, and his eyes like glowing coal when he looked at her, made a strong impression on her.

He saw that she was lying.

'Yes . . . so,' said he, looking at her and again lowering his eyes. 'I will go in there, and this place is at your disposal.'

And taking down the little lamp, he lit a candle, and bowing low to her went into the small cell beyond the partition, and she heard him begin to move something about there. 'Probably he is barricading himself in from me!' she thought with a smile, and throwing off her white dogskin cloak she tried to take off her cap, which had become entangled in her hair and in the woven kerchief she was wearing under it. She had not got at all wet when standing under the window, and had said so only as a pretext to get him to let her in. But she really had stepped into the puddle at the door, and her left foot was wet up to the ankle and her over-shoe full of water. She sat down on his bed—a bench only covered by a bit of carpet—and began to take off her boots. The little cell seemed to her charming. The narrow little room, some seven feet by nine, was as clean as glass. There was nothing in it but the bench on which she was sitting, the book-shelf above it, and a lectern in the corner. A sheepskin coat and a cassock hung on nails by the door. Above the lectern was the little lamp and an icon of Christ in His crown of thorns. The room smelt strangely of perspiration and of earth. It all pleased her—even that smell. Her wet feet, especially one of them, were uncomfortable, and she quickly began to take off her boots and stockings without ceasing to smile, pleased not so much at having achieved her object as because she perceived that she had abashed that charming, strange, striking, and attractive man. 'He did not respond, but what of that?' she said to herself.

'Father Sergius! Father Sergius! Or how does one call you?'

'What do you want?' replied a quiet voice.

'Please forgive me for disturbing your solitude, but really I could not help it. I should simply have fallen ill. And I don't know that I shan't now. I am all wet and my feet are like ice.'

'Pardon me,' replied the quiet voice. 'I cannot be of any assistance to you.'

'I would not have disturbed you if I could have helped it. I am only here till daybreak.'

He did not reply and she heard him muttering something, probably his prayers.

'You will not be coming in here?' she asked, smiling. 'For I must undress to dry myself.'

He did not reply, but continued to read his prayers.

'Yes, that is a man!' thought she, getting her dripping boot off with difficulty. She tugged at it, but could not get it off. The absurdity of it struck her and she began to laugh almost inaudibly. But knowing that he would hear her laughter and would be moved by it just as she wished him to be, she laughed louder, and her laughter—gay, natural, and kindly—really acted on him just in the way she wished.

'Yes, I could love a man like that—such eyes and such a simple noble face, and passionate too despite all the prayers he mutters!' thought she. 'You can't deceive a woman in these things. As soon as he put his face to the window and saw me, he understood and knew. The glimmer of it was in his eyes and remained there. He began to love me and desired me. Yes—desired!' said she, getting her overshoe and her boot off at last and starting to take off her stockings. To remove those long stockings fastened with elastic it was necessary to raise her skirts. She felt embarrassed and said:

'Don't come in!'

But there was no reply from the other side of the wall. The steady muttering continued and also a sound of moving.

'He is prostrating himself to the ground, no doubt,' thought she. 'But he won't bow himself out of it. He is thinking of me just as I am thinking of him. He is thinking of these feet of mine with the same feeling that I have!' And she pulled off her wet stockings and put her feet up on the bench, pressing them under her. She sat a while like that with her arms round her knees and looking pensively before her. 'But it is a desert, here in this silence. No one would ever know. . . .'

She rose, took her stockings over to the stove, and hung them on the damper. It was a queer damper, and she turned it about, and then, stepping lightly on her bare feet, returned to the bench and sat down there again with her feet up.

There was complete silence on the other side of the partition. She looked at the tiny watch that hung round her neck. It was two o'clock. 'Our party should return about three!' She had not more than an hour before her. 'Well, am I to sit like this all alone? What nonsense! I don't want to. I will call him at once.'

'Father Sergius, Father Sergius! Sergéy Dmítrich! Prince Kasátsky!'

Beyond the partition all was silent.

'Listen! This is cruel. I would not call you if it were not necessary. I am ill. I don't know what is the matter with me!' she exclaimed in a tone of suffering. 'Oh! Oh!' she groaned, falling back on the bench. And strange to say she really felt that her strength was failing, that she was becoming faint, that everything in her ached, and that she was shivering with fever.

'Listen! Help me! I don't know what is the matter with me. Oh! Oh!' She unfastened her dress, exposing her breast, and lifted her arms, bare to the elbow. 'Oh! Oh!'

All this time he stood on the other side of the partition and prayed. Having finished all the evening prayers, he now stood motionless, his eyes looking at the end of his nose, and mentally repeated with all his soul: 'Lord Jesus Christ, Son of God, have mercy upon me!'

But he had heard everything. He had heard how the silk rustled when she took off her dress, how she stepped with bare feet on the floor, and had heard how she rubbed her feet with her hand. He felt his own weakness, and that he might be lost at any moment. That was why he prayed unceasingly. He felt rather as the hero in the fairy-tale must have felt when he had to go on and on without looking round. So Sergius heard and felt that danger and destruction were there, hovering above and around him, and that he could only save himself by not looking in that direction for an instant. But suddenly the desire to look seized him. At the same instant she said:

'This is inhuman. I may die. . . .'

'Yes, I will go to her, but like the Saint who laid one hand on the adulteress and thrust his other into the brazier. But there is no brazier here.' He looked round. The lamp! He put his finger over the flame and frowned, preparing himself to suffer. And for a rather long time, as it seemed to him, there was no sensation, but suddenly—he had not yet decided whether it was painful enough—he writhed all over, jerked his hand away, and waved it in the air. 'No, I can't stand that!'

'For God's sake come to me! I am dying! Oh!'

'Well—shall I perish? No, not so!'

'I will come to you directly,' he said, and having opened his door, he went without looking at her through the cell into the porch where he used to chop wood. There he felt for the block and for an axe which leant against the wall.

'Immediately!' he said, and taking up the axe with his right hand he laid the forefinger of his left hand on the block, swung the axe, and struck with it below the second joint. The finger flew off more lightly than a stick of similar thickness, and bounding up, turned over on the edge of the block and then fell to the floor.

He heard it fall before he felt any pain, but before he had time to be surprised he felt a burning pain and the warmth of flowing blood. He hastily wrapped the stump in the skirt of his cassock, and pressing it to his hip went back into the room, and standing in front of the woman, lowered his eyes and asked in a low voice: 'What do you want?'

She looked at his pale face and his quivering left

cheek, and suddenly felt ashamed. She jumped up, seized her fur cloak, and throwing it round her shoulders, wrapped herself up in it.

'I was in pain . . . I have caught cold . . . I . . . Father Sergius . . . I . . .'

He let his eyes, shining with a quiet light of joy, rest upon her, and said:

'Dear sister, why did you wish to ruin your immortal soul? Temptations must come into the world, but woe to him by whom temptation comes. Pray that God may forgive us!'

She listened and looked at him. Suddenly she heard the sound of something dripping. She looked down and saw that blood was flowing from his hand and down his cassock.

'What have you done to your hand? She remembered the sound she had heard, and seizing the little lamp ran out into the porch. There on the floor she saw the bloody finger. She returned with her face paler than his and was about to speak to him, but he silently passed into the back cell and fastened the door.

'Forgive me!' she said. 'How can I atone for my sin?'

'Go away.'

'Let me tie up your hand.'

'Go away from here.'

She dressed hurriedly and silently, and when ready sat waiting in her furs. The sledge-bells were heard outside.

'Father Sergius, forgive me!'

'Go away. God will forgive.'

'Father Sergius! I will change my life. Do not forsake me!'

'Go away.'

'Forgive me—and give me your blessing!'

'In the name of the Father and of the Son and of

the Holy Ghost!'—she heard his voice from behind the partition. 'Go!'

She burst into sobs and left the cell. The lawyer came forward to meet her.

'Well, I see I have lost the bet. It can't be helped. Where will you sit?'

'It is all the same to me.'

She took a seat in the sledge, and did not utter a word all the way home.

A year later she entered a convent as a novice, and lived a strict life under the direction of the hermit Arsény, who wrote letters to her at long intervals.

IV

Father Sergius lived as a recluse for another seven years.

At first he accepted much of what people brought him—tea, sugar, white bread, milk, clothing, and fire-wood. But as time went on he led a more and more austere life, refusing everything superfluous, and finally he accepted nothing but rye-bread once a week. Everything else that was brought him he gave to the poor who came to him. He spent his entire time in his cell, in prayer or in conversation with callers, who became more and more numerous as time went on. Only three times a year did he go out to church, and when necessary he went out to fetch water and wood.

The episode with Makóvkina had occurred after five years of his hermit life. That occurrence soon became generally known—her nocturnal visit, the change she underwent, and her entry into a convent. From that time Father Sergius's fame increased. More and more visitors came to see him, other monks settled down near his cell, and a church was erected there and also a hostelry. His fame, as usual exaggerating his feats, spread ever more and more widely. People began to come to him from a distance, and began bringing invalids to him whom they declared he cured.

His first cure occurred in the eighth year of his life as a hermit. It was the healing of a fourteen-year-old boy, whose mother brought him to Father Sergius insisting that he should lay his hand on the child's head. It had never occurred to Father Sergius that he could cure the sick. He would have regarded such a thought as a great sin of pride; but the mother who brought the boy implored him insistently, falling at his feet and saying: 'Why do you, who heal others, refuse to help my son?' She besought him in Christ's name. When Father Sergius assured her that only God could heal the sick, she replied that she only wanted him to lay his hands on the boy and pray for him. Father Sergius refused and returned to his cell. But next day (it was in autumn and the nights were already cold) on going out for water he saw the same mother with her son, a pale boy of fourteen, and was met by the same petition.

He remembered the parable of the unjust judge, and though he had previously felt sure that he ought to refuse, he now began to hesitate and, having hesitated, took to prayer and prayed until a decision formed itself in his soul. This decision was, that he ought to accede to the woman's request and that her faith might save her son. As for himself, he would in this case be but an insignificant instrument chosen by God.

And going out to the mother he did what she asked—laid his hand on the boy's head and prayed.

The mother left with her son, and a month later the boy recovered, and the fame of the holy healing power of the *stárets* Sergius (as they now called him) spread throughout the whole district. After that, not a week passed without sick people coming, riding or on foot, to Father Sergius; and having acceded to one petition he could not refuse others, and he laid his hands on many and prayed. Many recovered, and his fame spread more and more.

So seven years passed in the Monastery and thirteen in his hermit's cell. He now had the appearance of an old man: his beard was long and grey, but his hair, though thin, was still black and curly.

V

For some weeks Father Sergius had been living with one persistent thought: whether he was right in accepting the position in which he had not so much placed himself as been placed by the Archimandrite and the Abbot. That position had begun after the recovery of the fourteen-year-old boy. From that time, with each month, week, and day that passed, Sergius felt his own inner life wasting away and being replaced by external life. It was as if he had been turned inside out.

Sergius saw that he was a means of attracting visitors and contributions to the monastery, and that therefore the authorities arranged matters in such a way as to make as much use of him as possible. For instance, they rendered it impossible for him to do any manual work. He was supplied with everything he could want, and they only demanded of him that he should not refuse his blessing to those who came to seek it. For his convenience they appointed days when he would receive. They arranged a reception-room for men, and a place was railed in so that he should not be pushed over by the crowds of women visitors, and so that he could conveniently bless those who came.

They told him that people needed him, and that fulfilling Christ's law of love he could not refuse their demand to see him, and that to avoid them would be cruel. He could not but agree with this, but the more he gave himself up to such a life the more he felt that what was internal became external, and that the fount of living water within him dried up, and that what he did now was done more and more for men and less and less for God.

Whether he admonished people, or simply blessed them, or prayed for the sick, or advised people about their lives, or listened to expressions of gratitude from those he had helped by precepts, or alms, or healing (as they assured him)—he could not help being pleased at it, and could not be indifferent to the results of his activity and to the influence he exerted. He thought himself a shining light, and the more he felt this the more was he conscious of a weakening, a dying down of the divine light of truth that shone within him.

'In how far is what I do for God and in how far is it for men?' That was the question that insistently tormented him and to which he was not so much unable to give himself an answer as unable to face the answer.

In the depth of his soul he felt that the devil had substituted an activity for men in place of his former activity for God. He felt this because, just as it had formerly been hard for him to be torn from his solitude so now that solitude itself was hard for him. He was oppressed and wearied by visitors, but at the bottom of his heart he was glad of their presence and glad of the praise they heaped upon him.

There was a time when he decided to go away and hide. He even planned all that was necessary for that purpose. He prepared for himself a peasant's shirt, trousers, coat, and cap. He explained that he wanted these to give to those who asked. And he kept these clothes in his cell, planning how he would put them on, cut his hair short, and go away. First he would go some three hundred versts by train, then he would leave the train and walk from village to village. He asked an old man who had been a soldier how he tramped: what people gave him, and what shelter they allowed him. The soldier told him where people were most charitable, and where they would take a wanderer in for the night, and Father Sergius intended to avail himself of this information. He even put on those clothes one night in his desire to go, but he could not decide what was best—to remain or to escape. At first he was in doubt, but afterwards this indecision passed. He submitted to custom and yielded to the devil, and only the peasant garb reminded him of the thought and feeling he had had.

Every day more and more people flocked to him and less and less time was left him for prayer and for renewing his spiritual strength. Sometimes in lucid moments he thought he was like a place where there had once been a spring. 'There used to be a feeble spring of living water which flowed quietly from me and through me. That was true life, the time when she tempted me!' (He always thought with ecstasy of that night and of her who was now Mother Agnes.) She had tasted of that pure water, but since then there had not been time for it to collect before thirsty people came crowding in and pushing one another aside. And they had trampled everything down and nothing was left but mud.

So he thought in rare moments of lucidity, but his usual state of mind was one of weariness and a tender pity for himself because of that weariness.

It was in spring, on the eve of the mid-Pentecostal

feast. Father Sergius was officiating at the Vigil Service in his hermitage church, where the congregation was as large as the little church could hold—about twenty people. They were all well-to-do proprietors or merchants. Father Sergius admitted anyone, but a selection was made by the monk in attendance and by an assistant who was sent to the hermitage every day from the monastery. A crowd of some eighty people—pilgrims and peasants, and especially peasant-women—stood outside waiting for Father Sergius to come out and bless them. Meanwhile he conducted the service, but at the point at which he went out to the tomb of his predecessor, he staggered and would have fallen had he not been caught by a merchant standing behind him and by the monk acting as deacon.

'What is the matter, Father Sergius? Dear man! O Lord!' exclaimed the women. 'He is as white as a sheet!'

But Father Sergius recovered immediately, and though very pale, he waved the merchant and the deacon aside and continued to chant the service.

Father Seraphim, the deacon, the acolytes, and Sófya Ivánovna, a lady who always lived near the hermitage and tended Father Sergius, begged him to bring the service to an end.

'No, there's nothing the matter,' said Father Sergius, slightly smiling from beneath his moustache and continuing the service. 'Yes, that is the way the Saints behaved!' thought he.

'A holy man—an angel of God!' he heard just then the voice of Sófya Ivánovna behind him, and also of the merchant who had supported him. He did not heed their entreaties, but went on with the service. Again crowding together they all made their way by the narrow passages back into the little church, and there, though abbreviating it slightly, Father Sergius completed vespers.

Immediately after the service Father Sergius, having pronounced the benediction on those present, went over to the bench under the elm tree at the entrance to the cave. He wished to rest and breathe the fresh air—he felt in need of it. But as soon as he left the church the crowd of people rushed to him soliciting his blessing, his advice, and his help. There were pilgrims who constantly tramped from one holy place to another and from one *stárets* to another, and were always entranced by every shrine and every *stárets*. Father Sergius knew this common, cold, conventional, and most irreligious type. There were pilgrims, for the most part discharged soldiers, unaccustomed to a settled life, poverty-stricken, and many of them drunken old men, who tramped from monastery to monastery merely to be fed. And there were rough peasants and peasant-women who had come with their selfish requirements, seeking cures or to have doubts about quite practical affairs solved for them: about marrying off a daughter, or hiring a shop, or buying a bit of land, or how to atone for having overlaid a child or having an illegitimate one.

All this was an old story and not in the least interesting to him. He knew he would hear nothing new from these folk, that they would arouse no religious emotion in him; but he liked to see the crowd to which his blessing and advice was necessary and precious, so while that crowd oppressed him it also pleased him. Father Seraphim began to drive them away, saying that Father Sergius was tired. But Father Sergius, remembering the words of the Gospel: 'Forbid them' (children) 'not to come unto me', and feeling tenderly towards himself at this recollection, said they should be allowed to approach.

He rose, went to the railing beyond which the crowd had gathered, and began blessing them and answering their questions, but in a voice so weak that he was touched with pity for himself. Yet despite his wish to receive them all he could not do it. Things again grew dark before his eyes, and he staggered and grasped the railings. He felt a rush of blood to his head and first went pale and then suddenly flushed.

'I must leave the rest till to-morrow. I cannot do more to-day,' and, pronouncing a general benediction, he returned to the bench. The merchant again supported him, and leading him by the arm helped him to be seated.

'Father!' came voices from the crowd. 'Dear Father! Do not forsake us. Without you we are lost!'

The merchant, having seated Father Sergius on the bench under the elm, took on himself police duties and drove the people off very resolutely. It is true that he spoke in a low voice so that Father Sergius might not hear him, but his words were incisive and angry.

'Be off, be off! He has blessed you, and what more do you want? Get along with you, or I'll wring your necks! Move on there! Get along, you old woman with your dirty leg-bands! Go, go! Where are you shoving to? You've been told that it is finished. To-morrow will be as God wills, but for to-day he has finished!'

'Father! Only let my eyes have a glimpse of his dear face!' said an old woman.

'I'll glimpse you! Where are you shoving to?'

Father Sergius noticed that the merchant seemed to be acting roughly, and in a feeble voice told the attendant that the people should not be driven away. He knew that they would be driven away all the same, and he much desired to be left alone and to rest, but he sent the attendant with that message to produce an impression.

'All right, all right! I am not driving them away. I am only remonstrating with them,' replied the merchant. 'You know they wouldn't hesitate to drive a man to death. They have no pity, they only consider themselves. . . . You've been told you cannot see him. Go away! To-morrow!' And he got rid of them all.

He took all these pains because he liked order and liked to domineer and drive the people away, but chiefly because he wanted to have Father Sergius to himself. He was a widower with an only daughter who was an invalid and unmarried, and whom he had brought fourteen hundred versts to Father Sergius to be healed. For two years past he had been taking her to different places to be cured: first to the university clinic in the chief town of the province, but that did no good; then to a peasant in the province of Samára, where she got a little better; then to a doctor in Moscow to whom he paid much money, but this did no good at all. Now he had been told that Father Sergius wrought cures, and had brought her to him. So when all the people had been driven away he approached Father Sergius, and suddenly falling on his knees loudly exclaimed:

'Holy Father! Bless my afflicted offspring that she may be healed of her malady. I venture to prostrate myself at your holy feet.'

And he placed one hand on the other, cup-wise. He said and did all this as if he were doing something clearly and firmly appointed by law and usage—as if one must and should ask for a daughter to be cured in just this way and no other. He did it with such conviction that it seemed even to Father

Sergius that it should be said and done in just that way, but nevertheless he bade him rise and tell him what the trouble was. The merchant said that his daughter, a girl of twenty-two, had fallen ill two years ago, after her mother's sudden death. She had moaned (as he expressed it) and since then had not been herself. And now he had brought her fourteen hundred versts and she was waiting in the hostelry till Father Sergius should give orders to bring her. She did not go out during the day, being afraid of the light, and could only come after sunset.

'Is she very weak?' asked Father Sergius.

'No, she has no particular weakness. She is quite plump, and is only "nerastenic" the doctors say. If you will only let me bring her this evening, Father Sergius, I'll fly like a spirit to fetch her. Holy Father! Revive a parent's heart, restore his line, save his afflicted daughter by your prayers!' And the merchant again threw himself on his knees and bending sideways, with his head resting on his clenched fists, remained stock still. Father Sergius again told him to get up, and thinking how heavy his activities were and how he went through with them patiently notwithstanding, he sighed heavily and after a few seconds of silence, said:

'Well, bring her this evening. I will pray for her, but now I am tired . . .' and he closed his eyes. 'I will send for you.'

The merchant went away, stepping on tiptoe, which only made his boots creak the louder, and Father Sergius remained alone.

His whole life was filled by Church services and by people who came to see him, but to-day had been a particularly difficult one. In the morning an important official had arrived and had had a long conversation with him; after that a lady had come with her son. This son was a sceptical young professor whom the mother, an ardent believer and devoted to Father Sergius, had brought that he might talk to him. The conversation had been very trying. The young man, evidently not wishing to have a controversy with a monk, had agreed with him in everything as with someone who was mentally inferior. Father Sergius saw that the young man did not believe but yet was satisfied, tranquil, and at ease, and the memory of that conversation now disquieted him.

'Have something to eat, Father,' said the attendant.

'All right, bring me something.'

The attendant went to a hut that had been arranged some ten paces from the cave, and Father Sergius remained alone.

The time was long past when he had lived alone doing everything for himself and eating only rye-bread, or rolls prepared for the Church. He had been advised long since that he had no right to neglect his health, and he was given wholesome, though Lenten, food. He ate sparingly, though much more than he had done, and often he ate with much pleasure, and not as formerly with aversion and a sense of guilt. So it was now. He had some gruel, drank a cup of tea, and ate half a white roll.

The attendant went away, and Father Sergius remained alone under the elm tree.

It was a wonderful May evening, when the birches, aspens, elms, wild cherries, and oaks, had just burst into foliage.

The bush of wild cherries behind the elm tree was in full bloom and had not yet begun to shed its blossoms, and the nightingales—one quite near at hand and two or three others in the bushes down by the river—burst into full song after some preliminary twitters. From the river came the far-off songs of peasants returning, no doubt, from their work. The sun was setting behind the forest, its last rays glowing through the leaves. All that side was brilliant green, the other side with the elm tree was dark. The cockchafers flew clumsily about, falling to the ground when they collided with anything.

After supper Father Sergius began to repeat a silent prayer: 'O Lord Jesus Christ, Son of God, have mercy upon us!' and then he read a psalm, and suddenly in the middle of the psalm a sparrow flew out from the bush, alighted on the ground, and hopped towards him chirping as it came, but then it took fright at something and flew away. He said a prayer which referred to his abandonment of the world, and hastened to finish it in order to send for the merchant with the sick daughter. She interested him in that she presented a distraction, and because both she and her father considered him a saint whose prayers were efficacious. Outwardly he disavowed that idea, but in the depths of his soul he considered it to be true.

He was often amazed that this had happened, that he, Stepán Kasátsky, had come to be such an extraordinary saint and even a worker of miracles, but of the fact that he was such there could not be the least doubt. He could not fail to believe in the miracles he himself witnessed, beginning with the sick boy and ending with the old woman who had recovered her sight when he had prayed for her.

Strange as it might be, it was so. Accordingly the merchant's daughter interested him as a new individual who had faith in him, and also as a fresh opportunity to confirm his healing powers and enhance his fame. 'They bring people a thousand versts and write about it in the papers. The Emperor knows of it, and they know of it in Europe, in unbelieving Europe'—thought he. And suddenly he felt ashamed of his vanity and again began to pray. 'Lord, King of Heaven, Comforter, Soul of Truth! Come and enter into me and cleanse me from all sin and save and bless my soul. Cleanse me from the sin of worldly vanity that troubles me!' he repeated, and he remembered how often he had prayed about this and how vain till now his prayers had been in that respect. His prayers worked miracles for others, but in his own case God had not granted him liberation from this petty passion.

He remembered his prayers at the commencement of his life at the hermitage, when he prayed for purity, humility, and love, and how it seemed to him then that God heard his prayers. He had retained his purity and had chopped off his finger. And he lifted the shrivelled stump of that finger to his lips and kissed it. It seemed to him now that he had been humble then when he had always seemed loathsome to himself on account of his sinfulness; and when he remembered the tender feelings with which he had then met an old man who was bringing a drunken soldier to him to ask alms; and how he had received *her*, it seemed to him that he had then possessed love also. But now? And he asked himself whether he loved anyone, whether he loved Sófya Ivánovna, or Father Seraphim, whether he had any feeling of love for all who had come to him that day—for that learned young man with whom he had had that instructive discussion in which he was concerned only to show off his own intelligence and that he had not lagged behind the times in knowledge. He wanted and needed their love, but felt none towards them. He now had neither love nor humility nor purity.

He was pleased to know that the merchant's

daughter was twenty-two, and he wondered whether she was good-looking. When he inquired whether she was weak, he really wanted to know if she had feminine charm.

'Can I have fallen so low?' he thought. 'Lord, help me! Restore me, my Lord and God!' And he clasped his hands and began to pray.

The nightingales burst into song, a cockchafer knocked against him and crept up the back of his neck. He brushed it off. 'But does He exist? What if I am knocking at a door fastened from outside? The bar is on the door for all to see. Nature—the nightingales and the cockchafers—is that bar. Perhaps the young man was right.' And he began to pray aloud. He prayed for a long time till these thoughts vanished and he again felt calm and confident. He rang the bell and told the attendant to say that the merchant might bring his daughter to him now.

The merchant came, leading his daughter by the arm. He led her into the cell and immediately left her.

She was a very fair girl, plump and very short, with a pale, frightened, childish face and a much developed feminine figure. Father Sergius remained seated on the bench at the entrance and when she was passing and stopped beside him for his blessing he was aghast at himself for the way he looked at her figure. As she passed by him he was acutely conscious of her femininity, though he saw by her face that she was sensual and feeble-minded. He rose and went into the cell. She was sitting on a stool waiting for him, and when he entered she rose.

'I want to go back to Papa,' she said.

'Don't be afraid,' he replied. 'What are you suffering from?'

'I am in pain all over,' she said, and suddenly her face lit up with a smile.

'You will be well,' said he. 'Pray!'

'What is the use of praying? I have prayed and it does no good'—and she continued to smile. 'I want you to pray for me and lay your hands on me. I saw you in a dream.'

'How did you see me?'

'I saw you put your hands on my breast like that.' She took his hand and pressed it to her breast. 'Just here.'

He yielded his right hand to her.

'What is your name?' he asked, trembling all over and feeling that he was overcome and that his desire had already passed beyond control.

'Marie. Why?'

She took his hand and kissed it, and then put her arm round his waist and pressed him to herself.

'What are you doing?' he said. 'Marie, you are a devil!'

'Oh, perhaps. What does it matter?'

And embracing him she sat down with him on the bed.

At dawn he went out into the porch.

'Can this all have happened? Her father will come and she will tell him everything. She is a devil! What am I to do? Here is the axe with which I chopped off my finger.' He snatched up the axe and moved back towards the cell.

The attendant came up.

'Do you want some wood chopped? Let me have the axe.'

Sergius yielded up the axe and entered the cell. She was lying there asleep. He looked at her with horror, and passed on beyond the partition, where he took down the peasant clothes and put them on. Then he seized a pair of scissors, cut off his long hair, and went out along the path down the hill to the river, where he had not been for more than three years.

A road ran beside the river and he went along it and walked till noon. Then he went into a field of rye and lay down there. Towards evening he approached a village, but without entering it went towards the cliff that overhung the river. There he again lay down to rest

It was early morning, half an hour before sunrise. All was damp and gloomy and a cold early wind was blowing from the west. 'Yes, I must end it all. There is no God. But how am I to end it? Throw myself into the river? I can swim and should not drown. Hang myself? Yes, just throw this sash over a branch.' This seemed so feasible and so easy that he felt horrified. As usual at moments of despair he felt the need of prayer. But there was no one to pray to. There was no God. He lay down resting on his arm, and suddenly such a longing for sleep overcame him that he could no longer support his head on his hand, but stretched out his arm, laid his head upon it, and fell asleep. But that sleep lasted only for a moment. He woke up immediately and began not to dream but to remember.

He saw himself as a child in his mother's home in the country. A carriage drives up, and out of it steps Uncle Nicholas Sergéevich, with his long, spade-shaped, black beard, and with him Páshenka, a thin little girl with large mild eyes and a timid pathetic face. And into their company of boys Páshenka is brought and they have to play with her, but it is dull. She is silly, and it ends by their making fun of her and forcing her to show how she can swim. She lies down on the floor and shows them, and they all laugh and make a fool of her. She sees this and blushes red in patches and becomes more pitiable than before, so pitiable that he feels ashamed and can never forget that crooked, kindly, submissive smile. And Sergius remembered having seen her since then. Long after, just before he became a monk, she had married a landowner who squandered all her fortune and was in the habit of beating her. She had had two children, a son and a daughter, but the son had died while still young. And Sergius remembered having seen her very wretched. Then again he had seen her in the monastery when she was a widow. She had been still the same, not exactly stupid, but insipid, insignificant, and pitiable. She had come with her daughter and her daughter's fiancé. They were already poor at that time and later on he had heard that she was living in a small provincial town and was very poor.

'Why am I thinking about her?' he asked himself, but he could not cease doing so. 'Where is she? How is she getting on? Is she still as unhappy as she was then when she had to show us how to swim on the floor? But why should I think about her? What am I doing? I must put an end to myself.'

And again he felt afraid, and again, to escape from that thought, he went on thinking about Páshenka.

So he lay for a long time, thinking now of his unavoidable end and now of Páshenka. She presented herself to him as a means of salvation. At last he fell asleep, and in his sleep he saw an angel who came to him and said: 'Go to Páshenka and learn from her what you have to do, what your sin is, and wherein lies your salvation.'

He awoke, and having decided that this was a vision sent by God, he felt glad, and resolved to do what had been told him in the vision. He knew the town where she lived. It was some three hundred versts (two hundred miles) away, and he set out to walk there.

VI

PÁSHENKA had already long ceased to be Páshenka and had become old, withered, wrinkled Praskóvya Mikháylovna,* mother-in-law of that failure, the drunken official Mavríkyev. She was living in the country town where he had had his last appointment, and there she was supporting the family: her daughter, her ailing neurasthenic son-in-law, and her five grandchildren. She did this by giving music lessons to tradesmen's daughters, giving four and sometimes five lessons a day of an hour each, and earning in this way some sixty rubles (£6) a month. So they lived for the present, in expectation of another appointment. She had sent letters to all her relations and acquaintances asking them to obtain a post for her son-in-law, and among the rest she had written to Sergius, but that letter had not reached him.

It was a Saturday, and Praskóvya Mikháylovna was herself mixing dough for currant bread such as the serf-cook on her father's estate used to make so well. She wished to give her grandchildren a treat on the Sunday.

Másha, her daughter, was nursing her youngest child, the eldest boy and girl were at school, and her son-in-law was asleep, not having slept during the night. Praskóvya Mikháylovna had remained awake too for a great part of the night, trying to soften her daughter's anger against her husband.

She saw that it was impossible for her son-in-law, a weak creature, to be other than he was, and realized that his wife's reproaches could do no good —so she used all her efforts to soften those reproaches and to avoid recrimination and anger.

* Páshenka is a familiar pet name. Praskóvya Mikháylovna (Michael's daughter) is the full Christian name and patronymic proper when formally addressing an adult.—A. M.

Unkindly relations between people caused her actual physical suffering. It was so clear to her that bitter feelings do not make anything better, but only make everything worse. She did not in fact think about this: she simply suffered at the sight of anger as she would from a bad smell, a harsh noise, or from blows on her body.

She had—with a feeling of self-satisfaction—just taught Lukérya how to mix the dough, when her six-year-old grandson Mísha, wearing an apron and with darned stockings on his crooked little legs, ran into the kitchen with a frightened face.

'Grandma, a dreadful old man wants to see you.'

Lukérya looked out at the door.

'There is a pilgrim of some kind, a man . . .'

Praskóvya Mikháylovna rubbed her thin elbows against one another, wiped her hands on her apron and went upstairs to get a five-kopek piece [about a penny] out of her purse for him, but remembering that she had nothing less than a ten-kopek piece she decided to give him some bread instead. She returned to the cupboard, but suddenly blushed at the thought of having grudged the ten-kopek piece, and telling Lukérya to cut a slice of bread, went upstairs again to fetch it. 'It serves you right,' she said to herself. 'You must now give twice over.'

She gave both the bread and the money to the pilgrim, and when doing so—far from being proud of her generosity—she excused herself for giving so little. The man had such an imposing appearance.

Though he had tramped two hundred versts as a beggar, though he was tattered and had grown thin and weather-beaten, though he had cropped his long hair and was wearing a peasant's cap and boots, and though he bowed very humbly, Sergius still had the impressive appearance that made him so attractive. But Praskóvya Mikháylovna did not recognize him. She could hardly do so, not having seen him for almost twenty years.

'Don't think ill of me, father. Perhaps you want something to eat?'

He took the bread and the money, and Praskóvya Mikháylovna was surprised that he did not go, but stood looking at her.

'Páshenka, I have come to you! Take me in . . .'

His beautiful black eyes, shining with the tears that started in them, were fixed on her with imploring insistence. And under his greyish moustache his lips quivered piteously.

Praskóvya Mikháylovna pressed her hands to her withered breast, opened her mouth, and stood petrified, staring at the pilgrim with dilated eyes.

'It can't be! Stëpa! Sergéy! Father Sergius!'

'Yes, it is I,' said Sergius in a low voice. 'Only not Sergius, or Father Sergius, but a great sinner, Stepán Kasátsky—a great and lost sinner. Take me in and help me!'

'It's impossible! How have you so humbled yourself? But come in.'

She reached out her hand, but he did not take it and only followed her in.

But where was she to take him? The lodging was a small one. Formerly she had had a tiny room, almost a closet, for herself, but later she had given it up to her daughter, and Másha was now sitting there rocking the baby.

'Sit here for the present,' she said to Sergius, pointing to a bench in the kitchen.

He sat down at once, and with an evidently accustomed movement slipped the straps of his wallet first off one shoulder and then off the other.

'My God, my God! How you have humbled yourself, Father! Such great fame, and now like this . . .'

Sergius did not reply, but only smiled meekly, placing his wallet under the bench on which he sat.

'Másha, do you know who this is?'—And in a whisper Praskóvya Mikháylovna told her daughter who he was, and together they then carried the bed and the cradle out of the tiny room and cleared it for Sergius.

Praskóvya Mikháylovna led him into it.

'Here you can rest. Don't take offence . . . but I must go out.'

'Where to?'

'I have to go to a lesson. I am ashamed to tell you, but I teach music!'

'Music? But that is good. Only just one thing, Praskóvya Mikháylovna, I have come to you with a definite object. When can I have a talk with you?'

'I shall be very glad. Will this evening do?'

'Yes. But one thing more. Don't speak about me, or say who I am. I have revealed myself only to you. No one knows where I have gone to. It must be so.'

'Oh, but I have told my daughter.'

'Well, ask her not to mention it.'

And Sergius took off his boots, lay down, and at once fell asleep after a sleepless night and a walk of nearly thirty miles.

When Praskóvya Mikháylovna returned, Sergius was sitting in the little room waiting for her. He did not come out for dinner, but had some soup and gruel which Lukérya brought him.

'How is it that you have come back earlier than you said?' asked Sergius. 'Can I speak to you now?'

'How is it that I have the happiness to receive such a guest? I have missed one of my lessons. That can wait . . . I had always been planning to go to see you. I wrote to you, and now this good fortune has come.'

'Páshenka, please listen to what I am going to tell you as to a confession made to God at my last hour. Páshenka, I am not a holy man, I am not even as good as a simple ordinary man, I am a loathsome, vile, and proud sinner who has gone astray, and who, if not worse than everyone else, is at least worse than most very bad people.'

Páshenka looked at him at first with staring eyes. But she believed what he said, and when she had quite grasped it she touched his hand, smiled pityingly, and said:

'Perhaps you exaggerate, Stíva?'

'No, Páshenka. I am an adulterer, a murderer, a blasphemer, and a deceiver.'

'My God! How is that?' exclaimed Praskóvya Mikháylovna.

'But I must go on living. And I, who thought I knew everything, who taught others how to live —I know nothing and ask you to teach me.'

'What are you saying, Stíva? You are laughing at me. Why do you always make fun of me?'

'Well, if you think I am jesting you must have it as you please. But tell me all the same how you live, and how you have lived your life.'

'I? I have lived a very nasty, horrible life, and now God is punishing me as I deserve. I live so wretchedly, so wretchedly . . .'

'How was it with your marriage? How did you live with your husband?'

'It was all bad. I married because I fell in love in the nastiest way. Papa did not approve. But I would not listen to anything and just got married. Then instead of helping my husband I tormented him by my jealousy, which I could not restrain.'

'I heard that he drank . . .'

'Yes, but I did not give him any peace. I always reproached him, though you know it is a disease! He could not refrain from it. I now remember how I tried to prevent his having it, and the frightful scenes we had!'

And she looked at Kasátsky with beautiful eyes, suffering from the remembrance.

Kasátsky remembered how he had been told that Páshenka's husband used to beat her, and now, looking at her thin withered neck with prominent veins behind her ears, and her scanty coil of hair, half grey half auburn, he seemed to see just how it had occurred.

'Then I was left with two children and no means at all.'

'But you had an estate!'

'Oh, we sold that while Vásya was still alive, and the money was all spent. We had to live, and like all our young ladies I did not know how to earn anything. I was particularly useless and helpless. So we spent all we had. I taught the children and improved my own education a little. And then Mítya fell ill when he was already in the fourth form, and God took him. Másha fell in love with Ványa, my son-in-law. And—well, he is well-meaning but unfortunate. He is ill.'

'Mamma!'—her daughter's voice interrupted her—'Take Mítya! I can't be in two places at once.'

Praskóvya Mikháylovna shuddered, but rose and went out of the room, stepping quickly in her patched shoes. She soon came back with a boy of two in her arms, who threw himself backwards and grabbed at her shawl with his little hands.

'Where was I? Oh yes, he had a good appointment here, and his chief was a kind man too. But Ványa could not go on, and had to give up his position.'

'What is the matter with him?'

'Neurasthenia—it is a dreadful complaint. We consulted a doctor, who told us he ought to go away, but we had no means. . . . I always hope it will pass of itself. He has no particular pain, but . . .'

'Lukérya!' cried an angry and feeble voice. 'She is always sent away when I want her. Mamma . . .'

'I'm coming!' Praskóvya Mikháylovna again interrupted herself. 'He has not had his dinner yet. He can't eat with us.'

She went out and arranged something, and came back wiping her thin dark hands.

'So that is how I live. I always complain and am always dissatisfied, but thank God the grandchildren are all nice and healthy, and we can still live. But why talk about me?'

'But what do you live on?'

'Well, I earn a little. How I used to dislike music, but how useful it is to me now!' Her small hand lay on the chest of drawers beside which she was sitting, and she drummed an exercise with her thin fingers.

'How much do you get for a lesson?'

'Sometimes a ruble, sometimes fifty kopeks, or sometimes thirty.* They are all so kind to me.'

'And do your pupils get on well?' asked Kasátsky with a slight smile.

Praskóvya Mikháylovna did not at first believe that he was asking seriously, and looked inquiringly into his eyes.

'Some of them do. One of them is a splendid girl—the butcher's daughter—such a good kind girl! If I were a clever woman I ought, of course, with the connexions Papa had, to be able to get an appointment for my son-in-law. But as it is I have not been able to do anything, and have brought them all to this—as you see.'

* 'Sometimes two shillings, sometimes one, or sometimes sevenpence.'

'Yes, yes,' said Kasátsky, lowering his head. 'And how is it, Páshenka—do you take part in Church life?'

'Oh, don't speak of it. I am so bad that way, and have neglected it so! I keep the fasts with the children and sometimes go to church, and then again sometimes I don't go for months. I only send the children.'

'But why don't you go yourself?'

'To tell the truth' (she blushed) 'I am ashamed, for my daughter's sake and the children's, to go there in tattered clothes, and I haven't anything else. Besides, I am just lazy.'

'And do you pray at home?'

'I do. But what sort of prayer is it? Only mechanical. I know it should not be like that, but I lack real religious feeling. The only thing is that I know how bad I am . . .'

'Yes, yes, that's right!' said Kasátsky, as if approvingly.

'I'm coming! I'm coming!' she replied to a call from her son-in-law, and tidying her scanty plait she left the room.

But this time it was long before she returned. When she came back, Kasátsky was sitting in the same position, his elbows resting on his knees and his head bowed. But his wallet was strapped on his back.

When she came in, carrying a small tin lamp without a shade, he raised his fine weary eyes and sighed very deeply.

'I did not tell them who you are,' she began timidly. 'I only said that you are a pilgrim, a nobleman, and that I used to know you. Come into the dining-room for tea.'

'No . . .'

'Well then, I'll bring some to you here.'

'No, I don't want anything. God bless you, Páshenka! I am going now. If you pity me, don't tell anyone that you have seen me. For the love of God don't tell anyone. Thank you. I would bow to your feet but I know it would make you feel awkward. Thank you, and forgive me for Christ's sake!'

'Give me your blessing.'

'God bless you! Forgive me for Christ's sake!'

He rose, but she would not let him go until she had given him bread and butter and rusks. He took it all and went away.

It was dark, and before he had passed the second house he was lost to sight. She only knew he was there because the dog at the priest's house was barking.

'So that is what my dream meant! Páshenka is what I ought to have been but failed to be. I lived for men on the pretext of living for God, while she lives for God imagining that she lives for men. Yes, one good deed—a cup of water given without thought of reward—is worth more than any benefit I imagined I was bestowing on people. But after all was there not some share of sincere desire to serve God?' he asked himself, and the answer was: 'Yes, there was, but it was all soiled and overgrown by desire for human praise. Yes, there is no God for the man who lives, as I did, for human praise. I will now seek Him!'

And he walked from village to village as he had done on his way to Páshenka, meeting and parting from other pilgrims, men and women, and asking for bread and a night's rest in Christ's name. Occasionally some angry housewife scolded him, or a drunken peasant reviled him, but for the most part he was given food and drink and even something to take with him. His noble bearing disposed some people in his favour, while others on the contrary seemed pleased at the sight of a gentleman who had come to beggary.

But his gentleness prevailed with everyone.

Often, finding a copy of the Gospels in a hut he would read it aloud, and when they heard him the people were always touched and surprised, as at something new yet familiar.

When he succeeded in helping people, either by advice, or by his knowledge of reading and writing, or by settling some quarrel, he did not wait to see their gratitude but went away directly afterwards. And little by little God began to reveal Himself within him.

Once he was walking along with two old women and a soldier. They were stopped by a party consisting of a lady and gentleman in a gig and another lady and gentleman on horseback. The husband was on horseback with his daughter, while in the gig his wife was driving with a Frenchman, evidently a traveller.

The party stopped to let the Frenchman see the pilgrims who, in accord with a popular Russian superstition, tramped about from place to place instead of working.

They spoke French, thinking that the others would not understand them.

'*Demandez-leur*,' said the Frenchman, '*s'ils sont bien sûr de ce que leur pèlerinage est agréable à Dieu.*'*

The question was asked, and one old woman replied: 'As God takes it. Our feet have reached the holy places, but our hearts may not have done so.'

They asked the soldier. He said that he was alone in the world and had nowhere else to go.

* 'Ask them whether they are quite sure that their pilgrimage pleases God.'

They asked Kasátsky who he was.

'A servant of God.'

'*Qu'est-ce qu'il dit? Il ne répond pas.*'*

'*Il dit qu'il est un serviteur de Dieu. Cela doit être un fils de prêtre. Il a de la race. Avez-vous de la petite monnaie?*'†

The Frenchman found some small change and gave twenty kopeks to each of the pilgrims.

'*Mais dites-leur que ce n'est pas pour les cierges que je leur donne, mais pour qu'ils se régalent de thé. Chay, chay pour vous, mon vieux!*'‡ he said with a smile. And he patted Kasátsky on the shoulder with his gloved hand.

'May Christ bless you,' replied Kasátsky without replacing his cap and bowing his bald head.

He rejoiced particularly at this meeting, because he had disregarded the opinion of men and had done the simplest, easiest thing—humbly accepted twenty kopeks and given them to his comrade, a blind beggar. The less importance he attached to the opinion of men the more did he feel the presence of God within him.

For eight months Kasátsky tramped on in this manner, and in the ninth month he was arrested for not having a passport. This happened at a night-refuge in a provincial town where he had passed the night with some pilgrims. He was taken to the police-station, and when asked who he was and where was his passport, he replied that he had no passport and that he was a servant of God. He

* 'What does he say? He does not answer.'

† 'He says that he is a servant of God. That oneis probably a priest's son. He is not a common man. Have you any small change?'

‡ 'But tell them that I give it them not to spend on church candles, but that they should have some tea. Tea, tea for you, old fellow.'

was classed as a tramp, sentenced, and sent to live in Siberia.

In Siberia he has settled down as the hired man of a well-to-do peasant, in which capacity he works in the kitchen-garden, teaches children, and attends to the sick.

Written in 1890, 1891, and 1898.

FRANÇOISE

FRANÇOISE

(*Tolstóy's Adaptation of a Story by Guy de Maupassant*)

I

On the 3rd of May 1882 a three-masted sailing vessel, *Notre-Dame-des-Vents*, left Havre for the China Seas. After discharging her cargo in China, she took on board a fresh freight for Buenos Aires, from whence she carried other goods to Brazil.

Apart from these long voyages, the vessel was so much delayed by damages, repairs, calms that continued for months, gales which drove her far out of her course, adventures at sea, and various accidents, that it was four years before she returned to France. At last however, on the 8th of May 1886, she reached Marseilles with a cargo of American tinned fruit.

When the ship left Havre she had on board a captain, a mate, and fourteen sailors. During the voyage one sailor died, four were lost in various adventures, and of those that had sailed from France only nine returned home. In place of these men struck off the list, two Americans had been engaged, besides one negro, and a Swede who had been picked up in a drink-shop at Singapore.

The sails were furled and all the rigging made taut. A tug took them in tow and, steaming noisily, drew the vessel to the line of ships moored at the quay. The sea was calm, only a slight swell plashed on the shore. The vessel took her place in the line of those ranged along the quay, where cheek by jowl stood ships large and small, of all sizes, shapes, and kinds, from every country in the world. *Notre-Dame-des-Vents* lay between an Italian brig and an English schooner, which had both crowded up to make room for their new companion.

As soon as the captain had got rid of the custom-house officers and port officials, he gave leave to the greater part of the crew to go ashore for the night.

It was a warm summer night. The streets of Marseilles were lighted up and were pervaded by the smell of food, the buzz of conversation, and the noise of traffic interspersed by sounds of gaiety.

The sailors from *Notre-Dame-des-Vents* had not been on shore for four months and now on landing went about timidly in pairs, like strangers unused to a town. They wandered about the streets nearest the quay, looking around them like dogs sniffing about in search of something. It was four months since they had seen a woman. In front walked Celestin Duclos, a strong and agile fellow who always took the lead when they went ashore. He knew how to find the right places and how to get out of a scrape when necessary. He avoided such broils as sailors frequently engage in when they go ashore, but he went the pace with his comrades and could stand up for himself.

For some time the sailors strolled about those streets which run down to the sea like sewers, filled with an oppressive smell rising from their damp cellars and musty attics. At last Celestin chose a narrow side-street where large, prominent lamps shone over the doors of the houses, and into this he turned. The others followed him, grinning and singing. Numbers were painted in huge figures on the coloured glass of these lamps. In the low doorways, on straw-platted chairs, sat women in aprons. They rushed out at the sight of the sailors, and running into the street threw themselves in their way, enticing them each to her own lair.

At times a door unexpectedly opened at the end of a passage, through which one saw a half-naked woman wearing very short skirts and a very low-cut velvet bodice trimmed with gilt lace.

'Ah! lads, come here,' such a one would cry from a distance, or even ran out herself and catching hold of a sailor dragged him with all her strength towards her den. She stuck to him like a spider seizing a fly stronger than itself. The fellow resisted feebly and the others stopped to see the result, but Celestin Duclos shouted:

'Not there, don't go in there: come farther!'

The fellow obeyed, tearing himself from the woman by force, and the sailors went on, followed by the abuse of the enraged woman. At the noise of the encounter other women along the street rushed out and fell upon them, shouting the praises of their wares in hoarse voices, but the sailors went on farther and farther. Occasionally they met a soldier with jingling spurs or a solitary clerk or tradesman making his way to some accustomed haunt. In other side-streets shone other lamps of the same kind, but the sailors went farther and farther, tramping through the foul-smelling slush that oozed from the yards. At last Duclos stopped at a house of better appearance than the others, and led his comrades in.

II

THE sailors were sitting in the chief room of the establishment. Each of them had chosen a woman companion from whom he did not part the whole evening; such was the custom of the place. Three tables had been placed together, and first of all the sailors drank, each with his lass. Then they rose and went upstairs with them. Long and loud clattered their twenty feet in their thick boots on the wooden stairs before they had all tumbled through the narrow doors into their separate rooms. From there they came down again to drink, and then returned once more upstairs.

The carouse was kept up recklessly. The whole half-year's pay went in a four hours' debauch. By eleven o'clock they were all drunk, and with bloodshot eyes were shouting disconnected phrases not knowing what they said. They sang, shouted, beat with their fists on the table, or poured wine down their throats. Celestin Duclos was there among his comrades and with him sat a large, stout, red-cheeked woman. He had had as much to drink as the others, but was not yet quite drunk: some more or less connected thoughts still flickered through his brain. He grew tender, and tried to think of something to say to his lass, but the thoughts that came into his head vanished again at once and he was unable to remember or express them.

'Yes,' said he, laughing. 'Just so. . . . Just so. . . . And have you lived here long?'

'Six months,' replied the woman.

He nodded his head, as if to show his approval of this.

'And are you comfortable here?'

She thought a moment.

'I have got accustomed to it,' she said. 'One has to live somehow. It is not so bad as being in service or working in a laundry.'

He nodded his head approvingly, as if to commend her for this also.

'Were you born in these parts?' said he.

She shook her head.

'Do you come from far away?' he continued.

She nodded.

'Where from?'

She paused, as if to remember.

'I am from Perpignan,' said she.

'Yes, yes,' said he and ceased questioning her.

'And what are you—a sailor?' asked the woman in her turn.

'Yes, we are sailors.'

'And have you been on long voyages?'

'Yes, long enough! We have seen places of all sorts.'

'Have you been round the world?'

'Oh yes,' said he, 'not once only—we have been nearly twice round.'

She again paused, as if remembering something.

'I suppose you have met many ships?' said she.

'Of course we have.'

'Have you ever met the *Notre-Dame-des-Vents*? There is a ship of that name.'

He was surprised at her naming his vessel, and thought he would play a trick on her.

'Why, certainly,' said he; 'we met her only last week.'

'Is that the truth?' she said, growing pale.

'The solemn truth.'

'You are not telling me a lie?'

'So help me God,' swore he, 'I am telling the truth.'

'And did you not meet a man on board named Celestin Duclos?' asked she.

'Celestin Duclos?' he repeated, astonished and even alarmed. How did this woman know his name?

'Why! do you know him?' he asked.

It was evident that she too was alarmed.

'No, not I, but there is a woman here that knows him.'

'What woman? Here in this house?'

'No, but near here.'

'Tell me where?'

'Oh, not very far away.'

'Who is she?'

'Oh, just a woman—like myself.'

'What has she to do with him?'

'How should I know? Perhaps they come from the same parts.'

They looked searchingly into each other's eyes.

'I should like to see that woman,' he said.

'Why?' she asked. 'Have you anything to tell her?'

'I want to tell her . . .'

'To tell her—what?'

'That I have seen Celestin Duclos.'

'You have seen Celestin Duclos! Is he alive and well?'

'He is quite well. But what is that to you?'

She was silent, again collecting her thoughts. Then she said softly:

'What port is the *Notre-Dame-des-Vents* bound for?'

'What port? Why, Marseilles.'

'Is that true?' cried she.

'Quite true.'

'And you know Duclos?'

'I have already told you that I know him.'

She thought awhile.

'Yes, yes, it is well,' said she softly.

'What do you want with him?'

'If you should see him, tell him . . . No, better not!'

'What shall I tell him?'

'No, never mind.'

As he looked at her he became more and more agitated.

'Do you know him yourself?' asked he.

'No, I don't know him myself.'

'Then what does he matter to you?'

She did not answer, but jumping up ran to the

counter, behind which the hostess sat. Taking a lemon, she cut it in half and squeezed the juice into a glass which she filled with water, and this she gave to Celestin.

'There—drink that!' she said, sitting down as before on his knees.

'What is this for?' he asked, taking the glass from her.

'To clear your head. Then I will tell you something. Drink it!'

He drank it, and wiped his lips with the back of his hand.

'Well, now tell me! I am attending.'

'But you must not let him know that you have seen me, nor tell him whom you heard it from.'

'Very well, I will not tell.'

'Swear it!'

He swore.

'So help you God!'

'So help me God!'

'Well then, tell him his father and mother are both dead and his brother also. A fever broke out and they all died in one and the same month.'

Duclos felt the blood rushing to his heart. For some minutes he sat in silence, not knowing what to say. Presently he uttered the words:

'Are you sure it is so?'

'Quite sure.'

'Who told you?'

She put her hands on his shoulders and looked him straight in the eyes.

'Swear you will not let it out!'

He swore it: 'So help me God!'

'I am his sister.'

'Françoise!' he shrieked.

She looked intently at him, and softly, softly moved her lips, hardly letting the words escape:

'So you are Celestin!'

They did not stir, but remained as though benumbed, gazing into each other's eyes.

Around them the others shouted with drunken voices. The ringing of glasses, the beating of hands and heels, and the piercing screams of women, intermingled with the singing and the shouting.

'How can it have happened?' said he, so gently that even she could hardly catch the words.

Her eyes suddenly filled with tears.

'They died,' she continued. 'All three in one month. What was I to do? I was left alone. The chemist, the doctor, the three funerals. . . . I had to sell everything to pay the debts. Nothing was left but the clothes I wore. I went as servant to Monsieur Cacheux. . . . Do you remember him? A lame man. I was only just fifteen. I was scarcely fourteen when you left home—and I went wrong with him. . . . You know how stupid we peasant girls are. Then I went as nurse in a notary's family —and it was the same with him. For a time he made me his mistress and I had a lodging of my own; but that did not last long. He left me, and for three days I was without food. No one would take me, so I came here like the rest of them.' And as she spoke the water flowed in streams from her eyes and nose, wetting her cheeks and trickling into her mouth.

'What have we done?' said he.

'I thought you were dead also. How could I have helped it?' whispered she through her tears.

'How was it you did not know me?' he answered, also in a whisper.

'I do not know. It was not my fault,' continued she, weeping yet more bitterly.

'How could I know you?' he said again. 'You

were so different when I left home! But you should have known me!'

She threw up her hands in despair.

'Ah! I see so many of them—these men. They all look alike to me now!'

His heart contracted so painfully and so strongly that he wanted to cry aloud, as a little boy does when he is beaten.

He rose and held her at arm's length; then, seizing her head in his great sailor paws, he gazed intently into her face.

Little by little he recognized in her the small, slender, merry maiden he had left at home with those others whose eyes it had been her lot to close.

'Yes, you are Françoise! My sister!' he exclaimed. And suddenly sobs—the sobs of a strong man, sounding like the hiccups of a drunkard—rose in his throat. He let go of her head, and striking the table so that the glasses upset and broke to atoms, he cried out in a wild voice.

His comrades, astonished, turned towards him.

'See how he's swaggering,' said one.

'Stop that shouting,' said another.

'Eh, Duclos! What are you bawling about? Let's get upstairs again,' said a third, plucking Celestin by the sleeve with one hand while his other arm encircled a flushed, laughing, black-eyed lass, in a rose-coloured, low cut, silk dress.

Duclos suddenly became quiet, and holding his breath looked at his comrades. Then, with the same strange and resolute expression with which he used to enter on a fight, he staggered up to the sailor who was embracing the girl, and struck down with his hand—dividing them apart.

'Away! Do you not see that she is your sister! Each of them is someone's sister. See, here is my sister, Françoise! Ha, ha . . . ha . . .' and he broke into sobs that almost sounded like laughter. Then he staggered, raised his hands, and fell with a crash to the floor, where he rolled about, striking the floor with his hands and feet and choking as though about to die.

'He must be put to bed,' said one of his comrades. 'We shall be having him taken up if we go out into the streets.'

So they lifted Celestin and dragged him upstairs to Françoise's room, where they laid him on her bed.

APPENDIX

THE PORCELAIN DOLL

A LETTER written six months after his marriage by Leo Tolstóy to his wife's younger sister, the Natásha of *War and Peace*.

The first few lines are in his wife's handwriting, the rest in his own.

21st March 1863.

Why, Tánya, have you dried up? . . . You don't write to me at all and I so love receiving letters from you, and you have not yet replied to Lëvochka's [Tolstóy's] crazy epistle, of which I did not understand a word.

23rd March.

There, she began to write and suddenly stopped, because she could not continue. And do you know why, Tánya dear? A strange thing has befallen her and a still stranger thing has befallen me. As you know, like the rest of us she has always been made of flesh and blood, with all the advantages and disadvantages of that condition: she breathed, was warm and sometimes hot, blew her nose (and how loud!) and so on, and above all she had control of her limbs, which—both arms and legs—could assume different positions: in a word she was corporeal like all of us. Suddenly on March 21st 1863, at ten o'clock in the evening, this extraordinary thing befell her and me. Tánya! I know you always loved her (I do not know what feeling she will arouse in you now); I know you felt a sympathetic interest in me, and I know your reasonableness, your sane view of the important affairs of life, and your love of your parents (please prepare them and inform them of this event), and so I write to tell you just how it happened.

I got up early that day and walked and rode a great deal. We lunched and dined together and had been reading (she was still able to read) and I felt tranquil and happy. At ten o'clock I said goodnight to Auntie* (Sónya

* 'Auntie Tatiána'—Tatiána Alexándrovna Érgolski (1795–1874), who brought Tolstóy up.—A. M.

was then still as usual and said she would follow me) and I went off to bed. Through my sleep I heard her open the door and heard her breathe as she undressed. . . . I heard how she came out from behind the screen and approached the bed. I opened my eyes . . . and saw—not the Sónya you and I have known—but a porcelain Sónya! Made of that very porcelain about which your parents had a dispute. You know those porcelain dolls with bare cold shoulders, and necks and arms bent forward, but made of the same lump of porcelain as the body. They have black painted hair arranged in large waves, the paint of which gets rubbed off at the top, and protruding porcelain eyes that are too wide and are also painted black at the corners, and the stiff porcelain folds of their skirts are made of the same one piece of porcelain as the rest. And Sónya was like that! I touched her arm—she was smooth, pleasant to feel, and cold porcelain. I thought I was asleep and gave myself a shake, but she remained like that and stood before me immovable. I said: Are you porcelain? And without opening her mouth (which remained as it was, with curved lips painted bright red) she replied: Yes, I am porcelain. A shiver ran down my back. I looked at her legs: they also were porcelain and (you can imagine my horror) fixed on a porcelain stand, made of one piece with herself, representing the ground and painted green to depict grass. By her left leg, a little above and at the back of the knee, there was a porcelain column, coloured brown and probably representing the stump of a tree. This too was in one piece with her. I understood that without this stump she could not remain erect, and I became very sad, as you who loved her can imagine. I still did not believe my senses and began to call her. She could not move without that stump and its base, and only rocked a little—together with the base—to fall in my direction. I heard how the porcelain base knocked against the floor I touched her again, and she was all smooth, pleasant. and cold porcelain. I tried to lift her hand, but could not. I tried to pass a finger, or even a nail, between her elbow and her side—but it was impossible. The obstacle was the same porcelain mass, such as is made at Auerbach's, and of which sauce-boats are made. She was planned for external appearance only. I began to examine her chemise, it was all of one piece with the body, above and below. I looked more closely, and noticed that at the bottom a bit of the fold of her chemise was broken off and it showed brown. At the top of her head it showed white where the paint had come off a little. The paint had also come off a lip in one place, and a bit was chipped off one shoulder. But it was all so well made and so natural that it was still our same Sónya. And the chemise was one I knew, with lace, and there was a knot of black hair behind, but of porcelain, and the fine slender hands, and large eyes, and the lips—all were the same, but of porcelain. And the dimple in her chin and the small bones in front of her shoulders, were there too, but of porcelain. I was in a terrible state and did not know what to say or do or think. She would have been glad to help me, but what could a porcelain creature do? The half-closed eyes, the eyelashes and eyebrows, were all like her living self when looked at from a distance. She did not look at me, but past me at her bed. She evidently wanted to lie down, and rocked on her pedestal all the time. I quite lost control of myself, seized her, and tried to take her to her bed. My fingers made no impression on her cold porcelain body, and what surprised me yet more was that she had become as light as an empty flask. And suddenly she seemed to shrink, and became quite small, smaller than the palm of my hand, although she still looked just the same. I seized a pillow, put her in a corner of it, pressed down another corner with my fist, and placed her there, then I took her nightcap, folded it in four, and covered her up to the head with it. She lay there still just the same. Then I extinguished the candle and placed her under my beard. Suddenly I heard her voice from the corner of the pillow: 'Lëva, why have I become porcelain?' I did not know what to reply. She said again: 'Does it make any difference that I am porcelain?' I did not want to grieve her, and said that it did not matter. I felt her again in the dark—she was still as before, cold and porcelain. And her stomach was the same as when she was alive, protruding upwards—rather unnatural for a porcelain doll. Then I experienced a strange feeling. I suddenly felt it pleasant that she should be as she was, and ceased to feel surprised—it all seemed natural. I took her out, passed her from one hand to the other, and tucked her under my head. She liked it all. We fell asleep. In the morning I got up and went out without looking at her. All that had happened the day before seemed so terrible. When I returned for lunch she had again become such as she always was. I did not remind her of what had happened the day before, fearing to grieve her and Auntie. I have not yet told anyone but you about it. I thought it had all passed off, but all these days, every time we are alone together, the same thing happens. She suddenly becomes small and porcelain. In the presence of others she is just as she used to be. She is not oppressed by this, nor am I. Strange as it may seem, I frankly confess that I am glad of it, and though she is porcelain we are very happy.

I write to you of all this, dear Tánya, only that you should prepare her parents for the news, and through papa should find out from the doctors what this occurrence means, and whether it will not be bad for our expected child. Now we are alone, and she is sitting under my necktie and I feel how her sharp little nose cuts into my neck. Yesterday she had been left in a room by herself. I went in and saw that Dora (our little dog) had dragged her into a corner, was playing with her, and nearly broke her. I whipped Dora, put Sónya in my waistcoat pocket and took her to my study. To-day however I am expecting from Túla a small wooden box I have ordered, covered outside with morocco and lined inside with raspberry-coloured velvet, with a place arranged in it for her so that she can be laid in it with her elbows, head, and back all supported evenly so that she cannot break. I shall also cover it completely with chamois leather.

I had written this letter when suddenly a terrible misfortune occurred. She was standing on the table, when N.P.* pushed against her in passing, and she fell and broke

* Natálya Petróvna Okhótnitskaya, an old woman who was living at Yásnaya Polyána.—A. M.

off a leg above the knee with the stump. Alexéy* says that it can be mended with a cement made of the white of eggs. If such a recipe is known in Moscow please send it me.

* Alexéy Stepánovich Orékhov (who died in 1882), a servant of Tolstóy's who had accompanied him to the Caucasus and to Sevastopol during the Crimean War. He was employed as steward at Yásnaya Polyána.—A. M.